DARE ME TO STAY

DEVILS & DARLINGS
BOOK TWO

AJ WILDING

ISBN: 979-8-9921643-6-7 (Pretty Boy Edition)

ISBN: 979-8-9921643-5-0 (Discreet Snake Edition)

Published by Rose Onyx Press

Editor: Nicole DiPatri Sheldon

First Edition, [January, 2025]

Cover design by IndieInkCovers

Printed in the United States of America

Visit www.AjWilding.com for more information about the author and upcoming books

"I'm fine."

No you weren't.
But this book is for you.

AUTHOR'S NOTE

Dare Me to Stay is the second book in a series of interconnected standalones. While each story focuses on a new couple, the timelines do overlap, and this book contains **major spoilers for book 1: No Promises, No Lies.**

For the best reading experience, it is highly recommended to read the series in **publishing order,** as the books and characters do interconnect.

You'll notice that certain events from the first book happen simultaneously with moments in this story. Those plot points won't be re-explored in full here—only referenced or explained as needed from this couple's perspective.

Now, little darlings, are you ready?

Because here we go... down the rabbit hole.

TRIGGER WARNINGS

Before diving in, a quick heads-up: *Dare Me to Stay* is a dark romance and deals with heavy, potentially triggering topics.

- Torture/interrogation
- Murder
- Sex trafficking/Human trafficking
- Stalking
- Voyeurism
- Emotional manipulation
- Gaslighting
- Threat of sexual assault
- Kidnapping and captivity
- Organized crime/mafia activity
- Concealed pregnancy/child
- Child endangerment
- Death of a loved one
- Strong language

- Explicit sex scenes
- Alcohol use/drug references
- Non-consensual drugging/incapacitation
- Panic attacks/mental health struggles
- References to disordered eating

PLAYLIST

The music that inspired the story
Dare Me to Stay - Only on Spotify!

SLEEPTALK- DAYSEEKER
CHASING CARS- SNOW PATROL
A$$A$$IN - BEAUTY SCHOOL DROPOUT
DIAL TONE- CATCH YOUR BREATH
RELIC- AWAKEN I AM
SORRY- NF, JAMES ARTHUR
HEAVENS IN ASHES- ELI
RUIN MY LIFE- ZARA LARSSON
KARMA- DUTCH MELROSE, BENNY MAYNE
PUT YOU THROUGH ME- ARROWS IN ACTION
STAY- GRACIE ABRAMS
FEAR- NF
BREATHING UNDERWATER- HOT MILK
DAMOCLES- SLEEP TOKEN

MY TATTOOED NIGHTMARE

BRIAR

THEN...

A little over four years ago...

"He's not going to be there."

"He's *going* to be there." I eye the bar across the street as if it's enemy territory.

Lily sighs, quick to recognize a losing battle when she sees one.

"Fine," she huffs out, throwing up her hands. "Let's go worst-case scenario. So what if he is? Get in there, find a guy, and make him regret ever letting you go. Show that *idiot* the fucking prize he fumbled."

I never should have left the house tonight. Never should have let Lily talk me into a borrowed crop top and tight-as-fuck mini skirt, and drag me out to a bar—*that's looking suspiciously like a club*—that the very ex-boyfriend I've been avoiding for weeks, would love.

No.

I should be at home, nursing my recent breakup with a pint of ice cream and a good book.

"Maybe I can catch a ride back and you can—"

"Briar Elizabeth Ralston." My best friend's hands go to her hips, and that sharp no-nonsense tone has my mouth snapping shut. "If you go home, I go home," she warns, hazel eyes flashing, daring me to try her.

Ah, hell.

"Fine," I concede. "But if Ben shows his lying, cheating face tonight, I reserve the right to bail. Or throw a drink in his face..."

"Fair enough. The refill's on me!" Seizing the opportunity, she drags me across the street, nearly killing the two of us in traffic before practically shoving me through the club doors before I can change my mind. *Again.*

I peer around at the dark, moody decor of Last Call, the newest sports bar to grace the streets of Boston. It just opened a few weeks ago, and Lily, an avid sports fan, has been dying to check it out. And unlike me, Lily thrives on social interaction, an extrovert through and through, and since she's been stuck in post-breakup hibernation in solidarity with me for the past three weeks, I figure I owe her one.

It's time.

Or at least, I thought it was. But now that I'm here, surrounded by a crowd of loud, obnoxious club goers, I'm second-guessing everything. Especially considering that Last Call is right up my ex's alley. Ben is *obsessed* with baseball and the Renegades, and judging by the amount of Renegades jerseys I see everywhere, this is the place to be tonight if you're a Boston fan. So unless Ben somehow scored tickets to tonight's game—which I'm really, *really* hoping he did—there's a good chance he's here.

You're a good friend, I remind myself as the urge to bail resurfaces. *Be a good friend.*

Last Call is packed, so I scan the crowded club—or bar. It's some sort of bar/club hybrid. I'm not quite sure how to describe it. But, admittedly, for downtown Boston, it's pretty nice.

The baseball game has in fact drawn quite a crowd. You can't go two feet without encountering someone in a Boston Renegades jersey or colors. Lily and I almost stand out, seeing as we're not dressed in the designated green and white for the baseball team.

"Cassie and Mia are at the back bar." Lily wiggles her phone at me, shouting to be heard over the loud music. I follow closely, keeping a light hand on her arm so we don't get separated in the crowd. As we make our way through the thick throng of people, a second, larger bar in the middle of the club comes into view. It separates the lounge area from the even busier dance floor full of people.

A rush of excitement shoots through me at the sight of the dance floor. *Maybe tonight won't be so bad.* We're halfway there when someone barrels into my shoulder hard enough that I lose my grip on Lily's arm, spinning me half around.

"Ow—watch it!" Rubbing my shoulder, I glare at the person responsible, my gaze traveling skyward. Up a lean, hard chest with broad shoulders straining against a black t-shirt, dark ink covers almost the entirety of one arm. I could almost appreciate the intricate sleeve design if I was looking at it under

3

any other circumstances. I have to tilt my chin to find his face, because he's so tall. He easily has a foot or more on me. Though that's not saying much; *my five-foot-two isn't making anyone look twice.*

Equally dark eyes glare down at me, unreadable under the club lights. He offers no apology, no flicker of surprise. Just cold, intense eyes watching me like a hawk does its prey. Even with the loud music, the silence is heavy.

"Well?" I bite out, breaking our staring contest, heat creeping up my neck. "Nothing to say?" I eye him up and down like I could even stand a chance in this argument. "Manners, ever heard of 'em?" Anger that I've been ignoring—burying for weeks, flares violently under my skin given its first opportunity, primed and ready to explode all over this unsuspecting asshole.

His jaw ticks, barely, like he's fighting the urge to either smirk or strangle me. And by the look in his eye, I'm fairly certain it could go either way...

Doubling down, I cross my arms and lift my chin, tilting my ear in his direction to show him I'm not hearing his still non-existent apology, refusing to be the first to look away. I'm so tired of fucking asshole men who think they can walk all over me and do whatever the hell they want without having to apologize for it.

Something in his eyes shifts when I challenge him—darker, quieter, and infinitely more dangerous.

Oh fuck.

Regret washes through me, cold and sharp. Maybe I should've kept my mouth shut. Maybe—just maybe—picking a fight with the massive, tattooed nightmare god *might* not have been the best idea I've ever had...

Maybe.

Either way, it's too late now. I'm stubborn to a fault, so I lock in, rolling my shoulders back, straightening my spine, and narrowing my eyes as we enter the most terrifying standoff of my life. Despite my racing pulse and every instinct in my body screaming at me to look down or to run away, I can't.

His gaze pins me there, steady and unwavering, like he's just waiting for me to flinch. *To break.*

I don't.

My heart thunders so loud I swear he can hear it even over the pounding beat of the music, but I don't look away. *I won't look away.*

Until, out of nowhere, a hand clamps around my arm, breaking the spell and my steely resolve. I flinch; my head, and my gaze, jerks sharply to the left.

"Hey, where'd you go? Are you okay?" Lily's familiar voice is an immediate comfort, but her question drags my attention away just long enough to answer, and I have to force my voice to sound steady. Anger, and whatever this other insane emotion I'm feeling, choking it up.

"Yeah, fine," I reassure her. "We just got separated in the crowd, thanks to this asshole."

I turn back, gesturing to my new arch-nemesis, but he's—gone. The spot where he'd just been standing only a few seconds ago has already been swallowed up by the crowd. I crane my neck to see over them, but there's no trace of that towering, tattooed nightmare anywhere.

"What did you say?" Lily leans in closer, unable to hear me over the surrounding noise.

Frustrated, I give up my search of the crowd. "Never mind." I relent, shaking my head before turning back around.

"I found Cassie and Mia. They're over here." She grabs my hand, holding tightly this time as she once again pushes her way through the packed club to find our friends.

"Briar! Hey!" Cassie shouts over the music when she spots me behind Lily, diving forward to wrap me in a tight hug. My body stiffens with the contact, not overly a fan of people touching me. Even if they are friends.

"Cassie... Hi." I force a smile to my face, waving to Mia, who's right behind her. They're in a few of my classes at the Conservatory, though they're more Lily's friends than mine.

Lily smirks at me over the rim of her own glass as Cassie squeezes me tight, my best-friend since kindergarten is well aware of my distaste for physical contact.

Cassie releases me, and I inch a respectable distance away given the first opportunity. "We heard about Ben. What a douche!" She takes a sip from her glass, allowing Mia to chime in.

"At least now you can have a hot girl summer!" She winks encouragingly.

"Yeah, that's the plan." I force a smile, wanting nothing more than to escape this conversation. Seeing the bar a few feet away, I seize the opportunity. "I'm gonna get a drink."

The girls nod, falling right back into whatever conversation my arrival had interrupted, and I blow out a tense breath. My mind is still reeling as I lean over the bar, waiting to catch the bartender's eye. He's in the middle of pouring shots for a group of rather boisterous frat guys a few stools down, and so I settle in for what might be a minute.

That's when I feel it—a prickle of awareness on the back of my neck that sends a dark shiver down the length of my spine.

I glance up, my eyes drawn like a magnet to the exact spot

where he's leaning against the far wall, arms crossed. All the way across the packed dance floor, through the sweaty, writhing bodies of people dancing to the sinful beat of the music. With the same dark, unreadable expression on his face.

My breath catches in my throat.

Because he's staring *right at me*.

2

FERAL LITTLE NIGHTMARE

BRIAR

Now

"Five, six, seven, eight. Step one, two, three, four... Good!"

Stifling a yawn, I straighten my shoulders as I call out the counts. Doing my best to shake off the lingering exhaustion. It's my fifth dance class I'm teaching today, on top of the two classes of my own I had this morning. My only saving grace is that I'm not on the schedule for the club tonight. The thought of being able to curl up in bed at a reasonable hour is the only thing keeping me going at the moment.

Well, that and my third, or was it fourth cup of coffee today?

"Hit one, two, three, four... hold!" The students in this class are third years, part of the Delacroix Conservatory's exclusive upper school. Some of the best up-and-coming dancers in the country. Though right now, they're just trying to get through a full run-through of their routine for the upcoming winter showcase without crying.

Which is harder than it sounds.

And once they've done that, I'll hammer them on technique and performance, but for now, I'm letting a lot slide.

"Your marks!" I call out, watching the girls scramble to their new positions right before the key change. "Get there, Ava!" I frown, watching Ava fail to cross the stage in time to hit her mark. Tears leak down her cheeks, but she falls right back into step on beat. I smile to myself. The mark of a true professional, the ability to keep going even when something goes wrong. She'll get it. For a moment, I remember what it's like to be in their shoes. Their very *expensive custom-made* pointe shoes.

Everything, possibly their entire careers, hinges upon this recital. If it sounds dramatic, that's because it is. This performance will determine who stays and who gets cut. Some standouts may even receive an audition offer from a local or national company. It will also identify the frontrunners for admittance into the Delacroix pre-professional program.

A program that could make or break them. A program that's currently breaking *me*. Though, granted, most students aren't also working two jobs on top of the already grueling training schedule.

"Jade, step it up. I can see you phoning it in back there!"

Nearly out of sight, in the far back line, Jade stumbles when I call her out. Immediately correcting and delivering the expected full leg extensions on her kicks. I might be tired, but I'm still me. I expect 100% effort every single time, even if this is our tenth run-through this hour.

The studio door opens, and I catch my best friend and

roommate, Lily, slipping inside. She's in the pre-professional program with me too. I pretend not to see her, avoiding eye contact and stifling any remaining yawns. Making my way around the room, I pause briefly to admire Hannah's enviable extension, with a few quick words of encouragement. Hannah beams at the praise, lifting her chin just a little higher before entering her pirouette.

I feel Lily's eyes on me and look just about anywhere else. She's been all over me since I took the bartending job at the club. She's worried the late nights are going to be too much with my already stretched schedule.

She's not wrong. It is too much. Not that I'll ever admit it, over my dead body in fact. But she knows as well as I do that it's not like I have much choice in the matter.

The music comes to an end, and I address the class in my very best and oh-so-posh-ballet-teacher voice.

"Very good, ladies. I want you all to practice your numbers overnight. Ms. Marie will be at rehearsal tomorrow, and she will expect nothing short of perfection." I hope my eyes convey the adequate level of warning required...

Since the girls are in the upper school, this is their last week before the Conservatory closes for winter break. Some stay in the dorms, but most travel home during the break, but as soon as we're back in session, it's non-stop until the show-case in mid December. But if Ms. Marie senses even the slightest hint of weakness, she won't hesitate to make cuts now.

The girls nod politely with my instructions before breaking from their strict practice lines and scurrying, in a very un-balle-rina-like manner, to pack up their things.

Lily wastes no time before she pounces. "I saw that yawn,

Briar, don't think you can hide from me. What time did you get in last night?"

I feign disinterest, heading to the corner before slipping off my ballet slippers in favor of my favorite worn pair of ankle boots. Carefully, I wrap the pink ribbons and tuck the slippers away in my dance bag. Pointe shoes are expensive, and I have to be extra careful with mine to try to make sure they last as long as possible.

"I don't know what you're talking about. And I don't know, around two—maybe?"

"So, three?" Lily challenges my nonsense, and I cover my mouth with my arm to hide my laugh.

"Fine." I cave. Far too tired to carry on with this argument. "It *might* have been three. But I brought home over four hundred dollars in tips. So, I'd say it was worth it."

"Is it going to be worth it when you literally die of exhaustion? I know you had studio choreography with Ms. Evans this morning at six. Did you even sleep?"

I did... one hour. But who's counting?

Lily... apparently.

"I slept. Besides, with the extra cash from the club, I've got the money for Remi's meds today and my half of the rent."

"Okay, I can't be mad about that," Lily admits with a huff. "But I'm worried about you. It's too much! You know it's too much."

"It's fine. I can handle it." I drop my voice low so only she can hear me, "And you know I still owe Gio..."

She frowns at my mention of the local loan shark. Dancers in the pre-professional program don't get fancy things like health insurance or a living wage, so the first time Remi ended up in the emergency room, the hospital bills alone threatened

11

to bury me alive. When the hospital then threatened to delay or suspend treatment if I couldn't come up with at least half of what I owed them, I didn't hesitate to do what I had to.

Was it the best decision I ever made? *No.* But would I do it again? *In a heartbeat.*

The initial loan amount wasn't bad, but with Gio's insane terms and close to a forty percent interest rate, the debt has been difficult to pay off. Even though I haven't borrowed any more money despite Remi's ongoing treatments, I've barely touched the principal after the interest eats up almost all of my payments.

So now instead of hospital bills threatening to bury me alive, I have Giovanni Moretti for that.

He's been patient, but I know I'm pushing the limit. When he approached me a year ago about a job opening at a local club he's got his hands in, I didn't exactly feel like I could say no. Gio's intimidating, sure, but he's just a loan shark. It's not like he's one of the Irish Devils or the Russian Bratva.

"Are you working tonight?" Lily interrupts my train of thought before it can run off its tracks.

"No. I took tonight off." I give her a look. "It's an injection day."

Lily winces.

"I should have just enough time to grab another coffee before picking Remi up for her appointment."

"Speaking of the devil..." The hesitation in Lily's tone immediately has my full attention. Seeing the flash of alarm in my eyes, Lily continues quickly, "The daycare called. They couldn't reach you, so they called my cell."

"And you waited until now to tell me?" Lily's been in here for at least five minutes. "Is everything okay? Is Remi okay?"

My mind instantly spirals into every possible worst-case scenario.

"Remi's fine. She's fine." Lily instantly picks up on where my mind's gone and rushes to reassure me before she winces again. "But you need to go pick her up. Your feral little nightmare just hit another kid."

"Fuck." I glance up at the clock. I was supposed to stay and lock up the studio after the girls left, and even though they had already been dismissed, they don't seem to be in any hurry, judging by how they're sprawled out across the floor chatting.

"I'll cover for you," Lily offers quietly, urging me toward the door. "I have class in an hour, anyway."

"Thanks, Lil!" I exhale, rushing to grab my bag and water bottle.

"Pancakes for dinner?" she asks, attempting to lighten the mood.

"Pancakes for dinner," I confirm. Breakfast for dinner is Remi's favorite. We always make them together on injection days.

"Alright, give your little devil-spawn a kiss from Auntie Lily, okay?" She smiles. "I'll see you guys later at home."

"I will!" I call back as I rush out the door to go pick up my daughter.

NO

BRIAR

Then...

"Briar... Earth to Briar." Lily shakes me, drawing my attention away from the tattooed nightmare god watching me and back to her.

"What?"

"Ali's here!" Lily links her arm through mine, dragging me away with her. I have just enough time to reach out and grab the glass I'd finally gotten the bartender to give me.

As Lily tugs me through the crowd, I throw back a few big gulps of my vodka soda. *Alcohol.* I'm going to need so much more alcohol to survive being dragged around by her all night.

"Oh my god, Miles is with them!" Lily reels on me, her expression an equal mix of horror and excitement. The sudden change of direction forces me to pull up short, and the liquid in my glass sloshes dangerously up the sides, almost spilling over the rim. "He's so effing hot! Did he see me?"

I huff out a breath, steadying my glass. Recovering, I peek over her shoulder, catching sight of Miles Phillips smiling at the back of Lily's head.

"Safe to say he saw you." I smile at her, attempting to spin her back around, but she doesn't budge. "Well, what are you waiting for?" I nudge her again in Miles' direction. "Go talk to him."

Lily's cheeks flush a bright scarlet. She's been crushing on Miles for weeks now, ever since she met him at the Harvard regatta Ben had invited us both to over spring break.

Wait a minute...

Because if Miles is here... An icy dread fills me. If Miles is here, that means Ben probably is too. *I knew it.* I feel totally vindicated knowing that I fucking knew it!

While Lily agonizes over the decision, it's actually Miles who makes the first move, heading our way. My eyes dart from her to him, warning her of his incoming presence just before he reaches us.

"Hey, Lily!" Miles grins over her head at me. "Hi, Briar."

I wave awkwardly at him, my eyes flashing at my best friend, who's gone completely still. She slowly spins back around to face him, her hazel eyes wide, and her entire body tense.

"Hi," I hear her say, almost too quietly to be heard over the music, her freckled cheeks reddening even further.

"Do you want a drink?" He points behind us, toward the bar she'd just dragged me away from.

"Oh, I—um." I feel her hesitation, and she looks back quickly over her shoulder at me. I shoot her a look, one brow raised—*Will you go already*? Gently, I shove her back in Miles' direction to really hammer in my point, while answering for her.

"Yes. Yes, she does."

Despite my urging, Lily still looks torn, turning to mouth at me: "Are you sure? I don't want to leave you!"

Considerate, seeing as she dragged me here against my will. "Yes." I nod reassuringly, pointing back to Cassie and Mia, who aren't far from us, and holding up my half glass of alcohol. "I'll be fine. Go!" My eyes flash as if to say, *Girl, if you don't go get a drink with him right now...*

Her smile brightens, and she turns back to Miles, finally agreeing to get that drink.

I watch them on their way back to the bar. Miles places his hand on the small of Lily's back, gently guiding her through the crowd. He's a good guy. He's got *terrible* taste in friends but, a good guy. My gaze continues past them, scanning the length of the bar only to find Tall-Dark-and-Tattooed at the end. And he is...

Not looking at me.

No, he has settled his dark gaze on the dance floor.

Why do I feel... *disappointed?* I should be happy he's finally redirected his attention elsewhere, though part of me still wants to wring that apology out of him.

"So, Briar, I've been meaning to ask—" I turn back at the sound of Mia's voice, "—what's it like being *the* Bridget Rousseau's daughter? I mean, it's no wonder your technique is flawless! She's a literal legend. Did she hand-train you herself?"

Gripping my glass tighter, I school my face into the well-practiced smile I save for when someone inevitably brings up my prima ballerina mother. I don't know Mia very well; we only share one class together, and while her question seems genuine, when one of my classmates brings up my mother, it's usually to throw her in my face. The dance world is cutthroat and cruel, and getting into other dancer's heads is an art form at this level.

But what I'm not going to do is tell her the truth. Did Bridget Rousseau Ralston want a ballerina daughter? Of course, she did. But just for the optics. Bridget Rousseau's daughter was supposed to *follow* in her mother's footsteps. Bridget Rousseau's daughter was under no circumstances supposed to *surpass* them.

"It's an honor to be her daughter." I can practically hear my mother's voice in my head, the constant criticism: '*Point your toe, lift your chin, fix your posture—it's an embarrassment.*' "I certainly learned from the best; she has very high standards." *Or make that... impossible...*

Mia and Cassie quickly lose interest and soon delve deeper into discussing the various strengths and flaws of potential partners for the fall semester. I scan the crowd again, my eyes catching on a familiar head of dark brown hair.

Ben.

My stomach drops, and I feel sick. I immediately avoid eye-contact. The panic is instantaneous. I can't do this, can't see him, not here, not now. I'm not ready.

I'd lost track of how many times he called me before I finally blocked his number. He was nice, cute, funny, and I thought he liked me. I let my guard down and lesson fucking learned. I won't be making that mistake again.

My panic is immediate, the threat very real, when I see Ben pushing through the crowded bar, headed my way.

My mind runs through my options. Ben is currently between me and the exit, so there's no escaping that way. I could hide in the bathroom. But I can't stay in there all night, and I'm willing to bet he'd be waiting outside for me when I came out. Even though he was the one who cheated, he's been borderline stalking me, near desperate in his efforts to convince me to take him back.

There's always the fire alarm...

My eyes scan for emergency exits, once again taking me right past *him*.

His eyes are on me, slightly narrowed, and it's unsettling how intense his gaze is.

A wild idea pops into my mind, and I'm moving before I can really even think it through properly.

He sees me coming, watching me dart through the crowd. I get as close to him as I dare. Something about the guy just seems to radiate danger. But by the time I reach him, his eyes are once again elsewhere.

"Hi," I say, brighter than I feel. Forcing myself not to take a step back when his eyes slide to meet mine. "Remember me?" I tilt my head rather adorably to the side. "The girl you owe an apology to?"

He arches a brow but doesn't deny it—Doesn't say anything, actually.

"I figured out how you can make it up to me," I continue, since he is giving me absolutely nothing.

His head tilts ever so slightly to the side as he considers me. "Is that so?" He speaks for the first time and, *oh god*, his voice. Deep and dangerous with an intoxicatingly addictive lilt of an accent that I'm far too distracted to place. It shakes my nerve, ignites my core, and I nod quickly—too quickly.

"Mhmm."

He eyes me as if to say, *Well, go on.*

"I need a favor."

"No."

"I—no?" The rejection is so immediate I don't know how to react, so I just freeze. *Do I keep going or...*

He just stares back at me as if he's silently asking, *And you're still here because?*

Wow. Amazing. Perfect. Love that for me. I'll just go die of embarrassment now.

Too bad for him—I'm desperate. I chance a glance over my shoulder and spot Ben standing with Mia and Cassie, his gaze flicking between me and Mr. Miserable. I recognize the storm clouds brewing in his eyes.

"Listen." I sigh, rubbing my hand down over my face, regrouping. "I know how this is going to sound, and I really don't have time to explain—but could you, like... pretend to be my boyfriend for a second?"

"Just for a second," I breathe out, almost desperately, before I give him a chance to answer. My eyes plead with him to say yes.

He leans in, studying my face, before dropping his eyes to run the length of my body. My breath catches under the intensity of it, my lungs forgetting how to work. I'm still breathless by the time his eyes find mine again and he leans back against the bar.

"No."

"N-no?" I stutter out in shock, my cheeks burning now.

"No," he repeats in confirmation before looking past me, resuming his casual surveillance of the club. A quiet dismissal. He offers no explanation and doesn't even bother to look apologetic about it.

"Why?" I blurt out, unable to help myself.

His eyes widen for a fraction of a second as they snap back to me, as if surprised that anyone, especially me, would dare question his choices. But the surprise vanishes as quickly as it came, replaced by a glare so icy I shiver.

I shift uncomfortably on my feet, caught between my tattooed nightmare's glare and the burn of my ex-boyfriend's watchful gaze on the back of my neck.

"Please?" I try, one more time. "You don't even have to do anything! Just stand there and look boyfriend-y." I wince when his gaze narrows further, because on what planet would *this* guy ever look *'boyfriendy?'* "I'll owe you one!" I bat my eyelashes a few times and force a small smile, nodding to coax a *yes* out of him.

He tilts his head as if he's actually considering the proposal before the ghost of a smile appears on his lips. Sharp and fleeting, like he's enjoying a private joke. The sight of it gives me hope, even if it feels like I might be selling my soul to the devil to avoid my ex-boyfriend, but desperate times...

"No."

Wow, he sure likes that word.

Heat rushes to my cheeks, humiliation snapping into anger at his repeat rejections. I release a small scream of frustration.

Reigning myself in, I take a deep breath, an unhinged level of calm falling over me. "Fine. Fine. That's—fine." I thrust my thumb back over my shoulder. "I'm gonna go. Enjoy being miserable, I guess." I roll my eyes, spin on my heel, and walk away from the asshole, flipping him off without so much as a backward glance.

Fuck. Him.

4

IF LOOKS COULD KILL

BRIAR

Now

"It is unacceptable behavior."

"Yes, I agree it is unacceptable. I just—"

"She tackled the little boy! Pinned his arms under her knees before she hit him. With a *closed* fist!"

I take a steadying breath, trying to gather my thoughts and calm my already racing nerves after running all the way over here.

"I'm just trying to understand what happened? Remi wouldn't attack another child for no reason." I glance down at my daughter, who's scowling in the chair next to mine. She might have her moments, but this is a stretch, even for her.

"We're worried she's falling behind for her age. This type of behavior is not acceptable in our preschool classroom. But we know Remi may not have the vocabulary to express herself properly..."

The hair on the back of my neck rises, and irritation grows. Remi has plenty of words. She just *chooses* not to use them. She's quiet for her age, thoughtful; she just has a bit of a temper. Not exactly out of character for an *almost* four year old; they don't call them the terrible-threes for no reason.

"Again, if you could just take me through what happened before she hit him?"

Mrs. Davis ignores me. "We have a zero-tolerance policy at our school for violence. This is Remi's second strike. One more incident and we may be forced to expel her."

Expel a preschooler?

"She's three," I say flatly. "I'd hardly call her a threat."

Mrs. Davis' eyes drop to my daughter, a wary expression on her face. "Be that as it may, given today's incident, I recommend we schedule a parent-teacher conference to discuss Remi's social-emotional development as soon as possible."

I stare at her, wondering what the hell it is we're doing right now...

"Okay." I agree, even though I still think they're over-reacting.

"Ideally, we would like both you and Remi's father to be in attendance. Are there any particular days of the week that are better?"

I blink at her, and I feel tension creep up my spine.

"Actually, it'll just be me," I say awkwardly. "And Mondays would be best."

Mrs. Davis peers at me over her deep purple frames. Her mouth thins into a frown. "It would be in Remi's best interest if *both* parents attended. We'd like for everyone to be on the same page."

I draw a deep, controlled breath before I lean down to talk to Remi.

"Hey Rem, is your backpack still in Miss Ashley's classroom?"

Remi nods.

"Can you go grab it for me? We're almost ready to go."

Silently, Remi hops down off the chair. I watch her walk across the hall, disappearing into Miss Ashley's classroom before I turn back to address Mrs. Davis.

"Remi doesn't have a father. It's just me. So seeing as how he *doesn't exist*, if we could get that appointment scheduled? Because I have somewhere to be." My words are clipped, dripping with irritation, and though a quick glance at the clock tells me we still have over an hour until Remi's doctor's appointment, I want out of this office.

"Oh, I see." Mrs. Davis fiddles with her glasses before going back to her computer screen, judgement rolling off of her in waves. *Of course, the problem child belongs to the single mom.* I bite the inside of my cheeks. "My apologies," she mumbles, without looking me in the eye. "I have next Tuesday at three p.m.?"

I sigh. Pulling out my phone to check the schedule for that day. "I can make it work." I type it in quickly. "Is there anything else?"

"That's all," she says with clear dismissal.

"Why did you punch Jack, Rem?" I wait until we're fully around the block before I ask her the question the school practically refused to answer.

Remi scrunches up her nose. "Jack pushed me. He pushed me three times!"

Okay, fair. I probably would have punched him too.

"But why didn't you use your words?" I ask *because parenting...*

"I did! I told him to stop, but he didn't listen!" The glower on her face tells me she'd hit him again just thinking about it. I'm about to suggest that she should've told a teacher at that point when she continues, "And then he pushed Grace and she fell. So I punched him." She shrugs, with an air of nonchalance I can only gape at. "He thought it was funny, so I punched him again. And then he was sorry."

Jesus.

"Are you mad at me?" She looks up, her big round eyes full of genuine worry, and I sigh, moving us to the corner of the sidewalk, out of people's way before crouching down to her level.

"No," I admit. As frustrated as I am with the situation, I'm not really mad at her. *Where the hell were the teachers when all of this was going down?* "I'm proud of you for defending yourself and your friend, but next time I need you to do it with your words—or tell an adult. No fists." I shoot her a look that says I'm serious.

She rolls her eyes, a perfect mirror of my own signature move. With her blonde hair and dark eyes, she may look nothing like me, but she sure has my attitude.

"Remi," I warn.

"Fine," she bites out.

"And I need you to apologize to Jack tomorrow morning when you see him."

"But that's not fair!"

My eyes narrow, and her mouth snaps shut. Temper flaring, she crosses her arms again, shooting me a wicked little glare. *If looks could kill...*

"Fine," she huffs out in defeat, a pout forming on her lips.

"Okay." I twist one of her long blonde curls with my finger before she swats my hand away. She's as much of a fan of physical touch as I am, though she is the exception. I just want to squish her given any opportunity.

"Well," I say, checking the time on my phone. "We still have an hour before Doctor Haven. Do you want to get some ice cream?"

I've done my parenting duty, demanded reparations, and now—yeah, I'm going to reward my daughter for not taking some boy's shit lying down.

"Cookie dough?" she asks, bouncing up and down excitedly. Irritation falling away at the drop of a hat. I wish I could get over things that quickly...

"You got it."

5

FRACTURED

BRIAR

Now

There's a new nurse at Doctor Haven's office today. I have to cover my mouth with my hands, hiding my smile when she attempts to soften up my daughter's scowl with a few jokes. They're funny and probably would have a normal child laughing, but not Remi.

"I'm Nurse Holly."

"Hi Nurse Holly," I say in greeting when Remi just glares at her.

"Remi, right?" She checks the chart quickly to be sure. "I've got a question for you. Why did the banana go to the doctor?"

Remi says nothing in response, and I hold back a laugh at the growing look of absolute disdain on my daughter's face.

"He wasn't peeling very well!" Nurse Holly throws up her

arms on the punch line, but my almost-four-year-old just shoots daggers at her.

"Hmm, tough crowd," Nurse Holly muses, finally throwing in the towel on the lame jokes.

"It's nothing personal," I reassure her. "She's... tough."

Remi has always been aloof with strangers. She really only likes Lily and me. *In that order.*

The nurse is just about done checking all of Remi's vitals and asking me the required medical history questions when she runs her light scope across my daughter's eyes.

"Oh, wow." Nurse Holly looks from her to me, and I know she's taking in the bright blue of my irises. "Her eyes are—beautiful!" She leans in to get a closer look, and my jaw tightens, as it does anytime someone *notices.*

"Green and—"

"Brown," I finish for her.

"They almost look black..." Nurse Holly muses, still marveling at Remi's eyes. "I've never seen anything like it!"

"It's a rare form of heterochromia," I explain without trying to draw more attention to it. *A beautiful little flaw.* One half of each eye is a deep emerald green, the other half a dark brown, almost black, fractured clean down the middle. The colors are so dark that the differences are distinguishable only in direct light.

"Gorgeous," the nurse says, remembering herself and straightening up. "Such a pretty girl!" She bops Remi lightly on the nose, and the glint of violence in my daughter's eye is a *little too familiar.*

"Open up." Nurse Holly presses a popsicle stick down on Remi's tongue, her fingertips unwittingly entering the danger zone. Remembering our last dentist appointment, I jump out of my seat, edging my way into Remi's field of vision. Over Nurse Holly's shoulder, I shoot my daughter a look promising retribution should she bite down on Nurse Holly's finger.

The dark edges of Remi's eyes sparkle when they meet mine, but the nurse withdraws her fingers without incident, and I let out a breath of relief before slowly sinking back into my seat.

"No attacks since the last injection?" she asks, picking up her laptop to type out a few notes.

"No. Her asthma has remained well-controlled."

"That's great news!"

It is. But the fact remains that Remi's asthma attacks got so bad that now she has to get monthly injections to keep them under control. And to a four-year-old, *that's not so great.*

The door opens, and Doctor Haven appears. "Hi Remi!" she says as she strolls in, a bright smile on her face, holding out her hand for a high five. My daughter eyes it with suspicion, distrustful of the doctor who's repeatedly held her down and stabbed her with needles over the past few months.

Inching away from Doctor Haven, Remi slides off her chair, climbing into my lap. I wrap my arms protectively around her. She hates shots.

Seeing she's been left hanging, Doctor Haven quickly whips her hand away. "Ope! Too slow!"

She turns her attention back to me. "I'm pleased to see the monthly injections are keeping Remi's asthma symptoms at bay."

I nod in agreement.

"She's set to receive this month's injection today, but before we do, I wanted to discuss with you a new treatment that's recently become available."

I sit up in my seat because anything's got to be better than *shots* every month. They also don't always work, and we're still frequent flyers in the ER.

Doctor Haven nods, resting her clipboard on her lap. "There's a new drug on the market; recently FDA approved, the medical trials are incredibly promising with a much higher rate of prevention than her current medication. It does still require an injection, but yearly rather than monthly."

The words hang in the air because, as amazing as it sounds, it sounds too good to be true. And the tightness around Doctor Haven's eyes gives me pause.

"That sounds... incredible."

"It is," Doctor Haven says. "The attacks should be much more manageable, and there is much less risk should she choose to play sports."

A fragile flicker of hope dares to light in my chest. Afraid to let it grow, I ask the question I know is about to bring the dream crashing down. "How much?"

Doctor Haven frowns. "It is expensive," she warns. "Very expensive." Remi's doctor is already well-aware that we are cash-only patients with no health insurance to help offset the cost of the medications. Picking her clipboard back up, she reads off the number. "Let's see, out-of-pocket, you're looking at $10,700 per injection."

Almost eleven grand? Fuck me.

My jaw tightens, not needing to run any calculations in my head to know there is no way I can swing that. "Any chance you offer payment plans?" I ask meekly.

"We do," she says with an air of reservation. "But the policy requires the balance paid in full prior to scheduling the injection." She nods in the nurse's direction. "Holly here can help get you set up."

Nurse Holly picks her laptop back up from where she left it on the table. "Did you want to set it up today? It would require at least a fifty percent down payment."

My cheeks flush with embarrassment. I only have enough for Remi's injection today.

"No, that's okay. I'll call later this week," I say in a rush.

She nods politely, offering me a kind smile, before Doctor Haven slides forward on her rolling stool, inching closer to the shiny stainless steel tray of instruments beside the table.

"Okay, Remi, are you ready to earn your sticker?"

I tighten my grip on my daughter right before all hell breaks loose.

6

RED FLAG?

BRIAR

Then...

"C'mon, Bri, just one drink."

I grit my teeth at the nickname. Ben wastes no time sidling up to me the moment I'm alone.

He sighs audibly when I don't answer him. Seeing as I've already politely declined his invitation for a drink *twice* now, I'd rather save my breath.

"It's been weeks; aren't you over whatever this is by now?"

"Whatever this is?" I give him a hard look. "It's a breakup, Ben. There's nothing to 'get over.' We're *over*. There's no getting back together. We were over the second you cheated on me with what's-her-face."

Ben's face reddens. "I've told you a million times, Harmony and I are just friends!" Ben half whines, having the audacity to look irritated with me. It's taking every ounce of self-control I possess not to slap him across the face. Maybe I should have taken him up on that offer to buy me a drink, seeing as my glass of vodka soda is empty...

"Last time I checked, *friends* don't shove their tongues down other *friend's* throats."

He blocks my attempt to shove past him, catching hold of my arm and wrenching me back against the bar top. I wince at the tightness of his grip.

"That never happened," he growls.

I roll my eyes, so over this bullshit. Seriously? "There's literally a photo of it happening!"

"Bri, I told you, I was so drunk that night. I don't even remember it!" His hand releases me, flying up in his defense.

I want to scream. "That doesn't make it okay!"

"C'mon, one drink? Just let me buy you one drink and we can talk." His expression flips from anger back to manipulative sweetness. The back of his finger comes up to graze the bare skin of my abdomen before he grips my side, trying to pull me closer to him.

I reach down and rip his hand off my hip.

He responds by leaning in closer, using the same hand to tuck a loose strand of hair behind my ear. My blood is boiling.

"Stop touching me!" I lean as far away from him as I can, the sharp edge of the bar top behind me digging into my spine. I feel a rush of panic when both his arms come down on either side of me, caging me in. He ignores me. His mouth finds my jawline, and there's nowhere left to recoil to.

"C'mon, baby," he breathes in between kisses, still thinking I'm going to change my mind. "I know you've missed me. I've missed you too."

"Ben—" I bring up both of my hands preparing to shove him away from me, but he's already—gone?

An inked hand circles around my waist from behind, lightly drawing me into the side of—

Oh, my god. Recognizable by his scowl alone, it's Mr. Tall-Dark-and-Miserable from earlier, but he's not looking at me. No, this time, his piercing gaze is fixed with deadly precision on my ex-boyfriend.

"Did you just put your hands on my girl?" There's a quiet fury in his words, his voice cold and controlled, but the threat within them is unmistakable.

Did he just say *my girl*?

Without letting go of me, my tattooed nightmare leans forward, speaking directly into Ben's ear. I can't hear what he's saying, but the blood drains from Ben's face; his skin pales, eyes widening in utter shock. The guy leans back, his grip on me is solid.

Ben looks in between the two of us, and he looks like he wants to say something, but the guy at my side tilts his head ever-so-slightly, and Ben goes ghostly white. His mouth snaps shut, and he turns, disappearing into the crowd without another word.

I stare after him in disbelief. "What did you—?"

"Follow me." The tattooed hand slips from my waist to grip my hand before stepping away from the bar. He pauses when his tug meets resistance, seeing as how I'm still frozen in place.

Partially in shock and still stunned by what just happened, I give in and follow, allowing him to lead me through the crowded bar.

The crowd parts for him like the Red Sea, and we have no trouble reaching the VIP section far off to the right. The bouncer unhooks the velvet rope without a word. There's fewer people in here, and I'm instantly grateful for a little extra space to breathe.

"Do you want a drink?"

I whip my head back to my still-unnamed savior. "What?" I shout over the loud music, processing his words only after I've already replied.

"A drink?" he repeats, but leans in closer this time. So close I can smell him, and—*oh*, he smells... *good*. I take a deep inhale of the dark citrus scent, only to realize he's still waiting for an answer.

"Oh, um... water. Please." I shoot him a nervous glance. "A bottle of water," I rush to add, swallowing hard under the intensity of his gaze. "If they have it."

He leans back, speaking into the ear of some other guy I hadn't noticed was lingering nearby. He nods, heading back to the bar.

I watch him go. I've never been in the VIP section of a club before, so maybe that's normal?

His hand is still on mine, but I don't pull away. He guides me up the stairs to an even more exclusive balcony section of the club, leading me to a set of empty armchairs. They're tucked into the far corner by the railing, but damn, you can see the entire club from up here.

I'm distracted, eyes scanning the scene below, so I'm defenseless when he takes a seat, tugging me backward. A yelp escapes me. He puts me on his lap, my back pressed against his hard chest, making me far too conscious of how I am straddling his knee.

I attempt to lunge for the empty armchair beside me, but his hand on my abdomen keeps me in place.

"He's still watching." That deep voice is in my ear, his

tattooed finger moving right past my eye, directing my attention all the way through the crowded bar until I find Ben.

So he didn't leave.

He's rejoined his friends, nursing some trash IPA, I'm sure, all while glowering in our direction.

I let out a deep sigh, my body relaxing slightly, and the hand drops away from my stomach, though the heat of his touch still lingers on that sliver of bare skin.

The man from earlier reappears with two bottles of water. Still sealed. He hands one to each of us before reassuming his post, watching our backs.

I furrow my brow, glancing back at my mystery man as he downs half of his bottle of water.

"You're not drinking?" I ask, surprised.

"Neither are you." He points to the still unopened bottle of water in my hand.

"Yeah, well—" I eye him carefully, gripping the bottle tighter. "I don't drink around people I don't know," I admit. Usually I would lie and say it's because I have an early morning or something along those lines, but something tells me lying to this man, even a white lie, is a bad idea.

"Clever girl." The corner of his mouth ticks up as he takes another sip from his water. His praise travels straight through to my core, and it's an effort not to squirm from where I'm perched on his knee.

"What about you?" I ask casually. *Too casually.*

"I don't drink when I'm working."

I sit up straight, glancing around us. "Working? You work here?"

"You could say that," he replies almost absentmindedly. His attention focused on something located over my shoulder.

I follow his eyes back to Ben, who looks like he's fighting an internal battle on whether or not to brave coming over here.

"He wants you."

"Very observant." I roll my eyes at the obvious, and my shoulders tense when I see a wicked gleam enter his eyes.

"But you don't want him."

It's not a question. I glance back in Ben's direction. We dated for almost two years, but mostly because of pressure from our parents. Close family friends and what-not. Ben was at Harvard; I was at Delacroix—it just made sense. Until it didn't.

"No." I steal a word out of his playbook, while offering no further explanation.

Fingers on my chin bring my face back around to him. He brings me close, drawing me in until we're only inches apart. His eyes are on my lips. Eyes that I notice are—fractured down the middle. I'd thought earlier they were a dark green, but up close I can see how each iris splits perfectly in half. Half green, half brown. It's unsettling, honestly, but beautiful. Angelic and demonic.

Those fractured eyes fix on me now, heated; they feel like fire on my skin.

"What was the plan exactly?"

My cheeks flush. "I don't know. It's not like I planned this. I just—we broke up weeks ago, and my roommate convinced me to come out, but then Miles was here..." I'm over-explaining, but this guy has me so off-kilter. "And then I saw Ben, and I—panicked." I look into his eyes, surprised to find he's listening intently despite my rambling. I swallow, twisting my fingers together. "Maybe part of me wanted to get back at him for cheating on me. And part of me wanted to show him I moved on and that I wasn't sitting at home for weeks in my pajamas eating ice cream and watching shitty-ass romance movies because of him."

I might be imagining it, but I think his hard gaze softens slightly.

"And how *far* do you want to go to prove you've moved on?" His eyes are anything but cool now. He drops his gaze back to my lips, leaning in further, invading my space, invading my... soul, when I inhale that dark citrusy scent of him once again. He hesitates, his hands are on my waist, just before his mouth lightly grazes against mine, giving me the opportunity to pull away, if I want to.

But I don't want to—I don't think. I stay where I am, my eyes flicking up to find him reading my expression.

"*Far*," I whisper.

His eyes flash—my only warning before his lips crash against mine. His hand slides up, gripping the back of my neck, and this man doesn't just kiss me... No, he claims my mouth. My lips part, and he takes full advantage. His tongue sweeps through, tangling with my own. Strong hands grip my hips, and I have no control over my thighs when they tighten around him, forgetting for a moment just how very much in public we are.

He's the first to pull away, and a small whimper escapes me at his sudden absence, my lips chasing his.

His face is a stone mask, but his eyes—his eyes are molten, staring at my mouth, slowly lifting. "Do you want to get out of here, love?"

That accent. I feel it twisting inside me. I'm still nearly breathless from his total invasion of my senses.

I bite my lip, trying to decide, and I swear I feel something harden underneath me.

I weigh my options. This guy is built. He's both exceedingly tall and muscled; I wouldn't stand a chance against him in a fight. Everything about him screams danger. Red flags all around. He's a wild card, but yet, every touch from him has been gentle, respectful. Except for his claim on my mouth... that was straight sin. And god if I don't need more.

"I—I don't even know your name," I sputter out, flustered and torn.

He stares at me for a long moment, as if deciding something.

"Rí."

I arch a brow, leaning back to look at him, my arms still wrapped around his neck. *Wait, when did they get there?*

"Ree?" I repeat, uncertain if I'm hearing him right, but he nods in confirmation. My eyes narrow with suspicion. "That's not your real name."

"No, it's not," he admits, to my surprise.

"What's your real name?"

"It's better if you don't know." His eyes flash again, and *oh, the flag, Briar. It's bright, glaringly red.*

"What's your name?"

I chew my lip, indecision muddying up my mind. Are we doing this? Am I doing this? Lily's words play back in my mind. And Rí looks like just what I need to blow off a little steam.

"Rose," I breathe out after some hesitation, keeping my eyes on his.

"Rose," he repeats, and *oh man,* it's not even my real name, and that Irish accent makes me want to melt. His eyes sparkle. "Now we're both liars."

He rises carefully, lifting me off his lap. He says something to the guy at our backs before his gaze finds me again. "Ready?"

"N-No," I stutter out, my nerves getting the better of me, and I watch his brows rise.

"No, I—" I let go of his hand, backing away from him and his friend, who is watching me now too. "I'm actually gonna go. Thanks for the, err—save. I owe you one!" I call out, before I bolt for the exit.

I don't look back even though I feel the burn of his stare on my neck the entire way out.

7

NOT MY GIRL

KOEN

THEN...

Intriguing.

Rose.

Dark hair, bright blue eyes that look almost ethereal in the neon glow of the club lights, and a face that looks like she'd been hand-carved by angels.

Most people know better than to look me in the eye. And those that don't, figure it out real quick the first time they make that mistake. They catch a glimpse of the dark soul radiating through my resting glare and they look away, finding any and every excuse to flee my presence.

But not her.

She's not from around here. Untouched and untainted by the dark side of Boston I call home. *Good.* Honestly, I should have left it that way, should have left her to deal with that shit-stain of an ex all on her own. But from the moment she glared up at me, stepping closer while demanding an apology, outright refusing to back down even once she glimpsed the darkness in my eyes... oh, she'd gotten under my skin.

Nothing gets under my skin.

No one.

She caught me staring. The little smirk on her face said as much. And then she had the audacity to ask me for a *favor*? Innocently unaware how favors are currency in my dark world.

It was tempting to take her up on it. I could've demanded just about *anything* from her. Her desperation was written all over her face. The possibilities were endless.

But pretend to be her *boyfriend*?

No.

Not my girl, not my problem, not my... *anything*.

I'd sent her on her way, though she hadn't exactly gone quietly. I almost wish I'd said yes and only so I could teach that mouth of hers a lesson.

Rose.

Still, I couldn't help the way my eyes tracked her. The way they watched her stand anxiously by the bar, looking around for the friends she'd arrived with. A guy—*her ex* I presume—wasted no time latching on to her.

He'd been watching her too. Watched her come to me, watched her get rejected, and then moved in, scenting blood in the water. He stood too close. It was clear by her body language she doesn't want him anywhere near her. I saw that fiery side of her flare again when he touched her, she shoved his hand away but he just smiled. The fucking asshole. He backed her up against the bar until she was trapped between his arms, uncomfortable, eyes darting wildly for help. People around her noticed but did nothing about it.

I was moving before I knew it.

How *dare* he touch what's *mine.*

My girl, I'd called her, wrapping my arm around her side, my fingers just grazing the bare skin of her back. I can still feel the electric shock that traveled into me when I made contact. Searing hot, a wicked thrill shooting through me with all the discretion of a lightning bolt, sparking something long dead back to life. I liked how she felt against me, the warmth of her skin, how she drew closer after I'd claimed her, finding safety under my protection.

He wouldn't touch her.

No one would ever fucking touch her again.

She got what she'd wanted finally: my attention. But when I asked her if she wanted to get out of here, she said no. Then practically ran out of the bar.

I let her go. Didn't try to stop her when she shakily climbed up off my lap, awkwardly waving goodbye and reminding me that she owes me one.

Oh, I know little Rose. I haven't forgotten.

Then she was gone. Made a beeline for the exit, like she felt the dark pull between us and the overwhelming urge to run from it just as much as I did.

She left her friends at the bar. Her ex was too busy getting thrown out the back by my guys to notice how she just slipped out into the night.

Alone.

Leaving me no choice but to follow her.

My bike is parked just outside the bar—one of the perks of being the owner. I hop on, the engine growling to life beneath me, powerful and built for speed, but I rein it in, gliding slowly down the street.

I keep my distance, hoping she doesn't notice the persistent rumble of my bike following her, keeping watch as she rounds the corner, heading for the nearest subway station.

She's halfway down the next street before she encounters trouble.

A group of about five or six college-age guys is headed for her. Her steps slow and I can see her consider whether or not to cross the street but there's a canal separating this side of the street from the other.

Lifting her chin she powers forward, passing the group without giving them another glance, but I see the moment *they* notice her. Too caught up in themselves to see her before. I watch as their heads turn and drop, checking out her ass and legs in that short as fuck skirt she's wearing.

One of them shouts something after her but she doesn't answer, doesn't turn, but I see her shoulders tense, how her fists clench at her side. The street light ahead of her is broken, leaving that end of the street cast in shadow. I grit my teeth, my grip tightening on the handle as I watch the scene play out.

One of the guys stops entirely, changing direction and walking back toward her.

Not willing to find out what happens next I pull in the clutch, adding a bit of throttle to speed forward until I slide up to the curb right beside her.

Both Rose and the guy following her stop in their tracks, looking over at me.

Rose backs away, moving toward the guy at her back, but

when I lift my visor I see the flash of recognition followed by a quick flash of relief. My gaze trails past her, to the man following her, and my eyes no sooner make contact before he's turning around, shooing his friends back down the street.

Rose follows my gaze, watching them.

"You want a ride?"

Her eyes are wary, and she doesn't answer the question. Instead, her sharp blue eyes narrow in suspicion. "Are you following me?"

"Yes."

Her brows lift at my admission. "Why?" She didn't expect me to admit to it, and her question comes out a little breathless.

"You're walking home alone—*at night*—in Boston," I say, like it should be obvious.

"I'll be fine."

I arch a brow. Are she and I on the same street? She's tiny and all five-foot-two of her doesn't stand a chance against what I know is out there.

I don't have an extra helmet, so I pull off the one I'm wearing and hold it out to her.

She doesn't take it, looking between me and the helmet like I just asked her to do a bump of coke or something.

"Get on."

Her gaze trails over the bike underneath me. "Is it safe?"

"No."

She blinks up at me but I just stare back. *It's not safe.* On the bike, nor with me, and I'm not about to lie to her.

"I—I'm going to pass," she says, reading the look in my eyes.

"You sure?" I question, watching her throat as she swallows

44

hard before nodding quickly. I resist the sudden urge to grab her by it, and force her onto the back rather than let her go. But instead, I tighten my grip on the helmet in my hands, dragging it back down over my head.

"Okay, have it your way," I shrug, leaning back on my bike and settling into the seat.

She's got a suspicious look on her face; I gave in way too easily.

"Thanks anyway. And thanks again... for before..."

I nod.

"Have a good night." She waves, awkwardly, and spins—too fast, nearly knocking herself off balance after tripping on the uneven sidewalk before taking off in the direction she was going before I'd stopped her.

I watch her go, letting her get a few feet ahead before I start my bike, edging it forward a little bit before allowing it to idle again.

Rose's pace slows and she glances back over her shoulder at me once, before continuing her walk down the dark street.

Again, I allow her to go a few more feet before I release the clutch, gliding the bike forward before stopping just behind her.

Rose looks back again, and this time I wave, placing both feet on the ground while I gesture for her to *please, keep going*.

Her eyes flash with anger and she whirls around, storming back to me.

I lift my visor and wait, sitting back in my seat and folding my arms across my chest. *Oh, she's cute when she's mad.*

"Are you going to follow me the whole way home?" she demands, looking me up and down.

This girl. Most people would be cautious around me... fearful, polite, careful. But not her. Not Rose. She sees the danger, sure, but snaps back anyway.

"Looks like it," I tell her with a bored expression on my face.

"I can handle myself," she snarks, straightening her shoulders back and lifting her chin before turning to walk away again.

"Is that so?" I arch a brow at her, my tone mockingly impressed. She freezes. "I seem to recall you asking, oh wait no —*begging* for my help earlier."

Her cheeks flush a bright pink, the color a distraction. *I wonder if they do that when she comes too...*

"You can stop following me."

"I can," I agree with a short nod.

Satisfied, she spins on her heel, gracefully this time, and stalks back off down the street. Her heels click loudly against the concrete sidewalk.

Once again, I pull the clutch and give the bike some gas, however, this time I don't stop. This time, I ride up right alongside her, keeping pace.

The withering look she gives me makes me smile. "Just because I can, doesn't mean I'm going to."

"Oh my god, you're relentless!" she seethes, stopping in her tracks and throwing up both hands in exasperation, before burying her face in them.

It's fun, needling her.

"In more ways than one." I smirk, spying a sliver of blue peeking out at me between her fingers.

"Listen," I say, seriousness taking over my tone. "You can either get on the bike and let me give you a ride home, or you can get used to me following you. Because I agreed to be your fake-boyfriend for the night, which means in good conscience, I can't just leave you out here alone." I stare down at her, my eyes dark and uncompromising.

She sighs, looking forlornly in the direction that must be home.

"Fine." She deflates, stepping closer to me and holding out a hand for my helmet. I slip it off, silently handing it to her, and she rolls her eyes before pulling it on.

"So where to?" I ask, watching as she fumbles with the helmet straps.

"Home, I guess." She shrugs and I pick up on a slight trace of disappointment in her voice. It's still early, just a little after eleven. She went to Last Call with her friends, probably hoping to have a fun night out, only for her ex to show up and ruin it.

And now she's stuck with me.

I tilt my head, studying her. "You sure? Do you *really* want to go home?"

She's quiet for a minute, her fingers still on the straps while she stares down at the pavement, debating whether or not to let honesty win.

"No." The admission is quiet but I hear it.

Reaching out, I grip under the chin of the helmet, pulling her closer, which brings her eyes flying back up to mine.

I hold her gaze, carefully looping the strap of the helmet through its cinch, and tightening it until it's snug. And *fuck*, touching her again, letting my fingers graze the delicate skin just under her jaw... it's addictive, this feeling.

"Okay, get on the back."

She does so without argument, holding onto my shoulders to keep her balance as she swings her leg over. As she settles around me, her hands tentatively snake around my middle,

47

lighting up each and every nerve along the way until she's fully wrapped around me.

Kicking the bike stand back with the heel of my boot, I'm just about to release the clutch when I feel her tense, her body growing rigid against my back.

"Wait, you're not a murderer right?" The words race out of her, half panic, half joke. "Like I didn't just jump on the back of a serial killer's bike?" She laughs nervously, her grip on my waist uncertain.

I smile quietly to myself. "Serial killer? No." I reassure her. "Murderer? Only sometimes." I spin around in my seat so she can see my face, giving her a little wink; she smiles back and a relieved laugh escapes her because she thinks I'm joking.

"So, where are we going?" she asks, settling back in around me.

"Not home." I smirk, revving the bike and feeling it vibrate excitedly beneath us. A dark thrill shoots through me when her arms tighten around my waist.

"Don't let go," I warn, before I release the clutch and speed off into the night.

8

AN OPPORTUNITY

BRIAR

Now

"No dancing," Remi pouts after I wrestled her into her pink leotard and tutu while hurriedly pulling her little ballet slippers out of her dance bag. The rest of her class is already warming up at the barre. She put up such a fight at Doctor Haven's office that we're running late.

Remi hasn't quite taken to dance the way I wish she would. I was hoping the more she did it, the more she'd love it, but if anything, she's only grown to hate it even more.

"Yes, dance," I tell her with a frown. The last thing I want to do is force her into an activity she doesn't like, so I need to figure something else out, but right now I need Remi in *her* class, so I can go to *mine*.

But when I reach down for her foot to put her slipper on, she rips it out of my hands, throwing it back on the ground with a wicked pout. I pause... I have to tread carefully because we *so* do not have time for a Remi-tantrum right now.

"No dance," she says again, crossing her little arms and lifting her chin up to glare at me.

I let out a slow breath, pinching the bridge of my nose. *She's had a long day—I've had a long day.* I just need to get us both to the end of it in one piece.

"Okay Rem, I'll make you a deal," I offer, not above bribery at this point.

Her little eyes flick up to meet mine with interest.

"You go to dance, and if Miss Emily says you did a nice job, I'll put chocolate chips in your pancakes tonight."

She visibly brightens, her arms falling to her sides. "Chocolate chips?"

"Mhm." I nod, seizing the opportunity to snatch her right foot, successfully getting the slipper on while she's debating whether or not my deal's worth it. "In all their chocolate-y goodness." I'm over-selling but... desperate times...

"Okay, chocolate chips," she agrees, and I let out a sigh of relief when she offers me her left foot all on her own.

"That's my girl!"

I deposit a light kiss on her forehead, leaving her in Studio C before turning and sprinting down the hallway. I dodge dancers and trailing glares of annoyance before attempting to slip into Studio A as quietly and unassumingly as possible.

I catch the warning look in Lily's eyes while I put my pointe shoes on as fast as I can. I already feel Mr. Carr watching me, clearly displeased at my tardiness. *At least he hasn't kicked me out. Small victories.*

I'm quick to the barre and fall into the warm-up routine with the rest of the class.

An hour in, I'm a mess of sweat as we go across the floor. But I'm distracted, unable to stop my mind from trying to work out how the hell I'm going to pay for that new injection. Apparently, it shows because Mr. Carr is quick to call out my mistakes, his tone growing sharper as the class goes on.

When he finally calls for a water break, it takes nearly everything in me not to collapse in relief.

"What's up with you?" Lily hisses, scurrying over as I down nearly my entire water bottle in one go, breathing hard. "You're so tense." And then lower, in a near whisper, "Did something happen at the appointment?"

Tense? Yeah, I'd say so. My body is so wound up, I feel like I might explode. An anxious feeling has settled deep into my chest, and it seems no amount of intense cardio is going to shake it.

I glance around, drawing Lily slightly away from the rest of the dancers in our group before quickly filling her in on what happened at Remi's appointment.

Her eyebrows nearly touch the sky when she hears the price.

"TEN THOUSAND dollars!" she exclaims, loudly, drawing attention from the other students.

"Shhh!" I nod, chewing on the inside of my cheek as I come up with ways I could get my hands on that money. But aside from pulling a bank heist, I'm falling short on ideas.

I'm in my final year of the pre-professional program at the Conservatory, and if it weren't for my scholarship, dance and I would've been finished a long time ago. The money Lily and I make teaching dance classes for the lower levels just about covers rent, groceries, and the bare necessities. This is exactly the situation that led to my having to borrow the money from Gio in the first place.

"You're not thinking—" Lily starts.

I shake my head. "I don't know that I have a choice..." Referencing borrowing more money from Gio. *Hell, I'm already in the hole, can I really make it worse?*

But she's adamantly shaking her head. "No. That's a bad idea. You're already in too deep with him."

"Maybe I can pick up some more shifts at the club?" Lily was correct earlier. I am at my limit, but I could still try to do more. *Who needs sleep, right?* "I could pick up dancing shifts?" I whisper under my breath.

The club Gio was nice enough to hook me up with is a strip club. While I have thought about picking up a couple of dancing shifts, I really hate when the men at the club try and touch me. So, I've only been working bartending or serving shifts. They don't pay as much but they sure as hell pay a lot more than they would at a regular restaurant.

Lily doesn't have time to respond because Mr. Carr calls the class back to attention.

He has us do the routine a few more times. My performance isn't great; I'm tired, but surprisingly Mr. Carr doesn't comment on it again.

"That's it for today. Remember to practice overnight. I hope to see better results in class tomorrow." His eyes stop on me, and I shift uncomfortably under his heavy stare. "Miss Ralston, a word?"

I feel the eyes of my classmates on me, so I nod stoically, straightening my shoulders back while scrambling to follow Mr. Carr into his office. He motions to a chair by the door, and I sit, uneasy, as he leans back in his.

"I hope you don't have plans to go home for winter break?"

Having not been home in four years, no, I don't have plans to break that streak anytime soon.

"I'll be staying in Boston," I confirm.

"Good." He nods sharply. "Because Catarina broke her ankle."

My mouth drops. "Oh my god, is she okay?" Catarina is the lead in the pre-professional piece for the upcoming winter showcase. *If Catarina broke her ankle, that means...*

"She's as you'd expect her to be." His eyes flick to mine. "Or well, you should know *exactly* how being forced to give up a major role in a show feels."

Ouch. That was pointed. He's never going to forgive me for getting pregnant my second year and having to drop out of all major performances.

"Anyway, Catarina can't dance the excerpt from Sleeping Beauty in the showcase. And *you* are our pick to replace her."

Those are words I never thought would come out of his mouth. "But I thought Julia was her understudy?"

Mr. Carr's mouth sours. "*Julia* can't handle the role." His gaze falls heavily on me. "Do *you* think you can handle it, Miss Ralston?"

No.

Yes.

Fuck.

"I think so," I respond, carefully, still processing the implications.

Mr. Carr frowns and I swallow the lump in my throat, the one reminding me how Lily's going home for winter break this year—and not to mention everything else I have going on with Remi at the moment.

"Yes, I can do it. I want it." I don't know how I'll do it, but I will. *I have to.* This role could change *everything.*

He smiles, *a rare sight,* sitting back in his chair. "This showcase is a huge opportunity for you, Miss Ralston. I didn't hesitate when I recommended you for it. But let me make myself clear: the showcase is a lot of work, both on and off the stage. And it is also our biggest fundraising event of the year. And as principal, you're expected to attend all rehearsals, meet with sponsors, and of course, attend the winter gala."

The annual fundraising gala. There is nothing I hate more than the idea of stuffing myself into a formal dress and rubbing elbows with Boston's high society. Nevertheless, I nod my agreement. Anything for this opportunity.

"If I see anything like I saw out there today, I will not hesitate to pull you from the showcase myself. Am I being clear?"

My cheeks are on fire when I nod. "Yes, sir."

"Showcase practice starts next week; it will be on top of your existing schedule. You'll make it work?" He eyes me questioningly, well aware of my *situation* with Remi and childcare.

"I'll make it work," I assure him, though I don't know how. But the showcase could land me a full-time job with the Conservatory or an audition with another dance company that could change *everything.* I could pay Gio back what I owe him, fund Remi's medical care, and not to mention get us out of Roxbury.

He nods approvingly. "I'll e-mail you the rehearsal schedule." I recognize the dismissal in his tone and rise from my seat, heading for the door.

"Oh, and Briar?"

I turn back. "The director of the Boston Ballet has just about confirmed attendance."

My heart skips a beat. Possibly even stops beating altogether. My *dream* company. Unlike my peers, I can't just audition for any role, or rather, any company. I have a child, so I won't be able to travel for work, go on tour, or even travel for auditions for stationary roles in other cities. The Boston Ballet is one, if not the *only* option. And their auditions are invitation-only. They only take the best of the best.

Mr. Carr reads the look on my face. "Good. Now that you know the stakes, go home and practice. Your pas de *chat* looked like a pas de *splat*."

9

DOWN BAD

KOEN

Now

Last Call is at capacity. From the private balcony above the main floor of the club my brothers and I own, I stand, arms crossed, scanning the crowd, the way I always do—practiced, methodical.

The bar maxed out over an hour ago and the line to get in now circles the block.

It's a good weekend for us. The colleges are back in session, and hockey season is starting up again.

My eyes catch on a tiny dark-haired girl squeezing her way through the dance floor, but just as soon as I give her a second glance, I already know... it's not *her*. I'm meant to be keeping an eye on the crowd, but somehow it always ends up with me looking for her.

They're never *her*.

The fact that I can't help it pisses me the fuck off. I hate the way my eyes catch on every five-foot-something, dark-haired girl, *just in case.*

For what reason, *I don't fucking know.* It doesn't matter. My little ballerina, forever dancing fucking circles around my head. If I had known that almost five years later I'd still be thinking about *her,* I never would have gone after her that night.

She *ruined* me.

My little Rose was a brand of drug all her own. One I've never been able to find anything close to. No one else compares. She crawled under my skin, injected herself into my bloodstream with a single kiss—the taste of her potent, like the sweetest of drugs, and after just one hit, I was hers.

But I couldn't have her, and I fucking hated her for it.

"What's Aidan doing?" Mac asks and that grabs my attention. He leans forward over the railing, signaling to both Jerrad and Garrett who are down on the floor tonight, backing up the bouncers.

I look down, easily spotting my brother stalking through the packed crowd. It parts easily for the growling six-foot-three hockey god as he prowls closer to the dance floor.

Both of my brothers are here tonight, and we have them to thank for this packed crowd, and the line curving around the block outside.

They're here celebrating the Boston Breakers, their pro hockey team's first pre-season win tonight. And they've brought most of their team and cheerleaders with them.

And where the team goes, sport fanatics and puck bunnies tend to follow, and I'm happy to reap the benefits. The better our legit businesses do, the less shady shit we have to run in the background.

I keep my eyes on my brother. He never leaves VIP when he's here with the team; he comes out of obligation only, typically bowing out at the first opportunity. Unlike our manwhore of a little brother who I can see over by the back bar. Liam's got a girl draped on each arm, neck-deep in shots of Jack, oblivious to everything going on around him as he takes his time making out with each girl, not an ounce of shame in sight.

Aidan's eyes are fixed on something up ahead, his fists curled at his side. It could be trouble, and instinctively, my hand trails over to the gun at my waist. Pushing through the crowded dance floor, he makes it to his destination, both Garrett and Jerrad not far behind, and now I can see just what has caught my younger brother's attention.

His little Russian obsession.

Aurora Kostalova, aka Rory, the Bratva princess, is talking to none other than Cam Reeves—or well, *was talking to him,* as Aidan sees to that immediate problem.

I shake my head, my hand leaving the handle of my gun to run down my face.

Mac sits back too, taking a sip from his beer and laughing, enjoying the show. "Your brother is down bad for that girl."

He laughs again when I growl into my cup, watching the situation play out below.

He's not wrong.

And Mac would know, he's known Aidan almost as long as I have.

While my brothers still do work for the Devils, neither of them wanted this life and chose to pursue hockey instead.

However, our father's recent death has pulled them back into the trenches, and, despite my repeated attempts to throw them back out, they insist on sticking around until we've gotten revenge on whoever it was that murdered him in cold blood.

My jaw tightens and I grind my teeth. Aidan's obsession with the Bratva's angel will undoubtedly be the match strike that lights the powder keg that is the Boston underworld right now. In the weeks following my father's murder, tension between the ruling families has just about reached a breaking point.

Rory storms out of the club, my brother trailing behind her, and I shake my head. I told him to stay away from her, to leave the Russians to their business, but he never fucking listens.

"What about you?" Mac asks.

"What about me?" I respond without looking at him. My eyes still scan the crowd, ignoring the girl lingering around the door to VIP, the one who's noticed us standing above her and keeps batting her fake eyelashes our way.

"I've clocked at least three girls in the last fifteen minutes making eyes at you, and you haven't so much as twitched."

"Make sure Jerrad and Garrett have a little chat with Cam Reeves I don't want to see him in our club again," I say, ignoring his comment and pulling out my phone to check on how *other* business is going, paying no attention to my best friend and his never-ending mission to get me laid.

Cam Reeves is known around our circles for drugging girls' drinks and taking advantage of them. He's got a lot of balls stepping into an O'Rourke bar. The bouncer at the door also needs a talking-to for allowing him in here.

Though my father's passing had been unexpected, he'd

ensured I was well prepared for the day I was to take over as heir to Boston's Irish throne. But as prepared as I'd been to assume the role of head of the family, not a single fucking thing has gone right since.

The human trafficking trade has exploded in our father's absence. The Russian Bratva and the Italian Mafia are making moves, pushing the boundaries of their territories. Testing my patience.

"Aye, Boss," Mac smirks, pulling out his phone to relay the message. "I'm just saying, that brunette down there looks like a lot of fun. Brunettes certainly do catch your eye."

I work my jaw. "Not interested."

"You didn't even look!" Mac laughs, peering back down at the girl with obvious interest.

"Who are you kidding, Mac?" Jace Reilly's voice drifts in from behind us. "Don't you know by now our Koen is allergic to fun? I reckon he's vying to take over for Father Lucent."

"Still, wouldn't hurt him to take a night off every once in a while," Mac grumbles. "Might help relieve some of that pent-up tension," he heckles and Jace shoves him playfully in the shoulder.

I pay them no mind, continuing to scan the crowd. Yeah, I've been in a bit of a dry spell. But only because I didn't find it to be worth my time or energy. I have more important things to worry about than getting laid.

Shit in the city was about to get ugly, and anyone connected to me is a target. The Irish have a lot of enemies. *I* have a lot of enemies. My brothers? They can take care of themselves. My sister? We keep her on lockdown, guards trailing her twenty-four seven. It would be the same for any woman I marry because my enemies would do anything to get to me, and if they can't get to me, they'll go for those closest to me.

Besides, now that I'm boss of the family, I'm expected to marry for alliances. That was always how it was meant to be. Hell, the pressure to marry had been pushed on me since before I'd even turned eighteen. It was never about love or connection but what a bride could bring to the table. What strategic advantages did she give the family?

And if I thought I'd known pressure before... As the heir, it had been a near constant conversation since I'd come of age. But ever since I'd taken over, there hasn't been a moment's peace from the clan leaders.

So I didn't let anyone close.

Simple. Easy.

That is until *she* happened.

I never got her name, her *real* name, because something in me knew that if I did, I'd never be able to leave her alone. My obsession with her didn't make sense. I'd felt myself claim her the first time I heard her voice.

It was one night, one dare, one *mistake*.

She was too good for me.

It scared me in the moment and I shoved her away. But now, even years later, it's *me* that pays the price because no matter what I do, I can't seem to let her go. I still scan every crowd—desperate for a glimpse of something I can never have.

My phone buzzes and I open it up to find an S.O.S text from Aidan. Reading it over, the corner of my lip ticks up.

Mac, not one to miss a thing, sees it and groans.

"Ah fuck, and here I thought we'd have a quiet night

tonight." He lifts his glass to his lips, draining the rest of his beer in one go.

I turn my gaze to Jace. "Get Liam, Jerrad, and Garrett and meet me by the bikes. We've got Volkov in the city." My smile turns dark.

"Who wants to go wolf hunting?"

10

ONLY WAY OUT

BRIAR

Now

"You're working tonight?" I jump at the sound of Lily's voice. Surprised to find her in the bathroom doorway as I set out my makeup and curling iron.

"Unfortunately," I huff, stifling a yawn. After reading the four agreed-upon stories with Remi, she demanded a fifth and I'd caved. I also let her talk me into laying with her until she fell asleep and nearly nodded off myself.

"You can't be serious right now? You're supposed to be off tonight!"

"I know. I'm sorry!" I wince.

"But didn't you work last night? And the night before that? *And* the night before that?" Lily points out. "We were gonna watch movies!" The pout that accompanies her whine gives Remi a run for her money.

"I was, but Giovanni texted me a little while ago that they're short staffed tonight. He asked if I could cover a shift. And given my current situation—" I say before looking up. Lily's glowering at me in the mirror's reflection, leaning with her back up against the bathroom door.

"I can't borrow any more money from Gio. I'm barely keeping up with the payments from the last time. She needs that new medicine." Not only would it mean one injection a year instead of once a month, but the current medication she's on isn't working all that great. Remi still has the occasional asthma attack, and we still find ourselves in the emergency room far more often than we should. Each time getting slapped with another bill.

Honestly, the up-front cost of the new meds might *save* us money in the long-run.

But as desperate as I am for that new medicine, Gio is becoming a much bigger problem. Despite me making regular payments, he has already sent his goons after me on more than one occasion. I assume whenever he's low on cash himself, he tries shaking it out of anyone who owes him. I've found his guys waiting for me outside my apartment and the dance studio twice in the last couple of weeks. It was only luck that Remi wasn't with me either of the two times they'd shown up, but it's only a matter of time. And how much longer until their threats become reality?

"I know," she laments. "I wish I could help more."

"Lily, no." I put down my eyeliner pen to face her. "You already do more than enough!" Seriously, I owe *everything* to my best friend. When I got pregnant with Remi four years ago and my own parents disowned me, she was there. Every step of the way, she was at my side. Together, we moved out of the dorms since I couldn't stay in them once I had a baby. We got an apartment, and she helps me out with Remi whenever she can.

But like me, she's in her final year at the Conservatory and works mornings at the diner down the street, on top of teaching dance classes at the studio with me. And unlike me, she doesn't have a scholarship paying her way. It's the only reason I was able to continue at Delacroix after my parents cut me off.

"I'm going to ask Gio if I can pick up some dancing shifts," I tell her, uncapping my blood red lipstick.

"At what cost, though?" Lily sighs, and I know she's frustrated with the situation more than with me.

"I know. But I'm just going to be dancing; I'm still not going to do any of the *extra* stuff some of the girls do." *Like whatever goes down in those private rooms...* "I've got one talent, and I might as well use every weapon in my arsenal to get myself out of this mess. The tips from the bar are great, but they don't compare to what I can make in one shift dancing." I look up at her. "You know Gio's guys have been hanging around, and I'm afraid to think what might happen if I *actually* start to fall behind on payments." Their threats keep me up at night. Gio's guys have made it incredibly clear that what I can't pay in cash they'll take in *other* ways.

"You really want creepy, old guy hands all over you?" Lily curls her upper lip with a grimace. "Or worse?"

I frown at the notion, my make-up brush frozen on my cheek. "The bouncers are good at their jobs and besides, it's only temporary."

With rent, daycare expenses, payments to Gio, and Remi's medical bills, I'm drowning. The water has been slowly creeping up, and now it's at my neck. I'm running out of time and air to breathe. The only way out is with money—money I'm going to get, one way or another.

I can tell by the look in Lily's eyes that I'm not going to like what is on the tip of her tongue. "Say it. Whatever it is. Out with it."

She frowns. "I was just thinking, have you considered asking your—"

"No." I turn away, reapplying a second coat of mascara in the mirror.

"Briar, I'm sure they wouldn't—"

I spin around. "No, Lily. My parents made themselves perfectly clear; if I decided to have Remi, they weren't going to help me." *Cut off. Disowned. Thrown away.* I embarrassed them with my little "mistake" and if I know my parents, I'm exactly where they want me to be. *On my own.*

"And besides," I sigh. "I already asked them."

Lily's mouth falls open. "You did? Why didn't you say anything?"

I shrug. "There was nothing to tell because they said no."

"Bastards," she bites out, shaking her head and tightening her fists.

"Everything will be okay. I'll pick up more shifts at the club, pay back my debt to Giovanni, nail the showcase and score an audition with the Boston Ballet, or at the very least a paid position with the Conservatory."

"That's a lot that has to go right," Lily warns.

"There's not a whole lot more that can go wrong." I twist the cap back onto my tube of mascara and drop it into my makeup bag. It's frustrating that no matter how hard I work, how far I climb, I just can't seem to get us out of this damn hole.

"Careful Briar, don't go tempting fate," Lily laughs. "We already know she doesn't like you."

11

WONDERLAND

BRIAR

Now

The night is shit.

Three hours in and I've barely made any money in tips. I lean across the bar, staring at Serenity up on the main stage. Watching as she effortlessly hooks a knee around the silver pole and spins her body around it while arching her back seductively. The men seated around the stage throw money at her feet. And not just dollar bills—I spy a few twenties and even a fifty, and they keep it coming.

I can do that.

"Deep in thought tonight, pretty girl."

I straighten from where I'm leaning across the bar, recognizing Daniel's voice, one of the bar's regulars. I smile at him. He comes in often and is always polite, never crosses the line. I heard from the other girls that he's a Boston cop, so whenever he's here, I feel just a little safer, given the general seedy nature of the business.

"The usual?" I ask, reaching for the bottle of bourbon.

"You know me so well." He returns my smile, sliding onto the stool at the far corner of the bar where he usually sits.

I laugh. "You're here several nights a week, and you only ever drink one thing." I slide his glass over to him. "I don't think you're as mysterious as you think."

"Fair enough." He smiles as he lifts the glass to his lips. His eyes stay on me as he drains it in one go. "Speaking of habits, what are you doing here? Thursday isn't your usual night?"

My eyes widen as I take his glass back, refilling it under his eye. "I picked up an extra shift." I shrug, ignoring the rising anxiety at the fact he knows my schedule so well. Though I guess a lot of the guys do, since most of them try to come in on nights when their favorite girls are working.

As if sensing my discomfort, Daniel politely thanks me for the second glass, pulling out a few dollar bills and leaving them on the bar. "I'll see you later." He winks before taking his drink and heading closer to the main stage, finding a seat with a few regulars.

Out of the corner of my eye, I spot Gio charging his way through the club, heading for the back. He's flanked at either side by the two guys he keeps with him when he's here.

I chew my lip for a few seconds, glancing between Gio and the pile of cash at Serenity's feet before dropping my rag in the bucket and skirting around the bar after him.

It's now or never.

I recognize the big, burly guy waiting outside the door as Marco. He recognizes me too, because he opens the office door for me before I can get a word out.

"Thanks," I say, slipping past his hulking form.

The door shuts behind me and my steps slow as I enter Gio's office.

"Well, well, well, if it isn't my pretty little Bella. Have you come to make a payment, sweetheart?" Gio's laugh is quickly joined by a few others, and I avoid his gaze as I take stock of who's in here.

My heart constricts when I find Lorenzo leering at me from the sofa near the door, puffing on a cigar. The buttons on his dark suit are straining to keep in the bulk of him. I sidestep a few steps to the right, giving him a wide berth. Lorenzo chuckles knowingly and sits up straighter, playing with the cigar in his hand, his eyes keen with sadistic interest.

"Briar." My real name on Giovanni's lips snaps my attention back to him. "What do you want? I don't have all day."

"Right, sorry," I apologize, looking around the room again, anxious over having this conversation in general, let alone in front of so many others.

"If you're looking for more serving shifts, I don't have them." Gio waves dismissively back toward the door. "But I'll have Celeste text you if I get any more call-outs."

"No, I wanted to ask about maybe picking up some dancing shifts?"

The hand holding his cigar freezes halfway to his mouth, and he looks me up and down. "You want to dance?" Doubt is evident in his tone. Which is fair, considering he's been trying to get me up on that stage since I started working at Wonderland months ago and I've always adamantly refused.

I nod, my eyes continuously scanning the rest of the men in the room. They are watching me a little closer now. "But just dance," I clarify, lifting my chin a little. "No extras, no... private rooms," I get out despite Gio's narrowing gaze.

"Get a load of this one!" Lorenzo scoffs, puffing on his own cigar. "That ain't how this works, sweetheart." His Boston Italian accent is thick.

Gio, thankfully, ignores him. "I thought you were too *delicate* for that kind of work, ballerina?" He teases, though I can tell by the way he folds his hands on his desk and leans forward that he's considering it. "What's changed?"

I let loose a shrug, trying to look as casual as possible in this room full of sharks, not wanting them to know how desperate I am. "I could use the money, finally pay off my debt, and you know they're always raising the rent."

"Mmm." Gio leans back in his chair again, studying me for a long while. "Fine." And my heart skips a beat. "But lap dances are non-negotiable." He points his cigar at me, and I bite my cheek to hide my wince.

"Okay," I agree, reluctantly. *Lap dances are fine. It's fine. I can do that.* Throw in a few lap dances and maybe I'll get to my goal faster.

"Alright, ballerina, you dance tonight. And you dance well." His eyes narrow on me. "Consider it an audition." He laughs, the rest of the room laughing with him. "You should know all about those. Have Celeste put you on the rotation. Now get out. We have business to discuss." He waves me toward the door, his interest waning.

Tonight? Fuck. I wasn't prepared for that.

I thought I'd have a day or two to mentally psych myself up for it, assuming he said yes. I don't get to vocalize the question though, because one of Gio's security guys tugs me back

71

toward the door, before pushing me unceremoniously out of it.

"You sure you wanna do this, sweetheart?" Celeste asks, watching me with a frown as I stare nervously at the thick red curtains blocking off the backstage area from the rest of the club. My palms are slick with sweat, and I'm almost certain I'm about to be sick.

I nod almost robotically in response to her question. Steeling my nerves, I climb the few steps up onto the platform like I'm headed to the gallows.

The black lingerie Celeste found for me to wear is a little small, the black mesh bodysuit just barely covers everything I need it to. Silver and black sequins glint in the neon club lights that stream through a crack in the curtain. A pair of black fishnet tights complete the look, held up by a garter belt fixed high up on my waist, and all on top of impossibly high clear heels.

At the top of the platform, I close my eyes as I attempt to drop into character. *It's just another dance—another performance. You're playing a character who has to tempt the icky men out of their cash,* I tell myself, fighting the rising vomit in my throat.

"Remember, they're just men. Appeal to their dicks and they'll pull out their wallets. It's that simple." Celeste smiles ruefully. She's been the dancer's manager for years now. I'm sure by this point, she's seen it all.

The music starts, and I hesitate for another half a second before cracking my neck, feeling myself drop into character right before I step through the curtains.

Just another performance.

"Please welcome to the stage, our newest dancer Bella!" Sam, the club's DJ, announces through the microphone before the music really cranks up. My hips move to match the seductive beat of the song. All eyes are on me, and I know it. It's what I've trained for, and while this isn't the Royal Opera House or the Mariinsky Theater, the same rules apply.

I reach the gleaming metal pole in the center of the stage, skimming it lightly with my fingertips as I circle it. Dropping my eyes to the small crowd circled around the stage, I allow a seductive little smile to grace my lips, drawing them in. I pretend to look them in the eye, but in reality I see nothing. My focus is on the music, and on the character I'm playing.

Tightening my grip on the pole, I spin around it, hooking one leg high and arching my back. A few dollars appear at my feet.

I lean into it, pulling out long-lost choreography from a few of my past, more *risqué* pieces. Catching hold of the pole, I drop, knees wide while arching my back. Gracefully sliding into a full split at the base of the pole.

The old man nearest me lets out a low whistle while dropping a fifty-dollar bill on the stage.

I haul myself back up just as gracefully, and just like that, I lose myself in the music, twisting, swinging my hips, letting my hands roam my body while I move.

They eat it up.

I have them eating out of the palm of my hand by the time I crawl, on my hands and knees, to the men waving the bigger bills. I try not to recoil at the touch of their fingers when they slip their bills into my panties, my bra, anything they can get their hands on.

When the music finally stops, I blow my audience a little kiss, heart pounding, before running off the stage with what has to be hundreds of dollars in tips. I've got money everywhere. Tucked into my bra straps, panties, garter belt. The rest I scooped up into a little tote bag Celeste handed me before I went out there.

And all that from one dance! And I didn't even have to get naked. They didn't seem to care.

Maybe this won't be so bad.

12

BULLET FOR BETRAYAL

KOEN

Now

There's a somber mood in the air when I ride up to the warehouse—Liam, Mac, and Jace close behind me.

Aidan is waiting for us outside, arms folded, leaning up against his own matte black sports bike.

"What happened?"

"Shipment got jacked," Aidan replies, his face tense.

"Who leaked it?" I ask, pulling off my gloves.

"Jake O'Leary." Aidan's mouth pulls down in a frown.

"Where is he?"

Aidan nods his head toward the warehouse, and my jaw tightens.

I take my time dismounting my bike, no part of me eager for what I'm about to do. *What I have to do.*

Problems like this have plagued the Irish Devils for the past few months. Ever since the death—no, *murder*, of my father, Declan O'Rourke, the former head of the family.

None of us had been with him when it happened. Liam and Aidan were away at training camp over the summer with the Boston Breakers, and I was busy with my crew, overseeing the brokering of a critical arms deal with the Cartel.

Someone was selling information on the Irish, and after months of sabotage, we are no closer to figuring out who it is. I'm certain it's the same someone who set up our father.

We know either the Russians or the Italians are responsible. We just have to prove it.

The Russians are the most likely; their Pakhan was on the move, expanding their businesses and pushing the bounds of their territory more than they ever had before.

But the Italians are also making unusual moves, cozying up to the Russians in a way I didn't like. A Russian-Italian alliance in a city already pitched on the edge of a mafia war did not bode well for the Irish.

"Alex traced O'Leary's financials back to a shell company with ties to Kostalov."

Adrik Kostalov, the Russian Pakhan. Perfect.

Alex would know; he'd been our spy within the Bratva for years.

"You want me to handle this?" Aidan asks, although he already knows my answer. He might be focused on hockey, but he is still head enforcer, and something like this would normally fall under Aidan's domain—or Mac's, in Aidan's absence—but disloyalty is something I see to personally.

Betrayal is a choice.

Betrayal can not be forgiven.

"No," I answer, my jaw tight. "I'll take care of it."

There are eyes on me the second I enter the warehouse, but I ignore them, feeling their stares on my back as I stalk right for the lockers. A shipment just came in, and my men are here unloading and redistributing the product for delivery.

I can smell the blood the second I turn down the hallway leading to the lockers, where we keep and interrogate prisoners. It's a thick, metallic scent, mixed with the overpowering scent of urine.

Alex stands guard, and I give him a slight nod as he unbolts the heavy metal door before sliding it open.

I step into the dank and dreary room.

Jake sits in the single metal chair, arms tied behind him, naked, and shivering from fear or the cold, I'm not sure. November is well upon us, and we don't heat the warehouse. It's cold enough in here to see my breath.

Jake lifts his head, eyes widening when he sees me in the doorway.

"Rí, please," he rasps out, his throat raw from screaming. The bruises and blood on his body evidence that my guys don't take too kindly to traitors either. "Alex is lying. I didn't do it! Please show mercy." He shakes his head, lips quivering. *Pathetic.* "I didn't—"

I lift my gun, firing a clean shot into the man's forehead—the pleading stops.

Silence.

Without another word, I turn and exit the locker, heading for my office.

"That was quick," Mac muses, pushing himself up off the wall of the hallway outside to follow me.

"A traitor's a traitor. I don't need to listen to their lying tongues trying to persuade me otherwise."

Seriously? He was trying to blame Alex. I should kill him again. My hand balls into a fist. Alex—or Alexei Ryan—is an easy target, having spent the last several years undercover with the Bratva. Even though Alex is half Russian, he had an Irish upbringing. Our father took him in after the death of his mother, raising him alongside us. He is one of us, an O'Rourke all the same. I trust him just as much as I trust Aidan, Liam, or Mac.

Loyalty and trust, they're everything. I need to know that the men following my orders have my back, without hesitation and without question.

And right now, I don't.

I can feel the cracks in the ranks. The man I'd just killed, a lowly soldier, hadn't been with the Irish long. Only a few months. I know he's not the one I'm looking for.

Too much shit has gone wrong to be bad luck. Someone high in the Irish has been leaking information. Likely to the Russians, if I had to wager a guess.

My brothers know it too. We all knew something wasn't right with how our father died. He shouldn't have even been there on that street, at that time of day, *alone.*

Someone set him up.

I am sure of it.

And that someone is after me, too. I'm fairly young, if you consider twenty-seven young. And there are those amid the Irish who think I might be a little *too* young to take over as head of the family, despite being groomed for it my entire life. A few clan leaders within the city have yet to bend the knee. I've been patient, but doubt is like a disease, and if I'm not careful, if I don't get a handle on the dissent soon, I'll be the next one with a bullet in my skull.

"The clan leaders aren't happy. They feel like you're excluding them from your plans," Mac warns.

They're right, I *am* excluding them from my plans. Since I don't know who I can trust, I've been keeping my circle small.

The Russians and Italians are testing me, seeing what they can get away with, how they can take advantage.

It ends now.

Loyalty is non-negotiable, and mercy is for the dead.

"Aidan, did you get a location on Carroza's warehouse?"

"Yes, you still want to do this?"

I meant what I said the other night... "Let's go fuck some shit up."

13

THE DARKSIDE OF BOSTON

BRIAR

Now

I'm hours early for my dancing shift tonight, but Lily took Remi to the playground after dinner, and even though I got through getting thrust onto the stage last night, I would feel a lot better if I had the chance to practice before tonight's performance.

There are a few cars in the parking lot already, probably the cleaning crew and maybe some bar or kitchen staff doing prep.

Finding the back door unlocked, I walk slowly down the long, darkened hallway that leads to the dressing rooms. The quiet here feels unnatural. It's weird being here during the day, while the sun's still up. Wonderland feels like the type of place that can only exist in the dark. There's no music, no shouts from the bar or kitchens, no half-naked girls racing up and down the hall to change outfits.

I'm not alone; I can hear the faint cadence of male voices coming from further down the hall.

Since the club floor is deserted, I realize it's a lot bigger than I thought. With the stage lights off, the room is lit solely by the red up-lighting along the walls. The main stage is the focus of the room, but scattered around the outskirts of the floor are smaller stages. Round platforms with their own poles and plush stools pushed in close.

To my left, a roped-off VIP section sits elevated from the rest of the floor. And back down the corridor I just came from are the private rooms. I don't know what happens back there, and I don't ask, though I've heard more than a few stories.

I'm not naïve. Illegal shit goes down inside of Wonderland every night. It's a strip club in a seedy part of town. When I first started bartending here, Celeste told me to keep my head down, mouth shut and eyes open. I'd found that to be solid advice, and following it has kept me out of trouble.

Circling back to the main stage, I drop my bag on the floor, pulling my long, dark hair up into a ponytail to get it out of my face before pulling off my sweats. To practice, I've just worn tight black dance shorts and a sports bra with a lightweight cropped sweatshirt over it. I leave my feet bare, better to get the basics down before I go adding six-inch heels.

Taking a deep breath, I climb up onto the stage, stretching and shaking out my limbs before finally reaching for the pole. It's cool under my fingertips, and it's the kind that spins on its own, giving the illusion that you're spinning around it but you're really not.

I've had some aerial training, just so I could put it on my resume, but this shit is harder than it looks. Bruises pepper the insides of my thighs from the bit of pole work I did last night, and my abs are sore. At least dancing here will be a good workout.

I'm glad no one's here because my first couple of attempts at lifting my body up on the pole are pathetic, to say the least. My muscles tremble with the strain, but I don't stop. My near-toxic perfectionism doubles down until I'm able to do it. Again and again I keep at it until it looks effortless, clean lines even Mr. Carr would have difficulty criticizing.

My stomach growls, and I check the time on my phone. I have just about an hour until everyone really starts showing up. I start packing up my bag to move to the dressing rooms. There, I can eat a couple of snacks I brought with me while getting ready for tonight.

Unease flutters through me as I turn down the still-dark back hallway. I've been here for over an hour, so it's a little weird I still haven't seen anyone around. As I get closer to the dancers' dressing room, the male voices I heard earlier, grow louder.

They must be having a staff meeting or something.

The voices sound angry, so I stop. Anxiety creeps down into my chest, something about this just doesn't feel right. Abandoning my progress down the hall, I back up, ready to retreat to the main floor and wait for some of the other girls to arrive, that is, until I hear crying.

I freeze.

"Shut. Up." The sound of the smack reverberates in my ears, and the sobbing only grows louder. The sound of a girl's terrified cries twists something in my gut, and I move cautiously toward the sound, tiptoeing down the hall.

The sound is coming from the next door down, which I

can see is just barely cracked open. *What if some guy has one of the dancers cornered in there?*

I get as close as I dare, my ears straining to make out what the angry voices are saying. Trying to work out what it is I'm walking into...

"—on a flight tonight. Security will look the other way, so long as you bring cash."

"And the others?" another voice asks.

Heart pounding, I inch closer to the door, desperately trying to steal a peek through the crack without whoever's on the other side seeing me.

"The others," I recognize Giovanni's accent, "we'll hold until the auction. They're higher value."

The girl sobs again, louder this time.

"Stop. You can't hit her again! I have a standard to uphold. My buyers expect to receive their product in pristine condition."

Buyers?

I stop trying to get closer, bringing a hand up to cover my mouth in order to silence the choking sound that escapes my throat.

I don't know what the fuck I've stumbled into, but I know it's bad. I should get the bouncers, call the cops, something... I move back rapidly, tripping over my own feet in my haste and practically crashing into someone.

My entire body stiffens at the contact, and I jolt away from them, twisting around to see who's behind me. My initial panic lessens when I realize it's Daniel behind me. *A cop.* Thank god.

I let out a breath of relief, but before I can explain the situation transpiring behind that door, Daniel reaches out, grabbing a fistful of my hair and propelling me backwards through the door before I realize what's happening. I barely fight him off before he releases me just as suddenly as he grabbed me. My head smacks hard onto the concrete floor as I fall.

"You idiots can't shut a fucking door?" Daniel huffs out, stalking back to slam the hallway door shut.

Peeling myself up off the ground, I find myself eye to eye with the girl I must have heard crying out in the hallway. Her red-rimmed eyes widen in terror as I take her in.

She's shaking, wearing only her underwear, silver handcuffs on her wrists, linked to a thick silver collar around her neck.

I stare at the thick metal circle in shock, scrambling to get back on my feet. Every instinct in me screams, *Run!*

I only make it to my knees before a hand lands roughly on my shoulder, keeping me on the floor. A deep, aching sense of dread fills me, and I swallow hard, glancing up to find Marco, one of Giovanni's guys, standing over me.

My blood chills as I take in the room. There's far more people in here than I thought. It's a conference room filled entirely with men. Most sit in plush executive chairs, circled around a large mahogany table. I recognize a few of the guys standing around the room as Giovanni's guys, as well as the cop Daniel. The men sitting, however, look well-to-do. Dressed in nice suits, puffing on what are probably expensive cigars, with drinks in hand. Some look down at me with mild disinterest, others crane their necks to get a better look, while some look downright alarmed.

"Bella."

My head turns toward the voice, recognizing it, finally finding Giovanni in the group. He wears a deep frown as he rises from the table, coming closer.

"I was looking for the dressing room—" I start, my eyes

darting around. All eyes are on me now, except for Lorenzo's. He's lurking at the back of the room. Still not sure what's going on, I look back at Gio. "I didn't—I didn't see anything," I say quietly, working to keep my eyes off of the trembling girl to my right.

Giovanni steps closer, bending down until he's at eye level, taking the time to tuck a loose strand of my hair behind my ear with a level of care that doesn't match the coldness in his eyes. "Ah, but unfortunately you did see something, didn't you, sweetheart?" I follow his gaze to the blonde next to me, and he clicks his tongue. "And now, I've gotta make sure you don't tell anybody else."

There's not a second of hesitation before I lurch away from him, falling onto my ass to escape Marco's grip, making a desperate attempt to reach the door. Lorenzo is closing in from behind Giovanni, and a scream rises in my throat at the sight of the white cloth he's holding outstretched in his hand.

"We-we can talk about this—I won't say anything, I won't."

I claw my way to my feet, tripping over myself as I bolt for the door, but I'm wrenched backwards by my hair before I can make it. I scream, kicking and fighting, but someone grabs hold of my hands, wrenching them behind my back. Lorenzo smiles as he leans over me, pressing his cloth tight to my face, covering both my nose and mouth.

I hold my breath, twisting and turning, trying to wiggle out of their grip. But there's too many of them. My wrists burn as I fight their hold, trying to get free, to wrench that cloth away from my face. My lungs burn, the need for oxygen becoming impossible to ignore, but I refuse to fill them.

Lorenzo's grip tightens, and I'm losing ground, but my legs

are still free. I kick at him, but it's no use, and having run out of time, I'm forced to inhale.

The cloying scent of chemicals fills my lungs, and the effect is near immediate. I falter, my knees buckling, vision tilting. I'm losing strength. My struggling becomes more and more pathetic, and my breaths come against my will as I lose control of my body, slumping helplessly in their arms. My lungs filling up with more of that nauseating scent.

I search the room, taking in their faces, some of them grinning excitedly at the scene. There's a man with dark, slicked-back hair, gold rings on every finger; another one with pale skin and sunken cheekbones who looks like he hasn't slept in weeks, he has a scar along his right jawline; the one closest to me is broad-shouldered, with salt and pepper hair and a nice suit—*he winks at me;* the one next to him is balding, with a sharp gaze and a sneer on his face I can never forget. Daniel's cold smile is the last thing I see before my vision blurs, finally tunneling out, as I free-fall into darkness.

14

THE LITTLE DARK-HAIRED GIRL

BRIAR

Now

Nausea hits me, and I groan, debating whether or not to wake up.

What the hell happened last night? I don't drink anymore, not since Remi. My days of drinking recreationally are far behind me.

I attempt to open my eyes, but they don't cooperate. I try wiggling my fingers, but I'm not sure I even feel them.

Something isn't right...

It's as if I'm trapped within a dense fog; perhaps I'm still half asleep with one foot in reality and one foot still in fucking dreamland.

The fog lifts slightly as I fight for clarity, and I relax a little when feeling returns to my body. My eyelids finally flutter open, but my hair is in my face. I try to brush it out of the way, and I can't. I'm unable to raise my arm, and panic surges as I realize it's stuck on something.

The rush of terror burns through the remaining mental fog enough for me to fully open my eyes and realize my hands are zip-tied together.

Thrashing, I fight against the restraint, only succeeding in tightening the plastic ties so tight that now it feels like they're cutting off my circulation. My chest heaves, my breaths coming hard as I realize two things: the first being I am not in my bed; and two, I am not alone.

I'm in a moving vehicle. It's dark, but as I look around, I find several pairs of eyes staring back at me. I try to sit up to better gauge my surroundings, which proves difficult as jolts and bumps send deep shockwaves of nausea through me while I'm still fighting the overwhelming urge to sleep.

No, I need to stay awake.

I've nearly twisted myself into a sitting position when we hit a bump, throwing me back to the floor, and I hit my head hard. For a moment, I feel dazed, like I'm going to black out again. *Fuck, that hurt.* But as much as it hurt, it seems to sharpen my senses, lifting the drug-induced fog just enough for rational thoughts to take over.

"You're awake!" The girl closest to me whisper-shouts before leaning closer, "We thought you might be dead."

With the fog lifting, it's far easier this time to push myself to sitting and, once upright, I lean my pounding head back against the cool, metal wall of the van I've determined we're in.

"Not yet," I frown. I'm still wearing the dance clothes I changed into at the club, and I'm relieved to find them all intact.

The van is dark, but I think I count at least twelve of us. All girls. All girls who look to be around my age or younger. No one else is unconscious, but all are in various states of disarray. The girl sitting next to me, the one who spoke, is sporting a nasty-looking bruise around her left eye. It's several days old, judging by the yellowing edges of the deep purple bruising.

The girl next to her has her face buried in her knees with her arms wrapped around them as she cries.

I clear my throat, my voice coming out hoarse and scratchy, and I'm near desperate for some water. "Where are they taking us?"

"I don't know," the girl next to me answers. "They've been picking up girls all night. One here, three there."

"How long was I out?" The van pitches, and I fight the rising urge to vomit, pressing my lips shut as well as my eyes, waiting for the wretched feeling to pass, as the effects of the drugs cling to me.

"I'm not sure."

I blink back at her.

"You were unconscious when they tossed you in here," she explains.

"When was that?"

She shifts nervously. "That was probably a couple of hours ago."

A couple of hours ago? Fuck. It can't be any earlier than two or three in the morning.

Remi's face is at the forefront of my mind, and I push away the dark thought. The one currently telling me *I'm never going to see her again.*

My fists tighten with grim resolve, and the plastic ties around them cut deeper into my skin.

I take in the van, the distressed and underdressed girls, and what I saw back in the club... *Traffickers*. These men are traffickers.

I'm hyperventilating, and my heart's racing, but I force myself to calm down. To survive this.

"Listen." I do my best to scoot closer to the girl on my right awkwardly. "When they open that door, it might be our only chance. We have to run—fight. There's probably way more of us than there are of them. Whoever gets free can go get help for the others."

My words don't have the effect I was hoping they would. Half the girls are so despondent, I'm not sure if they can even hear me—or maybe they don't understand me. And the other half, including the girl to my right, are giving me varying looks of horror.

"No," she says adamantly, shaking her head. "They'll kill you. I've already seen them do it," she whispers, with a haunted look in her eyes.

But before I can open my mouth to argue, the van slows to a stop. Everyone inside stiffens and shifts at the sound of the two doors up front opening before slamming shut again.

Fear, but also rage, floods through me. I know what this is, what they plan to do to me. And I'm not going to make it fucking easy for them. I will not be compliant; I will not yield or cry or beg. I will fight until my last breath because I have Remi back at home waiting for me. And I will not leave her alone.

The van doors open and armed men appear, roughly hauling out girls. "Let's go. Everybody out."

I don't move, sitting with my back up against the wall of the van until I'm the only one left inside.

There's one man left at the door, and he narrows his eyes at me. "C'mon, girl. I don't got all day." His accent is foreign... Eastern European, maybe?

I don't move.

My defiance finally garners his full attention, and he gives me a quick once-over that leaves me feeling gross. "Get your ass out of the van or you're gonna regret it." He smiles cruelly at me, tightening his grip on the rifle he's got strapped to his body.

I stay put. If they want me, they're going to have to come in here and get me.

Realizing I'm not, in fact, going to come out willingly, he does just that. Cursing under his breath, he ducks his head to climb inside, mumbling something in another language as he does. I bide my time until he's close enough and then I twist, kicking up at him with full force. He doesn't expect it, so the heel of my bare foot catches him square in the nose. I can't help but grin to myself when his hands fly to his face. He falls to his knees and howls in a fit of pain and rage.

"What's the matter, Mateusz? Can't handle one little girl?" I stiffen at the sight of a second man by the van door, coming back to see what's taking his friend so long. This one's Italian accent is very clear.

Mateusz glares at his friend as he moves his bloody hands away from his nose. "Help me get her out of this fucking van."

Grumbling something about incompetence, the new guy crawls into the van as well. He's quicker than his friend, grabbing hold of my feet before I have a chance to kick him too. I don't make it easy, but let's be honest; between the two of them, I don't stand a chance.

They drag me out into the night, kicking and thrashing like a wild animal.

Cursing, they shove me away from them as quickly as they can, toward the rest of the girls who are standing together outside a dark warehouse. Thankfully, a few of them are able to catch me, preventing me from face-planting onto the asphalt. The smell of low tide is heavy in the air. We're near the docks.

I take in my surroundings, planning out my next move, but there are more men here than I'd counted on. At least seven or eight men surround us; it's hard to tell in the darkness. Each one of them brandishes some type of firearm, though they look bored, standing together in groups and talking rather than patrolling the area properly.

One by one, the men at the front shove girls through the warehouse door. My eyes dart around, looking for a way out—but there's just too many of them.

Lorenzo appears, cigarette in his mouth, striding up the line of girls—inspecting them. I catch his eye, and he catches my darkest glare.

He moves fast. Faster than I would've thought possible for a man of his size, ripping me out of the group by my arm. I'm surprised, but still I resist. Digging in my heels, I fight against his grip.

Frustrated, he throws me against the van with a force hard enough to knock the wind out of me. My head is still questionable from the lingering effects of whatever it was they drugged me with, and my vision tunnels. My knees give out, and I feel myself sliding to the ground, but he catches me.

Fear yet again slices through the heavy fog when Lorenzo pins me up against the vehicle. I go rigid as he brings his hand up to my face. "So pretty," he murmurs, almost reverently, before he hits me—hard. The force of it whips my head to the side, and darkness once again clouds my vision. It's a fight just to stay conscious. "And so fucking stupid," he mutters, his grip on me the only reason I'm still on my feet.

I struggle, but it's pointless. My head is pounding, and nausea rolls through me. His sweaty, stinking body is pinning mine in place, and there's nowhere to go. He takes a long drag of his cigarette, a sadistic smile on his lips as he watches my pathetic struggle. "Don't worry, you'll learn, Bella. I'll take great delight in helping you." He takes the cigarette from his mouth, holding it in his hand for a moment before wrenching my head to the side and pressing the burning end to the soft, exposed skin of my neck.

My body jolts instinctively, frantically trying to escape the white-hot searing pain that tunnels deeper as he presses it even harder. I thrash and scream, but he covers my mouth, silencing me while laughing at the tears streaming down my face.

He finally pulls the cigarette away with a smug smile on his face. It's rage, not fear, that he's summoned with his actions, and I spit at him, hitting him in the eye.

The few remaining girls outside let out a collective gasp, and the men all go quiet.

Lorenzo looks from me to them, his face boiling with fury. A second later he lashes out, striking me so hard I hit the ground.

I spit again, this time blood—my own, onto the cold asphalt.

Fight. Keep fighting.

I'm not an idiot. I know how this ends. I know what fate awaits me on the other side of that warehouse door, and I won't accept it. *I won't.*

I push myself up onto shaky arms, trying to crawl away as

best I can with my hands bound in front of me. I have no chance, and I know it, but I have to keep *trying*.

Lorenzo looks down at me like I'm a cockroach he wishes he could smash with his boot. A snap of his fingers brings about two of his guys, who haul me back up to my feet and inside the warehouse.

15

FUCK AROUND AND FIND OUT

BRIAR

Now

Still dazed by Lorenzo's last hit, I'm dragged through a maze of wooden shipping crates, stacked high, until we reach a small clearing, somewhere near the middle of the packed warehouse. I lift my head as they drag me forward, but there's no sight of any of the other girls I arrived with.

There's a random couch, ancient, by the looks of its stained, eighties-era fabric, and a folding table covered in empty beer bottles and playing cards, with a few metal chairs scattered around it.

The men carrying me drop me without warning in the middle of the freezing cement floor. A groan of pain escapes me. I recognize Mateusz sneering down at me, his nose still smeared with blood from my kick. *I hope it's broken.*

The second I hit the ground, I attempt to push myself back up. But Mateusz quickly intervenes, shoving me back down roughly. "This one's spicy." The excitement in his tone is unnerving and I flinch away, but he grabs a fist full of my hair, keeping me in place.

While Mateusz holds me still, his friend rips my feet out from under me. I fall forward, smashing my face onto the concrete, too dazed to fight him as he ties my ankles together with rope.

"Good luck trying to kick me now," Mateusz chirps. I still try, though it's no use; there's barely any give in the ropes. *Fuck they hurt.*

Next, the guy grabs hold of my hands, hauling me forward while pulling another zip tie from his pocket. Swiftly, he connects my already zip-tied hands to the metal grate cemented into the floor.

I let out a yelp, attempting to wrench my hands away but he's too fast, and I only succeed at tightening the noose around my hands to the point of pain. My wrists are now slick with blood from my continued struggle to pull them free.

Satisfied, Mateusz releases my hair with a fit of laughter.

Awkwardly, I work my legs forward until I'm sitting on my knees. My tied ankles tucked underneath me. My hands, bound to the grate in front of me, keep me there. A tremble wracks through me at the vulnerability of the position—At the sight of the men circling around me.

One stares at me, grinning, all while rubbing at a bulge in his pants.

I force the vomit down as it climbs up the back of my throat.

Lorenzo steps into my field of vision, and I feel the blood drain from my face at the sight of the leather whip in his hands. I'm shaking now, out of options and fully at their mercy.

He massages the coiled dark leather as he steps closer. "Don't worry, sweetheart, you'll learn quick," he laughs. "They always do." He sneers down at me as he walks past, positioning himself at my back.

There's nothing to do but wait. My fingers dig into my skin as I curl them into fists, willing myself not to let them break me but doubting my resolve as soon as Lorenzo lets the whip loose. The leather cracks through the air and I flinch so hard I nearly fall over, though it hasn't touched me yet.

"Bad luck for you, you're not a virgin," he says somewhat empathetically. "We can sell you as-is, so what do ya say we have a little fun?"

The man standing in front of me, still rubbing the growing bulge in his jeans, grins wider. Winking at me when he notices my gaze.

My body shakes uncontrollably, anxiously awaiting Lorenzo's first strike. He's no doubt dragging it out to fuck with me. The anticipation perhaps worse than the punishment itself. *It won't be that bad.* I'm well aware that I am lying to myself. *Whatever you do, don't scream.* I repeat the words in my head: *Don't scream, don't scream,* until the next crack of the whip.

The sharp leather makes contact with a slicing sting through my shoulder blades and I fall forward with a sharp gasp, using my hands to brace myself. Tears spring from my eyes involuntarily at the sharp, searing heat of pain ripping through my back.

Fuck.

I hear the whip cut through the air before I feel it again. The pain far worse this time as it makes contact with the first wound. My arms buckle and tears stream freely, quietly soaking

97

my cheeks, but I bite down hard on my lip. *Don't scream. Don't scream. Don't you dare scream!*

Lorenzo brings the whip down again harder this time and I feel my skin break, warmth floods down my back. My shirt falls down my shoulder as he shreds the fabric from my body thread by thread. My breaths come hard and I try to focus on them, only them. *Don't scream, don't scream.* The fourth strike follows immediately after and hits harder. I hear Lorenzo grunt from the effort of it. Pissed off at my silence, I hope.

It's here I start to lose my resolve. The whip comes down so hard, snapping across the previous wounds, cutting from another angle, and while I don't scream, the tiniest cry of pain escapes me.

Gun shots ring out behind me and the circle descends into chaos. I dive forward, dropping down as low as I can, unable to use my hands to cover my head, so instead I watch as a masked man, dressed all in black, appears seemingly out of the shadows between the crates. His gun is fixed on Lorenzo and he quickly fires two shots into him in quick succession.

A second masked man appears behind the first, his gun pointed over my head before it fires. I track the shot, watching the man who was in front of me—the one holding his cock—hit the ground. His eyes frozen open, only a trickle of blood spilling from the small, circular wound in his forehead.

Another one of Lorenzo's men goes down, screaming out while clutching his leg, dropping his gun. I watch it slide across the floor to me, my heart dropping when it skids to a stop just outside of my reach.

More shots rain down and it's chaos as Lorenzo's men struggle to defend themselves, the shots seem to be coming from all directions now.

When no one in the small clearing is left standing, the gunfire pauses. Still alive and shaking uncontrollably, I push up on my elbows, stealing a glance behind me just in time to see the two masked men I saw earlier fully enter the clearing.

Lorenzo wails on the ground between us, clutching his knee. Blood covers his hand and I can't help but feel a dark sense of satisfaction at the sight of him writhing in pain. More gunfire rings out from the far back of the warehouse but I keep my eyes on the two masked men coming toward me.

They're tall, dressed in black, and my heart drops when I realize they're not police. They wear bulletproof vests, dark tactical pants and hoodies, with balaclavas obscuring their faces.

Lorenzo lets out another howl of pain at their feet.

One of the men steps forward, his gun trained on Lorenzo's forehead. His eyes, the only part of him visible through his mask, glimmer with a dark rage when he finally steps into the light.

"Tie him up," he growls before walking past to crouch down beside me.

His gloved fingertips reach for me, but I flinch away. Uncertain of his intentions, I keep my eye on him despite the gunfire still ringing out around us. Though, the shots are fewer and far between now.

More masked men step into the clearing, and together two of them heave Lorenzo up, throwing him into one of the metal chairs while he curses at them.

My eyes flicker between the masked man in front of me and the chaos happening at his back as his men make quick work of tying down a flailing Lorenzo.

My masked man's gaze stays fixed on me, trusting the men at his back to follow orders.

As I draw further away from him, reaching the max range the zip ties will allow, he holds up both of his gloved hands so I can see them. My eyes instantly fall to the gun he's holding in his left one. Tracking my gaze and moving slowly, ever-so-slowly, he holsters the gun at his waist, showing me his now empty hands.

He pauses for a moment as if to gauge my reaction before he reaches for me again. Not having anywhere else to go, I quietly tremble as he unties the ropes binding my ankles.

He levels me another look before drawing out a wicked-looking knife from somewhere at his side, swiftly cutting through the zip ties on my wrists. Flinching after he's already cut me loose, the knife disappears nearly as quickly as it appeared and he looks me over. His eyes darken as they trail over my back.

I'm hyper-aware of the state of my top, one thread away from falling apart entirely, and my hands come up protectively over my chest.

He stands, removing his bullet proof vest before wrenching his hoodie up and over his head before crouching down in front of me again, though not quite as close as he was before. Free of the grate, I inch away, putting a couple more inches of space between us.

"Here." He leans forward, closing the gap again, dragging the soft fabric over my head. It's still warm from his body, bringing awareness to just how cold I am. The hoodie is too big for me, but once it's on, its warmth and size brings me an odd sense of comfort. I inhale deep, trying to calm my still panicked breathing. The scent of him surrounds me, a dark citrus, triggering an overwhelming sense of familiarity.

My gaze shoots up, he's watching me with a dark intensity. Only his eyes are visible under that dark mask. And those eyes... a green fading into dark shadow at the edges, framed by lashes no man should have.

"You..." I whisper, my voice barely audible, but he hears it, the faintest flash of surprise in his eyes. Fractured eyes, as familiar as they are foreign...

"It's you."

16

YOU

KOEN

Now

It's her.

It's actually fucking *her*.

I knew it. I'd known it the second they'd dragged her out of the van, back out on the street.

And she recognized me, too.

Fucking hell.

Even with the mask on, she knew me. I could see it in her eyes, even before she spoke.

"It's you."

Her voice doesn't just sound familiar, it *feels* familiar. The memory of it has been echoing through my mind for years, had woven itself into the very fabric of my being. Something long dead flickers back to life inside of me at the sound. I stare down into ocean blue eyes, unsure of what to say, but before I can say anything, shouts at my back force my attention away.

Aidan and Liam have got the slimy bastard, the one who'd whipped her, tied to a chair. The man's bleeding from where I shot him in his hand and knee, pleading with my younger brother who's glaring down at him with the promise of death in his eyes. Aidan draws back his hood and slides down his mask, revealing his face before locking in on his target.

Here we fucking go...

"Don't move," I growl at the girl, who's still shivering at my feet before I rise, turning to fully assess the scene unfolding at my back.

The Italian's eyes dart wildly around, searching for help that's not coming. "Look, man, I—I'm just a hired gun," he jumbles out. "I only do what I'm told."

"And who does the telling?" Aidan plays with the gun in his hand, unloading and reloading the cartridge. His Irish accent comes out far thicker than usual, ensuring the guy knows *exactly* who he's dealing with.

The Irish Devils.

The Italian's mouth snaps shut, and he looks uneasy.

"Plot twist: it gets worse for you." Aidan clicks the safety off of his gun and there's a dangerous glint in his eye when he says, "Whatever comes out of your mouth next determines how much worse."

The man licks his lips, still looking between the three of us: Aidan, Liam, and me. His eyes calculating.

"Whose warehouse is this?"

My man doesn't miss a beat when he gives his answer, "Matteo Carroza."

Aidan and I exchange a look. He's telling the truth; it's the reason we targeted this warehouse in the first place. Matteo is the Italian's consigliere, second-in-command to Cole DeLuca.

Have the Italians finally expanded their business into the skin trade? My money had been on the Russians. Especially considering the Russian-manufactured guns we'd found inside some of the crates stacked up by the entrance.

My brother straightens, holstering his gun. The Italian visibly deflates, missing how my brother reaches instead for the baseball bat Liam's holding. He must have found it lying around somewhere.

"Wait, wait!!" The goon panics. His eyes flash between the three of us and the bat in Aidan's hands. "I have more—more information, please!" Aidan swings the bat casually in his hands, and the man's pants darken as he pisses himself.

"I'm waiting..."

The Italian looks between my brothers, a pained expression on his face.

"Time's up," Aidan grins, winding up the bat one last time.

"No!" the man screeches, struggling violently in the chair. "I know who ordered the hit on Declan O'Rourke!"

Everything stops. *Our father.* Information we've been chasing for *months* now. Aidan's bat freezes.

"It was the Lion, the Russian Lion—Adrik—Adrik Kostalov." He nods furiously, eagerly. "He put the hit out that left old Dec' dead."

I don't bat an eye when a second later, Aidan buries the bat in the pisser's face.

"Fucking hell," Liam mutters, looking over the mess.

Movement in the far corner has me drawing my gun, but I lower it immediately at the sight of Alex coming through another path in the crates surrounding us.

"There's got to be thirty girls back there. Did you call for back up?"

"Garrett, Mac, and Jace are on their way," Liam confirms.

"Keep the girls back there," I order, remembering where we are and what needs to be done to keep everyone protected.

"Ace."

There's nothing short of devastation on Aidan's face when he looks my way, but we've got a job to do.

"Put your fucking mask back on." I don't drop my gaze until that black balaclava is back over his face, hood pulled up, before I turn my attention to Liam.

"The guards?"

"All dead." A muscle in my jaw ticks. That leaves no one else to interrogate. Aidan should've left the Italian alive, so we could get more information out of him. But at least that means no witnesses, except...

The girl.

I turn slowly back around to face her. Even if Aidan hadn't pulled off his mask, she's already recognized me. She was quickly becoming a problem. Another *complication* we can't afford. Worse, considering when I turn around, the girl is *gone*.

The ropes and zip ties I cut away lie strewn about the floor, stained red with her blood, but there's no sign of *her*. My eyes dart to the opening in the crates, the one Liam and Alex came through earlier. The one no one had eyes on a few minutes ago.

I take off at a run.

The narrow path cuts haphazardly through the warehouse. Wooden crates are just thrown about, no sense of order.

"Fucking Italians," I mutter under my breath. The path only forks once and I cut left, praying my instincts are correct.

They lead me to a side door. A glowing red exit sign sits high above it.

Not good. Not fucking good.

I barrel through it. Finding myself on the docks. The *empty* docks.

Fuck.

Chasing down problematic ballerinas isn't exactly on my to-do list this week, but it looks like I'll have to make a fucking exception.

I stare out across the dock, my eyes trailing over every shipping container, every decrepit building she could be hiding in. There's too many to search, too many directions she could have gone. I growl low under my breath, knowing I have to go back inside and deal with that mess before dealing with her.

You can run, little Rose, but you cannot hide.

Not from me.

17

RUN, BABY, RUN

BRIAR

Now

Run.

The word circles through my mind as I sprint like hell away from the docks. Taking sharp, random turns, and not letting up on the breakneck speed I'm setting, even when I slide on a scattering of loose gravel, skinning up my left knee and thigh.

I hate cardio. I fucking hate cardio. But thank fucking god for cardio.

All that time spent on the treadmill is finally put to good use as I run for what seems like forever. Putting as much distance between me and the Irish Devil King as possible.

Koen O'Rourke. What was he doing there? I don't know if I want the answer.

Once I'm certain no one's chasing after me, I slow. I'm closer to downtown, and this area is much more populated.

I pull the hood of Koen's sweatshirt over my face as far as I can and push on. Trying not to draw any extra attention to myself from whoever might be wandering the downtown streets at this late—or rather, early—hour.

He recognized me. That flash in his eyes just before he cut my hands free. He *knew.* He *remembered.*

Why did I say anything?

Dumb.

Panic upticks my already pounding heart I run through all the possible implications.

I catapult myself onto a bus just as it's about to pull away from the sidewalk, relieved to find it happens to be heading in the right direction. It's late, so there's only one other passenger on the bus with me and he looks half asleep.

"Bus fare?"

I stop, staring blankly at the driver. After everything that just happened, being asked for something as mundane as *bus fare* has glitched my brain.

Right, shit. Buses cost money. And my wallet is back at the club...

The bus driver narrows his eyes, gripping the handle for the door, prepared to kick me out, when I remember I stashed some emergency cash in my bra earlier today. "Hold on!" I frantically check over my shoulder at the empty sidewalk, wishing he would just drive already while I fish a twenty out of my bra and shove it in the box.

"That's too much," he says flatly and I glare at him until he sighs, finally shifting the bus into gear.

I feel infinitely better once we're moving, hunkering down in the back of the bus, keeping my eye on the empty street behind us. I ignore my bleeding knees, curling them into my chest, sliding Koen's hoodie over them and hugging them close.

The adrenaline is finally ebbing away and shivers rack my body, both from cold and shock.

Koen.

He came out of the shadows like a demon summoned straight from hell.

He didn't even blink when he put that bullet in Lorenzo. One clean through his hand, forcing him to drop the whip. And another through his knee, taking him down. With barely a thought, from over a hundred feet away.

He was *lethal*. I'd heard the stories, heeded them too, but everything I'd heard paled in comparison to the *real thing*. Koen O'Rourke is Death incarnate. His brothers, too. I saw what his brother did to Lorenzo. Aidan O'Rourke, the Boston Breakers' star defenseman, had just smashed a man's face in with a baseball bat right in front of me.

And Koen *recognized* me.

Fuck, fuck, fuck.

They were distracted, and no one noticed when I slowly backed away, disappearing into the maze of crates before bolting out of a side door.

Lorenzo, Declan, Matteo, Kostalov, Aidan—The names ring through my brain, information I don't want. I wish I could rip them out of my brain and set them on fire. Knowing those names is dangerous. *They* are dangerous.

Lorenzo is dead. A small mercy. The only one of them who actually knew where to find me.

Declan O'Rourke. He used to be the head of the Irish Devils. Koen's father. Dead, last I knew. The incident had shaken the city for weeks. I'd read every article I could find on the car bomb that took out the notable Boston resident "with rumored ties to the Irish mob."

Matteo Carroza and Adrik Kostalov. I didn't know those two names. And I definitely didn't want to.

And *Aidan*. He'd taken off his mask. The hockey player is well known in this city, his picture is on a billboard somewhere for god's sake! And what I'd just seen him do...

If I didn't run, they would've killed me. No doubt about it. There was no way they were letting me walk out of there alive.

Car bombs, human trafficking—How none of them even flinched when Aidan killed Lorenzo? These are *dangerous* men. Men, I couldn't let anywhere near Remi.

Oh god, Remi. What would Koen do if he found out about her now? After all this time? Would he even care that he had a daughter? *Would he try to take her?* Would he *hurt* her? Would he hurt *me*?

Anxiety surges and I hug my shaking knees tighter, my fingers trembling where I've wrapped them around myself. Logic tries to put out the flames, reminding me that I never gave him my name.

My real name.

That night almost five years ago, I lied. I told him my name was Rose. So what if he recognized me tonight? He has no way of tracking me down. I'd lived in this city for four years and not *once* had we crossed paths.

Finally making it home, I race up the stairs to our fifth-floor walk-up, pulling the key out of my bra and locking every damn lock behind me. It doesn't feel like enough.

I stand there for god knows how long, palms pressed against the back of the door like I can keep out the devil at my back, breathing hard.

When I finally move, the shooting pain spiraling up my back almost brings me to my knees. Adrenaline, and likely fear, must have been keeping me from truly feeling the pain, but oh, it's coming roaring back with a vengeance. Worse yet, the blood on my back has started to dry, the wounds clotting and sticking to the inside of Koen's sweatshirt, ripping me alive with every little movement.

I should clean it but I don't. I'm on the verge of passing out from blood loss or adrenaline crash—I don't know, so instead I make a beeline down the hall. Quietly slipping in the second door on the right. Relief floods through me at the sight of my little girl, safe and sound, curled up under the covers. Her pink unicorn tucked under one arm.

The door clicks quietly behind me as I tiptoe through the room. Stepping over stuffed animals and matchbox cars—a new phase—until I reach the bed.

Doing my best not to disturb her, I crawl under the covers, pulling her into my chest and holding her tight. The fear of losing her was the worst part of it all.

Remi lets out a little sigh before drifting back off to sleep but not before her little hand wraps around mine too. I hold her close for the next couple of hours, shadowed green eyes haunting my thoughts, until I finally drift off.

18

TRUTH OR DARE?

KOEN

THEN...

Summer is right around the corner and it's a warm night; clear, the perfect night for riding. I take us through the nonsensical, winding roads of the city, turning the bright city lights into streaks of red and gold. Driving way too fast, seeing just how far I can push it—push *her*, but she just clings on tighter, my t-shirt fisted in her fingers, she's loving it.

As I take a sharp curve, I shout for her to hold on, having to lean deep into the curve in order to clear it. The pavement rises up to greet us, and I'm expecting a scream, but instead I get laughter.

She's laughing.

The wind picks up as I take her over the Longfellow bridge, the city lights sparkling in the Charles River beneath us.

Her hands disappear from my waist; she lets go of me, stretching her arms out wide. Holding them out to either side of her like she's flying, tipping her head back while she laughs wildly. I'm careful to keep the bike steady, catching a glimpse of her in my mirror, visor up, blue eyes sparkling, reflecting the glow of the city lights around us. That laugh turns to shouts of excitement just as fireworks illuminate the sky high above the river.

Rose's hands come back to my waist and I take us down to a secluded little spot I know, pulling to a stop right beside the river.

"Wow," she says, taking off her helmet and staring up at the bright lights exploding through the night sky.

I ignore the fireworks, choosing instead to watch her.

"Lucky timing," she says with a smile, looking up at me.

A little smile tugs at the corner of my lips. "Maybe not luck."

Her blue eyes flash with surprise. "You knew?"

I shrug like it's no big deal, even though it is. I don't even know this girl, yet she's got me unbalanced, doing things I never thought I would do.

She stares up at me and I notice how close she is. I study her face, memorizing every little detail. Rose is all soft contrasts; long, dark lashes frame eyes the color of the summer sky; a faint scattering of freckles decorate her cheeks. Her dark hair falls in loose waves down her back, a deep, dark shade of brown that you might mistake as black when the light shifts. It makes me wonder how it would look wrapped around my fist.

And then there are her lips—soft and full—and I'm reminded how they felt on mine. The taste of her still lingers on my tongue, and like the sweetest of drugs, I crave more. *Need* more. I lean in, wanting to kiss her again.

But she pulls away, forcing me to stop. My jaw clenches

and I look up. She's not looking at me, her eyes are in the direction of the fireworks but I know she's not watching them. There's a newfound tension in her body and I know she's watching me—my reaction—from the corner of her eye.

Her rejection was quiet, subtle, just enough of a reminder that *she's not mine*. I don't get to kiss her whenever I want. I shrug it off, sliding my hands into my pockets, but I'd be lying if I said her rejection didn't sting worse than a gunshot wound.

I keep my eyes on the sky overhead. The crackle and boom of the dynamite does nothing to soften the tense silence stretching between us.

"Do you want to play a game?" The sound of her soft voice surprises me and I glance down.

"Do you want to play a game?" she repeats when I don't answer her.

My eyebrows lift. "A game?"

"It'll be fun." She smiles, nodding, trying to convince me.

"I don't like games." My tone is harsher than I mean it to be but I stand by it, crossing my arms across my chest.

"Truth or dare?" she continues, as if she hasn't heard me.

"Isn't that a game for kids?"

"Depends on how you play." Her eyes sparkle and she bats those thick eyelashes of hers. *Is she flirting with me?*

"Truth."

She rolls her eyes. "Coward."

My eyes narrow on her. "Careful, little Rose."

Her answering smirk tests the boundaries of my restraint.

"What's your biggest regret?"

"I don't have one," I can say without hesitation. And I don't. I stand by every decision I've made. I own them.

"C'mon, everyone regrets something."

"Not me," I insist, shaking my head.

She frowns, while at the same time her eyes sparkle with mischief. "Well, if you can't answer the question, you have to do a dare. Those are the rules."

"I don't think that's the—"

"It is." She nods assertively, taking a small step toward me. Her eyes are locked on mine, stunning me into silence.

"And I suppose you get to decide what that dare will be, little Rose?" My voice is dark, and danger swirls in it. *If she thinks she's going to make me do something humiliating...*

"Kiss me."

I tense, my gaze snapping to her in surprise. Is this her idea of a joke? I just tried to kiss her minutes earlier and yet, she'd rejected me. My brow furrows, and I search her face. She's serious, all joking gone from her eyes, leaving behind only steady resolve.

"I dare you to kiss me," she says again, blue eyes locked on mine, unblinking. And then she licks her lips, and she not only has my attention, but the attention of my cock as well.

When I don't move, when I do nothing but stare down at her, she opens her mouth to speak again but hesitates when she sees me take a step forward.

I lean in slowly. She doesn't flinch, doesn't turn away, though her breath quickens right as my lips hover over hers, kissing her gently, carefully, waiting to see if she'll push me away. When she doesn't, I deepen the kiss, my hand going to the nape of her neck to bring her closer. A soft exhale escapes her lips, a whimper or maybe—a moan? The small sound travels straight to my cock and it's all the invitation I need.

My restraint shatters and I crush my lips to hers, exploring every inch of her mouth, my fingers curling into her hair. It's soft, silky, and I grab a fist full of it, tugging down to bring her face up higher. My other hand circles around her neck, holding her still, a possessive urge I can't justify taking over. I release her lips, looking down, certain to find a flash of fear or anger in her eyes. But instead, she melts against me, *like putty in my hands.*

'Oh, little Rose, you're playing a dangerous game." I squeeze my hand—the one around her throat—a little tighter. "My turn."

19

MY RIDE OR DIE
BRIAR

Now

I'm faintly aware of Remi climbing over me as she attempts to escape the bed without my notice. My eyelids are heavy, but I peel them open.

"Good morning, Remi-roo." Her perfect little face peers up at me, and I tense when her dark eyes linger on mine. The green in her eyes sparkles in the early morning sun that streams in through her little window. The same eyes that plagued my nightmares last night.

Remi's brow furrows with concern and she reaches for my chin. "Mommy, what happened?" she asks with a frown and instantly, I regret not cleaning up in the bathroom when I got home last night. What I must look like...

I push myself up, hiding my face from her as much as I can. "Umm, Mommy had an accident at the studio last night."

"An accident?" She blinks up at me, still sleepy. She's not a morning person.

"Mhmm." I agree, searching to change the subject. "Are you hungry? Auntie Lily went shopping yesterday and got your favorite cereal."

Her expression immediately brightens. "Cinnamon sugars?"

"Cinnamon sugars," I confirm, forcing a smile. "Let's go get some!'

She nods eagerly and I take her hand, leading her to the kitchen where I find Lily, sipping on a cup of coffee as she scrolls through videos on her phone.

"Morning, Remicoaster," she teases before her eyes lift to mine. "Jesus fucking Christ—" Lily catches herself before she falls sideways off of her stool.

"*Auntie Lily*, can you get some cinnamon sugars for Remi?" I say pointedly, my eyes boring into hers. "Mommy needs to shower before class."

Lily's mouth snaps shut, but she does nothing to wipe the horrified expression off her face. Her eyes promise me we'll talk about this later before she musters up a smile, jumping off her stool to scoop Remi up into her arms, flying her around the kitchen like an airplane before pretending to hit the brakes right outside the cereal cabinet.

Do airplanes have brakes? I don't know... My head hurts.

I duck quickly into the bathroom, closing the door behind me.

I breathe once, twice, before raising my eyes to face myself in the mirror.

Okay, it's not—*it could be worse.* I hardly recognize the sight of myself staring back at me. Dried blood trickles down from my nose; my lip is split in two places, and a dark purple bruise blooms on my left cheek—*that one will be hard to hide.*

I slowly peel Koen's sweatshirt off, hating that I'd slept in it, and hating that I can smell him on it... a dark, musky scent, a mix of leather and citrus. I wince as I struggle out of the heavy hoodie, inspecting the deep burn on my neck from Lorenzo's cigarette before turning on the shower.

Wanting nothing more than to wash away the horror of last night from my body, I climb right in.

It's a mistake.

The stream of water hits the slices in my back and I can't hold in my scream, clasping my hand over my mouth to keep the sound from reaching Lily and Remi in the next room, screaming into my palm.

The burn of the water against my raw back nearly causes me to black out and I twist out of the stream, leaning my forehead against the cool tile until it eases. I force myself back under the heavy stream when I think I can take it, only to cringe back out the second the water makes contact with the wounds.

I repeat this several times until I'm sure it's rinsed clean enough before climbing shakily out of the bathtub. Holding the towel tight to my chest, I'm unable to muster up the courage to attempt to wrap it around my back.

I open the bathroom door and nearly jolt back at the sight of Lily in the doorway.

"Talk."

"I don't want to talk about it, Lil." I shoulder past her into my little closet of a room, right across the hall from Remi's. Technically, it's not meant to be a bedroom. The apartment listing was for a two bedroom plus office, but we made do. The room is just big enough for a double bed and bureau, with no closet.

Lily doesn't take no for an answer, following me, her eyes catching on the exposed wounds on my back.

"What the fuck—" she starts.

"Where's Remi?" I ask, cutting her off.

"She's watching TV," Lily replies quickly. I can't even describe the level of concern in her eyes. "Briar, you need to go to the hospital."

"No. No hospital." I shake my head, sinking down to the mattress, wrapping myself in my comforter while carefully avoiding letting anything touch my back. "It's the first place they'll look."

I don't know that for certain. But it's what I would do if I were out there, *looking for me.*

"The first place *who* would look?" Her brow creases as she tries to make sense of what I'm saying.

"The O'Rourkes," I bite out, laying my head down,

Her eyes go wide. "The *Irish* did this to you?"

"No," I start. "They rescued me..." *I think.* Releasing a deep sigh, I fill Lily in on everything that happened last night.

"Oh my god."

"I know."

"That's—what could've—" She starts and fails.

"*I know,*" I say, quieter this time.

"Did you call the police?"

"No," I admit, staring at my toes.

There's a long pause before she speaks again. "Don't you think you should?"

I sigh. I've thought about it, almost did when I spotted a cop car parked around the corner from our apartment last night but...

"I think the police are in on it."

"You can't be serious."

"Remember Daniel? The regular from the bar?"

She nods. I'd mentioned him a few times. "He was the one that found me listening."

Lily blows out a breath. "Shit..."

"And we both know what Koen is involved with..." My eyes lift to find hers and she winces.

"*Koen* rescued you?"

"Koen was *there*," I state as a matter of fact.

Did he save me?

Yes? Maybe?

I didn't exactly stick around to find out what his intentions were. Somehow, I doubt the leader of the Irish mafia goes around breaking up trafficking rings in his downtime, seeing as how he's likely profiting from them himself.

And the way his brother killed Lorenzo... I can't get the image out of my brain; it's on an endless loop. A horror movie I can't shut off. *It was gruesome.*

No, there was something more going on, some *other* reason they were there. Maybe I stumbled into a mafia turf war or something.

"Do you regret not telling him about Remi?" Lily asks, dropping her voice lower.

"No. If anything, what happened last night only reaffirms

my decision to keep her a secret. Koen's dangerous. He doesn't even know me. If he knew about her, best-case scenario is dead-beat dad; worst case—he might try to take her from me..."

"Mommy!" Remi calls from the living room. I start to rise, but Lily stops me.

"Uh-uh, no way, lay your ass back down. You're not going anywhere today."

"I can't miss work," I protest.

"You can't turn up looking like *that* either... at the very least you need more sleep. Your eyes are bloodshot."

I can't argue with that.

"I can cover you at the studio today." I open my mouth to argue but she cuts me off. "Nope. I don't want to hear it. You can miss one day. Get your ass in that bed. I'll get Remi ready and drop her off at preschool on the way to the studio."

"Fine. But I want a Remi kiss before you guys leave!"

"Done." Lily smiles, satisfied.

"Thanks, Lil."

"Of course."

20

MY LITTLE LIABILITY

KOEN

Now

"Anything?"

"No, Koen." Liam levels me an irate stare from over his laptop screen. "I don't have anything new since the last time you asked me—thirty seconds ago."

I get up and pace the room.

"It might help if I had something more to go on other than *'her name isn't Rose.'* You wanna tell me how you know her? Maybe that will help?"

"*I don't* know her."

He scoffs. "Okay. Your reaction in the warehouse says otherwise."

"Just find her. Preferably *before* she starts running her mouth."

"We *did* save her ass. I doubt she's going to turn around

and narc to the police. But I am going to need a little bit more to go on..."

"That's all I got," I growl. Wracking my brain as I've been doing over the last twelve hours to recall any identifying information about the girl from the warehouse. I remember every fucking little thing about her: the silky feel of her dark hair when I had it wrapped around my fist; how she smelled of jasmine; and the eighteen freckles she has scattered across her cheeks.

I hadn't wanted to know anything more about her, didn't learn her real name, or where she went to school, because I knew if I did... I wouldn't be able to stop myself from making her mine. She was perfect, beautiful and too good for me.

"She was a dancer," I say, rubbing the back of my neck. "In school for it, I think. Definitely came from money."

"So *not* the stripper variety then?"

"No," I growl out. "Ballet, I think."

Liam looks up from his screen to watch me pace the length of the living room. "Why's this girl getting to you so much?"

"She's not!" I snap.

His answering smirk makes me want to punch him in the face.

"Will you just find her?"

"Find who?" A quick glance over my shoulder reveals my sister Reagan wandering into the room. She's still in her pajamas, her red hair in a messy bun on top of her head.

"None of your—"

"A *girl*," Liam supplies and I glare daggers at him.

Reagan's light green eyes sparkle with interest and to my dismay, she plops down on the sofa next to Liam with her coffee mug pulled up to her lips.

"Well this is intriguing. Tell me more."

"There's nothing to—

"Koen saved her life last night, and she ran away from him," Liam informs our sister.

"Ouch." She winces playfully before smirking at me over the rim of her cup.

"I'm going to kill you both," I seethe, pulling out my phone to check it for probably the hundredth time this hour. Mac and Alex are going through everything we stole from the warehouse, and talking to the girls we pulled out of there. I'm hoping at least one of them knows *my* girl's name.

"Oh, he's touchy." Reagan exchanges a glance with Liam, unfazed by my threats. "And what did you do to this girl to make her run away from you?"

"Nothing," I growl.

"Then why did she run?" she presses.

"I'm not talking to you." To prove my point, I press my phone to my ear, listening to a new voicemail from Mac.

Reagan turns her attention to Liam. "Spill the tea, what's the story?"

He shrugs before opening his mouth.

I tug the phone down to snap in his direction, "Do not tell her anything." Pinching the bridge of my nose, I take a deep breath to keep my calm. My head is pounding from lack of sleep and stress. "Reagan, so help me god..."

Whatever she's going to say gets cut off by the ding of the elevator. We all turn to see Alex and Aidan walking in, the latter looking a little worse for wear. Dark circles ring my brother's eyes. He's probably gotten just as much sleep as I have since last night.

Alex takes the long way around the sectional, rounding

behind Reagan and Liam. With his free hand, he reaches down and plucks Reagan's coffee straight out of her hands.

"Hey!" she shouts in protest, trying to snatch the drink back, but Alex has already got the cup tipped back to his lips, taking a long, drawn-out sip. "Thanks for the coffee, Rae."

He hands Reagan her cup back but she eyes it as though it's been poisoned, a pout evident on her face.

"The shipment?" I meet Alex's eye as he takes a seat a safe throwing distance away from Reagan.

"Secure." He nods, knowing what I'm referencing. *The girls.* It was important to move them out of the city—and out of the reach of Matteo and his little minions.

"And the clean-up?" My eyes slide to Aidan, who lets out a heavy sigh.

"Done." He leans back in his chair, his arms folded across his chest.

"Any new *complications?*"

His jaw flexes at my words. I love my brother, but he's gotten sloppy in his time away from the family business, leaving more than a few *problems* for me to clean up. He made a big mistake last night when he took off his mask before killing that Italian; he was lucky the warehouse didn't have cameras. But he did leave behind an eyewitness who could I.D. him and then we lost her.

"No."

"Good. Now we just need to locate the girl."

"C'mon Koen," Liam tries again. "You saved her from a world of hurt or worse, she's not going to tell anyone what she saw."

"The girl is a liability," I say almost robotically. "A loose end."

My gaze is drawn to Alex who's busy digging something out of his pocket. "Aidan and I found these while we were"—his eyes dart to Reagan before clearing his throat—"cleaning up."

She narrows her eyes, not fooled by our use of code words. *They were taking care of the bodies*, ensuring nothing could be traced back to the Devils.

He reaches out and I take the small stack of plastic cards from him.

"IDs." My eyes widen as I take in his discovery, shuffling through the stack, looking for my *little liability*.

"What are you going to do if you find her?" It's Aidan who asks. I don't look up, my entire body going still when I get to the second to last driver's license in the stack.

Briar Elizabeth Ralston, 301 Ironworks Street, Apt 5B, Roxbury, Massachusetts.

Found you little Rose.

Tucking *Briar's* ID into my back pocket, I hand the rest of the stack back to Alex before heading for the door.

"I'm going to take care of it."

21

WHEN I SAY DANCE...

BRIAR

Now

It's a little past noon by the time I wake up. After Lily and Remi left, I crawled back into bed, sleeping for hours, though I still feel as though I haven't. That could be because of the anxiety weighing on me over Koen, Gio... and how *everything* hurts.

I'm peppered in bruises from head to toe, but it's the burn on my neck and the whip marks on my back that bring tears to my eyes with every little movement. Wincing, I drag myself out of bed and change out of my now blood-soaked t-shirt.

Gathering up the bloody clothes and Koen's sweatshirt, I throw my shredded top and sports bra away and dump the rest into an empty laundry basket before beginning the long trek down to the basement communal laundry room. Our apartment is on the fifth floor and there are no elevators.

As I load the clothes into the wash, the hair on the back of my neck rises and unease trickles through me. I glance around the small room but see nothing.

I'm alone.

Chalking it up to potential post-traumatic stress and an overwhelming need for more sleep, I head back upstairs.

I should probably eat, or figure out what to do about Giovanni. He's the biggest threat; I saw something I shouldn't have at Wonderland and ended up in that warehouse because of it. Just because I happened to escape doesn't mean I'm safe from him. He's going to find out and he's going to come for me, but I don't have anywhere to run to, and I think I have $21.63 in my bank account at the moment.

All I want to do is crawl back under my covers and hide there forever.

One more hour wouldn't hurt...

Still, that feeling of unease doesn't let up, only growing stronger after I climb back up to my floor. I pause outside of my door, looking over my shoulder, but see nothing out of the ordinary.

The hallway continues down past my door before taking a sharp left. I keep one eye on the shadowy corner as I slip my key into the lock, turning it carefully.

My door cracks open and that's when they strike. Two men jump out from down the hall, running for me.

Shrieking, I bolt into my apartment, sliding on the hardwood as I try to slam the door shut behind me.

I'm not quick enough.

A steel-toed boot is shoved into the door jamb and it won't close. I throw all of my weight into pushing them out, but I'm thrown back a second later when the other one charges the door.

The gun.

I meet the man's gaze for a second before darting for the hallway in a mad dash to reach my bedroom. If I can lock him out then I can—

He catches me by my hair and I scream. A second later, there's a gun in my face, courtesy of his friend.

"Ah-ah-ah, none of that now."

My jaw snaps shut and I struggle in the hold of the first guy, but he's released my hair in favor of my arms, and his grip is firm. I'm not going anywhere.

"Bella, Bella, Bella, what are we going to do with you?" Giovanni's Italian drawl fills me with dread, and I fight with renewed passion when I see him waltzing in through the still wide-open front door like he owns the place.

"Remember when you told me you could be a good girl and keep your mouth shut?" he asks, shutting the door to my apartment behind him.

Despite the guy behind me having me locked down, I still struggle when Giovanni steps closer.

"I just want to talk." Gio holds his hands up innocently before snapping his fingers and pointing to one of the dining room chairs. Obediently, the man with the gun pressed up against my cheeks drops it, holstering it before shoving me into the chair Giovanni pointed to.

Just as soon as I land, I try to spring back up, but Giovanni's voice stops me again.

"Don't make me tie you to it." His voice holds a sharp warning, so, slowly, I sink back down. My eyes dart between the three of them, trying to watch all three at once, but my friend with the gun moves out of sight behind me, and the other goes to stand guard by the door.

Giovanni sighs loudly, taking a seat directly in front of me on the edge of the worn out coffee table, and looks me over. He takes out an expensive looking flask from his suit jacket's pocket, taking a long swig before offering it to me.

I shake my head while twitching nervously in the chair, my eyes flicking to the clock. It's almost two.

Lily and Remi will be home soon.

"Now, Bella," Giovanni starts, and my gaze snaps to him. "It seems you are the *only* living witness to a raid that took place at one of my warehouses last night."

I blink back at him in shock. *The other girls—they're dead?*

He smiles, leaning forward in his chair. It's a smile that's meant to be reassuring, kind even—but his cool eyes give it away, his smile doesn't touch them. "Now listen up. I'll make you a deal, okay?" He looks at me expectantly this time, and I manage a slight dip of my chin in response.

"Good." He grins at me and I have to bite back my glare. "Now you tell me everything you saw and heard last night, and I won't kill you." He leans back in his seat, still smiling at me.

I swallow hard.

"Did you see the men who attacked my warehouse last night?"

I nod.

"I need *answers*, Bella," he reprimands sharply.

I choke out a "Yes."

"How many of them were there?"

I hesitate for a moment before answering, "Four."

"Good." His shoulders relax a notch and I realize that was a test. He already knew how many there were."

"Who were they?"

"I don't know."

"What did they look like?"

"They wore masks."

"Did you hear any names? Did they call each other anything?"

"No." The lie rolls off my tongue easily—*too easily*, but Giovanni doesn't question it, continuing on.

"Accents?"

"No."

I protect them. I don't know why I do. It happens almost involuntarily, and once I've done it, there's no taking it back.

Gio's eyebrows rise, wanting more.

"I just heard gunshots, and shouting," I tell him, careful to look him straight in the eye. Utilizing my acting training, the little tremble I allow to shake my voice seals the deal.

He leans back in his chair, studying me... thinking. "How is it you're the only one who survived?"

My eyes widen in true surprise. *Did they... Did the Irish kill the rest of the girls?* I'm going to be sick.

"I ran."

He waits for more.

"They shot Lorenzo and I—I just ran."

He stares at me for a long while, and I have to resist the urge to look away, to check the clock. Until finally he says, "Okay," and rises from his perch on the coffee table.

My eyes follow him.

"So here's how this is going to go." He paces my living room. "You're going to keep your pretty little mouth shut about me, what you witnessed at the club, and that whole mess at the warehouse."

"I won't say anything, I swear." I stare up at him, meaning the words I say. *Anything* to walk away from this.

"Oh, I know you won't. Because I know that *you know* we own the cops. And I know that you know we own *you*."

A chill runs down my spine.

"And from now on, when I say jump... you ask how fucking high. You got that?" He leans in so close to my face, the scent of his menthols is hot on my cheek.

"And if you don't..." Gio's mouth twists into a dark smile before he holds his hand out to his right, someone from behind me puts something into it.

I jolt back at the sight of Rainbow Cupcake, Remi's stuffed pink unicorn. It was in her room, on her pillow. I never even heard the guy leave the room.

Giovanni grins at the look of horror on my face as I look between Rainbow Cupcake and him. "And if you don't, we'll handle you and *then* we'll take it out on her."

My whole body shakes and I grip the seat of the chair so hard my knuckles go white.

"Do we understand each other, Briar?" He brushes the side of my cheek with the little pink unicorn.

"We do," I bite out, looking him in the eye but hiding the murderous rage I feel burning in mine.

"Excellent." Giovanni straightens, rebuttoning his suit before tossing Rainbow Cupcake at me. I catch it, gripping the stuffed animal tight.

He motions to his men to take their leave. He gets two steps before he stops again, looking me up and down while I grip the seat of my chair. A flicker of distaste in his expression.

"Take the rest of the week off. I can't have you in my club, looking like that."

I clench my jaw.

"See you next weekend, Bella."

There's no hiding the look of what must be absolute dread on my face when Lily and Remi walk through the door just about forty-five minutes later.

The second they walk in, I scoop Remi up into my arms and squeeze her to my chest.

"Mommy! Too tight!" Her voice is muffled from where she's squished against my shoulder.

I relax my hold but keep her in my arms. "I'm sorry baby, Mommy just missed you so much. Did you have a good day?"

"Yes." She nods, squirming in my hold, eager to escape.

Reluctantly, I set her back on the floor and she goes straight for her room and her toys.

The second she's out of earshot, Lily whirls on me.

"What happened?"

"Giovanni stopped by."

Her breath catches and I nod solemnly. "He—He brought some friends."

"You didn't—they didn't?" Worry flashes in her eyes.

I shake my head sharply. "No. But he made it clear that he *owns* me now. I have to go back to the club next weekend."

She pales, and she and I share the same thought. There's no telling what he'll make me do there going forward.

"You can't."

"I don't think I have a choice. They threatened to hurt Remi..."

"Shit."

"I've got to get her out of the city—*we've* got to get out of the city." I'm panicked, but as many times as I've been over it, I can't find a way out. "I need an exit strategy, and I need one fast."

"You know I'm going home for two weeks over winter break. You guys can come with me!"

I chew my lip. "No. They'll find me there. If I'm going to get out from under Gio's thumb, that means paying him what I owe." Fuck. I don't even know where to start with that. I'm barely making rent right now, and paying off Gio is going to cost some serious cash, and *fuck*, I'm forgetting about Remi's meds. Not to mention the winter showcase; rehearsals start on Monday. I run my hands through my hair, feeling over-whelmed. My heartbeat doubles, and I'm on the verge of a panic attack. I don't know which problem to tackle first.

Sensing the rising panic, Lily places two hands on my shoulders. "Breathe, B. Breathe." I let out a shaky breath, not realizing I'd been holding it in.

What the fuck am I going to do?

"Okay," Lily says once I'm breathing again. Her Type A personality snaps into place and I see her formulating a plan in her hazel eyes. "What if Remi comes home with me anyway? My parents have been begging to see her. She'll be safe and out of the city for a couple of weeks, and you can work on getting the money together to either pay Giovanni off or run." She ends with a wince.

My frown deepens at the thought of being away from Remi for any period of time, but Giovanni's unpredictable. I don't trust him. I would probably still be in the warehouse—or worse—if the Irish Devils hadn't come along last night. For all I know, he could throw me in another van the second I step foot back in Wonderland.

Paying off my debt to Giovanni is the quickest way to try and get out from under his thumb. If I can pay it off fast, keep my mouth shut, then maybe he can forget this whole thing ever happened. I'll pick up as many shifts as I can between the studio and the club, pay off Giovanni, get Remi's medication, and maybe... it'll all be okay.

Lily looks at me with a question in her eyes. "And what about Koen?

My eyes snap to hers. "What about him?" Everything about Koen still screams danger to me. Would he help me if he knew what was going on? I'd have to tell him about Remi if I'm going to ask him to hide us. My hand shakes at the thought of it.

"Maybe—Maybe he could help. With Gio?"

I think about it. They're obviously not friends, seeing as how Koen and his men killed all of Gio's and tore apart his warehouse, but that doesn't mean he'd help me. But Gio said I was the only one to survive last night. *Did Koen kill the rest of the girls? Would he have killed me too if I stayed?*

I shake my head. "We can't trust him. Our best hope is that we stay off his radar while I try and get us out of Boston."

"So I'll take Remi to New York with me, and you'll stay here?"

I shift uneasily on my feet, not wanting to be separated from either of them. "Are you sure that's okay?"

"Yes, absolutely, even though I don't like the thought of leaving you here alone..."

"It's safer for you and Remi if you guys go. I'll handle things here." I nod, trying to look braver than I feel.

22

LITTLE ROSE

BRIAR

Now

After Remi's asleep, I spend hours in the old dance studio around the corner from our apartment, working on the routine I have to choreograph and perform for my senior piece at the winter showcase.

The studio sits right atop Mae's Diner, where Lily works a couple of mornings a week. Mae, Lily's boss, owns the studio too, but it's been closed down now for ages. Being the sweet, old woman that she is, Mae offered the space to Lily and me to practice in at no cost.

Some of the mirrors along the wall are cracked and broken, and the place is really in need of a good cleaning. Layers of dust and cobwebs coat the rafters of the old mill building, but the space is big and open and the floor is solid and that's all that really matters.

Music plays out of my phone speaker; it's not the sophisticated sound system the Conservatory studios offer, but it gets the job done.

After everything that'd happened, I'd tried going to bed early. Lord knows I could use the sleep, but lying there, alone in my bed, and in the dark... it only made my panic worse. My chest felt tight and, even lying still in my bed, my heart hammered inside like I was in the middle of a marathon. The walls began to feel like they were closing in, and my mind started to spiral into every possible way this could all go wrong.

Dancing is the only way I know how to make it stop.

I mark through the choreography I've been working on for my senior piece. I really shouldn't be dancing, and I'm not... *not really anyway.*

My ribs still ache and the lacerations on my back burn with every single movement I make; blood leaks out of the barely healed wounds every time I twist or stretch too far, preventing me from actually working through the routine properly, but even just being here, moving, working—it calms my brain.

As I mark the steps, I push myself further, losing myself in the music and the routine and forgetting the pain, the stress, and everything else I have weighing me down.

When I finally stop, my back is on fire, and sweat coats my body, but my mind is finally quiet.

I tug on my hoodie, welcoming the cold blast of night air against my hot face as I step out onto the sidewalk. Wet leaves litter the streets. It must have rained while I was in the studio, the wet sheen on the pavement reflects the faint glow of the street lights overhead. The further I walk, the heavier the night feels. A thin mist of fog creeps along the streets, giving the broken-down old buildings a ghostly appearance, keeping most pedestrians away.

I've walked the short walk from the studio to our apartment late at night many times, but tonight feels different...

The air feels off.

The street looks empty but I can't shake the overwhelming feeling that I'm being *watched*. I pull up my hood so that it covers my hair, keeping my head on a swivel as I quicken my pace, crossing the street for good measure, no sign of anyone else around.

But that feeling—*that feeling*—eyes watching me, burning into my back, it never leaves, no matter how many times I look over my shoulder, certain I'll catch someone following me, but every time I turn around, there's no one there.

All that work in the studio to center myself, to calm my racing heart, it's all for nothing because it's racing again now, my blood pressure rising, and the goosebumps along my arms are *not* from the cold.

My building comes into view and I'm practically running to it now. It's so dark outside; the slum lord that runs our apartment building hasn't replaced the doorway light in the entire three years we've lived here.

The lock on the front door is busted too, so I push my way through it, taking the stairs two at a time until I reach my apartment. Nervous, I fumble with my keys, too busy watching my back, and the dark end of the hallway, to get the goddamn key into the lock.

Finally, it slides in. I unlock the door and then the deadbolt, throwing myself inside like the devil himself is on my heels, quickly sliding the deadbolt back into place and the chain, too, for good measure. Standing on my toes, I peer through the peephole to check the hall one last time.

I see nothing. The hallway outside is empty, quiet at this late hour, and I chastise myself for my paranoia.

Get it together, Briar.

Safely inside my apartment, the panic I'd let take over ebbs away into exhaustion. I know I pushed myself too far in the studio tonight, purposefully pushing myself past my limit in hopes that it would help me sleep. Whatever sleep I got last night and this morning was plagued by nightmares, leaving me feeling more tired than if I had just stayed up.

I set my bag down by the door, leaving my keys and phone on the island. I pop my head in briefly on a sleeping Remi before crossing the hall and into my room.

The second I enter my bedroom, I sense it.

The room feels darker, smells... off.

I freeze at the sight of the open window. *I know I didn't—*

Movement in the far corner sends me skittering backwards, but he's on me in an instant. I go to scream, but a gloved hand comes up, covering my mouth while another snakes around my middle, trapping me against him.

I yelp at the sharp pain when the raw, angry cuts on my back are pressed against his front. My body jerks and trembles, and the searing pain brings tears to my eyes. I don't even fight him, too panicked, fear seizing my senses, paralyzing me.

"Don't scream," a dark voice whispers in my ear. "You'll only make a bigger mess for me to clean up."

Oh shit, oh shit, oh shit. He's holding me tight to his body and I can feel every hard edge of him.

Is he going to hurt me? Is he going to—

Oh god, Remi is right across the hall, and Lily is probably already asleep next door. Maybe if I scream loudly enough, and put up enough of a fight to wake her up, she can get Remi out while I distract him and—

He spins me suddenly, so now my back is to the wall, allowing him to cage me in, though he doesn't push me against it. The searing pain from my back subsides. His hand is still pressed to my mouth and I have to tilt my chin to see his face. He's wearing a mask, one that leaves only his eyes visible. A wave of both relief and inexplicable terror spreads through me at the sight of the darkened green eyes glaring down at me.

Koen.

My eyes must go wide because he tilts his head. "You know who I am?"

I nod slowly, my body shaking.

"Then you know what I'm capable of?"

I hesitate, but nod again. Never breaking eye contact, not even to blink.

He studies me for a moment, searches my face, considering something.

"I'm going to let you go. You're not going to scream when I do," he tells me.

I just stare wide-eyed at him.

Shadowed eyes narrow on me. "Nod, so I know you understand."

I hesitate again, searching those familiar dark eyes for any insight into his intentions.

I find nothing but cold, steady *intensity*.

His grip tightens on my mouth when I don't respond, his voice is darker now and he speaks slowly, enunciating every syllable, "I need you to promise me, you're not going to scream. Can you do that?"

Decision made, I dip my chin again with the lie. I make no

promises and reserve the right still to scream, dependent on whatever the fuck happens next. But *he* doesn't need to know that.

True to his word, he releases my mouth and I don't scream... yet.

"Good." He nods appraisingly at me and I fight the urge to squirm under the intensity of his gaze.

His fingers curl under the mask at his neck, pulling it off to reveal a face I feel like I know all too well, yet not at all.

He clenches his jaw, sharp enough to cut glass, while stalking like a predator would through my room. Six feet of coiled muscle moving with surprising grace within the tight space to close my door. I suppress the overwhelming urge to scream at the sound of the lock clicking into place. He holds me trapped in his piercing gaze as he crosses the room to also shut the window. The one leading out onto the fire escape.

Shit.

Closing my door and window seems to take all the oxygen out of the room. The tiny space feels ten times smaller with the mass of *him* in it.

I move back as far as I can without pressing my back against the wall, eyes darting around as I work to formulate a plan.

My bedside table holds the gun I'd gotten years ago for protection. Unfortunately for me, Koen stands directly between me and that table.

I watch him track my gaze to that very table, assessing it.

Double shit.

I tear my gaze away, taking the opportunity with his eyes off of me to bolt for the hall door. It's only locked from the inside.

Koen catches me easily, swinging me around until he has

me pinned back up against the wall. A whimper escapes me as a wave of pain rushes through me, and I watch his eyes darken.

He spins me again, and I feel his hands, rough against my skin, sliding up the hem of my shirt. I squeal and try to squirm away, but his hand finds my mouth again, suppressing any sound and holding me still.

"You're bleeding."

I rip his hand off my mouth, wanting to get as far away from him as I can. "It's fine."

"It's not fine. You didn't even clean it."

"I cleaned it."

"Not well."

"Here—" He goes to pull my shirt up a little higher and I flinch away violently.

"Don't touch me!" I spin, backing as far away from him as the wall allows.

Koen stays where he is, holding up his hands in surrender, even backing off a step, studying me—seeing my panic, my fear... *seeing too much.*

I fold my arms across my chest, uncomfortable under his scrutiny.

"What do you want?" I snap, my words come out stronger than I feel. "What are you doing here, Koen?"

His jaw tightens at the sound of his name on my lips.

"What do you want?" I ask again when he doesn't answer. Hating how hoarse and small my voice sounds.

God, Remi really is the spitting image of her father, I notice, getting my first good look at him after all these years.

He takes another step closer, stopping when he spies me edging away.

"It's nice to see you again, Rose."

I don't say anything, a little shocked he remembers me—or well, the fake name I gave him that one night, almost five years ago. But if he's standing *here*, in my bedroom, he very well knows that *Rose* isn't my name at all.

He moves again, shifting his attention to my bureau, pretending to study the knickknacks I have there. I'm instantly grateful there are no pictures of Remi in here. But, she's right across the hall. No less than ten feet away. *What if he sees her? Then he'll know.* The thousands of scenarios I've played out over the years flood my mind, and my heart races, but I shake them away. *I need him out. I need him out now.*

"You didn't answer my question," I shoot back at him, my voice gaining strength.

He notices, lifting his dark gaze to meet mine while holding my music box in his hand. His eyes drop back to the tiny dancer in his palm as though he has all the time in the world. He sighs, before placing it back down onto my dresser and turning to look at me.

"I'm here, because *you* little Rose." He looks at me, the streetlight pouring in from outside highlighting the cold glint in his eye. I take a step back. "*You* saw something you shouldn't have the other night."

The blood in my veins chills as I process his words. *Aidan. He's talking about Aidan.* I force away the horrific memory of him bashing in Lorenzo's skull.

"And I can't have you go running your mouth now, can I?" *Fuck.*

I straighten my shoulders and lift my chin to glare at him, my fists tightening at my sides. If he's here to kill me, I'm going to make it really fucking difficult for the asshole.

"I—I don't know what you're talking about," I hedge,

refusing to shrink under his narrowed stare. "I didn't see anything."

He looks away, and suddenly, I can breathe again with the weight of his gaze off of me.

"You didn't call the cops."

It's not a question but I answer it anyway. "No."

"Why not?"

I let out a dark laugh. "Because I like breathing."

A beat of silence and then, "You should leave town."

"Is that a threat?"

"It's not a suggestion." He takes a step forward and I steel my spine.

"I'm fine right here."

Koen's jaw tightens, the green of his eyes holding a warning. "The people who targeted you—"

"You killed them."

"I killed *lackeys*. This—" His jaw clenches. "What you've gotten yourself swept up in, it goes so much deeper than you know."

Oh, I know. Trust me. I know exactly what kind of shit I'm in.

"I'll take my chances."

He scoffs, taking yet another step and closing the gap between us, forcing me to tilt my chin so as to not break our shared gaze.

"What you saw the other night—"

"I didn't see anything," I say again, keeping my voice firm and even despite how my body shakes with fear.

He stares down at me for a long time, studying my face, my eyes...

"I might have saved you..."

Saved me?

"But let me be clear: I have no problem silencing you." His eyes flash, his threat clear.

"Understood," I breathe out.

We stare at each other for a long moment, both refusing to look away or even blink.

"How did you find me?" I finally gain the courage to ask.

He smiles, sending a shiver down my spine, reaching into his back pocket and pulling out my ID, holding it up before handing it to me. I take it with shaky fingers, staring at it, barely registering how he backs away, deeper into the room's shadows.

"Watch your back, Briar *Rose*," he says, before disappearing entirely through my window, pulling it shut again behind him.

23

STALK HER

KOEN

Now

What the fuck happened?

I'm standing in the alleyway that runs beside Briar's apartment building, concealed by shadows, watching her pace the length of her bedroom through the wide, dirty windows of her shitty-ass apartment.

She lives here. In this hellhole disguised as an apartment building.

I'd gained access to her room in two seconds with a simple switchblade. The door to the building itself doesn't even have a lock. Security is a joke. The drug addicts passed out on the first floor landing, the ones with needles half-stuck in their arms, even more so.

Last time I saw Briar, she had it all. Money, opportunity, dreams, and the ambition to bring them to reality. But something happened... Life had rolled her, tested her, drained the spark from her eyes.

Her edges are sharper, her voice colder, but that fire—that bold, beautiful fire that drew me to her in the first place, is still there. Hidden, buried even, but it still simmers inside her like an ember, flaring back to life when you've stoked it.

I'd seen it last night at the warehouse, in the way she refused to be a victim, and tonight after I'd held her by the throat and stared deep into her eyes. She didn't cower, cry, or plead for her pathetic little life.

No.

My little Rose has thorns and she's not afraid to use them.

What the fuck happened? How did she end up here? In this neighborhood, in the warehouse, in this life? And don't get me started on her fucking back.

It takes everything in me not to storm back up into that apartment and chastise her for not taking better care of the wounds. That piece of shit. He'd struck her *four* times. Guilt weighs heavily on me every time I think about it.

We'd been watching the warehouse, my brothers and I. It belongs to Matteo Carroza. Aidan had his reasons for wanting to fuck up his day, and I saw no reason to stand in the way. I was sure the Russians were the ones responsible for the sudden boom in the human trafficking business in the city the last few months. But, last night confirmed one of my worst fears: the Italians had jumped into the game too.

The night raised a lot of questions and I'm going to need some answers. I plan on continuing the Irish's long-standing *fuck you* to the human trafficking industry. And I don't give a fuck if it's Irish, Russian, Italian, or whoever the fuck's territory, it doesn't have a place in *my* city.

Briar lives *here*. They weren't just bringing girls *through* the city, they were picking them up right off the street *here*. The moment they did that, the second they touched *my* girl, they made it fucking personal.

I watched them drag her out of that van, and I recognized her immediately. Almost couldn't believe my eyes. Aidan had wanted to move in right then, but *I* stopped him. Attacking on the street, out in the open like that, wasn't good odds. I'd opted to wait. And that decision cost Briar. Those marks on her back... my fucking fault.

I walked away from her, all those years ago, to keep her safe from this world, and here she was, *drowning in it*. I thought I was protecting her by staying away, but did I really just abandon her to face it alone?

Now that I know, I can't make myself leave. I can't leave her unprotected. The men who targeted her before... they could be back, and the thought of them touching what's mine...

My hands tighten into fists.

Briar can't sleep. Even after spending hours drilling herself in that shitty little dance studio up the street, she's restless.

I suppose I didn't help matters... breaking into her bedroom and all, but she needs to know I mean business. And I do. Nothing is more important to me than family, and right now Briar is holding a match that could light mine up.

I still don't have any answers to my questions. How did she end up in the warehouse last night? The traffickers we're up against have been successful because they're smart, especially if they're taking girls from Boston. They can't be random, but rather targeted— ones no one will miss. The girls we pulled out of the warehouse last night, most of them fit that profile, broke with no family who would miss them. But Briar isn't someone no one would miss, I *would know*.

I eye the decrepit building she calls home. Her room is not what I'd expected. Mismatched furniture, mattress on the floor. That's a big fall from grace... What happened over the last five years? Did she get herself into a bind? Owe money to the wrong people? She doesn't look like she's on drugs, though that could be it.

God, she really did pick the worst fucking place to live. Her apartment sits on disputed territory between the Irish and the Russians. It's one of my uncle's neighborhoods. I'll have to remember to speak to him about ensuring we restake our claim on it.

Just because we took out one warehouse, doesn't mean anything. This won't end until we cut off the head of the snake. And we still have no idea who's calling the shots. If the Italians have jumped into the game, I know for certain Cole DeLuca has nothing to do with it. Like us, the Italian Capo doesn't fuck around with selling bodies.

The people running this are smart, and *connected*. We're talking police, government officials, and *money*. This whole operation screams money.

The city's restless. My father drew a hard line on selling bodies, and he made sure *everyone* knew it. But ever since his death, it's been a free-for-all. Seems like one hell of a fucking motive if you ask me.

Kostalov, the Russian Pakhan, has been making a lot of moves, running a lot of shipments, but he keeps it tight. We had a guy on the inside, but he'd been made, unfortunately before he could get close enough to find out anything of use.

It's almost dawn. Briar hasn't moved for almost half an

hour, finally laying down on the bed and I'm hoping... falling asleep.

I have to go. I've got shit to do. Picking up the phone and ringing Mac, I tell myself how we need to make sure she doesn't go to the police or the news. The last thing we need is an exposé on two Boston Breakers players wanted on suspicion of murder.

"Rí?" Mac answers with a yawn.

"I need you to run surveillance on someone today."

A groan sounds out over the phone. "That's a fucking shite job and you know it. Can't you get one of the recruits to do it?"

"No." My reply is hard and firm, and Mac stops his grumbling on the other end. "I need *you* to do it." While my brothers would be my first choice, I know none of them are free this morning.

"Fuck, Koen. Fine. What time?"

"Now." I hang up the phone as a string of far more colorful curses erupt out of my best friend, texting him the address and the picture of Briar's license I took before I gave it back to her. I stare at her picture, those blue eyes piercing through me, dredging up everything I've tried to bury.

24

EXPLICIT DETAIL

BRIAR

THEN...

"My turn," Rí says.

The dark excitement in his eyes gives me pause, and I'm suddenly regretting the game, underestimating the power I've given him.

He stares down at me. The heat from his kiss still stings my lips, I'm breathless, my heart fluttering. The first time he leaned down to kiss me, I panicked, turning away before instantly regretting it.

I wanted him to kiss me again...

"Truth or dare, little Rose?" Rí's Irish accent curls around each word and something deep inside of me twists at the sound.

"Truth," I say, the corner of my mouth ticking up when his eyes darken. The dark shadows at the edges of his irises overtake the green.

Two can play at that game, sir.

"Okay, Rose," he says, stepping closer, and I swallow hard as he begins to circle me. "*Truth*, ay?"

I nod, and it feels shaky.

"Alright." He's still circling me. "Tell me exactly what you want me to do to you."

I gulp, my eyes widening and watching the smile curve up his face. "I—I don't..."

"Say it." He stops behind me and I hear his voice in my ear, the edge of dominance unmistakable. "Don't hold back. I want to know *exactly* what you want."

You dug this grave, Rose. This was your idea.

"The truth, Rose, and don't you dare lie. I promise you, I can tell."

I believe him. The way this man stares at me, I think if so much as my pinky finger twitched, he would catch it.

"I want you." I swallow, refusing to look at him. Rough fingers curl around my chin, dragging my gaze up to his.

"You want me to *what*?" His voice is soft, his eyes staring intently into mine, not a trace of teasing in them. "Explicit detail, Rose," he reminds me.

"I want you... to make me come," I say, closing my eyes in horrified disbelief when I realize I've actually said the words out loud.

He's silent and I feel my cheeks burn red with embarrassment.

"It's my turn," he says, and I release a breath before I pass out from holding it in. "I pick *dare*," he says, without letting me ask the question. "Let's make it a dare."

He can't be serious.

Rí leans in, kissing me again... the scent of him... the feel of his hands, all of it invading my senses, making it impossible to think, impossible to resist.

Without warning, he picks me up. My legs wrap around him in fear, clinging tight in case he drops me. But his grip on me is firm, his lips trailing down my neck as he brings me back over to his bike, swinging his leg over it and settling me down on his lap.

He wastes no time, his fingers trailing up the length of my inner thigh. I shudder. He pushes past my panties, and the corner of his mouth ticks up at the wetness he finds there.

I expect him to shove his fingers inside, pump them in and out, but he doesn't. Instead, he just takes his thumb, pressing down lightly, slow circles edging along my sensitive clit. I inhale sharply, biting down hard on my lip to hold in a moan of pleasure when he increases his pace.

He smiles, well aware of what he's doing.

"Dare me to make you come *how*, little Rose?"

"Wh—What do you mean?" I ask, confused, tilting my head to the side.

"What's the challenge?" he asks. When I just stare at him, not sure what to say, he holds up his fingers, and ticks them off, one-by-one.

"Do you want me to make you come using only my fingers?" And then the second. "Or only my mouth?" I swallow and he smirks. His third finger falls as he says, "Or am I to make you come without touching you?"

Without even touching me? My brain struggles to wrap my head around that one when I notice he's stopped talking— taking note of my obvious confusion.

"Make. You. Come..." His accent rolls over my words,

enunciating each syllable as he repeats them, *really* hearing them this time.

I squirm uncomfortably hearing it back—at how embarrassing I must sound.

His head tilts to the side and I feel him assessing me. My cheeks must be a bright shade of crimson by now.

"Little Rose, has no one ever made you come?" His words are soft in a way I hadn't thought him capable, his fingers finding my chin and forcing my gaze back to his.

Way to let him know you're terrible at sex, Briar.

"It's my fault, I think I'm just broken or something..."

His fingers snap my head up so fast I swear I get whiplash.

"You're not broken," he growls under his breath and he looks... angry.

"I am," I insist, softly, searching his eyes as they stare down at me, trying to read them.

"Lay back."

My eyes widen. "*What?* Why?" Alarm fills my tone.

"It's still my turn, and I chose dare. Now do as you're fucking told and lay back."

His eyes are on mine, and his stare is... *intense.* It feels as though he can see right through me and into my soul.

I look around. For a very public space, we are quite alone. When my eyes find Rf's again, there's a near feral gleam in his eyes, though he waits patiently for my decision.

Swallowing hard, I lean back slowly; his hands stay on my hips, holding me steady as I arch my back over the bike's fuel tank, hating what his nod of approval does to my core.

"Hands on the handlebars," he orders and I comply, closing my fists tight around the rubber grips to keep from sliding off. I also tighten the grip my legs have around Rf's middle, crossing and locking my ankles together, and he smirks knowingly.

The position is... precarious and with my legs spread and open to him, I feel exposed—vulnerable.

Rí has both feet planted on the ground, keeping the bike upright and steady.

He runs both hands up my thighs, looking me over as if he's trying to memorize every inch.

"Truth or dare, little Rose?" he asks, his fingers reaching the hemline of my skirt, sliding it higher than it already sits.

My grip tightens on the handlebars, and I bite my lip to keep in the whimper that threatens to escape me at his touch. He's gently tracing my skin, teasing, traveling higher, but it's sending jolts of electricity from each point of contact, and they ricochet through me like bolts of lightning.

"Dare," I reply, because I know that's what he wants me to say and admittedly, I'm curious as to what it will be. I'm rewarded with another devastatingly beautiful smile.

"I dare you not to scream when you come on my fingers in the next five minutes."

I can't help but gape at him. *Five minutes?* My entire adult life, and he thinks he can change that in five fucking minutes?

Rí's fingers finally skim the edge of my underwear and I tremble. He takes the fabric between his two large hands and, without warning, violently tears through it and... *oh, fuck.*

Yep, there is definitely something broken in me because why did that make my stomach flip in ways I want to feel again?

The breeze picks up and the brush of cool air reminds me that I'm bare, stretched out, legs spread wide and wrapped around him. With no way to close them.

I expect him to touch me, but instead he leans forward and something *hard* presses into my most sensitive area. My breath hitches as he leans over me, his hand closing around mine, tightening the grip I hadn't realized I'd let go slack.

With his hand still covering mine, he twists, revving the bike under us and oh, lord—

My nerves are already alight, and the vibrations set off by the engine tease an already insatiable ache, stirring up a heat, a *need* I can't ignore.

Rí chuckles darkly, all too aware of what he's done. He keeps one hand on mine and the throttle, while reaching down with the other, running his fingers down my slit. I blush when we both realize how wet I already am for him.

His fingers pull away and my hips chase after them, starving for more of his touch, watching him bring his fingers to his mouth.

Tasting them.

Tasting *me*.

Smirking, he brings them back down, drawing small, lazy circles around the most sensitive part of me, all while throttling the bike, the vibration stoking the spark he's lit, fanning the heat—the flames as they slowly build into something all-consuming.

He increases his pace slowly and increases the pressure, all while staring deeply into my eyes, not looking at what his hands are doing, but rather looking right at me.

I bite my lip, holding in a whimper, and watch his eyes drop.

His thumb keeps up the relentless circles, while he slips a finger inside of me.

I can't hold in my whimper this time—it's followed closely by a moan when he moves his finger back and forth.

Slowly pumping, vibrating with the pulsing of the engine beneath me.

I tighten my grip on the handlebars, my body filling with tension. His persistent circles, the teasing, the look in his eyes... all of it pushing me further to the edge.

I arch my back as the deep ache inside of me becomes intolerable, tensing, gritting my teeth as I tamp down my scream.

Rí increases the pressure one last time and I can't—it's too much, my body shakes, and I cling on to the handles with white knuckles. It feels like I'm climbing higher and higher, and *oh, fuck,* when I crest that ledge... A scream bursts out in ragged, strangled gasps as I fight to hold it in, rough and raw, as I come all over his fingers. But Rí doesn't stop, and I whimper as he drags it out. "Please, please," I beg him because it's too much—I can't *breathe*—I can't *think*; I'm completely at his mercy.

"You do look pretty when you come." He smiles. "Truth or dare, little Rose?"

"I think it's your turn..." I mumble, breathless.

25

MYSTERY GIRL
KOEN

Now

Something's burning.

The overwhelming scent of charred... *something* hits me just as soon as the elevator doors open up into the loft.

"You're clearly doing it wrong."

"Reagan, I swear to god, if you say one more word—"

"What the fuck is going on?" I ask, stepping into the kitchen to what can only be described as utter chaos.

Liam's at the range, the pan he's holding is billowing out black smoke from under the lid he's holding pressed down tight. Meanwhile, Alex is in the middle of dumping yet another pan, this one still on fire, into the sink, scrambling for the sprayer to put out the flames. And in the middle of it all is Reagan, my menace of a little sister, sitting on the countertop, arms folded, watching the two of them with a frown on her face.

I scan the rest of the kitchen, finding Aidan brooding at the table, ignoring the chaos and staring out the window at the courtyard garden.

Reagan notices me first. "Well, well, well... look what the cat dragged in." Her eyes sparkle and the look I give her holds a warning.

Liam and Alex's heads both pop up. There's so much smoke, I'm surprised the smoke detector hasn't—

The alarm wails. Liam shoves his still smoking pan into the oven, shutting the door and looking irritatingly pleased with himself. I run a tired hand over my face and stalk over to the coffee maker.

It's empty.

Of course it's empty.

"Your job," Reagan chirps from her perch on the counter. "You missed breakfast. We thought you were dead."

"No we didn't," Alex chimes in, finally winning the battle over what I think was supposed to be pancakes. "You can't make jokes like that in a mafia household," he scolds, shooting Reagan a look.

Reagan just grins, swinging her feet.

I'm too tired for this.

I set about making coffee, my head pounding from lack of sleep.

Liam manages to turn the alarm off, and then the questions begin.

"So where were you?" My sister hops down off the counter, grabbing a mug and swapping the coffee pot out for it just as it starts to brew.

"I was out." My glare is sharp enough to cut throats, but she ignores me.

"Out with a *girl*?" She smirks over her shoulder. "*Mystery girl perhaps?*"

Not *with* a girl.

"No."

Reagan takes the mug, now full of fresh coffee, and I have to shove the pot back into place to prevent the rest of the brewing coffee from spilling all over the counter.

"Jesus Christ, you guys wouldn't last two seconds on your own."

"I'll have you know, I would do just fine." Reagan's playful tone sharpens slightly as she pours damn near the entire sugar bowl into her cup.

Liam and Alex abandon their smoldering pans and join Aidan at the table. I pull a clean skillet out of the cabinet, and head to the refrigerator for some eggs.

"Speaking of being on our own..." Reagan starts, leaning a little too casually on the island behind me.

"No."

"You don't even know what I'm going to say!" she whines with a pout.

I pinch the bridge of my nose, my headache worsening by the minute. "I already know what you're going to ask—and the answer is no. And I'm not in the mood to argue about it."

"I just want to go out with Effie tomorrow night."

"Well, in that case—no. But make it a double." Anything involving our cousin is bad news.

"You're being an ass." I can feel Reagan's glare through the back of my head while I take a whisk to the eggs. She tries again. "I just want to go out for one night!"

"You know we're on the brink of war with both the Italians and the Russians right now. Someone killed our father, on the street, in broad daylight." She winces. And after what the Russians did to Alex a couple of weeks ago? I'm willing to bet it's still open season on O'Rourkes, seeing as Liam was just shot at last week."

Her eyes widen as she looks quickly to her brother, and I almost feel bad.

"How am I supposed to know? You never tell me anything! You expect me to sit here all day with nothing to do. I had to drop out of college because it wasn't safe—"

"Only temporarily," I growl in my defense. "Once we get the Russians who killed Dad—"

"It'll just be another threat, and another and another, until I die from inactivity and boredom!"

"You're being dramatic." I turn to face her, eyeing my brothers, who are noticeably quiet as we have this argument yet again.

"I'm not a child anymore, Koen. I'm twenty-one. It's *my* life. At some point, I have to be the one responsible for it, not you."

"You have no idea what's out there—"

"And whose fault is that?" She sets her cup down, crossing her arms, and glares at me. "I want to go out with Effie tomorrow night."

"No." I don't even have to think about it. The city is volatile right now, not to mention the traffickers snatching girls off the street left and right. And not all the Irish clans in the city have bent the knee. My reign as the Irish King is still new, and since we don't know who we can trust, I only feel safe with one of my brothers keeping an eye on Reagan, and this week, I really can't spare one of them to babysit her.

Reagan lets out a little scream of frustration, turning on

her heel and stomping out of the kitchen. A few seconds later, I hear a door slam further down the hall.

"Ah yes, the picture of maturity," I mumble under my breath.

I feel my brothers' gaze burning on me in the silence.

"Something to say?"

"She's got a point..." Surprisingly, it was Aidan who spoke.

"I know she's got a fucking point. I *know*." I slam the pan of eggs down on the metal grate, my exhaustion splintering the usual tight control I have on my emotions. "But we've got a traitor in the Irish, traffickers in the city, and the fucking Russians and Italians breathing down our necks. It's not the right time." I bite out each syllable.

Aidan's jaw clenches, but he finally nods in agreement.

I sigh. "Where are we at with the warehouse?'

It's Liam who speaks up this time. "We're at a standstill. We know the Italian Consigliere's involved, since it was his warehouse that we found the girls in, but we know their Capo's stance on the trade."

It's true. Cole DeLuca, though the same age as me, has been Capo since he was eighteen years old and has always stood firmly against selling bodies.

"So, is Cole stepping into the dark side, or is Matteo stepping out on Cole?" Alex asks.

My eyes slide to Aidan, watching his face closely. "Matteo's set to marry Adrik Kostalov's daughter this weekend. Forging a blood alliance between the Italians and the Bratva." The latter have made a lot of money selling skin. "Unlikely coincidence."

Aidan's jaw ticks but he says nothing.

"Did you get anything useful out of the girls we found in

the warehouse?" I dump the pan of eggs on the table and crash into one of the chairs while they dig in.

It's Alex who speaks this time. "Not really, aside from that they were all grabbed within 24 to 48 hours of being taken to the warehouse. All local." *So they are after American product.* "We checked the rest of Matteo's warehouses but found nothing. His warehouse wasn't set up for holding girls. They had to be moving them somewhere else."

"Briar's local," I muse, not realizing I've said the words aloud until I notice all three of my brothers staring at me, their silence pointed.

"*Briar*, was it?" Liam's brow rises as he bites down on a forkful of eggs.

I ignore him. "Any intel on why they targeted the girls they took?"

"Likely hand-picked." Alex confirms one of my fears. "Young, pretty, and poor; girls unlikely to be reported missing. Most of them are either brand new to the city or traveling from out of town."

I run back over what I know about Briar, which isn't much. She's a dancer—ballet specifically. I'd thought she came from money, but then I remember her tiny apartment in that shitty-ass neighborhood. I might have been wrong about that, but she definitely has family and ties to the city.

"And the guard?" I ask. While we were sorting out the warehouse, another one of the Italians showed up for his shift. My guys have been working him over to wring out what information they can.

"Low level," Liam tells me. "Knew little, but confirmed the girls were inventory for an upcoming auction."

That piques my interest and I lean forward. "When?"

Alex shakes his head. "Sometime soon, but of course he's not high enough up to know specifics."

"This ring goes deep. The cops found all the trafficking evidence we left behind in the warehouse, along with our anonymous tip, and buried it." Liam frowns.

"What do our cops have to say?"

"Nobody knows anything."

I scoff, not believing that for a second. "Lean on them."

Liam smiles. "I can do that."

"And we need in on that auction." So far we've raided a few warehouses and clubs that have been trafficking girls, but it doesn't seem to matter. For every one we take out, two more pop up in its place. The only way to handle this is to rip it out by its roots, find the head of the snake and kill it.

WATCHED

BRIAR

Now

I can't sleep.

Restless energy vibrates just under the surface and, as tired as I am, as much as my eyes burn with exhaustion, I just can't seem to fall asleep.

I don't know how to deal—how to process this.

The walls of my bedroom should feel safe but they don't. Nothing feels safe anymore.

How did I get myself into such a mess? Giovanni is one thing, but Koen?

Koen *found* me. He fucking found me. *Fuck.*

He thinks I might tell someone about what I saw in that warehouse the other night. What if he's watching me? If he is, it's only a matter of time before he finds out about Remi. Will he suspect she's his?

Koen O'Rourke isn't known for his mercy. I might not

have known who he was when we met, but I sure as hell know who he is now. Everyone knows who he is, especially in my neighborhood. You don't cross him and you don't look him in the eye. Not if you want to live.

In the hours and days since I found him waiting for me in my room, I've been on high alert. Barely sleeping, nervously pacing, utterly fixated on the tiny, little, unshakeable feeling in the back of my brain that I'm being watched.

It could be Giovanni's men, it could be Koen's, or it very well could be nothing. Maybe I'm just imagining it. Paranoia setting in.

But what if it *is* Koen out there? He was worried I'd talk, tell the cops or go to the media, or whoever would listen, about his brother bashing some piece of shit's face in with a baseball bat.

I've only told Lily. *Oh god, does that put her in danger?* Even if I didn't know about Daniel, a cop who's clearly involved in whatever operation was going down in the dark... The cops couldn't be trusted and, even if they could, I wouldn't have said anything, because honestly... Aidan O'Rourke did me a favor.

Was it gruesome?

Yes.

Am I traumatized for life?

Probably.

But I'd gotten away. I'm alive. If the Irish Devils hadn't shown up... I don't even want to think about where I might be right now.

Throwing off the blankets, the cold leeches into my bare feet as I pad over to the window. It's large, dirty, and old. Our apartment building is the last one on this block that hasn't been condemned, but judging by the state of it, it's only a matter of time.

I hadn't bothered with curtains. The building next door has sat abandoned for over a decade. I haven't needed them—couldn't afford them, if I'm being honest. *Why the fuck do curtains cost so much money anyway?*

I lean up against my window frame, staring down into the dark alley under my window. It's empty, except for the dark corner of shadow I can't quite see into. My eyes narrow as the light bends and I swear I catch a glimpse of movement—

"You need me to drop Remi at daycare again tomorrow?"

I jump a mile at the sound of Lily's voice, finding her leaning in the doorway out to the hall.

"You okay?" There's concern in her eyes and alarm at my reaction.

A chill races up my spine, and I look back over my shoulder into the shadow of the alley below again, finding nothing, and rubbing my arm to comfort myself.

Stop it. You're fine. Maybe you have PTSD or something.

"What is it?" Lily comes closer, joining me at the window.

"Nothing," I pause, scanning the alley below us again. "I just—I don't know. I can't shake this feeling like I'm being watched." I force myself away from the window, collapsing on my bed and wrapping my arms protectively around myself, trying to calm the anxiety that feels like a live wire in my chest.

Lily looks between me and the window as if unsure what to do. Comfort me—or wage war on the empty brick alleyway outside.

"Briar, are you sure you don't want to call the police?"

"No police." I shoot up, and the look on my face is enough

to make my best friend throw her hands up in immediate defeat.

"Okay, okay, no police. But this—" She looks over and finds me jittery, anxious and fidgeting on the bed. "This isn't healthy."

"I'm fine," I lie.

"You're not." Lily's tone sharpens and she takes a seat next to me on my bed.

She's right. I feel trapped and I don't know how to find my way out.

"Is it Gio or Koen?" she asks, her voice softening.

"Koen." My answer is automatic, which is crazy, because Giovanni quite literally tried to sell me off in a fucking human trafficking ring, but at least I know what to expect. *With Koen, I have no idea.*

"Have you—have you thought about telling him?"

"About Remi?"

She nods, watching my face carefully.

I shake my head, staring down at my fingers twisting in my lap. "I can't."

"Do you think he's still watching you?"

My face goes toward the window. *Yes.* At least it feels like he is. "I don't know." My words sound haunted.

Lily and Remi are leaving in a couple of days. I rescheduled her parent teacher conference for now and if I can avoid being seen in public with Remi until they leave, that might be enough time for Koen to feel satisfied that I'm going to keep my mouth shut and move on. He didn't care before. The only reason he cares now is because of what I might say. Leaving me alive is a liability. Honestly, I'm surprised he left me breathing after our encounter in my bedroom the other night.

"Koen's dangerous," I whisper, like even speaking his name out loud could summon the devil himself. "You didn't see what I saw him do at that warehouse. He killed those men without batting an eye, precision shots to the middle of the forehead with barely a thought! He threatened me... If he ever found out about her..."

I shiver. "I can't risk it," I say, shaking my head. "Remi's *my* daughter, and it's my job to keep her safe." *Even if the threat is her own father.*

Lily nods, accepting my answer. She knows Koen's reputation just as well as I do. "How's your back?"

My shoulder twitches involuntarily. "It's okay," I lie again. "It doesn't hurt so bad anymore."

"*Doesn't hurt as bad* and *doesn't hurt* are not the same thing," she chides, reaching for the hem of my t-shirt and yanking it up so she can take a look. "You've torn them open again," she sighs, dropping the shirt back into place.

I just shrug in response.

"You should be resting more."

"I know." My eyes drop back down to my fingers, picking at the hangnail I have along my pinky. "But I have to dance, with the showcase coming up..." I trail off because that's a lie. The showcase is everything, but that's not why I've been in the studio every night. "If I stop *moving*, I start *thinking*, and when I start thinking..."

Lily wraps an arm around me, pulling me into her, sniffing out a laugh when my body tenses up. "Let me love you, dammit!"

I can't help but let out a tight laugh. "I'm sorry. I can't help it."

She releases me and I stare into her hazel eyes. "I'm sorry,

Lily, I feel like I've been leaning on you too much with the day care runs and the babysitting. Are you sure you want to take Remi with you to New York?" I love my daughter but she's a lot of work. Work that doesn't seem fair for Lily to have to take on.

"Don't you dare apologize for that. You would do the same for me and we both know it. And for the hundredth time—" she sighs audibly rolling her eyes, "—yes. Honestly, I think my parents and my brothers are more excited to see Remi than they are me." She crosses her arms in mock annoyance, drawing a smile to my face. "We're in this together. I meant it back then and I mean it now. You're stuck with me, girl. For the long haul."

"I don't deserve you," I tell her, tears threatening the corner of my eyes.

"Maybe not," she teases. "But you're stuck with me anyway."

We both laugh and, for a moment, the stress, anxiety, and weight of everything is lifted.

"Now, you owe me a movie night if I remember correctly. And I'm cashing in!"

I groan, watching her bounce toward the door, knowing she's about to go gather enough snacks to make us sick.

"My pick!" she calls back over her shoulder.

I rise to follow her, throwing back a tense gaze over my shoulder at the darkest parts of the alley before following Lily out, closing my door behind me.

27

THIS FUCKING GIRL

KOEN

Now

Briar dances every night. After midnight, while the rest of the world sleeps, she's up—working through whatever's haunting her. At least, that's what I think she's doing in the old dance studio around the corner from her apartment.

I know because I've been watching her.

Every night so far this week.

Just a quick check-in, a drive-by that sometimes lasts for hours. I need to be sure Briar isn't going to go to the cops about what went down in that warehouse. And her refusal to leave the city means she could still be a target. Despite digging, I haven't uncovered any fresh leads on who might be running the trafficking organization within the city. At least, that's what I tell myself— and Mac and Jace, who I've appointed to watch her when I can't.

For the past few days, I've spent my nights on the rusty old fire escape across the alleyway from her window. Every spare second I have, I spend it watching Briar. Which often means showing up long after she should be asleep but, like me, she's a night owl. And more often than not, I find her awake, either practicing in the studio, in her living room, or staring up at her bedroom ceiling, tossing and turning. Somehow surviving on the couple hours of sleep she banks each night.

She hasn't gone to the cops, hasn't gone much of anywhere according to Mac and Jace. Briar is either in her shithole of an apartment or at the dance studio down the street, often late at night. That is until about mid-week, when she started going to the Delacroix Conservatory downtown for most of the day.

I flip through the surveillance photos Jace sent me earlier. Briar must be a student there, attending classes. Teaching them too, by the looks of these photos. I stare at the one of her surrounded by mini ballerinas in fluffy pink tutus. They look to be about four or five at most, gazing up at her adoringly as she demonstrates the proper way in which to hold their arms.

It's cute, but that's not why I can't stop staring at it. *She's smiling.*

With a quick look around the nearly empty street, I slip into the alleyway unnoticed. Keeping to the shadows as I maneuver over to my favorite spot. Taking up a seat on the steps of the abandoned building next door, I lean up against the brick.

I'm right on time.

Lights flicker on from the second floor dance studio and, through the floor-to-ceiling windows of the old factory building, I make out Briar.

The light spills over into the alley, and instinctively I shift back further into the shadows, but she's not looking outside.

She never does.

Unlike the past couple of nights, there's a spring in her step. An obvious thrum of excitement in her body. I study her, realizing she's got something in her hands. And by the looks of the pink ribbons, they're ballet slippers.

Briar makes quick work of lacing them up and once she's up, I realize they're not just ballet slippers, they're pointe shoes.

The nights usually start out intense. Her rigid, structured —sometimes angry—routines break down as the night wears on into haunted and heartbreaking movements. Stories she tells with her body.

Briar's dancing is haunting.

And once she starts, there's no taking your eyes off of her.

She's mesmerizing, and she's talented. Ever since the first night I stayed and watched her, I couldn't help but come back night after night. Craving just one more hit.

She's beautiful. She's dangerous. She's *mine*.

She just doesn't know it yet.

Barefoot Briar doesn't hold a candle to Briar en pointe. She dances with an elegance even *I* know can't be taught, a refinement and artistry one can only be born with.

I don't know anything about ballet, but I know I can't look away.

Especially once I see the smile stretched across her beautiful face. The way it changes her, lighting her up from within. I've never seen her happier. Usually it's rage or sadness she's channeling but tonight, nothing but pure joy emanates from the tiny dancer.

Many nights, she runs her routines over and over again, each time perfect... mesmerizing. But she never seems satisfied; no matter how perfectly she executes it, it never quite seems to be good enough for her.

She pushes herself too hard.

Again.

My fists clench at my sides when she turns and I see the bright red blood soaking through the back of her pale pink leotard.

This fucking girl.

The wounds that Italian piece of shit left on her back were deep, but they should be further along in the healing process by now. If only Briar would properly care for the wound and actually *rest*. That word doesn't appear to be in her vocabulary.

Unable to help myself, I broke into her apartment again this morning. After confirming with Jace that both Briar and her roommate Lily, another dancer, were at the Conservatory, I scaled the fire escape outside of her apartment again. Leaving behind a prescription-strength antibiotic cream, fresh bandages, and tape on top of her dresser.

The blood is evidence she hasn't used the bandages and I curse under my breath.

It's going to get infected.

Briar calls it a night somewhere around two a.m., but I linger. Watching, making sure she makes it back to her apartment. Leaning back against the wall until she finally collapses into bed. Resisting the urge to go up there, pin her down and bandage her up myself.

I keep an eye out. Not moving until dawn breaks over the horizon, the sunlight never touches the little alley.

It's been a few days now and she hasn't gone to the cops, but I can't seem to stop watching her. I tell myself it's because Briar is likely still a target. Anyone who makes a move on her would have information... information we need.

So I keep watching.

28

HE'S A DEAD MAN

KOEN

Now

Stalking Briar last night was a mistake.

It took everything in me to walk away the first time, but now that I know where she lives, where she dances, *her name...*

She'll be the ruin of me, I know it. Like a drug burning in my veins, she's the poison I crave. One hit and I'm already looking for the next one.

But she's innocent, a little taste of heaven I can't allow myself to have. I still don't know what happened, how she ended up in that neighborhood or in that warehouse that night, but the facts remain: we're from two different worlds and I won't drag her down into mine.

I stalk through the dark mansion, stepping over piles of broken glass and furniture, a strong smell of gasoline in the air. I nod briefly at our guys tearing the place apart before descending down into the hidden basement.

We've been sitting in a powder keg for months now, the entire city at a stand-still just waiting for the inevitable spark that will set it off.

I'm tired of waiting, and my—and my brothers'— reasons are as good as any.

Let's light a motherfucking match.

Reaching the basement, I shut the door behind me. The sounds of breaking glass and shouting from upstairs fades away, replaced with the sound of someone screaming. It's music to my ears. I lean back against the wall, folding my arms across my chest to watch in appreciation as Aidan circles the man hanging by his wrists from a hook in the ceiling. I watch stone-faced as Aidan holds a red-hot fire poker to the underside of the man's balls. The screams emanating from him are raw, until they break down further into sobs and pathetic pleas.

My brother notices me for the first time, pulling back the poker to look my way. The man sags in his chains at the brief reprieve, coughing before spitting blood to the floor.

The bastard's barely recognizable after the pummeling he took from Aidan when we first picked him up hours ago. There's a pretty good chance Aidan would've beat him to death right then and there if I hadn't pulled him off. Aidan's focus may be on hockey right now, but he's still head enforcer for a reason. When it comes to violence, he can be merciless, brutal if he wants to be, and tonight, *he wants to be.*

"Don't kill him yet," is all I say to my brother, who nods before sucker punching the guy, knocking his face so hard to the right he could've snapped his neck. The man lets out a groan and slumps over, half conscious; there's blood every-where. Aidan's been *busy* while I checked on things upstairs.

My phone rings and I answer, as Aidan pulls out the knife he keeps in his jeans.

"Yeah?" I answer, recognizing the incoming number as Garrett's.

"All the money leads back to the Volkov."

"I can't—" I press the phone closer to my ear, unable to hear Garrett over the guy screaming when Aidan suddenly slices off a finger. "Hold on." I step out of the room, walking further down the hall until I can hear the intel Garrett's dug up. Seeing as how the warehouse we'd found the girls in was Matteo Carroza's, Garrett and Alex have been doing a deep dive into Matteo's financials to try and find us some leads into who's pulling the strings. It would seem gaining access to the Italian Consigliere's study has opened more than a few doors.

"You're sure about the Volkov's involvement?" I ask Garrett.

The Russian Wolves, aka the Volkov, have been at the top of my list but I need to be sure. Oleg Volkov and his five sons are a force to be reckoned with. They practically own Russia and had been busy in their attempts to take over New York. Apparently, Boston has started looking pretty attractive as well.

"It's them," Garrett says, his tone certain. "Carroza's been getting deposits from the Volkov for months now. We were able to trace it through a network of off-shore Volkov shell corporations created to clean the cash. He's moving girls, weapons, and product for them.

"Volkov's men were the ones who went after Kostalov a couple of weeks back. It makes sense they would be the ones running the pipeline from Eastern Europe." The Volkov are well known to grease the hands of officials and politicians if it benefits their agenda. "If Matteo was getting paid directly from the Volkov, there's a good chance DeLuca doesn't know."

My jaw tightens. I can't stand the Italian Capo, but disloyalty pisses me the fuck off. Betrayal... is a choice. Betrayal... can not be forgiven. It's a knife in the back of someone you've sworn to protect. Disloyalty is like a cancer, a rot that will fester and spread if ignored. It has to be cut out clean, no matter how deep you have to dig or how many times you have to cut.

Garrett and Alex have dug up some names of the Volkov involved and more locations to check out in the city.

The screaming down the hall intensifies and I have to hold my hand up to my ear to hear the rest. I frown. The network is bigger than I'd thought.

"When did the payments to Carroza start?" I ask, remembering that he said it was a few months ago.

"Uhm—let me check." I hear typing and few clicks and then, "Six months ago." My jaw tightens.

"Okay, get the rest of what you need and then wipe it."

I don't hear Garrett's response because it's then I realize just how *quiet* the basement has become. Slowly, I walk back down the hall.

"What the fuck?" I hiss, rounding the corner and staring at Carroza's lifeless body. He's dead, there's no doubt about it. "I stepped away for like three minutes!"

Aidan's standing off to the side, a knife still in his hand. He's drenched in the man's blood, staring down at his handiwork, a wild and shadowed look in his eyes.

"I told you not to kill him." I hang up the phone and take in the scene before me. There's blood everywhere. So much so that there's a pool of it at Aidan's feet, too much for the drain in the concrete floor to keep up with.

"You'll get over it." Aidan's voice is low, and there's a dark edge to it that keeps me from pushing him. Letting out a breath, he pockets the knife, dropping off the blowtorch I hadn't seen in his other hand on the metal table of instruments by the door before trying to shoulder past me.

"Did you at least get a name?" I ask before he's fully out of the room.

"Giovanni Moretti," he replies without stopping and I let him slip by me, disappearing down the hall. Leaving his mess for someone else to clean up.

So the Italians and the Russians are working together on this. Suddenly, the arranged marriage between Carroza and the Russian Pakhan's daughter makes a lot more sense.

Staring down at the dead body of the Italian Consigliere, it gives me pleasure to have disrupted their best laid plans, though killing the Italian's second-in-command won't be without its consequences.

And neither is the fact that Aidan not only *killed* Matteo, but he's stolen his *bride* too.

Aurora Kostalova, the Russian Angel, is currently holed up in our family's loft. Aidan's officially laid claim to her.

"Fucking Russians," I curse under my breath, thinking over the shitstorm we've found ourselves in and what we'll need to do to survive it. I slide my phone out of my pocket to make some calls and set a few plans in motion.

One of those plans includes setting up a meeting with *Giovanni Moretti.*

We need to find out how far this goes. A ring this big has help. Carroza's warehouse, the one I'd found Briar in last week, was on the south side. *In Irish territory.*

That was bold. Even for the Italians.

Our father's murder, the arranged marriage between the Russians and the Italians, the trafficking ring, and the sudden appearance of the Volkov... Somehow, it's all connected. I don't believe in coincidences, not in my line of work, and all of them seemed to be gunning for the Irish.

But the question was why?

Our father had prepared us well; even with the Irish patriarch Declan O'Rourke gone, the Irish remained strong. In fact, his death had drawn both of my brothers, Aidan and Liam, back into the fold, which arguably made us even stronger. Picking a fight with us now was a suicide mission. The Irish are out for blood.

But yet... It had been weeks now of shipments going missing, drops getting raided...

They'd messed up when they took something of *mine*.

Briar might not belong to me, but I laid claim to her almost five years ago and I've yet to take it back. Whoever targeted her is still out there, and she won't be safe until we burn the whole thing to the ground.

I strike the match and let it fly.

Watching the old Italian mansion go up in flames, its consigliere with it.

One down... however many more to go...

29

COME FOR ME

KOEN

Now

Needing to take the edge off after our little bonfire, I stop by Briar's on my way home.

Careful to park my bike down the street, I keep both my hoodie and my neck gaiter pulled up over my nose *just in case* before walking the rest of the way to her building.

The seasons have just about crossed over into winter so no one looks twice as I stalk down the street, my motorcycle gear giving me a pass for my covered face. Not that anybody would say anything about it in *this* neighborhood. Hell, I could drag Briar into the alleyway in broad daylight and have my way with her and I doubt anyone would blink a goddamn eye.

The teenage drug dealers hanging out on the corner scatter when they see me coming. Likely recognizing my bike. Good instincts, if poor decision making skills.

It's been nearly a week since I pulled Briar out of that warehouse.

I've watched her nearly every night. Only mafia business has kept me away from her, but as soon as it wraps up, I'm here. In the shadowed alcove at the end of this forgotten alley, or on the fire escape of the abandoned building next door—watching.

No one's come for her.

I also can't find a reason why she was targeted. I know from my guys that she spends most of her day at the Delacroix Conservatory uptown. Other than that she stays home, hangs out with her roommate, and she dances.

It's becoming more and more obvious now that she doesn't need my protection, but I can't make myself stop.

She practices at that abandoned studio nearly every night. Sometimes after spending all day in the studio uptown. Setting out just after ten p.m., every night like clock-work.

I click my tongue.

She should vary what times she leaves, what days she goes. It's too easy for someone to learn her schedule and it pisses me off how she's putting herself at risk.

I follow her, making sure she gets to and from the studio safely.

I want to follow her up the rickety wooden stairs and watch her dance from inside, but I tell myself that's getting too close. Because if I were to see her—*really* see her—or catch an inhale of her sweet scent, I might never leave. *I might never let her go.*

The building next to Briar's is abandoned, and after the first few nights tucked deep into the shadows of the alleyway, I've begun climbing the old fire escape, giving me a better view into her room. I climb two floors higher, allowing me to see right into her bedroom. There's less cover up here, but if she looks out her window, she's more likely to look down than up.

I settle in, taking a seat and allowing my legs to hang off the edge as I lean over the iron bars, taking a long, deep, pull from my cigarette.

It's not long until she appears, tossing her dance bag on the floor before disappearing back out into the hall for her evening shower. Reappearing a short while later, she's in an oversized sweater that just brushes the tops of her thighs, and thick socks that come up to her knees.

Oh.

Briar turns out the light and climbs into bed. Her room is illuminated in the red glow from the old neon sign above me, a few of the letters still working. She has no curtains. With the building abandoned next door, I'm sure she thinks she doesn't need them. Doesn't think about who might be watching.

But I do. I think about it every night.

She lies very still. Too still. Staring up at the ceiling.

What are you thinking about? Do you ever think about that night? Did it ruin you like it ruined me?

The darkness in me wants to corrupt her, mark her as mine and drag her with me straight to hell, and I grip the bars tight to keep myself from storming across the street and claiming her.

I'm here to make sure she keeps her mouth shut. That's it. Making sure that no one else tries to take what they have no right to—that no one tries to touch what's mine—is an added benefit.

But she's not yours and she never will be.

She was too good for me then, and she's too good for me

now. I had to let her go—shove her away so she wouldn't follow after me like I wanted to follow her. I left her after that night. Left the goddamn country to stop myself from trying to find her. *She deserves better than me.*

My hands are stained with blood, my soul hollowed out after submitting to the darkest parts of me to do what's necessary to survive. She's everything I'm not. A bright light to my endless darkness, soft and delicate to my serrated edges.

But she's not all soft.

There's a darkness to her too. I saw it years ago, and so did she. The shadows in her were drawn to the shadows in me, like a moth to a flame. She's not as innocent as she seems. She fought back at the warehouse, and I saw the way she looked at Lorenzo on his knees, her blue eyes flashing with violent thoughts, a dark wish for retribution even through her fear, and that makes me wonder what happened to her.

Briar tosses and turns. She hasn't been sleeping well.

A pang of guilt flickers through me. I hope it's not because of me.

I wasn't thinking too clearly after I'd found her. I broke into her room. I *scared* her. *I needed to.* It was a necessary evil. I wasn't going to hurt her. But I had to make sure she wasn't about to go off to the police with what she knew. The need to protect my brother stronger than my moral compass. Fucking Aidan and his goddamn mask. I ought to superglue the thing to his fucking head next time we run a raid.

Briar throws off the covers and I watch her check the locks on her windows one more time.

Ah, shit.

The overwhelming urge to let her know that I'm watching, to let her know she's safe, overtakes me but I reel it back in.

That might not be how she'll see it. I tighten my fist on the iron railing I'm leaning over to keep me from stomping over there and yelling at her to fix the locks on her goddamn windows.

Then maybe I wouldn't have to sit out here, watching.

Briar turns back to the bed. Stopping to stare at it, her head tilts to the side in thought.

After about a minute, she climbs back into bed but she doesn't lie down. No, instead she stays on her knees, the oversized sweater she has on slipping down and revealing the soft golden skin of her shoulder. Her back is to me but it's the smallest movement that catches my attention.

Fuck.

My heart skips a beat. I should look away, I should—

Briar's head falls back as she picks up the pace, building herself up, and it's too late. I can't look away. I stand frozen, captivated by the late night performance, her fingers teasing, stroking—her mouth falling open, and the way she bites her lip immediately to withhold the sound.

I can almost hear the little whimpers.

Before I know it, I'm imagining my fingers shoved into that perfect little mouth, having her suck on them while I bury my cock in her.

Her hand moves faster and she falls forward, her back arching as she gets herself close, giving me a better view.

It's the same position I had her in that night and *fuck—* that does it for me.

Unzipping my jeans, I grab hold of myself, stroking hard, fast, matching her rhythm. Remembering how it felt with her dark hair wrapped around my fist, and oh, how I long to pull it back, forcing her to deepen the arch of her back.

My cock throbs and I squeeze tighter.

Her hips lift and her movement grows more desperate as she spreads herself wider.

Christ, I nearly come at that.

There's a growing tension in her hips. I see the way she's winding herself tighter and tighter until she starts to tremble, in desperate need for release.

"Come on baby, come for me," I mumble under my breath, fisting myself hard, needing to come myself, but holding off— *waiting for her.*

She stiffens, burying her face in her pillow to silence the cry as she falls apart, shaking from the intensity of it. I imagine the way her clit pulsates, the way her muscles contract, heating with her arousal and tightening around her fingers.

I spill into my hand with a low groan, not taking my eyes off of her as her body collapses into the sheets. Still at last.

Completely spent, breathtakingly beautiful, and blissfully unaware of the dark shadow watching from outside.

30

TWO WEEKS

BRIAR

Now

"But I want you to come, too!" Remi whines, stomping her foot, as she refuses to leave the apartment. And here I was thinking we were past the tantrum stage...

Keep it together, Briar. "I know, baby, I wish I was coming, too, but Mommy has to work. And you're going to have way more fun hanging out with Lily and Uncle Jim and Aunt Patty than having to go to pre-school everyday right?" She and I aren't technically related, but seeing as I practically lived at her house growing up, Lily, her brothers, and her parents are the only family Remi's ever known.

"I guess..." Remi's got her pout working overtime and the sight of that quivering lip almost sends me racing back to my room to pack my suitcase.

"Two weeks will go by quicker than you know it."

"You promise?" She blinks up at me with tears in her eyes

and I feel my heart break inside of me. If I didn't think Giovanni would follow my ass to New York, putting not only Remi and Lily but her entire family at risk, I would absolutely do it. Gio hasn't shown back up at my apartment since the morning after *everything,* and neither have his guys, but he's been blowing up my phone with not-so-subtle reminders.

"I promise."

I trap Remi's head in my hands while landing a kiss on her forehead long enough that she starts squirming away, distracting herself. "Mom! Stop!"

Reluctantly, I release her. "Go find your shoes, and don't forget your bag of snacks for the ride!"

While Remi searches for her shoes, my gaze meets Lily's.

"Are you sure you can't come?"

"Not you too," I groan.

A hint of a smile appears on her face but it's still heavy with worry. "I feel like I shouldn't leave you alone. It's not too late to see if one of the girls—or even one of the guys—from the Conservatory can stay with you, or vice versa?" She shakes her phone in her hand, but with Giovanni haunting me, and Koen's reappearance, I don't want to put anyone else at risk. This is my mess and I need to be the one to clean it up.

I shake my head and Lily lets out a disappointed sigh. "Text me if you change your mind. I'll have Dash or Sam come pick you up."

"I will." *I won't.*

She narrows her eyes but thankfully doesn't call me on it.

"No sign of you-know-who?" she asks, lowering her voice, though Remi is fully distracted, poring through the snack bag I put together earlier in the kitchen.

"No." I haven't seen or heard from Koen since that night

he broke into my bedroom, and I've been on high alert. I'm willing to bet he's watching me but I haven't been able to prove it. Aside from a black SUV I've started noticing parked outside of the Conservatory during classes, nothing else seems out of the ordinary.

But I always have that little feeling—especially at night. A little prickle of awareness, a feeling deep in my gut when I'm at the studio, that I'm not alone, but when I turn around to check, no one's ever there.

"Probably for the best." Lily nods and I start grabbing bags, helping her load up the little Toyota Corolla that Mia let her borrow.

Even without any verified Koen sightings, I've been careful to avoid being out in public with Remi just in case he decides to drop in, ensuring I remember to keep my mouth shut.

Seeing him again has stirred up doubts over whether or not keeping our daughter a secret from him was the right choice. And while I still feel immense guilt and a nagging feeling that I've done something wrong, the events at the warehouse should only reinforce that I made the right decision.

Nothing could've prepared me for seeing Koen in that warehouse. The way he moved—practiced, methodical—fire fights and murder... it was just another night to him.

His life is dangerous. *He* is dangerous. And I need to do everything I can to keep Remi as far away from him as possible.

Which is why I absolutely have to get that audition from the showcase.

Once I pay off Giovanni, I'd have access to health insurance for Remi, and we could move out of the city.

It's all within my grasp, and there is no way I'm going to blow it. Everything is riding on these next two weeks.

"Do you want me to say hi to your parents if I see them?"

Lily's tone is teasing but I have to resist the urge to throat punch her for even bringing them up.

"No. And don't you dare let them anywhere near our girl."

Lily salutes me. "I shall use my body as a human shield should it come down to it."

"Not funny," I say, remembering how Gio threatened her.

Not that they were ever really parents to me. They were always out of town, and as I got older I spent more weekends, more holidays, with Lily's family than I did my own.

I take my time buckling Remi into her car seat, fighting back tears. "Call me every day, Remi-Roo. And be good for Auntie Lily or else," I warn her, doing my best not to crack a smile when she rolls her eyes.

"I will, you already told me that."

"I know," I sigh, forcing myself out of the car. "I love you, baby. I'll see you in two weeks."

I hold up two fingers and she mirrors me. "Two."

Lily slides the car into gear, and I reluctantly shut the door. Watching my best friend drive away with my whole world. The sudden emptiness that fills me the second they disappear around the block is enough to send me running, crying, to my bed, but alas, I have to be at work.

It's my first night back at Wonderland.

31

ARE YOU DAFT?

KOEN

Now

The next afternoon, I'm in my office at our main warehouse, discussing with Liam our mess of a situation with the Italians and Russians, when my uncle Conor barges in.

"Tell me you didn't kill the Italian's consigliere and set his mansion on fire?"

I look up at my uncle with a straight face. "Okay." There's a flash of relief on my uncle's face as I speak. "I won't tell you," I finish, and that relief turns to rage, Conor known for his hot temper.

"Christ above, Koen!" he curses. "I suppose I don't need to ask if the rumor that your brother married the Russian Pakhan's daughter in an unauthorized ceremony is true then, too?"

I just shrug, reaching for my glass of whiskey. "Father Lucent officiated."

He hisses and I hide my smile with my glass.

"You think this won't start a war?" He's pacing the room now, hands running anxiously over his balding head.

"The war already started," I tell him. All we did was make it official.

He lets loose a string of curses and I narrow my gaze at him, not that he notices, too caught up in his own fury.

"Pissing off both the Italians and the Russians in one night? What were you thinking?"

"Technically it was a weekend," Liam adds, and I watch our uncle struggle to keep his composure. He's not wrong; we killed Matteo on Friday night, and Aidan and Rory got married earlier today.

Conor Reilly is our mother's older brother. Their family had strong ties back to Ireland and he's been in the game now for decades. Best known for his ability to fly into a fury at the drop of a hat. Since my father died, he and my uncle Seamus— on our father's side—have been acting as pseudo advisors to me.

"And what about your sister? Did you think on how this would affect her?" He frowns down his nose at the two of us.

"Aye, of course I did. Which is why she's with Alex on her way to one of the safe houses right now." I'd sent Reagan, as well as Aidan and his new wife Rory, out of the city for a few days to help the heat die down and give me a chance to sort out this mess so everyone doesn't end up dead. It dawns on me that I haven't checked in on either of them today and I reach for my phone. Reagan was pissed when I shoved her in a car and sent her away. By the looks of the unanswered thread of texts, she's still not talking to me. I pull up Alex's contact.

"Do you really think you can trust him?"

"Trust whom?" I don't look up from the screen, typing out a quick message.

"Alexei."

This has my attention and I glance up, leaning back in my chair, and take my uncle in fully.

"*Alex*, you mean?" I ask, for clarification. There's a warning in my tone, asking if he really wants to go down this path with me.

"Are you really asking us that?" Liam fumes from beside me, and I feel the tension in the room pull tight. As my mother's brother, he knows as well as anyone that Alexei Ryan was the child of his sister's best friend. When his mother died, he came to live with us, and our parents raised him as their own.

And *Alex*, even though he's lived with the Bratva the past couple of years after reconnecting with his father, is just as much my blood, as Aidan and Liam are. And he's just as much a brother to Reagan, too. There's no doubt in my mind that he would protect her with his life if it came down to it.

Sensing my darkening mood, my uncle holds his hands up innocently. "I know, I know, you grew up with him, I know! But we've had a lot of *problems* lately—" My jaw tightens as I realize where he's going with this. "—a lot of shipments gone missing or destroyed..."

"It's not Alex."

"As the newcomer, I think we have to consider the possibility—"

"It's *NOT* Alex." I slam my fist down on the desk, shaking everything on it, before rising to my full height to stare down at my uncle. "And he's not a fucking newcomer," I bite out.

He relents, letting out an exhausted sigh. "Fine. Fine. But if it's *not* Alexei, then who? Someone's running their mouth to the Russians. I can't prove it yet, but I know it's them intercepting our cargo."

I run my hand down my face. "I don't know." And while Alex has my full loyalty, Conor isn't wrong. There's still a traitor amongst the Irish.

A knock sounds at the door, pulling our attention.

"Am I interrupting something?" Uncle Seamus asks, poking his head in.

No," Uncle Conor says, waving him in. "Come on in. You ought to hear this too."

My two uncles couldn't be more at odds. Conor is huge. Our height came from our mother's side clearly, as he's a bulky six-foot-five. He's got wild and unruly red-gold hair and a thick beard that makes him look like he may as well live off in the Irish cliffs. Seamus, on the other hand, looks like our father. His graying hair is always slicked back, his suit neat, and he prefers strong-armed negotiations to backdoor alley threats.

Seamus looks between us for a moment, reading the room before entering, and closes the door behind him before helping himself to a glass of whiskey at the cart.

Conor continues, "Like I was saying, cash is low, the territory war in the city is only growing worse, and the men are restless. I don't think I need to remind you that if you don't get this shit under control, the clans won't stand for it."

"I'm working on it," I seethe. Turning to pace the space behind my desk, I spy Seamus, out of the corner of my eye, slip a fresh glass of whiskey onto the desktop.

"You have a lot of enemies right now, you might want to consider making a few *friends*," Seamus says smoothly, taking a sip from his own glass, watching me with a knowing look in his eyes.

"You already know my opinion on that," I spit out, not even considering it.

"Aye, I knew your opinion on it when your father was alive and kicking, but—" he lets out a humorless laugh, "—things have changed."

I glare at him sharply.

Still he presses on. "Alliances are important, but now that your father is dead, it's even more crucial that you produce an heir."

I can't help but scoff, making eye contact with Liam, who sits by silently taking measure of the exchange. "An heir? I've been head of the O'Rourke family for six months and already I'm expected to *produce an heir?*"

"Many say that as the heir, you should have already married in preparation for this."

I let loose a low growl, reaching for the glass on the desk.

"There's been talk among the other clan leaders that you're not ready."

"Bollocks!" Conor bellows loudly from where he's still pacing by the door.

I stop my own pacing, turning slowly to face Seamus, and he holds up his hands in defense, as if declaring innocence.

"Hey, hey don't shoot the messenger. All I'm saying is, getting married and having a baby will show them you're serious and want to settle down into this new role. *And* it's the perfect opportunity to strengthen ties. The Quinn girl, for example, would be an excellent choice, and a union that would strengthen the Boston Devil's ties back to Ireland."

"Ah, leave the boy alone, Seamus," Conor chides, looking appraisingly at me. "Aside from this recent business with the Italians, he's been doing a fine job, ain't you "boy?"

I sigh, irritation running through me at being called 'boy.' And I run a hand down my face at the emergence of a familiar argument. It's not the first time Keira Quinn and I have been pushed together, and while I have no intention of marrying her, I'll never hear the end of it if I don't at least pretend to think it over.

"I'll consider it. But for the moment, I think we have more pressing concerns."

My eyes travel to Seamus. "The Montreal shipment's gone," I say flatly. "Two containers. Vanished. Someone's lining their pockets with our cargo."

Concern etches at the corner of Seamus' eyes and he leans forward in his seat. "First I'm hearing of it."

"Was Alex on that run?" Conor's mouth twitches up before he hides it with his glass.

Both Liam and I glare at him. "No, he wasn't. Like I said, I have him guarding Reagan while we sort out all this business with the Russians and Italians."

Conor mutters a few choice curses under his breath, pacing the back of the room like a caged lion.

"But did Alex *know* about the run?" Seamus asks, his tone careful.

"Everyone in my inner circle knew—and the guys we had on both the run and the warehouse," I admit, and Conor slams his glass down on the table before flexing his fists. Not known for his subtlety.

"You need to send a message. Line up every last one of them and take 'em all out," Conor seethes. "You want loyalty? You remind 'em what happens when they cross you."

If I did that, I would have even more to answer for from the clan chiefs.

Seamus looks at Conor as if he's gone mad. "Are you daft? Are you *trying* to get the boy killed?"

Conor blows out a breath, continuing to pace the office like a barely contained storm.

"Someone's gotta pay. That's all there is to it." Seamus turns to face me. "If you let this slide, the men will talk, and the Callahans and Murphys will see you as weak and all hell will break loose."

Liam rises after quickly checking his watch. "We gotta go," he says to Conor, striding for the door. "Shipment's coming in."

Conor grumbles, following him out, but not before adding his two cents, "Think about what I said, Koen. You're playing with fire here." He leaves shaking his head.

I blow out a breath, draining the rest of my whiskey, silence falling over the office until my eyes find Seamus, still sitting in the leather chair across from me.

"Conor Reilly ain't known for his thinking. You know that, don't you? Could be costly if you trust him blindly." Seamus shrugs, sipping from his glass.

I grunt in response, too much on my brain to read too much into it.

"But Reilly's right about one thing, we need to find the man—or men—responsible for sabotaging our runs. Which clan was in charge of the Montreal run?"

My jaw tenses. "The Reillys," I admit.

There's a subtle sharpness in Seamus' eyes when they meet mine. "Perhaps put the *Reillys* on another run next week, something not terribly valuable, just to see. You know your father had Conor on the shite work ever since your mother left, and ever since he's been gone, Conor's been in here every other day, making a fuss about this or that, vying for more responsibility, more control."

My eyes narrow at the implications. "What are you saying?"

"I'm a man of detail, Koen." As if to emphasize his point, he rises out of the armchair, adjusting his impeccably tailored suit, picking a thread of invisible lint off his sleeve. "I pay attention. And I know you do too. You get that from the O'Rourkes. You have to watch who you let close. Even *friends* can make *mistakes*... or worse."

32

RECKLESS REIGN
KOEN

Now

"We've got a problem."

My grip tightens on the phone as I hear Mac's words on the other end of the line.

"What now?" My irritation comes through in my tone. I swear, ever since my father died it's been one fucking thing after another.

"Shipment never made it to the docks."

I start pacing the room. "What do you mean *it never made it?*"

"The truck disappeared somewhere between Quincy and Southie. We haven't heard from Donny. No sign of him—and no sign of the cargo. Liam is doing his best to track him down."

Fuck.

My phone's been ringing off the hook all day.

Cole DeLuca and Adrik Kostalov are pissed, and neither of them are fucking around, both out for blood. The Irish aren't too thrilled about my brother's new little Russian bride either but they'll get over it.

"You think it was the Russians?"

"Russians or Italians. Who do you think hates us more at the moment?"

I sigh. "Keep your ears on the ground and double-up guard rotations on every warehouse from here to Revere. Trusted men only. No new guys."

"Understood." Mac's reply is tight and I can tell he's got something else to say.

"Out with it."

"Do you want me to cancel the meeting tonight?"

My jaw tightens. With the intel we tortured out of Carroza, I was able to confirm that Giovanni Moretti is our *in* to the human trafficking trade currently exploding in the Boston Underworld.

"No. We have to keep up appearances. The Bratva and the Italians might be out for blood, but we can't look like we're scared. Business still moves forward. We can't afford to look weak. Got it?"

"Loud and clear, Rí," Mac confirms, and I hang up the phone, sinking into the couch and leaning my head against the back. Just killing guys on the ground won't do anything to throw a wrench into this operation. I want this shit out of my fucking city, so I need to figure out who's involved. This is no rinky-dink organization. Not with Kostalov and the Volkov involved. When we intercepted the Volkov attack on the Kostalov mansion a couple of weeks ago, it was clear the Volkov are funding the Kostalov Bratva. But to what end?

How far up the chain does this thing go? Police, city officials... maybe even state politicians?

My brothers and I decided the best course of action was to go in as an interested buyer. Seeing as how I'm the reigning mob boss for the Irish, it wouldn't be out of the ordinary for me to take an interest in the trade. And that means a meeting with Moretti is the first step.

We raided their warehouse of girls, but *they* don't know that.

Time to lean on Moretti and see what exactly I can squeeze out of the Italian rat.

The elevator dings and instinctively I reach for the gun at my waist. It's a little too early for Liam to be home yet and I sent Aidan and his new wife, Rory, out of the city until the heat dies down, as well as Reagan with Alex for protection. Neither Aidan nor I will ever forgive ourselves if anything happens to our little sister because of this mess. But with all of them gone, no one else should have access to the loft.

Lifting my gun, I train it on the elevator doors, only to pull it up hard when none other than Reagan herself comes storming through it. She stops dead at the sight of the gun, surprise quickly turning into a glare.

"What the fuck?" I growl, flicking the safety back on and shoving the gun away.

"Really, Koen?" She puts a hand on her hip like *I'm* the one being unreasonable.

"What the hell are you doing here? Where the fuck is Alex?"

Not a second later, Alex trails out of the elevator after Reagan.

Perfect. He looks guilty as all hell.

"I tried to call—"

I remember seeing all the missed calls from him on my phone.

"What the hell am *I* doing here?" Reagan snaps, stalking closer, her heels clicking sharply against the hardwood. "I live here, do I not?"

"Yes," I growl out, stepping closer, but she doesn't back down. She *never* backs down. "But *you're* supposed to be in a safe house in Vermont."

I point my finger at her and she lifts her chin, arms crossed while looking me in the eye. "I don't think that's your call to make."

"Not my—" I start but she keeps going, cutting me off.

"I'm not one of your little soldiers you can boss around, or a pawn to move around on your chessboard. It's my life and it's my decision."

My eyes slide to Alex, hovering uselessly by the elevator doors, looking like he'd rather be in a Bratva torture cell than stuck between two siblings at war.

"I'm sorry Rí, she was relentless. When I stopped for gas she started walking back to Boston... refused to get back in the car unless I agreed to take her home. I tried to call—"

Honestly, it's no surprise she managed to berate him into turning around. He has a soft spot for her. I pull out my phone, scanning through the calls to see a few I missed from Alex. With all the chaos happening after Aidan's impromptu wedding, I haven't been able to get back to everyone yet. I let out a sigh, running my fingers through my hair.

"I'm not a child," Reagan hisses, and I peer down at her. "You can't keep shipping me off like a piece of luggage every time you piss off someone in the city."

"It's to keep you safe." And I mean that, I know what men like the Bratva and the Italians or the Cartel would do to her if they ever got their hands on her. I couldn't live with myself if I let it happen.

"I'm tired of safe. *Safe* is killing me. I have to be able to *live*, Koen." Tears well up in her eyes before she wills them away, clenching her jaw—as well as her fists—as she stares me down, throwing her energy into her anger to keep from breaking down. "I'm here all day, in this apartment. I have to *ask* permission to go out. I have to have an escort. Two of your guys, if not one of my brothers." She rolls her eyes. "You've built me a prison."

"Better a prison than a grave," I mutter, but my words lack conviction because I know she's right. Growing up as the youngest daughter in a mafia family hasn't exactly been easy. Her life already wasn't her own before, but since our father died and I ordered a lockdown, it's not a question that she's gotten the shortest end of the stick.

"You're not wrong. I'm not disagreeing with you but the Bratva—"

"It's never a good time! There's always going to be someone, somewhere, who wants to hurt me. I can't just sit around waiting for it to happen. I won't." Her chin lifts and the glint in her eyes grows sharper—unyielding. I recognize it, I've seen it before; it's a silent promise that no threat in the world would move her.

I look away, toward the sky while I try and figure out what the fuck to do with my rebellious little sister.

"Fine. No Vermont. But you don't leave this apartment."

She rolls her eyes and I take a step toward her, my eyes

narrowed. "I mean it, Reagan. I'm not fucking around this time."

She glares at me for a long while. "Fine," she spits out with a small snarl, turning on her heel and storming down the hall. A moment later I hear her door slam shut.

For not wanting to be treated like a child, she sure knows how to throw one hell of a tantrum.

I sigh, looking over to Alex.

"I'm sorry, Rí." He hangs his head, looking away from me.

"It's fine." I wave it off. "I know how she can be."

My phone buzzes and I read over the incoming text about another potential distribution issue.

The elevator dings again and we both look up to see Liam strolling into the loft, hockey bag over his shoulder. He stops when he spots Alex, looking between us in confusion, knowing just as well as I do that he is supposed to be in Vermont. "What's going on?"

"Don't ask," I mutter.

He drops the bag, coming around the couch to join us. "Reagan threw a fit, didn't she?"

I glare at him.

"Called it," he says, amusement in his tone.

Ignoring him, I turn my attention back to Alex. "Since you're back, I need all hands on deck tonight. Get cleaned up. We have a meeting with Giovanni Moretti at Wonderland down by the docks at midnight. Call Mac and have him put a couple guys on the door downstairs." My gaze travels over to Liam. "You're coming, too."

Liam makes a face. "Are you sure that's the best idea, considering we're already on the Italians' shit list?"

My jaw ticks, having already fielded this question from Mac. "No. But I want to fuck with the Italians some more," I shrug.

Liam shakes his head. "This is a terrible idea." And then a dark grin spreads across his face. "I'm in!"

33

DOWN THE RABBIT HOLE

BRIAR

Now

Walking back into Wonderland feels wrong.

For about the millionth time, I wonder if I would be better off running. But I don't have the money or resources and I have nowhere to go, no one who will hide me. They'd find me. Probably pretty quickly.

The bouncer on the back door nods at me in polite greeting as I walk past, the music a dull rumble until he opens the doors and the sound comes tumbling out. Alongside a burst of cigar smoke that sets my anxiety on edge, the back hallway feels more claustrophobic than it already did.

I teeter on the threshold. I can feel the bouncer's eye on me, but he doesn't say anything. Straightening my shoulders, I let out a deep breath, lift my chin, and step inside. Resisting the urge to scream out when the door shuts behind me.

You're okay. Giovanni will keep his word. Make money. Pay him back. And get the fuck out of this place.

Do I trust Giovanni? *Fuck no.* But really what choice do I have?

In my mind I go back to my call with Remi earlier. I'd read her a story over the phone before wishing her good night. *I'm doing this for her.*

I stiffen at the sight of Gio walking around the corner, dressed in his usual suit and tie. His eyes land on me and he smiles warmly like we're old friends. "Bella! Welcome back. I was beginning to think you weren't going to show." A dark smirk pulls at the corner of his lips and I tremble slightly, getting the feeling that showing up was far better than what they had planned for me if I didn't. He checks the clipboard in his hand. "You're on bar tonight. And the main stage later."

I release a strangled breath. *Okay my normal schedule—that, I can do.*

I nod, squeezing by him on my way to the dressing room.

"Move it, Bella. You're already late."

I clench my jaw, tightening my grip on my bag, quickening my pace and practically diving through the curtain of the dressing room up the hall. I pull up short when I find two girls inside, taking stock of who is in the room. I relax slightly at the sight of Sierra and Jade, both arriving, like me, for the ten p.m. shift. They're annoying, but hardly a threat.

"Bella!" Sierra whines when she spots me in her mirror trying to sneak over to an empty makeup table. "We missed you! Where've you been?"

"I thought you quit," Jade laughs, eyeing me through her mirror while applying a bright pink shade of lipstick to match the neon lingerie she's wearing—If you can even call it lingerie, it's more like... strategically placed string.

"I—Giovanni gave me a week off," I blurt out.

Both Sierra and Jade turn in their seats to stare at me. "Who did you have to blow to make that happen?"

My eyes widen in shock but Sierra just pouts, looking at Jade. "I wish Gio would give me a week off. You're so lucky, Bells." They both turn back to their respective mirrors and I let out a slow exhale.

"Yeah, lucky. *That's me.*"

As quickly as I can, I slip out of my ripped jeans and t-shirt and into a sheer, black lace corset. It's revealing, while also covering everything I need it to. A garter belt fastens over my waist, holding my black fishnet stockings in place. I disconnect from myself a little bit more with each snap of the clasp.

It's just another routine, a performance just like all the rest, practiced and perfected to draw the *right* kind of attention from the audience.

Sheer ruffles of lace flare off my hips, delicate and teasing, softening the dark look I picked for tonight.

Leaning into the mirror, I darken my makeup. The bold, dark liner and burgundy lips feel a lot like slipping on a mask. Typically I wear little to no makeup, a little eyeliner, a sweep of mascara—anything else would be washed off in sweat by my second class. But inside these walls, inside Wonderland, I'm not *Briar.* I'm who I need to be to survive. I'm playing a role—a character— I'm Bella.

And *Bella* is all sinful curves, coy smiles, and is just elusive enough to keep the men out there drooling and opening up their wallets.

My rigorous ballet training has honed my body to my

control and now I've weaponized it; choreographed every mannerism so as to better manipulate men. Every movement has purpose; every toss of my hair, every swing of my hip, and every curl of my lips meant to charm, tease, flirt...

And as long as I keep hold of that—that control—I can make it through this. I can do this.

Disassociation is my new best friend.

Temporary. It's only temporary.

I try to push away the thought that it's not just tonight. It's *every* night, until Gio finally decides to let me go. If he wanted to, he could have me thrown in the back of a van again and brought to another warehouse that I'm sure he has waiting.

Finished, I stare at myself in the mirror, barely recognizing the girl staring back.

Good. I don't want to know her.

Celeste barges through the curtains, giving me an assessing look and subsequent nod of approval. "Sierra, you were supposed to be on stage five minutes ago. Move your ass." She glowers at Sierra a moment longer before her eyes fall back on me. "Bella, you're on bar."

I give her a quick nod to let her know I've heard her and she disappears back through the dark curtains.

Looking back into the mirror, I push away an errant strand of dark hair from my face with trembling fingers as I rise, retreating into myself as I head out to the floor.

34

WE'RE ALL MAD HERE

KOEN

Now

"We should wait for Aidan," Liam says, a look of unease in his eyes as we arrive outside of Wonderland, the strip club Giovanni uses like it's his personal conference room.

"Aidan's not coming," I say. "He's staying at the Lake House with Rory. You, me and Alex can handle Giovanni Moretti. Aidan needs some time to sort shit out with his new wife."

"I'm sure they're getting in plenty of cardio," Liam muses, shooting a wink at Alex who rolls his eyes.

We step into the club and immediately are approached by a blonde with huge tits. They're spilling out of the tight black dress she's squeezed them into. "Mr. O'Rourke," she says, her smile eager. "Mr. Moretti is expecting you. Please come this way."

It's a Friday night and the place is busy. As we get closer to

VIP, I notice they have some high roller football players in. It's causing quite the stir among the dancers in the club as they try and hustle their way into the lap of one of the professional athletes.

The blonde leads us to a private table, off to the right of the center stage, in the VIP section.

Another blonde is curled around the pole in front of us, her body contorted in ways that defy gravity, but my attention is on the Italian in a sleek navy suit headed our way with a huge smile on his face.

"Koen! Good to see you." Giovanni offers his hand and I take it. "Welcome to Wonderland." He winks at me but I just scowl at him. I'm not known for my warm personality.

"Giovanni."

"Come, come." He smiles, motioning for us to sit.

We take a seat. Liam and I on one of the couches opposite the one Giovanni sinks into. Alex slides into one of the arm chairs.

"How's business?" he asks, eyes dancing with excitement at what he thinks is the possibility of drawing the Irish into his web.

"Good," I say, keeping a cool expression on my face.

"Do you own this?" Liam asks, glancing around at the club.

"Wonderland?" He smiles. "No. But I do conduct a lot of business here."

"I didn't realize we were meeting in a brothel," I say, watching girls lead men through a door near the back. Disappearing into a hallway lined with private rooms.

Giovanni laughs, a gold chain glinting from inside of his open shirt. "It's a gentlemen's establishment, my friend. Best girls in Boston! Let me know if any strike your fancy." He winks and I look away.

"I have to admit, I was surprised to hear from you." Giovanni takes a sip of his drink. "Heard you O'Rourkes got yourself into some hot water recently with both the Russians and the Italians."

I fix my gaze on him, giving nothing away as he begins to squirm under my dark intensity, realizing he's tiptoed into dangerous waters.

"You owe me girls," I say, leaning forward in my chair and watching him shift. He can't hide his discomfort.

"Listen, I didn't know you were one of the vendors." *I wasn't, but he doesn't know that.* "We hit a little snag, and the delivery is going to be—delayed."

"What do you mean *delayed*?" Liam growls, looking surprisingly convincing, and Giovanni looks anxiously between the two of us. "There was a—a complication, with the latest shipment," he rushes out, watching our faces for our reactions.

I shoot a dark look Liam's way when the corner of his mouth ticks up at Giovanni's admission, though it's an effort to keep a straight face myself.

"We're a little low on inventory at the moment—"

"That sounds like a *you* problem." I take a sip of my drink. Giovanni pales.

Liam zeroes in. "So, the auction is... off?"

His eyes widen as he takes in the three of us. "Who told you about that?" he hisses, narrowing his eyes.

I ignore the question, leaning forward to rest my elbows on my knees. "We want in."

Gio swirls the ice in his empty glass nervously. "It's not that simple, buyers for such an event need to be vetted. There's a process."

"So vet me."

Giovanni mumbles some more about "process" but I don't hear him; movement on the stage across the room catches my attention, forcing me upright.

Look away.

I don't.

Since the moment she walked out on that stage seconds ago, she's had my full attention. *Why?* I'm still trying to figure that out.

I don't normally care for strippers but the way this one moves... She doesn't move like the others. I notice each careful step, how she stretches up on her toes before she turns, the subtlest little flick of her wrist. I've spent hours watching Briar dance. Over and over and over... the same routines, the same moves, practicing, perfecting, obsessing...

The girl on stage arches her back up against the mirrored pole and I lean forward in my chair, sliding my glass onto the table and resting my elbows on my knees.

It's her. It's Briar. I haven't seen her face but I don't have to. I *know* it's her.

Rage boils, warring with shock and something darker, sharper twists deep inside me at the realization. *Why is she here?* Briar doesn't work here, she's not a stripper, but yet she sure looks like she knows what she's doing up there.

She turns and I finally catch a glimpse of her face. It's her, but it's *not.* Gone is the girl I've been watching all week. The quiet focus, intense discipline, and overwhelming innocence— gone. This isn't that girl. The black lingerie clinging to her body is a sharp contrast to the oversized sweats and dance clothes she's been living in for the past two weeks. Her dark brown hair, usually pulled back and half falling out of either a messy bun or braid, is down, cascading in loose, polished curls down her back. Under the club lighting it looks nearly black, highlighting the equally dark winged liner accentuating her eyes.

Her eyes.

They're unfocused. She smiles, bats her pretty little eyelashes at the men at her feet, but it's almost as if she's looking through them. Her mind is elsewhere, disconnected from the body crawling along the floor, pandering for men's attention. They call out to her, requests, beckoning her closer, wanting to *touch* her, waving dollars at her. But it's as if she can't hear them.

Her body, usually loose and free when she's dancing, is tense; the delicate curve of her shoulders are stiff, and her fingers grip the pole in front of her just a little too tightly.

She's on edge. My fists clench and my jaw tightens. I sit perfectly still, and I know I should look away but I can't. Afraid that if I do, she'll disappear and I'll lose her again.

Fury burns hot under my skin but I force myself to stay in my seat.

"Gorgeous, right?" I hear Giovanni say, taking notice of my attention.

I don't say anything, don't look at him, keeping my eyes locked on her.

"She for sale?" I hear Alex say, and I break my gaze on Briar for the first time to shoot him a dark look. He just cocks his head at me.

Giovanni, to my surprise, looks uncomfortable. His mouth

tightens when he looks up at Briar, not answering Alex's question.

Instead, he turns his attention back on me. "You like her, yeah?"

Look away.

"That's Bella."

No. That's Briar.

I force my eyes away from the stage again and reach down to pick up my drink.

The music finally stops and my little dancer disappears backstage, and it takes everything in me not to follow her.

Giovanni leans over to tell one of his men something. The man nods and disappears.

Moments later a couple girls are brought over, though none of them are Briar.

A girl with short, bright purple hair that has to be a wig slithers up to me, attempting to take a seat on my knee.

"No," I growl, lightly shoving her away.

She's not too broken up about it because a half a second later she's crawling into Liam's lap alongside the blonde he's already got curled around him, whispering something into his ear with a smile on her face.

I want to find Briar. I want to find out why the fuck she's here but I sense Giovanni's eyes on me. I've already piqued his interest when I stared at Briar for too long.

He calls her Bella. *How many fucking names does this girl have?*

"So about those girls you owe me." I fixate my narrowed attention back on to Giovanni.

The waitress appears, slipping a fresh glass of sambuca con la mosca into Giovanni's hands but I don't look up, enjoying watching Giovanni squirm under my hardened gaze a little too much.

"What can I get for you?"

I see her at the exact moment she sees me, and she straightens up with surprise, nearly dropping the glass in her hand.

Briar.

"Your best Irish whiskey," Liam chirps, oblivious though he looks my way, tilting his head questioningly.

Briar doesn't move, doesn't write down the order. No, she just stares at me. A fawn's response, deer in headlights, which slowly morphs into panic and fear as her eyes dart between Gio and me.

"Ah, Bella." Giovanni's Italian accent draws out her name, and I almost reach for my gun when his hand wraps around Briar's wrist, tugging her down and into his lap.

I grip the arm rest on my seat in order to stay in it.

He smiles at her, but her body language is tense, and she leans away from him, attempting to slide back off his lap, but he tugs her back and she stops trying to get away. That faraway look reentering her eye.

My grip on my glass tightens.

"This girl can move." Gio grins and I want to punch him. "Are you going to dance for us later, Bella?" he asks, gesturing toward the small elevated stage that's actually the table between us.

Briar's eyes dart between Gio's and mine before she answers, her voice tight. "I'm on drinks right now, but maybe later."

"We can get someone else on that." He snaps his fingers,

and just like that another girl appears, taking in our waitress on Gio's lap with mild disinterest. "We need a new waitress, this one is busy." She nods, taking out a pad to take our orders. "And send a few more girls over, will ya?" He grins at the three of us but my expression never changes, my eyes never leave Briar's. All while she's doing everything she can to avoid looking at me.

A moment later, more girls appear and Giovanni perks up when he spies a busty brunette among them. "Cherise! I didn't know you were working tonight." He practically shoves Briar at Alex, who has to catch her to prevent her from falling to the floor. "That one looks like he could use a little pick-me-up. Show him a good time, Bella," he instructs before directing his full attention to the brunette in the orange fishnets who is more than delighted to have it.

But my brother's eyes are on me, and I know he reads murder in mine. "No offense, sweetheart, but I'm going to pass on this one." Alex gently guides Briar off his lap and lightly deposits her into *mine.*

She's as pale as a ghost. In an effort to steady her, my hand wraps lightly around her wrist and I can feel her pulse racing under her skin. She's so tense, her spine rigid, trembling atop my knee.

Terrified.

She's terrified of me.

I throw back the last of my scotch before leaning forward, pressing my mouth to the back of her ear. "*Bella*, was it?" My words are full of spite and she flinches.

Giovanni sees Briar in my lap, his eyes flashing with excitement.

"Ti ho visto guardare prima," he says, switching to Italian, presumably so I can understand him but *she* can't. "Da vicino è ancora meglio, immagino."

He raises his brows at me and lifts his chin. His laugh is low and vile.

Briar looks at him confused. I was right. She doesn't understand him, but *I do*. Every goddamn word. My father saw to it I was trained in several languages.

I saw you watching her before. Up close, she's even better, I imagine.

I can already see where this is going and I don't fucking like it.

Briar quietly tries to slip off of my lap but my hand on her thigh stops her, the look in my eye is enough to keep her from trying it again.

My attention is on the girl trembling in my lap, her eyes darting everywhere but at me.

Giovanni continues on in Italian

"She's a beautiful whore."

My vision goes black at the edges.

He doesn't notice. Keeps talking, keeps smirking, keeps looking at her like he has the right. "*I can let you try her. Just one night. On the house.*" He winks.

He fucking winks.

Briar shifts uncomfortably on my lap. She might not know what he's saying but she knows something's off. Her eyes dart between us.

It's a test. This is the game, remember? You're supposed to be one of them. A buyer. Another piece of shit who treats women like they're currency.

"I need a refill on my whiskey." Briar's too busy taking

stock of everyone around us that she doesn't notice at first that I'm talking to her.

"Go," I growl, nearly under my breath.

But she hears me, surprise on her face when she turns to stare at me.

When she doesn't stand up, I lock eyes with her. Cold. Everything about me is cold, hard, and angry when I say the word again. Louder this time, practically yelling at her.

"I said go!"

She jumps off my lap, backing away, taking in Giovanni's frown before trying to disappear out of sight.

But she'll never be out of my sight again. And even though I'm watching Giovanni, I track her through the crowded club, heading for the back hallway.

I sense Liam watching me from the corner of my eye and turn to lock eyes with him completely, accompanied by a slight nod in the direction Briar disappeared. He returns with a nearly imperceptible nod himself.

"Restroom?" I ask Giovanni.

"In the back, to the left," he replies, gesturing in that general direction.

I rise and Liam speaks up, seizing the opportunity to pepper Giovanni with financials, distracting him.

I reach the bathroom but instead of going in, I pass right by. Heading further down the hall to where the private rooms are. Finding an empty one, I lean casually against the wall of the darkened hallway, pulling my hat from back to front to better conceal my face, though the hallway is pretty busy. Crossing my arms, I wait, eyes peeled on the dressing room door further down the hall.

The hallway is busy enough that nobody questions it. I do

my best to disappear into the shadows while I wait for Briar to reemerge.

Just as I'm contemplating busting right in, she appears. Still looking flustered, her expression tense, and she trips over her own feet in her rush down the hallway. *It's almost too easy.* She's distracted, so she doesn't notice me standing there until it's too late. Just as she goes to pass me, I grab her. Catching her off guard so that all she gets out is a little squeak as I redirect her with ease into the private room across from me.

Once inside, I close and lock the door, turning to set my sights on the girl I've only watched from a distance for weeks.

The room is small, barely six by eight, but she's pressed herself into the far wall. Just about as far away from me as she can get. Fear shining bright in her eyes.

I smile.

"Briar Rose, what the fuck are you doing here?"

35

MINE
KOEN

THEN...

I want to give her a dare I know she'll never do. My eyes roam over her perfectly tan skin.

"I dare you to get a tattoo."

"A tattoo?" She gapes at me.

I lean back in my seat to fully appreciate the shocked look on her face.

"Right now?"

I tilt my head in a way that says, *obviously.*

"But don't you have to make an appointment? It's the middle of the night!"

I can't help but bark out a laugh, which earns me a glare from Rose.

"I know a guy." Leaning forward, I start up my bike, watching and waiting to see if she's going to climb on the back.

She eyes the bike then looks at me, chewing her bottom lip.

"Having second thoughts, love?" I grab the helmet hanging from my handlebars and hold it out to her. A silent dare in my eyes. "It's okay to chicken out." I shrug, folding my arms across my chest and trying not to smile when Rose's cheeks burn pink.

Her eyes narrow and her mouth drops into a slight frown. "No I—I'm just thinking about what to get."

Likely story. "Oh that's easy. I get to pick for you."

"What?"

"Mhm." I'm sure she's about to back down any second.

To my surprise, a wicked gleam enters her eye and I start to get the feeling I've done it now.

Rose leans back on her heels, drumming her perfectly manicured fingers atop her arm. "Truth or dare, Rf?"

My eyes narrow and I approach this one with caution. I know she knows my game now. I'm not going to pick truth. I let the tension drag out a little longer between us before I speak.

"Dare."

She smiles. "I dare you to get a tattoo, too."

I glance down at my body. I'm already covered on most of my chest and back, and a full sleeve on my right arm. I can't think of why she looks so excited, so I shrug again.

"Fine. What's one more?"

Seemingly satisfied, I arch a brow when she suddenly struts forward, taking my helmet out of my hands and pulling it over her head, remembering how to do the straps.

Swinging her leg over the back, she settles in and leans up against me.

"Alrighty then, but remember I get to pick for you."

Bloody hell.

"Ay, Rí!" Jace shouts over the loud metal music blasting in his tiny shop, spotting me as we walk in, and I'm holding the door open for Rose. "What can I do for you?" He closes the distance and I'm greeted with a familiar palm slap, pulling me in close and clasping me tight on the back.

I feel Rose poke her head out from behind me. When my cousin's eyes drop down, before meeting mine again with the addition of two raised brows, I narrow mine, silently telling him to *keep his fucking mouth shut* and he nods in understanding, holding out a hand to the girl at my back.

"I'm Jace. Rí's cousin. Nice to meet you."

"Rose, and likewise." She takes his hand, giving it a solid shake, and looking him in the eye when she gives him her name, which says so much about her, since Jace is an intimidating motherfucker. He's just as tall as me, short hair bleached silver, tattoos and piercings as far as the eye can see. Well, she gave him her *fake* name; that is, I know *Rose* isn't her real name just as well as she knows *Rí* isn't mine, but it's part of the game. I don't know her, she doesn't know me, we can just be us without any of the expectation. A novelty I didn't realize I needed.

"What can I do for you guys?"

"Sorry to bother you, but err—" Rose's eyes flick up to mine and I help her out.

"Rose here has got a dare to complete." I take off my motorcycle gloves, sliding them into my back pocket.

A grin spreads across Jace's face. "Is that so?"

She glares up at me, cerulean eyes bright with challenge. "So does Rí."

"Interesting." My cousin smirks but one look from me and he spins, motioning us to follow him back to his chair, stopping to turn down the music a fraction along the way. "Let me guess, it involves a tattoo."

"If it's too late—" Rose hedges and I give her a look.

"It's never too late to tattoo," Jace says, and he means it. The guy doesn't have an apartment above his shop for nothing. I've spent the night here more times than I can count. He does his best work after midnight.

"But if you want to back out..." I offer, not wanting her to do anything she doesn't want to, as much as it gets me off to push her outside of her comfort zone.

"Never." She lifts her chin defiantly. A surge of heat travels south and my fingers flex at my side, resisting the urge to grab that chin and tug her closer.

"Ladies first." I gesture to the open chair beside us, ignoring the shit-eating grin on Jace's face as he pretends to be busy prepping his tools. My keen eye picks up how Rose's gaze lingers a little too long on the needle.

"Is this your first tattoo?" Jace asks.

She nods and he, too, gives her another out. "Tattoos are forever," he says seriously. "No one'll blame you if you don't go through with it." He points to me. "I'll even kick his arse for ya." He winks and Rose laughs. The sweet melodic sound drowns out everything else. I want to hear it again.

"No," she pauses, her brow furrowing before she replaces it with a small smile. "No, I want to. Let's do it." Her words bring a smile back to Jace's face.

"Alright, I ain't gonna argue with that. So what'll it be?"

I clear my throat. "That," I say, "would be up to me." I pull out my phone, typing out a quick text addressed to him before holding up the device and giving it a little shake.

Jace's phone chimes and he gives it a look, earning a shake of his head before he looks back to Rose. "You sure you want to give him this kind of power, lass? It'll only go to his head."

She looks between the two of us, and I raise a single brow, awaiting her answer.

"What the hell?" she breathes out finally, settling deeper into the chair, gripping tightly to the arm rests. "Let's do it."

Jace looks my way and I nod. He picks up his tattoo gun, rolling his chair closer. "Alright, where's it going?"

Rose's eyes slide to mine and she slowly hooks a thumb into the waistband of her skirt, dragging it down and pointing to the soft swatch of skin just south of her hip bone.

Jace sets about prepping the area, lowering the chair back so she's more comfortable.

Her eyes never leave mine.

I need to take a walk. I need to do *something*, but instead, I stay, holding her gaze, watching her hold mine. Another challenge, the thrill of it awakening something primal in me, begging to be let out to play.

"Ready?" Jace's voice breaks the tether between us, reminding us where we are, and Rose nods once, swallowing a lump in her throat, "Ready."

I lower myself into one of the chairs, sitting on it the wrong way so I can lean my arms over the chair back while I watch.

Jace lowers his gun to her skin, and I can see the instant he makes contact. Pain flashes through her beautiful face and her grip tightens on the arm rest, eyes squeezing shut for all but a second before they fly open again, seeking me out.

Breathe, I mouth to her, and she does, slowly getting used to the annoying scratching of the tattoo needle.

She doesn't look down to check Jace's work. Doesn't try to peek and see what it is I've chosen for her. Instead she watches me, letting me be her anchor through the pain, trusting me, in blind faith, that I haven't decided to mar her with an infinity symbol, an anchor, or some other stereotypical generic tattoo.

The tattoo I've chosen for her is simple and small. Jace makes quick work of it and it's over before she even realizes.

"All done," Jace confirms, wiping the last of the blood away before she sees. "What do you think?"

There's a nervous rhythm to my heart as her gaze falls, skimming over the new and permanent dark mark upon her skin. Her attention drawn to the black club, like that on a playing card, and the letter "K" that sits just above it and just under a small crown.

"It's actually cute." She lifts her head, approval glinting in her eyes, and Jace has to walk away to hide his face.

I smile too—because she doesn't realize... I've just branded her as *mine*.

That smile falters, however, when I catch the shift in her expression. A wicked spark flickers there and her smile turns sinister.

"Your turn."

36

DEATH SENTENCE

BRIAR

Now

Koen.

I stare at him, still not fully convinced I'm not hallucinating, and it's really him.

Koen O'Rourke.

He reaches up to twist his hat rim back behind him; a few dirty blond locks escape out onto his forehead.

He lifts his head and eyes me expectantly.

That's when I remember, he'd asked me a question.

"I—I work here." My voice sounds stronger than I feel.

His expression darkens, and I swallow.

He takes a step forward and I take one back, pressing myself further into the back wall, wondering why the hell he looks *so angry.*

The private room is up-lit in red lighting, and the eerie red glow making him look every inch the devil he is.

I think he's going to stop, but he keeps advancing until he's got me trapped against the wall, his hands closing around my hips.

He leans in, and I squirm in his hold until his mouth finds my neck.

I still.

Confusion, and something else, hits me as I let him trail light kisses up my neck, and he releases one of my hips to tuck my hair behind my ear.

"What are you—?"

"Cameras?" His deep voice, soft against my skin, sends a shiver though my body that I can feel in my core. It takes another second to register that he's talking about the room. "Just nod once if yes," he breathes again, his voice so low that I can only hear him because his mouth is right up against my ear.

I dip my chin in confirmation that there are, indeed, cameras.

His mouth slides further down my jaw as his hands tighten on my hips. "Microphone?"

Slowly, I shake my head. *No.*

He pauses, seemingly thinking something over, before he pulls away. I have to fight the urge to pull him back, my body instantly missing the warmth of his. His touch feels familiar in a way it shouldn't. His eyes scan the room.

It's one of the smaller rooms, dark, with only a red leather sofa against one wall, and a small stage with a pole on the other. I see him locate the camera, mounted just over the door.

Koen shifts, taking me with him until his back is fully to the camera, blocking me entirely from its view. For a moment, he says nothing, studying my face. Scanning over my eyes and dropping down to my mouth.

His own face is cold and unreadable. His eyes are more shadowed than I remember.

"Knees, now."

He moves off me just enough to give me space, but I blink up at him stunned. "I don't—" I start to tell him that I don't do *extras,* but his hand whips out, grabbing hold of my jaw and cutting me off.

His eyes narrow into thin, cold slits. "I wasn't asking."

I swallow hard, and watch his eyes drop to my throat. The cameras are supposedly for the dancer's safety, but I know for a fact club security has a habit of *overlooking* certain things—and I'm sure he does too. Especially for a client like Koen O'Rourke. No bouncer is about to rush in here and tell the Irish King what he can and cannot do.

I'm on my own.

My glare is smoldering when I finally lower myself on shaky knees. Resolving to bite his dick off if, and when, he takes it out.

"That's a good girl." Koen's smile is dark, and my eyes are murderous, when he unzips his jeans with one hand while fisting my hair in the other. He tugs me closer until I'm face level with his dick.

I stare at the bulge, hidden still by his black boxers, with my lips pressed tight. He's already hard, but he doesn't take it out. Instead, he tilts my chin up with his free hand, forcing me to look at him.

"Briar Rose," he whispers.

I wonder if he can feel my body shaking through his fingertips.

"What are you doing here?" he asks me again. And it might be my imagination, but the edge in his voice softens slightly.

When I don't answer, he sighs, "I drag you out of hell, only for you to run right back?" He shakes his head, disappointment showing on his face. "My, my... how far my little ballerina has fallen. It's no wonder you ended up in Giovanni's warehouse. You're just another whore for hire, aren't you?" To prove his point, his grip tightens on my hair, pulling me closer toward him, but yet he still doesn't take himself out.

I can't speak, too busy fighting back the tears that form, his words landing like knives.

"You owe him money." That brings my eyes snapping up. I'm not sure how, but he comes to the conclusion all by himself. *How could he possibly know that?*

He takes the look on my face as confirmation. And if I didn't know better, I'd say he was pissed. Especially since his fist tightens in my hair.

"You should've run, left town..." His judgmental gaze trails over me, looking down at me like I'm just a stupid girl.

"I'm handling it," I growl, my fists tightening at my sides, fingernails digging deep into my palms.

"Not well," he scoffs. "Seeing as how you walked right back into the lion's den."

Anger flares and his last comment sends me over the edge. I shove him away from me, and he allows it, letting go of my hair. "*You're* judging *me?*" *Is he fucking serious?* "Well, good thing it's none of your business."

"None of my business?" he growls, but I'm done.

I stand, cheeks burning with repressed rage. "I'm doing what I need to do, which, by the way, what I do is none of your concern. I'm not yours. I'm not anyone's. Now get out." I shove my finger to the door at his back, staring down the growing storm raging behind green eyes. Yeah, let's see how *he* likes rejection.

"I said, *get out.*"

He doesn't move. Instead, his hand whips out, wrapping around my throat. Both of my hands fly up, trying to pry his fingers from my skin, but his grip is unyielding. "You don't get to tell me what to do, *Bella*," he hisses.

"Here's what's going to happen, and listen closely because I don't repeat myself. You owe me a favor."

I open my mouth to disagree—because *I absolutely do not owe this man fucking shit*—but his darkening eyes at the barest hint of my dissent has me snapping it shut.

"We're going to leave this room together. You're going to keep that pretty little mouth of yours shut and let me do the talking."

Without warning, he starts toward the door, his hand wrapped around my upper arm, dragging me with him.

It's work to keep up with Koen's long strides as he half walks, half drags me down the hallway. He stops so abruptly, his hand on my arm is the only thing keeping me on my feet.

We're in Gio's office.

"I'm taking this one."

Koen hauls me roughly forward—far rougher than is necessary—so I'm standing in between him and Giovanni. The amusement on Gio's face fades away as he looks from the Irish boss and back to me.

"I believe the offer was for one—"

"You owe me girls, Moretti." Koen cuts him off. His voice is dark and dangerous. "And I require a little *collateral*. So until you make good on what you promised, I'm keeping this one with me." He tugs me back toward him while I plead silently with Gio.

To his credit, the man looks torn, looking between me and Koen.

Don't you fucking dare. My eyes narrow.

Oh my god. He's gonna cave. I can see it written plain as day on the bastard's face.

Giovanni sighs deeply. "There's an auction in three weeks. I'll have your girls by then." He takes a sip from his glass before his eyes slide back over to me, but not looking me in the eye. "She's untrained," he warns, his gaze going back to Koen.

"That's fine," Koen says casually.

Trained? Trained in what?

"And she's not a virgin."

My head whips back to Gio at the same time Koen tightens his hold on me.

"Even better," he smirks, his eyes meeting mine.

Giovanni stares at Koen for a long time before speaking again, "I want her back in one piece, O'Rourke." His eyes narrow on Koen, and the uncertainty in them feeds my growing anxiety.

"I'll try my best," Koen says, and I know he feels me trembling.

"Fine," Gio huffs, throwing back the rest of his scotch. "But before you go, I require a private word with Bella here." He points at me.

Koen's grip on my arm tightens, and he looks like he's about to argue right before he suddenly releases me.

"Five minutes," he growls, and then he's gone. Leaving me alone with Giovanni.

Giovanni leans back in his desk chair, a smug look on his face.

"Well, Bella," he says, shaking his head in almost disbelief. "I don't know how you did it but you caught the eye of the Irish Devil." He looks pleased, as if I've accomplished something by attracting Koen's attention.

"This is a fucking joke, right? You can't just—you can't just *sell* me to him!"

"Bella!" His mock surprise at my attitude makes me want to hit him. My fingers curl into fists. "I did no such thing! It's only temporary. Three weeks max." He shrugs like it's not a big deal. Like he didn't just gamble my life away to one of the city's most notorious mafia lords. "You go with him, and your debt... I'll consider it paid."

I perk up slightly at that. But there's a sly look on Gio's face that tells me it's too good to be true

"So if I do this..." I swallow. "Go with him? You and me, we're square? My debt is paid. I won't have to work here anymore, and you'll leave me alone?"

The smile that spreads across his face has the hair on the back of my neck rising. "I said it would cover what you *owe*. As for what you *saw* a couple of weeks ago—"

"I didn't see anything," I'm quick to say—too quick.

"—that's an extra cost."

Extra? As in more than being sold to a mafia boss for just short of a month?

"What do you want?"

"Koen O'Rourke wants you as his for the next three weeks.

You make him happy, you do everything he asks, and you tell me *everything.*"

I just blink at him.

"He wants in on my operation and I need to know I can trust him. You—" he laughs, smiling to himself. "You will be my little spy. If your information is sound—useful..." He gives me a look. "Then we can call it even."

Spy on Koen. On the O'Rourkes?

"That's a death sentence."

"Only if you get caught." He shrugs.

"Gio, he's the head of the Irish mafia. He'll *kill* me."

"Then I suggest you don't get *caught,* Bella." He looks at me like that should be obvious.

My thoughts are racing.

"It's simple. He's only taking you for collateral. Once he has what he wants, he'll give you back to me, your debt will be paid, and you'll be free to go. And that business at the warehouse? Forgotten."

My mouth opens and closes, unsure what to say. I feel like I'm making the decision of who I would rather have kill me. Get caught betraying Koen and he'll kill me outright, or possibly get trafficked by Gio if I refuse...

"Listen Bella, I'm going to level with you here. You saw something you shouldn't have. It's a problem, but logistics— they're working out in your favor. So, you either take the deal, or you face the auction block. And Bella, trust me when I say that neither of us wants to see you up there." He eyes me. "See *your daughter* up there."

Horror cuts through me like a knife.

There's a gleam in Gio's eyes. "*Remi,* right?"

My hands are trembling and I feel like I'm going to pass out.

He leans forward over the desk. "Don't look at me like that, Bella. You know I like you. You went and caught the Devil's eye. I don't know that there is much I could do to save you. But I am a capitalist, and can't help but seize this opportunity that's presented itself. You go with the Irish, Bella. I'll be in touch. And if you even think of breathing a word of this to them..." The look he gives me is threat enough.

Seemingly satisfied, he pushes a button on his office phone for the intercom. "Tell the Irish they can pick up their package at the back door. She's ready for them."

37

I'D HAVE TWO NICKELS, WHICH ISN'T A LOT, BUT...

KOEN

Now

My little ballerina is silent as I escort her out the back of Wonderland and into Liam's waiting SUV.

I keep a firm grip on her arm, seeing how her eyes dart around the dark alley behind the club, desperate for a way out.

I open the back door and thrust her through it, far too forcefully to be considered gentle. I'm being too rough with her because there are cameras back here, and because I'm not willing to take a chance on her bolting on me.

Again.

Inside the SUV, she turns to face me, and wordlessly, I motion for her to slide over, climbing in to sit in the seat beside her.

Her lip curls and she slides as far away from me as possible, pressing herself into the other side of the SUV, stiffening when she notices both Alex and Liam staring over their shoulders at her from the front seat.

"Hi." Liam smiles at her, and she stares back at him like he's crazy.

"Just drive," I order. Sinking down into my seat, I keep my gaze fixed outside and away from Rose—*Briar*, as I try and work through the chaos playing out inside my mind.

We make it nearly two blocks before a small click draws my attention, and I'm momentarily confused when the interior lights of the SUV turn on. But just as I put two and two together... I lock eyes with Briar just as she shoves open her passenger door, evading my hand and diving out of the moving vehicle.

A string of curses erupts out of my mouth when Briar disappears from view. The car door slams shut in my face before I can follow, and I'm grappling for the door handle.

"Fuck, Liam. You didn't child-lock the doors?"

My brother slams his foot on the brake, and my face hits the back of the front seat hard, causing me to let out a grunt.

"No, I didn't. This wasn't exactly the *plan*, was it? How the hell was I supposed to know you were going to kidnap a stripper?" He looks to Alex for backup. "Honestly, if I had a nickel for every time..."

I don't hear the rest of it, finally getting the door open and launching myself out of the car to hunt Briar down. She's not getting away from me again that easily.

I look back down the street, sure I'll find her still curled up on the ground. She would have hit hard; she'll be lucky if she didn't break anything hitting the asphalt like that. Liam was going at least thirty miles per hour when she dove out of the car. But to my surprise, Briar's already halfway down the street by the time I catch a glimpse of her, sprinting like her life depends on it.

I take off after her. I'm fast, and with far longer legs than her, I easily close the distance. Briar never looks back, but she must hear me closing in because, just as I've about caught up to her, she darts down a narrow side street before quickly turning down another, nearly losing her footing on the loose gravel in her attempts to shake me.

I smile to myself, knowing it'll be over soon.

But that smile quickly turns to a frown when I notice how she's favoring her left leg. Probably injured it jumping out of the fucking car. She's still got a bit of a lead on me, so I increase my speed, having had enough of these shenanigans.

I lose sight of Briar when she takes another tight turn down yet another narrow side street but, when I make the turn, she's nowhere in sight.

A delivery truck is parked at this end of the street, blocking a good portion of the alley from view. A few dumpsters line the street to my right, and I also take note of a few metal doors leading into the abandoned warehouse that stretches tall over the alleyway.

The turn to the next street is too far away. I was too close for her to get away, so I start walking slowly down the road, the sound of my boots echoing in the late-night quiet. She's somewhere nearby.

"Might as well come out now, Briar Rose," I call out, eyeing the dumpsters to the right, craning my neck to see if I can get a look in them before moving deeper into the alley. "There's no escaping me, love."

My words are met with silence, and I sigh.

"Your choice, remember."

That's when I strike. One second I'm on my feet, and the next, I'm chest-down on the pavement, arm outstretched underneath the truck, my hand closing around a slender, delicate *ankle*.

I yank hard, and Briar screams as I drag her out from under the truck. She fights me, clawing the ground in desperation, trying to find something to grab ahold of. Her attempts to kick me away are futile.

"Stop."

Swapping out her ankle for an arm, I haul her up while she thrashes against me, her fists flying, falling uselessly against my chest. Once she's on her feet, she does everything she can to twist out of my grip.

In a shock to me, she actually manages to slip out of it. Her eyes widen when she realizes she's free. She barely makes it two steps before my hand closes around her wrist again and she yelps when she meets resistance. Whirling her around, her back hits the brick wall of the alley, and I pin her there. Yet she still doesn't relent.

"Let me go!" she screeches, attempting to drop out from under me, but I reach down, wrapping a hand around each wrist, forcing them up over her head and pinning them there against the brick. At the same time, I lean in, using the weight and size of my body to cage her in until she has nowhere left to go. By the time her eyes meet mine again, my forearm is pressed firmly against her throat—threatening but not yet cutting off air—just letting her know if *I wanted to, I could.*

"Stop. Running. Away. From. Me."

She finally goes still, blue eyes alight with fury.

I cock my head to the side as I look down at her, finding her rage at being caught amusing. "You done?"

She struggles again, bringing our attention to just how *close* our bodies are. How I'm pressed up against her. She makes an attempt to free her hands, but I tighten my grip and watch as the rage and fury in her eyes fall away to reveal sheer panic and utter terror, before she releases a low whimper. Her entire body trembles beneath me.

At first, her reaction confuses me, but then—realization. "Fuck, I'm not—I'm not going to hurt you, okay?"

My grip on her loosens slightly, but I don't let go. I don't trust her. I keep her pinned in place.

"You *bought* me." Her voice comes out cracked, full of broken accusation.

I let out a sigh. "I know, but—"

"I heard what you said in there about..." *breaking her*, she doesn't say it. Trailing off, her gaze darts to the right, flinching violently at the appearance of my brothers.

I move my forearm off her neck, holding up a hand to ward them off. They freeze a couple feet away, watching me and waiting on my next order.

"Please let me go. *Please*, Koen," Briar begs. Falling apart now, tears rim her blue eyes as she stares up at me, pleading with me to let her walk away from this.

Something cracks deep inside me at the sight—and the way she says *my name*—but I only tighten my grip.

"No."

Her eyes once again fill with panic, and she trembles against me.

I rub my free hand down my face. "Shit. Look, it's not— it's not what it seems. I just... need you to trust me. I can explain, but not here." I release her hands, taking hold of her arm again as I ease my weight off of her, guiding her in the direction of the street, but she resists. "If you'll just get back in the car and—"

"I don't know you." She cuts me off, trying to watch both me and my brothers behind me at the same time.

I stop. Looking down at her.

"No, you don't." In all fairness, we'd spent one night together, nearly five years ago, and all I've done since then is threaten her.

"Alright, I get it, this is... a lot. But if you get back in the car with me, I promise, no one will hurt you. I'll take you back to your apartment. And we can talk."

She stares at me, searching my face, my eyes, for a reason to believe what I'm saying is true. That I'm not trying to trick her.

"Okay," she says finally, letting me lead her back to the SUV. Her eyes full of distrust.

38

NO EXPIRATION DATE
BRIAR

Now

Koen keeps his word, and after an uncomfortably silent car ride home, we arrive outside of my apartment. He escorts me upstairs, leaving his men in the lobby.

He doesn't say anything as I fumble with the keys, my hands are shaking so badly it's a struggle to get the keys; into each of the three locks needed to open the door. He waits silently at my back with his hands in his pockets.

Koen stays by the door when we finally get inside, scanning the length of my pathetic excuse of an apartment. I really wish I'd picked up more before leaving for work tonight. There are dishes in the kitchen sink, wrappers on the counter, and some of the living room pillows are still on the floor from earlier when Remi was playing The Floor is Lava.

The apartment building might be shit, but Lily and I have done what we can to make our space as cute as possible. The exposed brick of the old mill building helps to lend a bit of charm. A few thrifted rugs cover up the most worn areas on the hardwood floors. The living room is big enough to get some dance practice in if we move around the furniture. We have a basic, but plush, couch and a super comfortable reading chair we scored off a neighbor when they moved out last year. The television might be small, but the bookshelf is overflowing. The thrift store sells used books for $1, and we go a couple times a month. Bright and colorful children's books line the bottom shelf, easily accessible to Remi.

Fuck. The children's books.

As inconspicuously as I can, I move so I'm standing in between Koen and the books, blocking them from his line of sight and hoping he doesn't notice. Not that he's probably all that interested in what I'm reading. Quickly, I scan the rest of the small space, looking for anything else of Remi's that might have been left out.

My eyes flick to the pictures of her on the fridge.

One of her in her pink leotard and tutu, pouting with her arms folded at the ballet studio; one of Lily, Remi, and I laughing with ice cream cones ; and the most damning one of all, a close-up of Remi sticking out her tongue at the camera, her round, green-brown eyes wide and clear.

Koen's still standing by the door, his back to the kitchen and the fridge. It's late, it's dark, maybe he won't notice.

My eyes go to him and he's not looking at the fridge—he's looking at *me*.

There's nothing soft about the man standing before me. He's all sharp edges and quiet menace, but the dark shadows in his eyes seem to lighten when they meet mine.

I clear my throat, breaking some of the tension in the

room. "What do you want, Koen?" My words are slow, careful, and I don't dare take my eyes off of the Irish King. Despite his assurances he won't hurt me, I have no reason to believe anything he says.

Speaking his name appears to break him out of whatever thoughts he'd been lost in, and he steps further into the living room space and away from the kitchen.

"You owe me a favor."

"A favor?" My eyes widen with confusion and I shake my head, crossing my arms across my chest. I'm still in the fucking lingerie from the club. "I don't owe *you* any favors."

He picks up the book lying on the coffee table, examining the cover and spine before setting it back down. "You don't remember?" He clicks his tongue as though disappointed. A smirk appears on his face and my heart rate picks up. "A few years ago, you promised me a favor if I helped you out of a certain *situation*?"

The blood drains from my face at his mention of *that night*.

"You can't be serious," I say, shaking my head in disbelief. "You can't call in a favor now. That was over four years ago!"

He just watches me, his expression unchanging, a predatory gleam in his eye as he takes another step closer. The apartment is starting to feel even smaller than it is.

"Did you not give that favor freely?" he asks, and I feel like I'm walking into a trap, a web he's spun just for me when I give him my answer.

"Yes, but—"

"Was there an expiration date agreed upon for that favor?"

My palms grow slick and my arms tighten around me. He's got me there. "No, but again—"

"Then you still owe me a favor." He's close now, *too close*, within arm's distance, and I catch a whiff of his dark citrus scent

He stops. His head tilts to the side as he takes in the sight of me again. "I'm here, Briar Rose, to collect on that favor."

I swallow the lump that's formed in my throat, the weight of his words falling heavy onto my shoulders. "What do you want from me?" I ask, doing my best to keep my voice level, though I fear it betrays me.

His dark eyes are locked on me, books forgotten. It's only the deep intensity of his gaze that holds me in place.

"You," he breathes.

My lips part in shock but no words spill out. My knees weak under that *gaze* of his.

"You're close with Giovanni." He clears his throat before continuing on.

I open my mouth in protest but quickly shut it when he shoots me a warning glare.

Do not interrupt me.

"You've already been taken once. I think you have some information I might find... useful."

He wants to interrogate me.

"But mostly, I just need a girl to play the part and be mine, help me to convince Giovanni, and the people he works for that I'm one of them. I need access to that auction. To their list of buyers."

"I won't help you with that." My anger, making me brave. "I won't help you traffic more girls." I steel my spine and set my jaw, hoping he can see the resolve in my eyes.

There's a wild gleam in his when he closes the gap between us, and despite my trembling knees, I don't back down, tilting my chin so that I hold his eye. He towers over me. I always seem to forget just how tall he is.

I steel my gaze, ready to take whatever comes out of his mouth next, but I'm unprepared when he says, "Good. I don't want you to."

My voice stutters. "I—I'm confused."

"I don't want you to help me traffic more girls." His face is serious. "I want you to help me stop it."

"Stop it?" I blink at him, not quite sure what to believe. "But back at the club..." I trail off, searching his face for any sign he's trying to manipulate me. But his face is stone. I don't know what to believe. I don't know Koen very well but I do know *his world*—men who will say anything to get what they want.

"How do I know I can trust you?" I say finally.

He shrugs, picking up a lock of my hair and letting it run through his fingers as if he couldn't help himself.

"You don't."

I stare at him, long seconds passing us by. "Do I have a choice?"

"You always have a choice, Briar." His voice is low, and the way he's looking at me... I can't quite read the look on his face. "You can stay with me and we can further discuss terms, or I can bring you back to Giovanni." He shrugs, but I still see the violent gleam in his eye when he says Giovanni's name.

Not really a choice... I think, weighing which of the two is more of a threat.

Koen checks the time. It's after two.

"You need sleep. We'll talk more tomorrow. Someone will be outside." He heads for the door.

Like a guard?

248

"So I'm not allowed to leave?"

He turns, his hand still on the knob. "You're mine now, Briar Rose." I shiver at the way he says my name. "And I protect what's mine."

Considering the matter finished, he turns the knob.

"Yours ... *temporarily*," I correct.

He freezes, not turning around, though I see his head tilt slightly back in my direction. Rolling his shoulders, he steps fully out into the hall, shutting the door behind him.

I sigh, finally alone.

A deal with the Devil? Sounds too good to be true. Won't cost much... only my soul.

39

YOU'RE A BAD IDEA

BRIAR

Then...

Freshly tattooed, I hop on the back of Rí's bike. I don't ask where we're going, just enjoying the spontaneity of it all. I don't know what time it is, and I don't care. He brings us underground into what looks to be an empty private parking garage. Pulling into a parking space, Rí kills the loud engine, and the sudden silence is a shock.

To break the tension, I decide to crack a joke as I dismount the bike, sliding the helmet off of my head. "So... is this the part where you kill me?" I laugh, but you can hear the nerves in it.

"Kill you?" He arches a brow, amusement on his face. "Oh, now, little Rose, why would I do that? I'm not nearly done with you yet." He steps closer, one hand taking the helmet from me, the other tucking a lock of hair behind my ear. I swallow hard. "Still looking to go *far*, love?"

I stare up into his eyes—his beautifully fractured, soulful eyes.

"Yes," I breathe, almost inaudibly.

The corner of his mouth ticks up in a smirk, and he steps back, holding out his hand for me to take.

"C'mon."

I stare at him—at his hand for another second before taking it, letting him lead me to a waiting elevator, the door held open by a man in a dark suit. "Rí," the man says, nodding respectfully at the both of us.

That's the second person to call him that tonight... I'd thought it was a fake name, but Jace, back at the tattoo shop, had also called my tattooed nightmare *Rí*.

I have little time to think about it though, because Rí releases my hand, standing next to me as the man steps out, leaving the two of us in the elevator alone. And as the doors slowly inch closed, all I can think about is *him* at my side. Feeling his eyes on me, I blush, biting my lip.

The door still has another couple of centimeters to go when he grabs my waist, spinning me, the two of us falling back against the far wall, his mouth on mine, his hands in my hair, tasting, consuming, exploring. I break the kiss with a whimper, looking to the sky when his palm finds my breast, cupping it over my shirt. His mouth drops to my throat.

I'm nearly breathless when I say, "*You're a bad idea.*"

"*The worst,*" he whispers right up against my neck, his breath hot, soft lips trailing featherlight kisses all the way up and down my jaw before they stop, hovering just over mine. "But something tells me you're tired of pretending to be the *good girl.*"

I pull back to stare at him, cheeks growing hot. "I am not—"

He smirks at me, his devil eyes seeing through to my soul. I stare at him—really stare—and something passes between us in that moment, something deep, indiscernible, and inescapable.

"Fuck it," I breathe, and kiss him.

I'm aware of everything, yet it's all a blur... his mouth is on mine, my fingers tangle in his hair. He picks me up, and I wrap my legs tight around his waist.

I barely hear the ping of the elevator when we reach our destination. It's dark, but that doesn't disguise the sheer size of the loft we walk into. The lights are off, but it's lit up by the city surrounding it, the lights and moonlight shining through floor-to-ceiling windows.

Rí doesn't set me down, doesn't even lift his lips off mine as he carries me down a darkened hallway. Together we crash through a door and into a bedroom. He has me naked in seconds.

"So fucking beautiful," he says, stealing a glance at my body.

His words, and the look in his eyes when he said them, gets past all of my defenses, burrowing down deep into my heart.

He pulls his shirt off and, *holy fucking shit*, I can't stop my mouth from falling open.

I saw his chest back at Jace's, the bandage just over his heart covering the new ink is proof, but here, the shadowed lighting highlights every curve, every ripple of muscle; the ink he has covering most of one arm and his chest appears even darker, nothing but black or gray, not a trace of color to be seen.

Next thing I know, his pants are gone and...

Oh.

I gasp, letting my eyes drop. No, there is nothing *soft* about this man at all.

He's already stalking for me, catching me, claiming me, walking me back until we're under the archway separating the bedroom and bathroom. There, he drops to his knees.

"What are you—*Oh my god.*" I shiver when he licks me, a deliciously dangerous feeling exploding out from my core.

I lean back against the threshold, keeping my balance as he devours me, clinging to the wall behind me with one hand while twisting my fingers into his hair with the other. His tongue flicks my now wicked little clit, and I almost lose it. I swear I feel him smile when I scream out.

One of his hands pushes the underside of my thigh, pushing my leg until it's over his shoulder, arching my back off the wall. He gives me no warning when he suddenly stands, taking me with him, my upper shoulders sliding up the wall. Rí throws my other leg over his shoulder, and I have just enough time to grab hold of the top of the arch above me before he goes back in. I groan deeply when he sucks down hard on my clit.

He zeroes in with his tongue, and I cling to the wall, his hair, anything I can when I come for the second time tonight, hard, all over his face.

When it's over and my screams turn to ragged breaths, he steps back, sliding me off his shoulders, I plummet to the floor. I let out a yelp, right before he catches me, I wrap my hands tightly around his neck.

"I thought you were going to drop me." My words come out in a trembling rush. I'm still breathless from what just happened.

He smirks down at me, the green in his eyes sparkling.

"Never."

I cling to him as he carries me over to the bed, lying me down gently before running his hands up my body as he leans over and kisses me. His fingers trail back down my side, and I shiver.

A little scream sneaks out when he slips two fingers roughly inside of me, the intrusion unexpected, his thumb pressing down on my still-pulsating clit, sensitive from the orgasm he gave me just minutes ago.

"That's two, love, shall we go for number three?"

My breath catches, because until a couple of hours ago, I would have been shocked that *one* happened, but *three*?

I swallow, my eyes dropping to take in the sheer size of him again.

"Umm, okay?"

But he backs up, shaking his head.

"Oh no, love, if you want me to fuck you, I'm going to need nothing other than a *yes* out of you."

My eyes widen, and I stare up at him, frozen in shock.

He tilts his head, patiently waiting for my answer. After a few seconds, he goes to push off of me entirely, but my hand shoots out, stopping him.

"No, stay I—" I bite my lip. "*Yes*, I want to..."

But he still looks unconvinced, and my eyes narrow a little. I need his hands back on me like I need oxygen to breathe right now.

"Rí?"

"Aye?" he says, looking down into my eyes.

"I dare you to fuck me." I smirk, giving him a devilish little look.

His jaw ticks, and that's my only warning before he rises,

grabbing hold of both of my ankles and flipping me to my stomach. A gasp escapes me when Rí grips my hips with both hands and tugs me back until I'm bent over on my knees.

"I accept." His grip on my hips tightens just before he drives himself in deep.

He wraps my hair around his fist, tugging hard, forcing my back to arch even more but then... *Oh*. The new angle redirects his thrusts, and I whimper as he pounds mercilessly into an increasingly sensitive area.

A now familiar heat builds—similar, but different from before. It feels wilder, far-reaching and uncontrollable. Moans and screams flow freely from me now. I can't stop them—can't do much of anything—as Rí drives me straight over the edge.

My whole body shakes, and it doesn't stop, the cascading waves of pleasure crashing through me until my eyes roll back in my head.

"Fuck," I hear Rí say, and there's one last thrust before he pushes deep, releasing my hair and falling down over me, both arms on either side of my head. I can feel his dick twitch inside of me as he comes, holding himself deep until it's over.

He pulls out, and I collapse down fully onto the mattress. Rí drops next to me on his back, reaching down to drag me further up, until my head is on his chest and I'm listening to the sound of his heart.

We're both quiet, and he runs his fingers lazily through my hair. I exhale. I have no idea what time it is, but his slow, gentle strokes are lulling me to sleep.

There's one thing I need to know first.

"Rí?"

"Mmm?" The sound of his voice is soft, like he might be falling asleep, too.

"One question?"

He hums his agreement, moving down from my hair to trace light circles across the bare skin of my back.

"Back at the tattoo shop, Jace called you Rí... and then, the doorman downstairs... is that—is that your real name?" I'm dancing into dangerous territory here.

"No, it's a nickname," he confesses.

"What does it mean?" I ask, curiosity getting the better of me, even as my eyelids grow heavy and fall... sleep beckons.

"It's Gaelic," he says, his voice low, "for *King*."

40

BUT I BROUGHT DONUTS...

BRIAR

Now

Koen keeps to his word and my apartment is quiet for the night. Not that I'm able to sleep... After a never-ending night of restless tossing and turning, I finally throw in the towel and shuffle into the kitchen around seven a.m.

First thing I did after Koen left last night was purge the apartment of photos of Remi.

Her toys and books are all safely locked away in her room. The photos, in a box tucked deep into her closet.

I spent the night in her room last night, missing her and Lily. Fighting the urge to escape down the fire escape and hitchhike out to Lake Placid just so I could hold her.

Before I have a chance to fill up the coffee pot with water, there's a knock at my door.

I steal a panicked glance at my own reflection in the microwave; no makeup, though my hair isn't terrible—the curls from last night falling into loose, but tangled, waves. And I'm still in shorts, wearing a t-shirt that's three times too big for me with no bra.

Finger combing the tangles from my hair, I lift onto the tips of my toes to check the peephole... finding Koen on the other end.

I take a deep breath and brace myself as best I can for whatever's about to come.

I abandon my hair, letting it stay wild. He wanted me... he's got me, tangles and all.

Pulling the door open, I lean casually against the frame while crossing my arms, blocking the way in.

"Well, well, well, would you look at that? He *does* know how to use a door."

Koen's eyes narrow and he lets out a grunt of acknowledgement, his gaze falling to my bare legs before finding my face again. "Good morning to you, too."

He waits for me to invite him in, but I don't, seizing the opportunity to study him instead.

He's dressed casually, in a pair of black jeans and boots, and a faded leather jacket over a dark gray henley. His hair is darker than usual, the dirty blonde locks tamed down, still wet from a shower. The scent of his body wash begins to permeate the apartment along with...

"Is that coffee?"

Some people are addicted to drugs, but me... I'm addicted to coffee, and Koen's holding a tray of two cups from my favorite coffee shop two streets over.

He pulls the tray back toward him, and I track it with my eyes.

"Depends... Can I come in?"

I pretend to think about it, but who am I kidding? There's little I won't do to get my caffeine fix. "Fine." I retreat back into my apartment, leaving the door open behind me.

Koen steps inside, shutting the door behind him.

Rubbing my eyes, I slide my ass onto one of the island stools and watch as he makes himself at home in my kitchen. Setting down the tray of drinks and a plain brown bag, I hadn't noticed in his other hand.

Without a word, he slides one of the cups to me before claiming the other for himself.

My need for caffeine is at war with my sense of self-preservation, and I eye the drink I was so desperate for just a second ago suspiciously.

What if he put something in it?

Not that he'd need to. Between his height, his muscles, and what I'm guessing is a morally grey compass, he could very easily overpower me. *He already has.*

Koen sips from his own coffee cup before catching me staring down at mine with a look of apprehension.

"It's not going to bite you."

"It might." I eye both him and the cup with newfound suspicion. My brain slow from lack of sleep and caffeine.

He lets out a sigh that sounds an awful lot like exasperation before reaching for my drink, and taking a sip out of it before placing it back down in front of me.

Crisis averted. I reach for the cup, finally getting my fix, while his dark eyes assess me.

"I think you and I both know, I don't need to drug you to fuck you."

I nearly choke on the coffee in my mouth, and he shoots

me a wicked little grin and a wink before pushing the paper bag my way.

Feigning interest in the bag, I ignore the way my body heats. That look he gave me awakens something deep down in my core. His words, that *wink*...

Koen clears his throat, leaning on my counter on his elbows, confirming he's still hot as sin. He's quiet, watching me from the other side of the island as I take another sip of my coffee.

"Wait," I pause, pulling the rim of the cup away from my face. "This is a caramel latte," I say, stunned, looking back in Koen's direction. His expression remains unchanged. "How did you—?"

"I remembered." He drains the rest of the coffee from his own cup, tossing it into the trash by the edge of the island before changing the subject. "I thought we'd start by going over what you know that may be of interest."

He keeps talking but I'm no longer paying attention.

He *remembered*? That I liked caramel lattes? I don't even remember telling him that...

"Briar."

"Yeah?" My name snaps me from my thoughts.

Koen gives me a look when he has to repeat the question I ignored. "How long have you worked at Wonderland?"

"Uhm." I think back. "About one year. As a waitress." *Since Remi's first asthma attack*—but I withhold that last bit. Need to know.

"Why?" The question is simple, but loaded, and I sit my cup down on the counter, curling my fingers around it. Savoring the warmth on my cold hands.

"Money got tight," I admit finally, averting my eyes and giving him a shrug. "I did what I had to do."

I peek up at him. But to my surprise, there's no judgement in his eyes, and he nods as if he understands.

"That's when you borrowed money from Giovanni?"

"Mhm." I sip at my coffee, pulling open the mystery bag and my jaw drops at the sight of donuts inside.

"And you defaulted?"

The question has me shifting anxiously in my seat, but a quick glance at Koen reveals no emotions—no judgement.

"Not my intention," I start. He arches a brow, and my defense flares. "I broke my ankle, couldn't waitress and couldn't dance. With an eight-week recovery, it wasn't hard to fall behind," I bite out, peering up at him to gauge his reaction, but he's just staring at me. If I'm not mistaken, his jaw seems tenser.

"By all means, continue with your interrogation."

"This isn't an interrogation."

"Are you sure? Because it feels an awful lot like an interrogation to me."

"I brought donuts."

I blink up at him. "Are you saying this can't be an interrogation because you brought donuts?"

"Yes," he confirms, reaching into the bag and biting into a Boston Creme.

"Pretty sure cops and donuts are synonymous."

He shakes his head. "Cops wouldn't give you donuts if they were interrogating you."

"And how would you know? Spend some time in an interrogation room?" My tone is teasing but his answer is immediate.

"Yes."

I immediately regret the question, and a tense silence fills the room.

"Oh."

Koen pushes up off the island, rising to his full height.

"Now that we've cleared that up, you're free to go about your day. I'll pick you up later tonight."

"Tonight?" I ask warily before adding, "I'm supposed to work."

Koen's gaze darkens and I resist the urge to shrink back in my chair. "Where?" The word comes out as more of a growl than anything else.

"The club," I reply, softly.

"You don't work there anymore."

My mouth drops.

"While you're mine, you're only working for me."

Annoyance flares at the audacity he has thinking he can just dictate my whole life now. "I have to work! And I have classes to teach at the Conservatory."

"Cancel them." His phone chimes and his attention drops to it. His words coming out like an afterthought, not realizing I'm growing more and more irritable by the second, and how quickly I'm starting to spiral.

"I can't just cancel them! It's my job, and I need the money. I can't afford to—"

"*I'm* fucking paying you." His gaze snaps up from the screen of his phone, his grip on it tight, like he's losing his patience.

I blink at him. "How much?" It's a bold question but I've got my priorities.

He sighs, running a hand through his hair. It's almost dry

now, and he messes it up while letting out a deep breath, looking out the window like he'd rather be doing anything else other than having to talk to me.

"How much do you want?"

"Ten thousand, seven hundred," I say without thinking.

That gets his attention. "Ten *thousand* dollars?" He stares at me, and I nod.

"And seven hundred," I say, doubling down. Standing by that number despite the look on his face. *Enough for Remi's medication.*

"Are you out of your fucking mind?"

"Ten thousand, seven hundred dollars, and I'll be your willing little slave for two weeks." I don't stop to think of all the ways I could live to regret those words...

Koen's eyes flash and I have to fight the urge to run and hide under the covers of my bed.

"A month," he counters, and I chew my lip. Remi will be home in two weeks. There's no way I can keep her a secret from Koen if he's still around by then.

"Three weeks." I lift my chin and narrow my gaze, staring him down. "No club and no lessons, but I can't compromise my studio and rehearsal time. I have a showcase coming up. I have to be able to practice."

"Fine," he says, leaving me shocked. His attention drops back to his phone, no longer interested in me. "Three weeks. You'll get the ten thousand... *seven hundred,*" he adds when I look at him expectantly, "at the end. Assuming you deliver."

"Okay, and what do I have to do?"

He looks up at me and the corner of his mouth ticks up.

"Whatever I want."

41

THE AUDACITY

BRIAR

Now

There's a man named Mac sitting outside my door.

A *large* man named Mac.

I know this because, when I tried to leave for the studio about an hour ago, I almost fell running into him.

He winces. "Sorry lass, but you can't be doing that now. Rí says you stay here."

"Rí?" I ask. Surprised he's using the name Koen gave me when we first met.

"Aye Rí. The *boss*, Koen," he confirms, and my lips press tightly together.

The audacity.

"Okay, well, you can tell your *boss* to shove it. I need to get to the studio."

My attempt to slide past him fails miserably.

"Now, now lass, we can do this the easy way—or the hard

way." The look of amusement on his face has me seeing red. I grip the strap of my bag tighter. The man is built like a linebacker, with a ruggedness that feels as though he was ripped straight from the Highlands. With messy copper curls and blue eyes, despite his size, there's a teasing warmth about him. A charming, playful, arrogance and a smile that I'm sure has all the ladies just falling at his feet.

"Fine. Fine. That's—Fine," I spit out, throwing up my hands in defeat before turning on my heel and slamming the door in *Mac's* face.

Tossing my bag on the floor, I storm around the apartment feeling like the walls are closing in. The apartment is small, but now it feels suffocatingly so.

Pulling out my phone, I stare at the screen, my thumb hovering over the glass after realizing I don't even have Koen's number. For a moment, I contemplate calling the police, but quickly toss out the idea, considering the circumstances.

Instead, I shoot off a text to Melanie at the Conservatory, requesting to be taken off the schedule for lessons for the next couple of weeks, citing my need to prep for the showcase.

"No problem."

Her response is immediate, and I'm left with an emptiness at the suddenly freed-up calendar and empty apartment. Nervous energy ripples through my body, and I can feel the anxiety creeping into my chest, my heart rate picking up.

Dropping my phone on the counter, I move quickly for the living room. Taking out my anger on the poor, unsuspecting couch when I shove it back hard against the wall. The coffee table gets it next, and I keep going until I've cleared as much space as I can and start to warm up.

Letting out a tethered breath, I sink into my stretch.

Letting the familiar burn and pull of the movements relax my racing heart, my mind following suit.

Using the reflection in the window, I do what I can with the space for the next couple of hours. Cursing the fucking O'Rourke name as I go.

After a couple of hours, I stop when I hear my phone ringing from the island where I left it. I race over, hoping to not miss a call from Lily and Remi, but deflate slightly at the sight of *Unknown Number* flashing on the screen.

Sliding my thumb across the glass, I ignore the call. My stomach rumbles, so I open the fridge, only to stare at its emptiness instead. Lily does most of the shopping, and with her and Remi out the house, I'm in desperate need of a grocery trip.

Not less than thirty seconds later, there's a knock at my door.

I sigh, letting the refrigerator slowly close in front of me before trudging over and dragging open the door, not bothering to check to see who it is, considering Mac's been out there all day.

It is, indeed, Mac at the door, and he thrusts a cell phone in my face. I look up at him, confused.

"It's for you."

I arch a brow but take the phone from him, holding it up to my ear. "Uhm—hi?"

There's no hello, no greeting, just a familiar, irritatingly deep voice cutting through the other end.

"Answer when I call you."

I glare down at the device and then up at Mac, who gives me a knowing look. "I don't have your number, how was I supposed to know it was you?" I move away from the door, leaving it open for Mac while wandering slowly back to the kitchen.

There's silence on the other end. *Haha, got you there, tough guy.*

That look of amusement is back on Mac's face as he makes himself at home on my couch while waiting to get his phone back.

"Did you need something, darling?" I say sweetly, into the phone.

"We're going out. I'll be by to pick you up in an hour. Be ready to go."

"Where are we going?" I ask, bypassing the urge to hang up the phone on him, or give him a piece of my mind about locking me inside my apartment all day. *And how the hell did he get my phone number?*

"Out."

I roll my eyes. "Clearly. But I need to know what to wear to said *outing.*"

"To a club." He pauses before continuing, disdain dripping from his tone now, "One of your little *stripper outfits* would probably do nicely."

My cheeks heat with the judgement I hear in his tone. "One hour. Save this number to your phone." And he's gone.

I'm tempted to throw the device before remembering it's not mine. Straightening my shoulders, I waltz calmly over to Mac, who's still watching with interest from my couch. "Your *boss* will be here in an hour." I hand the phone back to him without bothering to jot down the number. Koen can go fuck himself.

The living room is a mess, but the couch still faces the television, so I slide the remote over to Mac. "You can wait in here if you want."

"Thanks." He takes the remote, turning the TV on, and settling in after he finds a hockey game to watch.

Pretending the sight of a mafia guard stretched out on my tiny sofa is normal, I retreat into my bedroom, closing the door. Once inside, I take a few minutes to regroup before turning to face my dresser.

What does one wear as the newly minted property of a mob boss?

The selection is admittedly lacking. These days, I practically live in dance clothes. The Conservatory has a strict dress code for dancers, so—while I own plenty of black and pink leotards and tights—aside from a handful of shorts, sweats, and sports bras, there isn't much else...

I have a couple of outfits I wear to bartend—tight jeans, corset tops—but somehow I don't think that's what Koen's looking for.

My gaze slides to my bed, it's unmade, a mess of tangled-up blankets, and it takes everything in me not to climb inside and hide from the rest of the world.

I'm in way over my head, and I know it.

There's no room for mistakes. The same rules as Wonderland applies: I need to keep my head down, mouth shut, and eyes open.

And maybe I'll survive this.

I hear the apartment's front door open. *Did I forget to lock it?*

Quickly, I pop my head out to check.

Koen stands there. His eyes travel between me in my bedroom doorway and Mac on the couch.

"You're supposed to be watching the door," Koen growls at Mac, and I'm instantly defensive of my new... guard? Lookout? I don't know...

"He's fine where he is."

Koen's gaze ticks slowly back over to me, and I fight the urge to swallow the growing lump in my throat. Picking his battles, he decides to let this one go in favor of my outfit.

"You're not ready."

I follow his gaze down to my own body. "What? Yes I am."

"You're not wearing that."

"What's wrong with this?"

"I think she looks great," Mac adds, unsolicited, and Koen's glare is sharp enough to cut. Though, Mac's answering smile shows he's undeterred. I get the feeling Mac loves to bust Koen's chops and it makes me smile. I think he and I are going to get along just fine.

"No," he says, like that's just the end of the discussion.

I put my hands on my hips, narrowing my eyes at him. "You said to wear one of my little 'stripper outfits,' remember? Well, here it is!" My hands travel the length of me, showcasing myself for him.

His face doesn't change; cool ambivalence stares back at me.

"Put this on." He hands over a black garment bag I hadn't noticed he was holding.

He bought me an outfit?

"No." There's really no need to be a pain in the ass, but I'm still mad about being locked inside all day and this is where I'm choosing to draw the line.

"Briar Rose," Koen warns, but I'm shaking my head and crossing my arms over my chest.

"No. I'm not wearing whatever that is," I argue, gesturing to the bag. I haven't set eyes on it yet but... No. Fuck that, and fuck him, too.

"Mac, could you give us a moment please?" I feel myself pale. Koen's eyes don't leave mine as I watch Mac leave. I have an overwhelming urge to go with him. Still, I hold my ground when the Irish King closes the space between us. My entire body going tense.

"You're mad."

I blink at him. Of all the things I thought he was going to say, *that* was not one of them.

"Yes," I bite out, eyeing him uneasily, unsure exactly how far I can push him before he snaps. "I missed my studio time this afternoon because *you* ordered me locked inside my apartment all day."

He stares down at me, an unreadable expression on his face, but I make sure to hold eye contact. If I let him walk all over me now, there's no telling where I'll be in three weeks.

"When do you have to be at the studio?"

"Monday through Friday it varies, but usually I'm there all day, starting early. The weekends, I book extra studio time if I can get it."

"Fine. Send me the full schedule and I'll make the arrangements."

I just stare at him, anger still thrumming in my veins, I still want to fight despite getting what I wanted.

He tries handing me the garment bag again. This time without a word.

I let it hang between us, chewing my bottom lip before reaching out to grab it with a roll of my eyes.

"Fine."

42

THE SOVEREIGN

KOEN

Now

Briar's been quiet the whole drive.

She's wearing the dress—the one I bought her. And it's a good thing I did. The outfit she'd come up with—a cut off band t-shirt, shorts, and black fishnet tights—while I enjoyed it, clothes like that won't cut it at the club we're going to.

The Sovereign is exclusive, catering only to the rich and powerful. And seeing as how she's mine, I need her to look the part.

The black silk clings to her the way I knew it would. Simple, expensive, and tight—and short enough that it might as well be lingerie. The sight of her in it, knowing that I bought it for her... it's all I can do not to drag her back into her bedroom and rip it off.

But we have places to be.

Briar fidgets in her seat, pressed up so close against the door

272

that I'm glad I engaged the child-lock, because even if she doesn't try to run again, she might just fall out.

She's staring out the window. Her hands play anxiously along the hemline of her skirt, which is so indecently high, I think I might have an aneurysm if it creeps any further.

It's what I wanted, I bought the fucking dress, but the thought of anyone else seeing her in it has me seeing red.

I should check on her, see if she's okay, but every time I go to open my mouth, I can't make the words come out. So instead, we sit in silence as I try, and fail, to keep my eyes off of her.

When we pull up to the club, Briar shifts in her seat, shooting anxious glances my way with nervous flicks of her eyes.

"What?" I clip out, looking up from my phone after I feel her gaze on me a third time.

"What's the plan again?" she asks nervously.

"You do everything I say."

"Oh, of course, how could I forget?" She rolls her eyes. "Excellent plan, *boss*."

I clench my fist to keep from wrapping it around her throat.

I slide my phone away, turning so that I'm facing her. I don't miss how she swallows, her throat bobbing as she meets my gaze.

"This club is known for—" I pause, carefully choosing my words. "Trading," I say finally.

"In girls?" she asks, her expression borderline horrified.

One look gives her her answer.

"Oh."

"While we are in there, you're going to act like you are

273

mine. You know, just like you do for all those guys back at Wonderland every night." She works for Giovanni. I know Wonderland's reputation, what his girls are known for doing in those back rooms of his. This should be right up her alley.

Her eyes darken. It's a low blow, but I can't resist. If she can do it for them, she can do it for me, too.

"You just have to pretend like you want me; it's really not that hard."

"Says you," she mumbles. "And what are you doing in there?"

"I have business to attend to. Your job is to look at faces. I want to know if anyone in there looks familiar to you from that night in Wonderland." Before we left her apartment, I made her fill me in on the circumstances that got her sent to that warehouse.

"Got it?"

I look back at her, annoyed to find she's not looking at me. Her eyes are on the club, a far-off look in them as she chews on her thumbnail.

"Briar."

The sharpness in which I say her name elicits a little flinch, pulling her out of whatever memory or imagined scenario she'd been lost in.

"I got it."

This girl has got me so distracted I almost forget to give her the chain. I reach under my collar to unfasten the twisted silver chain from around my neck. I rub my thumb over the little charm, a Celtic trinity knot, before holding it out to her.

"Here."

Briar turns slowly to face me, eyeing the chain before looking back at me.

"What is it?"

She still hasn't taken it.

"Just put it on, will ye?"

She eyes the twisted silver chain in my hand like it's poison.

"Why?"

My fingers tighten around the chain and I grab her hand, depositing the necklace directly into it before closing her fingers around it. "Because I told you to, that's why."

I bring my fist back to my side before it tightens again, and I force myself to look out the window so I don't wrap the damn thing around her neck myself.

I catch Liam's smirk in the rear view mirror and notice how he and Mac exchange amused glances. I glare at the both of them. I'm relieved to find Briar fastening the chain around her neck out of the corner of my eye.

"Can't just answer a simple question..." she mutters, keeping her gaze steady out the window.

I breathe in deep, not entirely conscious of the decision to answer her before I do.

"It's mine. If you're wearing it, everyone will know who you belong to." I look over to find her staring at me. "No one will touch you."

She releases a shaky breath and dips her chin, and I relax back against the seat, considering the matter done with.

"Never take it off," I add, right before Liam pulls up to the door, and the valet steps forward to take the keys. I step out, buttoning my suit jacket before walking around the SUV to let Briar out.

As I open the door for her, the look on her face tells me she tried and failed to open it herself, and she sure as hell knows why. It's work to hide the smirk on my face when I offer her my hand.

She thinks about refusing, but when my gaze hardens, she sighs, reluctantly placing her palm in mine, yanking it away the second her feet are on the pavement. I give her a look but allow it, placing my hand on the small of her back instead, to guide her the rest of the way to the door.

When we reach the main floor, Briar visibly stiffens and I feel a slight tremble ripple through her body, not missing when she inches closer to me. The first floor of The Sovereign is just a strip club: tables, stages, a bar. As we weave our way through to the back, I don't miss the attention Briar attracts... how men lean back in their seats as she passes to steal an extra look at her ass.

My jaw tightens when I catch her lagging behind. Reaching out, I snatch hold of her hand and pull her in close. Her body is stiff in my grip while I lead her toward the elevator.

"Relax," I hiss into her ear as we wait for the doors to open. She's going to blow this whole thing with how tense she is. Her reaction is odd—doesn't she do this every night? At least here, she won't have to take her clothes off.

Eyes follow us through the club. First, looking to me, then taking an interest in her. I make sure my hand stays on her at all times, keeping her close. Liam trails closely behind.

The host brings us to the table, the men I'm looking to meet are already waiting. I slide into the booth, setting Briar down on my knee, my hand moving to her lower abdomen to steady her.

The eyes of all three men flash with interest at the sight of the girl I've got with me.

"I didn't know you were bringing company?" Filip smiles,

leaning in while licking his lips. He gives her an appreciative once-over, and my fingers tighten on Briar's side when I feel her stiffen.

The way he's looking at her makes me want to reach for my knife and gouge his eyes out but instead, I lean back in my seat, forcing my expression to stay lazy, indifferent.

The waitress automatically places a glass of whiskey in front of me. My hand grips it but I don't take a drink, wanting to keep my wits sharp tonight. "Thought we were here to talk shipments," I say, redirecting the conversation.

Dominick speaks up, nodding to my brother seated on my right. "Liam here said you wanted to meet to discuss changing up the routes." The Polish mafia may be small, but they do control several key ports and ships along the East Coast.

"Aye. We've encountered a few snags in operations over the past few weeks. I may be looking to expand my horizons, test out some new waters."

"That so?" Dominick's eyes gleam with interest. He's got a terrible poker face.

"She really is exquisite." Filip hasn't taken his eyes off Briar, and he's staring at her chest. "Where'd you get one like that?"

My mouth pinches, irritation growing at his continued interest in the girl on my lap.

"Giovanni," I clip out and watch their brows rise.

"Fuck." Filip smiles, looking away from Briar, and finally to his boss. "I might have to change my mind about attending that auction next month."

"I didn't know the Irish were involved in all that," Aleksander, the oldest of the three, says, speaking for the first time.

"Like I said," I say smoothly, slowly tracing a finger up and down Briar's side. A wave of delight goes through me when she shivers. "We're looking to try new things." My gaze moves back to Dominick. "The trade routes?"

The business talk circles, we go back and forth on various ports and shipments we need to land. Liam wants reassurance that the Polish still have no deals with the Russians.

"You'd sooner see me dead than striking a deal with a fucking kacap!" Dominick hisses angrily, snatching his glass off of the table and draining what's left in it.

I believe him.

"Heard your brother snatched the Bratva's little angel right out from under Kostalov's nose," Aleksander says casually, swirling his glass but keeping a keen eye on me.

My jaw tightens.

Filip laughs at that. "I wouldn't want to be her. Ace ain't known for his soft side," he says, winking at me. "Word is he's making their little angel pay for what her family did." He lifts his glass to me. "My condolences on your father by the way." I grit my teeth but he continues, "I admit, I'm jealous. You can't buy premium virgin ass like that on the street, that's for sure. She must've been fun to break." His eyes slide back over to Briar, who's trembling now on my knee. "The Irish do seem to have good taste when it comes to their pets."

Every muscle in my body goes tight, and I feel Liam shift beside me. He looks my way and I give him a small, nearly imperceptible shake of my head. Liam looks pissed but he stays seated, though I'm certain, like me, he's resisting the urge to launch across the table at Filip for the way he's talking about Rory.

My brother didn't *take* the Bratva Princess; he *saved* her. Married her to keep her safe from the arranged marriage her father had set up with the monster that was Matteo Carozza. Another *problem* we'd seen to.

I don't correct them. If we're to get into the upcoming auction, rumors like that can only help us.

Liam clears his throat, wrangling the discussion back to the matter at hand, and finalizing the deal for an upcoming shipment we have coming in from down south.

Briar hasn't moved in minutes. She sits atop my lap, stone still, back rigid. To anyone watching, she appears to be the perfect accessory: poised, pretty, and obedient. But I can feel the truth in every tiny tremor that runs through her. The way I can feel her heart racing when my hand circles her wrist, wanting to feel her pulse.

I lean in, letting my mouth brush against her ear, low enough so that only she can hear me.

"Go to the bathroom," I murmur.

She tenses, nearly jumping at the sound of my voice, too caught up in the conversations playing out around her. My thumb moves in small circles on the outside of her thigh.

"Take a breath," I say, trying to reassure her, and wait until I see her inhale deeply.

"Good. Now go, take a lap, freshen up, and remember why you're here." My hand finds her chin, turning her face to mine, silently reminding her of her mission—*to see if she recognizes anyone from that night in Wonderland.*

I sit back, my expression bored and unreadable. It takes her a second, but she slowly rises. Keeping her head down as she makes her way through the crowd, though I catch her eyes darting up, taking in faces. I keep my eyes on her until she disappears into the bathroom.

"Well-trained," Filip compliments, and I grab hold of my glass, pulling it closer so I don't bury my fist into his throat.

43

PANIC

BRIAR

Now

My heart hammers in my chest, a frantic rhythm that refuses regulation.

The scent of perfume, sweat, alcohol, and... sex hangs heavy in the air. My breaths are shallow, the air feels hot, the room... too small.

Men watch me as I pass; their gazes leave me feeling gross, violated by their eyes alone.

The club is similar to Wonderland, but *worse*. It's high class, and most of the men have on designer suits, Cartier watches—the whole place is dripping in arrogance and privilege.

There are poles, and women dancing, and I walk by several couples openly having sex. When I pass a girl on her knees, a collar wrapped around her neck, and the man she's animatedly sucking off holding the chain connected to it, I quicken my steps.

Briar, you idiot. What have you gotten yourself into?

My heart rate grows more erratic, my breaths coming in shallow and uneven.

Fuck. Not here. Not now. Please don't let it hit me here.

A panic attack. I've gotten them on and off since high school. The prize you get in exchange for the pressure of being an overachiever. I'm supposed to be taking anti-anxiety meds but I can't afford them. Instead, I resort to raw-dogging my anxiety, holding it at bay by sheer force of will and luck.

I glance back, connecting with Koen's gaze as he follows my path to the bathroom. There's no softness in his eyes, just that familiar hard edge and overwhelming intensity.

I swallow, spotting the women's restroom and darting into it.

Once inside, my hands grip the countertop. I turn on the water, letting it run, but don't touch it. I stare at the water pouring out of the faucet, watching it swirl around the drain before disappearing. I take a shaky breath before counting in my head, *One, two, three, four....* I focus on the sound of the water; it drowns out the sultry, sexy beat of whatever it is the DJ's playing outside. I keep counting in my head, *five, six, seven, eight...* Trying to ground myself.

"Hey, are you okay?"

I jump at the voice behind me, having not realized I wasn't alone. Whirling around, I find two girls talking further down the counter. The one who spoke to me is leaning up against the far wall, the other is bent over the countertop, her face close to the mirror as she applies a fresh coat of lipstick to her lips.

"You look tense," the girl applying lipstick says, assessing me through a side-eye as she continues with her task.

I swallow, trying to stay calm. The spike in heart rate at discovering them almost undoes all my efforts to calm it down.

"First time here?" one of them asks, tilting her head as she inspects me.

I nod, unsure of what to say.

They're both dressed like me, in tight dresses and expensive heels. The first one—the blonde—smiles. It's meant to be friendly, but her eyes stay sharp. "I'm Tara. This is Margot." She gestures to the redhead who's now wiping streaks of mascara I hadn't noticed were running down both cheeks.

Tara releases a dark chuckle at my confirmation. " The first time is always... a lot." She smirks, looking at her friend through the mirror's reflection. "You remember your first time, Margot?"

Margot huffs a laugh, straightening up. They're both far taller than me in their heels. Tall and thin, like models. "Do I ever." She rolls her eyes. "It gets easier, sweetheart, I promise." She shoots me a jaded smile.

Tara pushes off the wall. "I know something that will help. Give me two minutes." She gives my shoulder a reassuring shake as she passes me, exiting the bathroom.

Margot and I stare at each other for a minute.

"Do you want to touch up anything?" she asks, pointing to her open make-up bag on the counter.

I shake my head. "Oh, no thanks. I think I'm... good." The last part feels like a lie. *Am I good?*

Filip, one of the Polish guys Koen and Liam are meeting with, hasn't stopped leering at me all night. Koen's been ignoring his comments, but I'm terrified of what he'll say if

Filip proposes a trade. *Would he trade me?* If it furthered his own agenda—I think he might. He'd warned me in the car about the *trading,* but I hadn't thought he meant *I* was on the table. Now I don't know what to think.

And what the men had said about his brother Aidan... Koen had made it seem like their entire family is against this sort of thing, but what they said he's been doing to that girl...

My stomach flips and I rush to the sink. Flipping back on the water, I splash some of it on my face this time.

My head snaps up at the sound of the bathroom door opening, finding relief when Tara slips back in, shouldering the door open, three double-shots of a clear liquid in her hands.

Margot brightens, dropping her eyeliner pen, her heels clicking against the marble tiles as she scurries over to us. "Ooh, gimme, gimme!"

Tara smiles, carefully handing her the glass on her right before offering the one in the middle to me.

I hold up my hands. "Oh, I probably shouldn't—"

Tara hushes me, her hand snapping out and grabbing hold of mine, pushing the glass into it. My fingers close around it so it doesn't drop to the floor when she lets go. "Trust me, it'll calm your nerves." She holds up her own glass. "One shot. Helps take the edge off." She smirks at me before exchanging a look with Margot standing next to me.

"You'll feel better in a minute." Margot nods, pinching her nose closed before downing her own shot. Screwing up her face, she gives Tara a little glare. "Ugh, vodka? Tara, really?"

Tara just shrugs, downing her own shot in one go.

I feel both of their eyes on me—the shot of vodka still in my hand. My heart is still beating wildly out of control, and the hand holding the glass shakes a little as a result.

Staring down at the glass, I weigh the pros and cons. I mean... it can't hurt, maybe it'll help keep me from slipping into a full scale panic attack, which is probably the last thing I need to happen right now. If I fall apart now, Koen might get annoyed enough and just leave me here in a huddled ball for the vultures to pick on.

"What was your name again?" Margot asks, but I haven't told them yet.

"Briar," I say.

"Bottoms up, Briar!" she hollers, shaking my shoulders a little in her excitement.

"What the hell," I say, giving in, lifting the shot and downing it. I wince at the sharp burn when the alcohol hits my throat.

"Your night is about to get a whole lot better." Tara grins.

44

I DON'T SHARE

KOEN

Now

There's something off about Briar. She's moving through the crowd, on her way back to me. I watch her the whole way. I can't quite put a finger on it, but something doesn't feel right.

She reaches the table and stumbles back as every head looks her way, and she pales under the attention.

Filip leans back in his chair, rubbing the upper part of his thigh and smiling at her. "Welcome back, beautiful. I got a seat for you right here."

My hand lashes out, wrapping around Briar's wrist and tugging her down onto me.

"Whoa," she breathes, her eyes going subtly out of focus while her body sways slightly on my lap.

My brow caves in, concern weighing heavily, but Filip's grating tone drags my attention up.

"Alright Irish, consider me interested. What do you want for her?"

Briar inhales sharply, her body freezes, and it feels as if she's holding her breath as she awaits my response.

My gaze turns lethal when I meet Filip's eye. "I don't share."

Liam sits up straighter in his seat when he hears my tone. Aleksander shoots a worried look over to Dominick, who tries catching Filip's attention. But his *attention* is fixed on the girl sitting in my lap.

"Come on Irish, don't be like that." He leans forward, his hands folded in front of him but traveling dangerously close to Briar. "Everything has a price."

My hand travels up Briar's waist, closing around her middle and dragging her into me until her back is pressed up against my chest. Keeping my eyes on Filip's growing scowl, I lean down. My lips graze lightly against the soft skin of her neck as I kiss it, feeling her shiver.

Briar's breathing is strangled but she doesn't stop me. When I reach her jawline, I grab hold of her chin, my touch firm—possessive—tilting her head back toward me.

I catch a glimpse of her face, eyes wide, pupils dilated, surprise flickering in them as I lean in, pressing my mouth to hers. My hands grip her chin, holding her in place. The kiss isn't sweet or soft, and my hand drops to wrap around her throat as I claim even more. At first I'm met with resistance, the little whimper that escapes her makes my dick twitch.

I keep one eye on Filip the whole while, enjoying the way his expression sours as he watches. I keep going just long enough until I'm sure I've hammered in my point. I release

Briar, sitting back in my chair with a dangerous smirk on my face.

"Not this."

Filip doesn't ask me to trade again. He excuses himself from our table not long after my little possessive display.

We're just about finished, finalizing the last few terms for our new trade agreement. Aleksander and Liam go over details at the end of the table. Across from me, Dominick is busy with a girl he's summoned over, so my attention zeroes in on the dark-haired little rose I have seated in my lap.

I spin her around, one of her legs to each side of me.

My hand goes to the back of her head, guiding her face to my neck.

"Kiss it," I order.

Briar hesitates, her breath warming my skin as her mouth hovers just above.

The hand I have on her outer thigh tightens, reminding her of my command, and she closes the distance, landing a tentative kiss on the side of my neck.

I let out a breath as she continues to move slowly up. When her ear nears my mouth, I ask my question.

"Did you recognize anyone?"

She freezes, and my hand flies again to the back of her head, keeping her pressed to me as she starts to pull away. "Don't," I say, keeping my voice low. "Whisper it to me in my ear." No one's watching us, and we've done a good job blending in so far, but I'm not willing to take any chances.

"Yes," she breathes into my ear, the sound igniting every nerve in my body.

"Who?" My hand moves to stroke her hair.

She swallows, chewing her lip nervously. "By the bar."

My eyes shift up.

"Older, dark suit, red tie," she mumbles into my ear, speaking slowly, her words slightly slurring together. "The one that's balding, with the sneer on his face..."

I scan the crowded bar ahead of us, freezing on the man she's described.

"Him?" I ask. Needing confirmation, I lift my chin in his direction and watch as she tracks my gaze. I clench my jaw when she dips her chin nervously.

Fuck. Justice Thompson. Suddenly Giovanni's obsession with Briar makes a lot more sense. The information in her head could be key to bringing down the network.

I'm so busy thinking about the possible implications that I don't notice Briar slumping forward. Her forehead falls into my shoulder, and her body goes lax in my arms.

"Hey," I try pulling her back, my voice sharpening, especially when I see her eyes are closed—she looks like she's falling asleep. "Briar. Look at me."

She does, but her gaze is unfocused. Her pupils blown wide, her eyes glassy in a way that has my blood pressure rising. I check the table. I ordered her a drink when we first arrived but she's barely touched it. Sure enough, it's still nearly full, ice melting just in front of us.

"Koen?" Briar says my name, instantly earning my full

attention. She sways on my lap, her lids heavy. "I—I don't feel so good."

That little voice inside needles me again. Something isn't right, she's acting like she's wasted, yet she's hardly had anything to drink. She's been with me the whole time except for—

I grip her chin, bringing her head back up to face me. The sudden movement catches her by surprise, and I'm faced with wide blue eyes staring back. Her pupils are blown wide now, there's no mistaking it.

"What did you take?" I demand, my tone sharpening.

She blinks slowly at me. Confusion etching her delicate features.

"When you went to the bathroom, what did you take?" I ask again, growing more annoyed. I hadn't thought of it before but, fuck, that would explain how she ended up indebted to Gio—her apparent money problems. I reach for her purse, lying abandoned next to us on the booth, peering in quickly but not finding any evidence of drugs.

Briar's eyes soften, and start to close again.

I shake her roughly. She needs to stay awake until I can figure out what the fuck she's on.

"Not nice," she grumbles, her bottom lip poking out.

"Briar." I have to say her name twice to get her attention, asking her again, "Briar, what did you take?"

She doesn't respond and I glare down at her, my voice growing more commanding, "Tell me what you took."

"Nothing," she mumbles out. She falls forward again, trying to rest her head on my shoulder, but I shake her again.

She scowls back at me this time. "Stop it."

"Don't lie," I bite out, my voice full of venom. I have no patience for drug addicts or liars.

"I'm not." For a second, her eyes clear, her focus sharpening with her growing irritation. "I didn't take anything! I'm not a drug addict."

I scoff and she glares at me.

I grab hold of her chin and lean in. "Tell me what happened in the bathroom." I enunciate each syllable in an effort to keep my control from snapping.

"That's private. No boys allowed." Her words slur again and she smiles to herself.

"Briar." I say her name, sharply enough to get her to finally open her mouth, and she rambles over her journey to the bathroom, the girl on her knees—and the collar—but when she gets to the part about taking a shot in the bathroom, I stop her.

"What shot?"

She shrugs. "Tara gave it to me."

"Who the fuck is Tara?" I growl, losing my patience. By this point, Liam's joined me, looking at Briar with concern in his eyes.

"They said I was too tense and I needed to loosen up. It was vodka, I think." Her nose scrunches up in a way that would be adorable under any other circumstance. "I hate vodka."

I study her. One shot wouldn't do this. Briar's acting like she's at least ten shots deep.

My head lifts and I scan the crowd, spotting a pair of girls only a few yards away, watching us.

"Hold on to her." I stand, sliding Briar off of my lap and into Liam's next to me, before storming across the room.

"What the fuck did you give her?"

"What?" The girl blinks up, and I see a flicker of fear in her eyes before she masks it with faux innocence. "I don't—"

"What's your name?" I ask, cornering her up against a nearby table.

"I—" She looks to her friend for help, but the girl she was standing with has already made herself scarce. Her face turns slowly back to me and she gives me a nervous smile, brushing her hand up against my arm in a sorry attempt to flirt with me.

I reach up, grab her hand, and remove it from my bicep, glaring at her. "Don't make me ask you again..." I warn.

She swallows, her eyes darting between me and Briar at the table behind me.

"Tara," she finally admits, and my eyes darken.

"Listen up, *Tara*, you're going to tell me exactly what you gave my girl over there, or you're going to find out what it feels like to pray for mercy and not get any."

"It was just a little shot. She needed to loosen up."

"Do you think I'm a fucking idiot, Tara?"

"N-no, no," she stutters out, shrinking back as far as she can into the table at her back.

"What did you give her?"

"Just a little liquid X!" Tara rushes out. "She'll be fine!"

Fucking Christ. GHB. I turn to check on Briar, who is teetering dangerously on the edge of Liam's lap. He's doing his best to keep her upright, while also trying to touch her as little as possible.

My gaze falls back on *Tara*. "If anything happens to that girl... and I mean *anything.*" She gulps. "I will be back here, and I will make sure I do ten times worse to you."

She pales, her eyes flicking between me and Briar as if to measure just how bad off she is.

Without another word I release her, stalking back over to our table and hauling Briar up onto her feet.

"Hey!" she protests, swaying precariously on her heels.

"Time to go."

Briar goes to take a step toward the elevator and stumbles. I catch her, wrapping my arm around her waist to keep her from falling. We go a few more feet like this before my frustration wins out and I pick her up.

She watches me, surprise on her face as I carry her out of the club. She makes it as far as the elevator before her head falls down on my shoulder, her eyes fluttering as she tries to stay awake.

No one in the club even bats an eye at the clearly inebriated girl in my arms.

"So pretty."

"Who?"

"You." She smiles and reaches up, her fingertips touching my cheek. "Such a pretty boy."

Pretty? I frown. I'm not sure how I feel about that.

"Mhm." She half-laughs at the frown on my face, as if she can read my thoughts.

"What did you eat today?" How much she has in her stomach might affect how long the drug will affect her.

"Donuts," she replies, and I grind my teeth.

"I know that. What did you eat after?"

She shakes her head. "Just donuts."

Christ Almighty. She hasn't eaten since breakfast?

"Why didn't you eat?" I ask, frustrated.

Briar shrugs. "I forgot."

Forgot to eat? I have nothing to say so I just shake my head, staring out the window and letting silence fall over us.

After a little while, I feel her fingers graze my chin. I look back down. She's looking up at me, her eyes glassy, studying me.

"You haunt me."

Her fingers move higher and I don't stop them, allowing her fingertips to trace lightly along my jawline and trying to ignore just how *good* it feels. "Your hair, your eyes..." Her fingers move back down to my mouth. "She got your smile too. It's not fair." Briar's brow furrows and she scowls. "It's not fair that the best part of *me*, looks like *you*."

"What the hell are you talking about?" She's not making any sense. Briar continues on as if she hasn't heard me, her eyes distant, lost to her thoughts.

"These eyes. Can't get away from these eyes."

I stare at her, as she searches mine. I want to tell her she's haunted me too, but I don't. Instead, I say nothing.

She sits up, and I watch her eyes drop to my mouth. She leans in but at the last second, I pull back—away from her. She's messed up in the head, drugged, not aware of what she's doing.

"Sorry. Not interested."

For a second, something flickers in her eyes—hurt, maybe —but it's gone before I can be sure.

She sinks back against the seat, quiet now, her hand slipping away from my face.

For a while, she drifts, half-asleep, drifting in and out of consciousness. I keep an eye on her breathing, counting her respirations, ensuring her chest continues to rise and fall.

The SUV comes to a stop and she's out cold. I circle around, opening her door and scooping her up and into my arms once again. She doesn't wake, even as I carry her up to the apartment, trying not to focus on the way she nuzzles her cheek into my chest.

As gently as I can, I lay her down on the bed. And for a moment, I just stand there, taking her in. She looks almost peaceful like this, sharp edges gone, the defiance she wears on her face whenever she looks at me is muted. Her lips are parted as she inhales in and out, soft and pink against the soft gold of her skin.

She's beautiful.

Too fucking beautiful.

A strand of dark hair lies across her face and I brush it back with the backs of my knuckles, barely skimming the soft skin of her cheek.

Briar's lashes flutter, her eyes open—a startling blue, even in the dim light. They lock onto me and sharpen, dark and burning.

"I hate you."

The corner of my mouth ticks up, the ghost of a smile on my face when I reply, "I hate you too, love."

45

A ONE NIGHT STAND ISN'T A FAIRY TALE

BRIAR

Then...

The orange glow of the early morning sunrise wakes me, and I stretch out beneath soft sheets, my muscles and body sore in the best way. Movement from the other side of the bed draws my attention and when I look over, I find Rí.

He's already up, sitting on the edge of the bed, jeans on, chest bare. The skull tattoo that stretches across his entire back is on full display, his muscles tense underneath, like he's gearing up for a fight instead of a conversation.

"Hey," I say, clearing my throat. My voice gravelly from having just woken up. "What time is it?"

He doesn't answer.

Instead, he rises off the bed, turning to face me. Instinctively, I pull the sheets up higher, tightening them around me. I'm naked underneath. The guy glaring at me from the other side of the bed is almost unrecognizable. Gone is the hot, dangerously sexy man from last night. And in his place stands someone colder, harder, *dangerous*. It rolls off him in waves, and I'm reminded of my first impression of him back at the club.

The danger emanating from him is not the kind of danger you flirt with, but the kind *you run from*.

"Get out."

At first, I just blink at him, confusion clouding my still muddy morning thoughts. "What?" I let out an awkward laugh, thinking this has to be a joke.

His eyes slide to meet mine, and they're full of disdain. Cold, dead, heartless. "I said get out."

The laughter dies in my throat and I clutch the blankets a little tighter. "You're serious?"

"You got what you wanted. So did I. It's over." He shrugs in a way that's anything but casual, moving to lean against the door frame, crossing his arms and watching me—*waiting*.

"Wow," I scoff, shoving the sheets from my body, and I notice that he averts his eyes. "You don't waste any time, do you?"

His jaw ticks and he shifts slightly, his gaze on the ceiling, as I pick up my shirt off the hardwood floor, pulling it over my head. "Don't make this into something it's not. It was a one-night stand, not a goddamn fairy tale."

"No," I huff, dragging on my skirt as fast as I can without falling over, hands shaking. "And you're not a *King*, you're just another asshole."

I spot my bag on top of his dresser and scoop it up, fishing through it for my phone while storming for the door. *I'll call a cab or ride-share or something once I'm outside.* I move fast, needing to be anywhere but here immediately.

"I'll have my driver give you a ride home."

A driver? *Who the fuck is this guy?* "Don't bother," I snap, trying to dart past him to get out of his room, but he catches me. His hand wraps around my arm like a vice, bringing me to a quick halt.

Anger boils over and I spin to face him, tilting my chin so I'm glaring at his face. "You've got a lot of nerve, you know that?" I rip my arm out of his grasp, unable to stand it. His touch burns against my skin. He lets me go, peering down at me with cold, dead eyes.

"Take the ride, Rose." His words, like his eyes, are cold and measured.

I don't know why I flinch at the sound of the fake name on his lips, but I do. "I don't need your help. I can find my own way home."

Again I try to squeeze around him, but he shifts, not grabbing me again, but blocking my path with his body. He doesn't say anything else, just stares down at me with a glare that could set me on fire.

"Are you always this controlling?" I snap, without thinking.

"Are you always this impossible?" he bites back. His eyes flare with molten flames before he seems to catch himself, and like flipping a switch, they're cold again.

I let out a slow breath and regroup, straightening my spine and realizing I don't have a choice. "Fine," I seethe between my clenched teeth. "I'll take the goddamn ride. If you *insist*."

He stares at me for another breath before turning on his heel and disappearing down the hall. I chase after him, struggling to keep up with his long strides, almost crashing into his back when he comes to a sudden stop at the elevator.

Impatiently, he presses his index finger to the glass panel, and the elevator dings, the doors opening, and I practically charge through them.

He follows after me.

"You don't—" I start to tell him I don't need him to escort me down, but he's already pressing the button to close the door. Shutting us both into the tiny space that's made even smaller by my growing rage.

I move as far from him as possible, watching the numbers light up as we slowly make our way down. *This is Hell.* I steal a glance over at him and find him staring hard at the floor, hands in his pockets.

Yup. Hell, I'm in actual Hell.

I never realized how loud silence can be. It *screams* in the air between us, grating across my nerves like broken glass. I *feel* his eyes lift, the heat of his stare burning the side of my cheek... but I refuse to look up.

After what may very well be an eternity, the elevator dings, finally reaching the basement level. I'm through the doors before they're fully open, walking out to find a sleek black SUV waiting by the curb, and who I assume is Rí's driver standing outside of it.

I turn to look at Rí, one eyebrow raised, but his attention is on the driver. *Seriously, who the fuck is this guy?*

"Take Rose here home for me, Garrett?"

Garrett nods. "You got it, Rí." The driver steps forward, opening the rear passenger door for me, and while I'm momentarily caught off guard, I only waste another second before I dive into the back of the vehicle.

Looking back, I catch Rí watching me, arms across his

chest again, tense as he works his jaw. He says nothing when I meet his gaze, still watching me with that icy expression.

Just as Garrett goes to shut the door, I lean forward, holding my middle finger high, and flashing him my teeth until the door cuts off his view of me.

He doesn't move. Holding my stare through the mirrored glass as if he can still see me, and it's not until Garrett pulls the SUV away from the curb, that the connection is finally severed.

46

NOTHING HAPPENED

BRIAR

Now

My head is pounding. Like a hundred tiny ballerinas are simultaneously curb stomping my skull. Forcing my eyes open, I let out a groan when I'm assaulted by the bright sunlight streaming in. I shut them tight again, reaching for the blankets, pulling them up to cover my face.

The material is —soft? Plush even. My eyes fly open under the protection of the dark blanket, immediately hyperaware that I'm not at home. I'm not in *my* bed. My sheets are nowhere near this nice.

Panic surges and I brave the light, sitting up with a start. I regret it seconds later, when the sudden movement throws my head into the spins, my stomach rolling alongside it.

Shit. "Where am I?" The question is unnecessary because a half second later, I know exactly where I am. The room... familiar, his scent... *everywhere.*

"You're in my bed," a cool, dark, and overly familiar voice answers, and I close my eyes tight. The clipped tone triggering my memory.

His *rejection.*

"Right... okay." I swallow, opening my eyes and doing a sweep of the room until I find Koen. He's not in the bed. Instead, he's leaning up against the window alcove, holding a cup of coffee. Fully dressed, his eyes are locked on me.

An awkward silence falls over us and I move to get out of bed, freezing when I realize I'm not wearing my dress—just my panties, since I went braless last night.

"Nothing happened."

My eyes slowly rise to meet Koen's.

Oh, I know.

I remember.

He brought me back to his apartment.

He brought me back to his apartment... *Why?*

Koen didn't have much to say, tossing a pair of girls' sweats at me before handing me over to be Mac's problem for the day.

I don't linger. I get dressed quickly, so I can get a ride back to my apartment to change before heading to the Conservatory for showcase rehearsals.

Mac attempts to start a conversation, but after a few times of me shutting him down, we ride together in silence. I'm not in the best mental headspace. It turns out my memories from last night are patchy and my mood sours as I try to remember anything after we arrived at that club Koen brought me to, but there's only bits and pieces.

'Not interested,' however, plays on repeat in my head.

The fact that I make it through rehearsals without triggering Mr. Carr's radar is a goddamn miracle. But he's distracted today, we're in the theater and he's busy berating the techs in charge of lighting to pay too much attention to what's happening on stage.

I'm dehydrated. I can't seem to get enough water; no amount of it is quenching my thirst. And I'm tired. My muscles feel weird, slow, and my balance is off, my timing is off —*I'm off.*

They're playing with the lighting, and the constant on-and-off of the hot lights in my eyes has my brain pounding in time with the music. I fake a smile and get through it, but my mind is elsewhere.

Mr. Carr also reminds us about the benefit next week.

Shit. With everything going on, I'd almost forgotten.

"Mr. Carr?" I ask, slowly approaching him in the auditorium seats after rehearsals have wrapped for the day.

"Yes, Miss Ralston?" He doesn't look up, too busy scanning the half-crumpled documents he's holding in his hands.

"About the benefit?"

"Be there no later than seven thirty" he replies automatically, his eyes still on the papers.

"Right. I—uhm—I—"

His gaze snaps up, cool brown eyes locking on me. "Whatever it is, Miss Ralston, do spit it out. I'm busy." He holds up the papers in his hands with an air of annoyance.

"Sorry," I grimace. "I was just wondering if it was possible to get a ticket for a plus-one?"

"A plus-one?" he repeats, confused.

"Yes. For my—for my boyfriend." I say the last part while masking my wince. The benefit is a requirement for participating in the showcase. It's the Conservatory's biggest fundraiser of the year. The city's elite pay big money to throw a party and meet the premiere dancers. It's a tradition that's gone on for decades. The only reason I'm facing this embarrassment is that I'm certain Koen won't let me go, or if he does, he'll insist on accompanying me.

The event is a big deal and there will be security everywhere. Without a ticket there's no way he's getting in, and without him, there's no way I am either.

Mr. Carr turns up his nose in disgust at my mention of a *boyfriend*. "No, Miss Ralston. The dancers are not permitted to bring a plus-one. If your boyfriend would like to accompany you, he will have to buy a ticket."

Right. I was afraid of that. I try not to wince, my cheeks heating with embarrassment. "Okay, thank you." I spin on my heel, anxious to leave this conversation behind us.

With rehearsals over for the day, and given my current state, I should call it a day, go home, sleep whatever this is off, but me being me, I don't. Of course I don't. I stay. I push myself too far until sweat coats every inch of me and I struggle to catch my breath.

I'm in Studio C. It overlooks the street, and when I move by the window, I can see the dark SUV with its blacked out windows waiting outside.

I told Mac to stay outside, needing space from all things *Koen*, from this world I'd fallen down into, and he listened. I almost feel bad. He's been out there all day; it's late afternoon now.

My head hurts and I'm so tired. It's still early, but I need sleep and a shower, possibly in that order. I start my cool down routine.

"Bella."

I freeze at the sound of the voice at my back, my gaze snapping up to find Gio in the mirror. I twist quickly so I have him in front of me.

"You haven't been answering my messages."

My eyes drop for a fraction of a second to my dance bag by the door, where my phone's been all day.

"I've been busy."

He moves further into the studio, taking a look around but staying far away from the windows. At this angle, Mac won't be able to see him. "And were you too busy last night too?"

I frown, not answering since he seems to already know the answer.

"I hear from a very good source that you and Koen O'Rourke are getting on... well." He smirks. "You spent the night at his place last night." He sniffs. "I'm impressed. Until he saw *you*, he had no interest in taking a little pet."

I swallow. *He's watching me.*

Of course he's watching me. I've been so fixated on surviving Koen, I've almost forgotten to worry about Giovanni.

Sliding the towel down my face, I scowl at him. *Someone from the club, obviously.*

"I'm just doing what you asked," I say, like I'm *actually* in control of any of this.

He smiles, turning to casually inspect the studio while keeping up his conversation with me. "The Irish want in on my operation. I need to know I can trust them." He stops, giving me the full weight of his stare. "Have you seen any reason I should doubt them?"

"No," I say. The lie rolls easily off my tongue. Koen told me he wants to take down Giovanni's network. Telling Gio might get me out of Koen's hands faster than expected, but if there's a chance that what Koen told me is true... I need more time. I still don't know if I can trust him.

Gio frowns. That wasn't the answer he was looking for.

"Did you hear anything else that might be useful for me, Bella? He's had you for a couple of days now."

I shake my head, keeping the distance between us, moving in parallel with him around the studio. He stops, and I do too.

"Really, Bella?" His eyes narrow and I catch a glimpse of the real man inside. "You haven't heard *anything*?"

I shrug, playing dumb. "I don't think so."

Gio sighs, pulling out his phone. A second later, I hear mine vibrate in my bag.

"You might want to check that." I look at him, and his face is a cold mask, waiting for me.

Slowly, I walk over to my bag, drawing out my phone and unlocking it before navigating to the last incoming text message.

There's no text, only a photo, and I swear my heart stops upon opening it.

"I think you might find you know more than you realize," Giovanni hedges. His words feel like a bucket of ice water over my head but I can't pull my eyes away from the photo.

It's a picture of Remi. She has a big smile plastered across her face. She's running through a field I know all too well, sunlight reflecting off her blonde curls. She's wearing the new Breakers jersey Lily's parents got for her the day before yesterday. The one they sent me a photo of last night before I left with Koen.

"How did you get this?" I snarl, standing up and taking a few steps in his direction before thinking better of it. "You piece of shit." I clutch my phone tighter to keep from chucking it at him. "You sold me to the mafia as collateral. I'm doing what you asked! You leave her out of it."

He waives me off. "Ah Bella, always so dramatic. When you needed something, I was there for you, yes? Now I need something from you in return. I scratch your back, you scratch mine. Yeah?" I'm standing in the middle of the studio now and he circles me, his Italian loafers echoing across the empty space. "And I need information. And you—" he points at me, "—aren't providing any."

I stare at him

"He met with the Polish mafia last night. He and his brother."

"Which one?" Gio asks, interested in this.

"Liam," I say, glaring at him.

"Keep going."

"They were discussing shipments, ports, dates... I don't know—I blacked out last night. I don't remember much." I look up at him warily, not sure if he'll believe me.

He assesses me as if trying to detect a lie. His eyes slowly flick up and down the length of me, slow enough to make me shift uneasily.

"Get closer to him." His tone is hard. It's an order.

"I don't know if that's possible," I argue. "He doesn't trust me."

He comes closer and I straighten my body, tensing with his

incoming proximity. The smell of his cologne is overpowering and bile rises up in my throat as nausea creeps back in.

"Figure it out, Bella. You're a smart girl."

I grip my phone tighter.

"Good talk, sweetheart. I'll be in touch. Don't make me chase you next time," he warns one last time before he's gone, and I sink down slowly to the floor. Remi's smiling face still lighting up my phone.

I bury my face in my hands. Crying for the first time in days. *I miss her.* I miss Lily. This is all such a mess. Such a fucking mess.

I throw the phone. Thankfully it misses the studio mirrors and lands with a crack on its side. I can see the splinter of glass across the screen, the damage I've done.

What am I going to do?

47

COLLATERAL

BRIAR

Now

My phone buzzes and I reach for it quickly, relieved when I see Lily's name flashing on the Caller ID. We've been playing phone tag since the night after last, and I'm desperate to talk to her and hear Remi's voice after Gio's threats this afternoon.

I do a quick scan of the empty studio, even peering out into the darkened hallway before answering. Can't be too careful with Koen and his guys lurking about.

"Briar?" Lily's nervous voice comes through on the other end when I don't immediately say anything after accepting the call.

"Yeah, it's me," I breathe out once I'm sure I'm alone, pacing slowly around the studio with the phone pressed up against my ear.

"You alive?" Her tone is teasing, but I can detect an edge of concern.

"I'm surviving," I admit.

"I've been so worried. You didn't text me back, and when I couldn't reach you last night..."

"I know. I'm sorry."

"What's going on?" she asks, picking up on my tense tone.

"Are you alone?" I ask, not wanting Remi to overhear Lily's half of the conversation.

"For now..." Lily confirms. In a house with both of her parents, two brothers, and my daughter, that's got to be the best case scenario.

"He found me again."

"Who?" There's a pause before she continues,"Oh Shit! Koen?" She whispers his name, as if he can hear her on the other end.

"Yeah. He showed up at Wonderland."

"Holy shit."

"I know. I—I'm kind of stuck with him for now." I bite my lower lip.

"What does that mean?"

"I guess he and Gio had some sort of business arrangement," I start, deciding how much information to give her for her own safety. "Gio reneged on his end of the deal, and Koen —" My lips press tightly together. "He sort of took me as collateral."

A choking sound comes through the other side of the phone. "I'm sorry—He *what*? He *kidnapped* you?" she hisses.

"No!" I defend, until having to admit, "Yes? Maybe a little bit? It's a bit of a gray area..."

"Maybe a little bit?!" she squeaks. "Briar!"

"I'm fine." I attempt damage control, not wanting her to worry. "Just keep Remi safe. I'll—I'm handling it," I say, hoping I sound braver than I feel, considering I just had a mini-meltdown on the studio floor not too long ago. "The plan is still the plan. He's paying me," I say slowly. "By the end of this, I'll have the money I need for Remi's medication, and my debt to Giovanni will be settled."

"Koen is... paying you?" Lily's question is laced with horrified apprehension.

"Not for that!" I clap back, immediately realizing where her mind went.

"Well if not that... for *what* exactly?"

I check around the studio again, careful to keep my voice as low as possible. "He just wants me *with* him. To hold me over Gio's head, I think. And he's bringing me places—clubs. He wants to know if I recognize anyone from that night at Wonderland and the warehouse."

I don't tell her how Koen admitted he and his brothers are trying to take down the trafficking network I got swept up in. One, because I'm still not one hundred percent sure *I* believe him, and two, if it's true, and I tell her and he finds out, he might go after her.

There's a pause, and then her voice comes in softer, "Are you going to tell him?" And I know she's not talking about familiar faces.

I stop my pacing, turning to stare at myself in the mirror for a long second. The question has been at the forefront of my mind ever since I saw Koen that night. It's a question I'd shoved away for years, constantly reminding myself that the man I'd spent the night with, Rí—with his devilish charm and quiet smiles—wasn't real. He'd flipped the switch on me so quickly, he left my head spinning for days. The real Rí— Koen O'Rourke, is ruthless, all hard edges sharpened by near constant violence. The man wouldn't hesitate to kill me if it furthered his agenda.

But yet... he hasn't hurt me, even when he thought I was a threat and might expose his brother. And last night, he carried me home and put me to bed instead of taking advantage. He could have, I wouldn't have been able to stop him. The few flashes of memories I have, I remember how gentle his touch had been...

"I don't know," I admit. To her... myself... my voice barely audible.

"If you don't tell him, and he finds out about her—" Lily whispers anxiously into the phone.

"He's not going to," I say firmly. "I can't risk it. There's no telling how he'll react, what he'd do to me. What if he tries to take her?" My voice betrays my fear and I feel my hand shaking. I'm not mafia, but I know enough to know those families are insular as all hell. He's never going to marry me. Girls in families like his are nothing but currency. Like his brother's new wife, Rory, I think her name is. An object to be traded for one means or another. I can't let that happen to Remi. I have to keep her safe.

Koen can't be trusted.

"Just be careful," Lily breathes, her anxiety transferring through the phone and feeding mine.

I let out another sharp breath before diving in to what I really need her to know. "That reminds me," I pause, working through my words on how to say this right, "have you noticed anyone following you?"

There's a long silence on the other end, long enough I have to verify she's still there. "Lily?"

"No. Why?" I feel like I can see Lily peering through her curtains as we speak.

"Gio found you. He sent me a photo of Remi. She was wearing that jersey your parents got her."

"Oh my god."

"I don't think he'll do anything. I'm doing everything he wants, but—he knows where you are. I'm so sorry I dragged you into this." I press my forehead against the glass, shame burning through me. This is all my fault. I've put everyone I love in danger.

"It's not your fault, Briar."

I sigh. It is though. But she knows me too well. "Just stay close by your brothers, alright? Is Dash there?"

"Yeah," she agrees, and I breathe a little easier.

Lily's two older brothers are a force to be reckoned with. Growing up, my parents were always out of town, and instead of staying home with the hired au pair, I found myself spending more and more time with Lily's family until they'd all but adopted me as their own.

I spent far more time with her family than I ever did mine. My house was always clean, cold, and empty. But Lily's house was every bit the opposite. Her house was messy, loud, and pure chaos the majority of the time. Her parents made sure I knew I was always welcome. *Always. I loved it.*

Her two brothers, Dash and Sam, were pains in our asses growing up, ridiculously over-protective of their little sister, and by extension, her best friend. I can't prove it, but I'm almost certain the pair of them are the reason Lily and I stayed single all throughout high school. No one wanted to piss off the resident hockey gods of Lake Placid. *Especially* Dash. He was built like a tank, strong, dependable, good with guns, and he could fight.

Sam, too. While smaller than Dash, he had sharp instincts and noticed things others didn't. He was a brick wall, both on and off the ice. Dash was lucky enough to score a Division I scholarship at Northgate University right in our hometown, but both Dash and Sam were home for winter break.

"Ok good. He won't have to do anything if I just do what I'm supposed to do...bide my time with Koen, and keep my head down, and we all just might survive this."

I hope.

"Can I talk to Remi?" I ask, my voice thin.

"Of course," Lily breathes out, the heaviness of our conversation weighing on her. Guilt nags at me again for putting her through this. "Just give me one second, I think she's still outside with the boys."

There's a shuffle and the sound of Lily moving through the house, another shuffle, and then a sweet little voice fills the line, "Mommy?"

My entire body softens and tears prick at my eyes, and I lean back against the mirrored glass of the studio to keep myself upright. "Hi, sweetheart." I swallow hard, brightening my voice for her benefit. "How's Auntie Lily's? Are you having fun?"

"Yeah. Yeah. Mommy, guess what?"

"What?" I ask, smiling at the excitement in her voice.

"Uncle Dash taught me how to skate."

"He did, did he?"

"I'm a hockey player now!" she boasts, sounding so proud of herself. "I scored a goal on Uncle Sam! Can you believe it?"

I'm pretty sure it's Sam I hear in the background, shouting about how she just got lucky. I can't help but laugh.

"You did? That's amazing! I'm so proud of you!"

"Do they have hockey in Boston?"

I can already see where this is going. "I think they do." Looks like we might be trading in ballet slippers for ice skates. *Shit. Hockey is expensive, isn't it?* The only reason I can afford ballet for her right now is because the studio lets her take lessons for free since I teach there. But maybe if I get that audition...

Remi's excitement quells and her voice quiets. "Do you think I can play?"

I wince. I can't make any promises, but I swear to god I'll figure it out. Of course her asthma is a concern too, but that new medication is supposed to work better...

"I think we can figure something out, baby."

She screams with excitement and the phone clatters to the floor. The sound of little feet bouncing up and down on the hardwood fills my ears.

"Hi," Lily laughs, picking the phone back up.

"How's her asthma?" I ask, chewing my bottom lip, worried about her skating.

"It's been good. No attacks so far."

"Not even on the ice?" Lily's family has a small pond behind their house that freezes over in the winter.

"No, but we've been watching her closely," Lily assures me.

"You have her inhaler?" Remi just had her monthly injection two weeks before she left, so she should be okay, but still I worry.

"Of course." And I relax a little. "Okay, can you hand the phone back to her? I want to say goodbye."

"Yeah of course. Remi!" Lily shouts, and I pull the phone away from my ear to save my ear drums.

"Mom!"

"Hi, babe."

"Mommy! When are you coming here?"

"Oh, honey, I thought we talked about this." I swallow, my throat thick. "I have to work."

"But don't you miss me?" Remi whines, and I know it's getting close to her bedtime and she's tired, but her words still cut deep. "I miss you..."

"Of course I miss you!" I press the phone closer, wishing I could reach through it and wrap her in my arms. "More than anything," I add, my eyes burning as I get choked up, and try to keep it from my voice. "I'll see you soon. I promise."

I hear a commotion in the background and Remi laughs. "Bye Mommy! I love you!" she shouts out, happy once again.

"I—" The call disconnects before I can tell her I love her, too. I tip my head back, staring up at the ceiling, hoping that will keep the tears in this time. There's a prickle of awareness at the back of my neck and my head jerks to the right. Koen's standing there, leaning up against the doorframe leading out to the hall, dark eyes settled on me, watching, *listening*.

My spine snaps straight and I stare at him like a deer in headlights, phone still pressed up against my ear.

I push myself up, hoping the evidence of my tears isn't flushed across my face. I cross the studio as nonchalantly as I can. Sliding my phone into my dance bag like I'm burying evidence, before lifting my eyes to meet the burning gaze I can feel following me.

"Ready to go?" I ask, keeping my voice level.

Koen doesn't answer me, just continues to stare with those shadowed eyes of his, and I force myself not to fidget under his scrutiny.

"Who was that?"

48

MAKE. ME.

BRIAR

Now

"Who was *who*?" I reply, a little too quickly, and his eyes narrow as he takes a step into the room.

"On the phone," he purrs out in that Irish accent of his, and sweat coats my palms as he takes another step closer.

I break eye contact, pretending to be busy packing myself up, and that his question isn't about to launch a full scale panic attack. I'm far too aware of my breathing when I turn my back to him, walking slowly across the room to retrieve the sweatshirt I left hanging on a folding chair.

"Oh, um... No one important," I call back, as if it's an afterthought.

Fully packed up now, I force myself back around to face him. The way he's looking at me, I fear he can read every traitorous thought I have in my head. The conversation Gio and I had earlier, Remi's very existence... His gaze is sharp, assessing, and a flicker of suspicion flares in the green of his eyes.

"If you say so," he says finally.

I nod, clutching the bag tighter while shrugging like it's not a big deal, praying he doesn't demand to see my phone. I can just picture him scrolling through it, finding all the evidence I've worked so hard to keep from him.

"Have you been here all day?"

"I—" My response is delayed, unprepared for him to so easily change the subject. "Yes."

His glare grows volatile, and I gulp, fighting the urge to take a step back, not quite sure why he's pissed about that.

"What the fuck have you eaten?"

Shit. He's mad. But it's better he be pissed about my not eating than continue to stew over who I was just on the phone with.

"I, uhm, well, you see—" His eyes darken the longer I talk. "I had a granola bar in my bag."

Studio time is precious to me. I can't afford it, so I can only get it if no one else booked it first, which is why I end up spending most of my time practicing at the studio above the diner. And when I do get studio time here, I use it. It's not typical for me to take a break for lunch.

Plus, takeout in this area is expensive, so I usually just eat when I get home.

Koen closes his eyes, his fingers pinching the bridge of his nose. He looks to be on the verge of combusting. I seize the opportunity, with his eyes off of me, to shift uneasily on my feet, immediately straightening when his eyes open again. He sighs, audibly, picking up his own phone and typing something into it before putting it up to his ear. He glares down at me.

"What are you doing?" I ask, feeling as though I can't make it worse.

"Ordering you food," he snaps back, irritation apparent on his face.

Annoyance flares through me, and I cross my arms while glaring back at him. "I can feed myself."

"Apparently not." He gives me an appraising look, garnering a glare back from me, before he starts speaking into the phone, rattling off a Chinese food order to be delivered to my apartment. We have the same taste in food, it would seem, and my stomach growls as Koen lists off all my favorites.

"Twenty minutes," Koen informs me, while pocketing his phone.

I just stare at him. His frown deepens. "I thought you were ready to go?"

"I am," I huff, staring at him like he wasn't the one delaying us.

He motions for the door, stalking toward it himself when I don't move. He's already annoyed with me as it is, so why not go ahead and really rip off the band-aid?

"One quick thing," I call out, keeping my feet planted in the studio.

Koen stops on a dime, turning around slowly, looking like he's just about ready to strangle me.

My gaze drops to my feet. "So, part of this showcase I'm doing for dance, there's a requirement for participants to attend this gala. It's a charity event raising money for the Conservatory," I explain, peeking up to check on his reaction, but his face is unreadable. "It helps fund the scholarships, equipment, and facilities," I ramble on—over-explaining.

"When is it?" His tone gives nothing away of his opinion

on the gala, but he pulls out his phone as if he's actually going to check his calendar.

Stop it, Briar. He's probably just texting Mac to come and get me himself because I'm annoying him.

"It's this upcoming weekend but—" I trail off, my nerves getting the better of me.

Koen's eyes flicker up at my sudden silence, his growing irritation coming out in his tone. "But what?"

"Only dancers are given tickets. I asked, but—" I look up at him. "I can't get an extra ticket. So, I'll have to go alone."

Koen's expression turns stormy at that, his attention dropping back to his phone. "I'll go with you. Not a problem."

I tilt my head, unsure I heard him correctly. "What do you mean *not a problem*? What, are you going to drop in double-oh-seven style? Wearing that mask of yours?"

He looks up at me. "Would you like that, Ballerina?"

I huff out a breath, not knowing how to respond to that.

Koen's phone chimes and he checks the incoming text. "It's not a problem because I just bought a table." He holds up the phone like he just placed an Amazon order or something. "Come on. I'm going to be late." He turns and strides out of the studio, and I have to run to keep up with him. He's quick on the stairs, too, and I don't fully catch up to him until we're both on the street outside.

He points to the bike parked up against the curb, his attention back on his phone.

"Get on the bike."

I stop, staring at the bike while shaking my head in confusion.

"You just—you just bought a *table*?"

"Yes." I think I see him roll his eyes. "Now get on the bike. You're testing my patience." He shoots me a warning look.

I don't move, in fact, I'm cemented to the sidewalk until we figure this out.

"A table? You're sure?"

His brow furrows sharply, jaw tightening as his eyes darken, exasperation breaking through his cold, emotionless mask. "Quite sure, Briar Rose. Now will you get your pretty little defiant ass on the fucking bike?"

"A table costs one hundred thousand dollars," I continue.

"I know."

I just stare at him and he steps closer, forcing me to tilt my chin to keep his gaze. "I'd be quite happy to discuss this further little Rose, but right now I need you to get on that bike." His words come out carefully controlled, and I realize that I'm actually getting to him.

Koen grabs hold of the handlebars while swinging his leg over the motorcycle with ease. Settled into his seat, he looks at home on the massive bike. Even though there's a bite of frost in the evening air, Koen's only wearing a tight black t-shirt. The muscles in his arms ripple as his finger feathers the throttle, his abs tightening when he kicks away the kickstand, supporting the weight of the bike to keep it upright. It's attractive as fucking hell, and my pulse betrays me, quickening at the sight. A familiar warm heat flares to life deep in my core.

I'm overwhelmed with the need to either wrap myself around him, or slap him for making me feel this way.

Just as Koen goes to start the bike, his hand freezes on the throttle, looking up to find me still standing on the sidewalk, feet from the door, hand wrapped around my bag strap. The nylon strap's rough edges cut into my palm.

"Maybe I should just catch a ride with Mac." I shift, uneasy under his heavy gaze, looking up and down the street for the now familiar SUV, anxious over the thought of riding on the back of Koen's bike again.

"I sent Mac home." Koen's voice sounds darker than it did before. He sits back, assessing me for a moment before he says, "Get on." His gaze goes back to the dash.

Annoyance flares in me at the assertiveness in his tone. Like I'm just going to jump when he says fucking jump. As much as I don't want to get on the bike right now, I *really* don't want to be *told* to get on the fucking bike right now. And the way he just looked at me... like he *owns* me... expecting me just to do everything he says without question...

What if he asks you to kill someone, Briar? What if he demands it? Are you going to just do as you're told?

"No."

Koen stills, and I stiffen. His head tilts slowly back in my direction. It's predatory, dangerous, and it's as if he's giving me a chance to correct my answer.

"I wasn't asking."

I swallow hard.

"Get on the bike, Ballerina." The dominance in his tone sets off an unrecognizable flare of defiance in me. After waking up in his bed, whatever the fuck happened last night, Giovanni's threats, Remi's hurt little voice on the other end of that phone... I am *not* in a good mood, and like it or not, I'm about to make it *Koen's* fucking problem.

"I said *no*."

"You really want to test me tonight?"

Sure, you know what? Why the fuck not? What else do I have to lose? I'm tired of tiptoeing around, wondering where the line is. Time to find out just how far Koen's willing to go to make me kneel.

I cross my arms across my chest and sharpen my gaze. "I'm not getting on that bike. It's cold."

His jaw ticks, the muscles in his arms flex as well. "Last chance, love. Get. On. The. Bike."

I lift my chin, my voice mimicking his clipped, dark order. "Make. Me."

A deadly silence stretches between us, and neither of us moves. His shadowed gaze is fixed on me, and I don't dare look away. He moves slowly, first lowering the kickstand, then climbing off the bike with slow, deliberate precision. My nerves are on fire, every instinct screaming at me to fold, give in, or even run, but I stand rooted in place.

He prowls closer, and I fight the urge to flinch away from him. He keeps coming, until he's inches from my face, forcing me to tilt my chin to keep his eye and *oh, if looks could kill.* The green in his eyes is gone—they're nearly black now when they drop from my eyes to my mouth.

"You want me to? Because I don't think you know what you're asking for." Something dangerous sparks in his eyes and I feel a tremble ripple through me. He sees it too. "You're already shaking. I have a feeling you won't like it very much when I put you on your knees and fuck that attitude right out of your pretty little mouth."

"You wouldn't dare." The words I intend to come out with a bite, instead, sneak out in a half whisper, my breath failing me.

Koen smiles, and I think I stop breathing.

"Oh, I think I would."

My eyes narrow, and I go to open my mouth again, but his

hand shoots up, wrapping around my throat. His thumb falls just over my now thunderous pulse. The shadows playing in his eyes darken, his grip tightens until he cuts off my air. My hands fly to his, scrambling to pry his fingers off of me—to loosen his grip—but he doesn't budge. Darkness edges along the corners of my vision and I stop fighting him, my hands going still. It's only then he releases me, and I fall against him, sucking in air.

"Just giving you a little taste of what you're asking for." He winks, and I glare up at him, too busy returning oxygen to my lungs to bite back.

He leaves me gasping for breath against the wall of the studio, stalking back to the bike. "Get on the goddamn bike, Briar Rose." His gaze cuts back to me and he smiles again. "I dare you not to."

49

RÍ

BRIAR

Now

I haven't seen Koen since our little stand-off outside of the Conservatory days ago.

Realizing he's even more unhinged than I thought, I gave in. Freezing my ass off on that *goddamn bike* all the way home.

The Chinese food was waiting for me when I got there, and Koen took his leave. But not before giving me one last order to *eat*.

Fucking prick.

If I hadn't been on the verge of my stomach eating itself, I would've left the food on the counter, untouched. But your girl is a sucker for some good Chinese takeout, and Koen called the good place, ordering up enough Lo Mein and Teriyaki sticks to last me a week.

I was greeted once again this morning by Mac, who drove me to rehearsals, and sat outside again all day keeping watch.

It's after dark when I decide to brave the night, surprised to find Mac waiting for me outside in the SUV. I felt sure it would be Koen finally, but I haven't seen or heard from him since Monday night, even checking my messages again to be sure. I quickly bury the spike of disappointment his absence brings on the ride home.

Good riddance, honestly. Maybe he decided I'm just not worth the trouble, and I only have another week of free rides back and forth to dance to worry about now.

Giovanni's not thrilled about it, wanting constant updates, but I can't exactly work over the mafia boss if he's not around, can I?

I get home, eating some of the leftover Chinese food, before taking a shower and throwing on some dance shorts and an oversized t-shirt to sleep in.

Even after putting in extra hours at the studio today, I feel restless. It's pretty late by the time I finish everything, but I already know I'm not going to be able to sleep, so I try turning on the TV. After spending about a half-hour watching streaming previews with still no idea what to watch, I shut it off. I pick up the book I left cracked on the arm of the sofa, only to drop it back there a few minutes later. My mind too keyed up to focus.

I check my phone again. I said goodnight to Remi at the studio and she's likely been asleep for hours now, so there's nothing from Lily. Still no text from Koen, and Gio's finally left me alone. Dropping the phone on my bed, I wander over to the window, looking down into the dark alleyway.

For weeks, I've felt like I've had eyes on me, an inexplicable feeling that I'm not alone, but not *tonight*. Tonight, I feel more alone than I ever have. The apartment is quiet, cold, and dark without Lily and Remi here. I wrap my arms around myself, making the decision to go to bed. I'd rather go to sleep than feel this sorry for myself.

I toss and turn for hours. At some point it starts to rain, the droplets careening off the window, falling hard on the ceiling above. Usually I love the sound of the rain, not rain machines —ew—but actual, real life rain. It's soothing. But tonight, every single drop that hits the glass is like a stone to my brain. The sound is driving me crazy. I lay there, my arms hugging the pillow, eyes closed, reminding myself that studies show even resting with your eyes closed is still better than just staying up.

I don't know how to explain it, but I sense him before I see him.

My eyes fly open just as a large shadow moves across my window five stories up. I push myself up on my elbows, my heart hammering as I watch the dark shadow, tall with broad shoulders, make its way across the narrow bridge of the fire escape and stop at the window that leads into my bedroom.

His hood is up, and through the wet glass, I see him pull out a knife.

I should scream—should grab my phone or make a run for it, but I don't. My fist tightens around my blankets as he slips the blade through the crack in the metal, running it up, and with the smallest click, flicks up the latch.

My eyebrows rise when he pushes the glass in, opening the window and climbing inside with an ease and grace I wouldn't have guessed from a man of his size. He's soaked. Water drips from his hood, dirty blonde hair falling into his eyes. Reaching up, he pushes his hair out of his face, freezing when he finds me looking at him.

"I have a front door," I sigh with a defeated huff.

"I know," Koen says, his voice quiet.

"What are you doing here?" I'm exhausted, and if he thinks we're going in on yet another battle of wills, I'm just going to tell him to shove it.

"I don't want to stay outside tonight," he shrugs, taking a step closer, turning and closing the window behind him, reaching up and resetting the latch.

My brow furrows in confusion. "Stay outside? Why would you—" My breath catches, fisting the blankets in my hand harder when I realize. *Koen's been outside—watching?* I didn't imagine someone out there watching me. It was *him.*

He moves closer, stepping into the warm glow from the light outside, his body is stiff, and he's moving weirdly, holding one arm tucked into his side.

"I—Wait, are you bleeding?"

Without thinking, I push off the blankets, rushing toward him. *He is bleeding.* Crimson rivulets drip from his fingertips, his hand falling uselessly to his side. I notice the blood is coming from inside the sleeve of his hoodie. His other hand is holding that arm tightly, applying pressure to somewhere on his upper arm.

"Did you get shot?" My eyes widen as I get closer, my hands going instinctively to where the blood is still soaking through his sweatshirt..

"It's fine," he grumbles, rolling his shoulder in an attempt to shake me off, only to wince, a flash of pain appearing on his face before he schools it back into a frown.

"It's not fine. Sit down." I attack the other side of him, nudging him toward my bed. My room isn't very big, so it's only a foot away. To my surprise, he lets me guide him there, sinking down to the mattress with a slight groan of pain.

"Can I—?" My hands hover over him, pointing to where his hand is wrapped tight around the blood soaked fabric, hoping he'll let me take a look. He stares at me for a long second, an unreadable expression on his face, before he dips his chin, shifting over to make space for me on the bed.

I sink down next to him, realizing I can't see anything through his clothes. I reach down, hooking my fingertips under the hem of his hoodie. "We have to take this off."

His eyes slide to mine, and he nods silently, helping me pull the sweatshirt off of him.

I frown at the blood soaked gray tee underneath. "You don't own *any* color?" I say without thinking, and his gaze meets mine, sharing a look while my question goes unanswered. My attention snaps to the blood gushing out of his arm. "Holy shit! You actually did get shot!" I don't know what I expected, but the sight of the real live gunshot wound takes me aback, and I feel the blood rush out of my face, leaving my head a little dizzy.

"It's just a graze."

"A graze? You have a *hole* in your arm!"

"It went clean through," Koen says, shifting his weight on my mattress. "I just need to sleep it off."

My mouth falls open. "You want to *sleep off* a gunshot wound? Mister *'you didn't clean your wounds properly'* wants to *sleep off* his own?" I shake my head at him, and the corner of his mouth ticks up, amused.

"You need to go the hospital."

He stiffens and his eyes go hard. "No hospital."

"But..." My eyes drop to the *literal* gun shot wound in his arm.

"No hospital," he growls, and I can't help but roll my eyes.

"Stay here. I'll be right back." I feel his eyes track me all the way out of the bedroom, and again when I return, bringing with me the first aid kit from the bathroom and some warm, damp towels.

Settling back down on the bed, I start to wipe away the blood. I'm no med student but I've watched enough television to know we have to clean it or it could get infected. They usually end up having to stitch the wound closed too, but I shake away the thought. One thing at a time.

"Can you take off your shirt?"

He nods, reaching back over his shoulder with his good arm, and ripping off the gray t-shirt—saturated in blood—with one hand, and *holy hell*, I forget how to breathe. His muscles are larger, thicker since the last time I saw them, water coats his skin, the wet sheen highlighting the deep contours of his body. My fingers twitch to roam over his defined abdomen, to feel the ripples beneath my touch.

He's covered in dark ink. Only black, shaded with gray. There's hardly any skin visible on his right arm, the ink spreading over his chest. My heart stutters at the familiar hawk he has flying over his heart, but it stops entirely at the small red rose just above it.

A single splash of color amongst nothing but dark ink.

He still has it.

My eyes pull to his. He catches me looking, and a soft smile appears on his lips. And for a moment, he's not the hardened mafia boss controlling me for his own gain, or the violent and dangerous father of my child I need to run from. For a moment, he's just *Koen*. Hard eyes soften when they look at me, all his defenses; his barbed wire and guns have been ordered to stand down. Right here is the guy who took me to a midnight firework show, dared me to get my first tattoo, and who made me come for the first time.

Ri.

His throat clears and I'm snapped from my train of thought, seeing the blood and remembering I'm supposed to be doing something. I move slowly, lifting one of the damp towels to start cleaning away some of the blood.

Koen sits *very* still.

"What happened?" I ask softly, wondering if he'll tell me.

"Ambush." My eyes fly to his. "Bratva—Russians," he adds for my benefit. I continue to wipe away more blood, swapping out the soaked towel for a fresh one. "It was a trap. They made us think they had our sister." He rolls his shoulder back in annoyance. "They didn't. Should've seen it coming." He shakes his head.

I bite the inside of my cheek. What happened—his injury —is a harsh reminder of how dangerous Koen's world is.

"I know they do it in all the movies, but I don't think I'm going to be able to stitch this for you." I make a face, barely keeping it together as it is.

Koen releases a chuckle. "It'll be fine. Do you have any large bandages or medical tape, maybe?'

I remember I still have some of that medical wrap Lily bought me for my back. "Yes, hold on two seconds for me. I dart out of the room, grabbing the medical wrap, then going back to the bedroom and taking some fresh gauze out of the first aid kit.

Carefully, I press the gauze to each side of the wound, packing it in tight with the wrap as I wind it around Koen's bicep. Every so often, my fingertips graze his skin and I feel a tingle in my spine.

Once I have the wound wrapped to my liking, I stop, cutting off the excess wrap and freezing. Shit! I have nothing to hold it in place. With my free hand, I feel through the first aid kit but I don't find anything I can use.

"Uhm. Can you hold this for a second?"

Koen's hand moves over mine, keeping the wrapping in place when I slide my hand out from under his. Darting back across the hall into the bathroom, I search the counter and the medicine cabinet for anything I can use. My eyes fall to a box of unicorn Band-Aids.

I let out a laugh, exhaustion or crazy winning out, and I clasp my hand over my mouth so as to not lose it entirely. I take a few extra minutes to wash myself up in the bathroom, washing Koen's blood off into the sink with a few rounds of soap and water. Snatching up the box, I head back across the hall to Koen.

Proudly keeping a straight face, I pull open the box. Using three unicorn Band-Aids, I secure the medical wrap around the gunshot wound. Satisfied that it's not going anywhere, I release a breath, stepping back to admire my handiwork.

Koen's staring at the Band-Aids with an arched brow.

"Unicorns?"

"Mhm," I say, not trusting myself to open my mouth right now, fighting a bubble of hysterical laughter brewing in my throat.

"What are you, *two*?" he teases, and I laugh. The unicorn bandages amongst all his dark and gloomy tattoos is a little bit funny.

"Three actually. Almost four," I say jokingly, the words losing their amusement halfway through, and the last two words come out in nearly a whisper.

My eyes shift to his, horrified to find him watching me. I press my lips together, sweeping up the last remnants of supplies and dumping them onto my dresser to clean up later. Without thinking, I pull open one of the drawers, ripping off my blood stained t-shirt to replace it with a fresh one. My back is to Koen, and I've got the new shirt halfway over my head when I remember he is, in fact, *right there.*

I can feel the burn of his stare on my back like a brand. My movements slow and I pull on the rest of the shirt. It falls nearly to my knees, covering my shorts almost entirely. Hesitantly, I turn back to face him, remembering how he said he didn't want to *stay outside tonight,* and for the first time, I really think about what he meant by that.

"Are you staying here?" I want to pat myself on the back for being bold enough to ask.

"I'm on ballerina watch tonight," he says, a faint smile tugging at his lips, but I can see exhaustion wearing on his features. He's a little pale from all the blood loss.

"I'll give you the night off."

He huffs out a half-laugh.

"What's wrong with your place?"

"The windows are broken," he shrugs. "Can't get them fixed until tomorrow." I try making sense of what he just said. He lives on the top floor... "Your *windows* are broken?" I ask for confirmation, but he ignores me, pushing himself further up my bed until he's able to lie back. His head hitting my pillow.

"What are you doing?"

"Sleeping. It. Off." He has the audacity to arch a brow at me. "I believe this was discussed already."

"In *my* bed?" I'm unable to hide the alarm in my tone.

"I'm wounded." He bats those long eyelashes at me. "You're really going to make me take the couch?"

If I'm not mistaken, his expression is almost... playful.

I stare down at him. Half annoyed, half—I don't know what I am. But the tattooed god from my nightmares is currently lying in my bed, half-naked. So I start for the door.

"Don't you dare, Briar Rose. I know you're dancing first thing in the morning. You get your ass in this bed right now."

"But..."

"No buts. Injured or not, I'll pick you up and put you in here if I have to."

Sure that I'll live to regret this, I let my shoulders drop, ripping back the covers and climbing inside. Careful to keep to the far edge of the mattress, as far away from Koen as I can manage.

"Just pretend I'm not here."

Oh, sure, no problem.

50

MY SWEATSHIRT

KOEN

Now

I wake with the first rays of sunlight. I start to push myself up but freeze when I'm met with resistance—a dark-haired girl asleep on my chest.

Briar.

Not wanting to wake her, I slowly relax my shoulders back down to the mattress, all but holding my breath until I confirm she's still out cold.

Her cheek is snuggled into my chest, one of her legs curls around mine, the other pressed close. She's clinging to me like her life depends on it. And maybe it does, since it's fucking freezing in here.

I eye the window, making sure I didn't accidentally leave it open last night when I climbed in, frowning when I find it shut tight. With my uninjured arm, I slowly reach down to pull the blankets up so she's fully covered.

I just barely remember waking at some point in the middle of the night, Briar's shivers sending little tremors through the mattress. She was curled in on herself; her skin was as cold as ice when I touched her. I didn't think twice before dragging her body against mine.

With the blankets fully around her shoulders, my arm wraps back around her, holding her to me. I'm instantly conscious of the way her arm is draped so casually across my torso. Her fingers falling right atop my lower abdomen, lightly brushing my skin as I shift around.

Briar's breath catches and her fingers curl into my skin, sending a shockwave of warmth radiating throughout my lower body. I stiffen, and she stirs further with the movement.

I should wake her up. Move her off of me and get on with my day. There's so much shit to work out after everything that went down last night. But looking down at her, she looks so peaceful in her sleep. The usual tension missing from her beautiful face.

My breathing steadies and I keep it even. Lifting my hand, I run a couple of my fingers through the silky strands of her dark hair.

Her body goes tense with the contact, but she lets out a soft sigh, relaxing back into sleep once again.

Fuck. What was I thinking coming here? Last night was a shit show in every way possible. We knew the Russians had set a trap, but that hadn't stopped Aidan from walking into it anyway. Seeing as how it was *his* girl on the line, I guess I can't blame him.

He got out. Rory was safe. Everybody was safe. But when everything was going down, my first thought was *her*.

Briar.

That's probably how I ended up outside her apartment, climbing her fire escape, watching like I'd done every night for the past two weeks. Making sure she was okay. And maybe it was the blood loss, but I just couldn't stop myself from slipping my knife into the crack in her window, freeing the lock and going inside.

It wasn't enough just to watch from outside. I *needed* to see her. I wanted to—

I just wanted to see her.

My eyes trail over to my other shoulder. The warmth from Briar's body and her sweet jasmine scent are a distraction, but overall the wound doesn't hurt all that much. The bandage Briar had wrapped so carefully is still white and clean; it doesn't look like the wound is going to need stitches after all.

Briar's breathing hitches and I feel her stiffen, her eyelids fluttering.

I close my eyes, wanting to see what it is she'll do when she wakes up on my chest.

All at once, Briar goes unnaturally still. She's holding her breath before she ever-so-carefully attempts to untangle herself from me.

I relax my right arm, letting it fall heavy, setting a deliberate trap.

Smiling to myself at the existential crisis Briar goes through on my chest, as she tries to work out how to escape the weight of my arm without waking me, only realizing too late there's no way out.

I decide to put her out of her misery. "Think you can get away that easily?"

"You're awake." Shocked blue eyes peer up at me, searching mine.

"Mhm." I just look down at her. "Have been—for a while now."

Her brows knit together and her head tilts to the side in the most adorable way. "Then why—?" At the same time, she seems to notice how very much attached to me she is and launches herself away, nearly falling off the other end of the bed like it's on fire.

She would have too, if I hadn't rocketed forward, grabbing hold of her arm just before she goes over.

For a moment, we just stare at each other.

"You looked comfortable." I shrug like it's no big deal, dropping her arm once I'm sure she's scooted her ass a safe distance back onto the mattress.

She pushes herself up, the comforter falling away and revealing the tiny pair of shorts she wore to bed last night.

Her body jolts from the shock of the cold air.

"It's fucking freezing in here," I tell her. Briar tucks her arms into herself before crawling out of the bed in search of more clothing. My eyes trail her. "Don't you have heat?"

She winces. I catch it right before she tries to hide it, quickly smoothing out her face. "Consistently?" Her tone rises an octave as she tries to play this off. "No," she admits, reluctantly, when I dip my chin. "It goes out sometimes."

My eyes narrow on her, sensing the lie. "Sometimes?"

She winces again, but this time it's harder to hide.

"Okay, fine," she huffs. "It goes out more than it doesn't." She shrugs like it's no big deal.

Well that pisses me off. "What the fuck?" I sit up fully now. It's December. Why the fuck is her heat not *consistently* working?

She makes a run for her dresser across the room. Quickly

grabbing a pair of sweat pants from the bottom drawer, she refuses to make eye contact with me while she drags them on over her shorts.

"Why don't you call your landlord?" I'm on my feet, too, searching her bedroom floor for my shirt.

She snorts and I glare at her, confused as to how she can find any of this *funny*. She's still refusing to look my way, finger combing her hair into a low ponytail. "What makes you think I haven't?"

I frown, finding my blood soaked tee from last night and picking it up off the floor. "How long has this been an issue?"

Her face sours, which is answer enough. She starts chewing her bottom lip, finally turning to face me. Her eyes drop to the now dried blood staining the t-shirt I hold in my hands.

"You can't wear that." She frowns. "Hold on." Twisting, she starts in a few different directions before changing her mind and rushing back to the side of her bed. I watch as she tears through the covers before dragging out a dark sweatshirt from underneath her pillow.

My sweatshirt.

She tosses it at me without looking. I catch it before it hits my face. "From the other night—I uh, I laundered it."

"Uh-huh." My jaw works and I try not to smile, looking down at the mess of pillows on the bed.

"Will you just get dressed already?" She paces lightly by the window, still trying to avoid looking at me.

Unable to keep the smirk from my face, I drag the sweatshirt over my head. Noticing the faintest trace of jasmine within the threads.

Some of the tension ebbs out of her body once I'm covered up, and she levels me a glare when she catches me staring.

"What?" she snaps, and I shake my head.

"Nothing."

She rolls her eyes, and my dick twitches in my jeans, thinking about what she would do if I threw her down on the mattress right now.

My phone buzzes and she's saved. *For now.*

My jaw tightens as I read over the incoming text from Reagan. She holds half the blame for last night's catastrophe, thanks to her running off. The endless string of apologies she's firing at me are proof she knows it, too.

I swipe out of the message thread without replying. I'll deal with her later.

Briar, once again, catches my gaze, and anger burns through me when I realize I can see her breath on the cold air.

I sigh, shooting off a message in the group thread I have with my brothers.

"Pack a bag."

Briar's face snaps to mine before looking around the tiny room like I could be talking to anyone else. "What? Why?"

I eye her over the phone, typing one more thing into it. "It's like thirty fucking degrees in here, Briar. You're not staying in this apartment."

She backs up a step, shaking her head.

"I don't—that's not—"

"I believe we agreed you would do whatever I say."

"I don't know that *this* qualifies," she mutters, folding her arms across her chest.

My eyes flick up for a second to meet hers before dropping back to my screen.

"It qualifies."

Her mouth opens and shuts, and my lips twitch at the internal war she's busy fighting.

"You can pack a bag, or you can wear nothing." My eyes sparkle when her eyes narrow into slits, glaring at me.

"Your choice, Briar Rose."

51

JUST BREATHE

BRIAR

Now

The backpack Koen asked me to pack sits ominously by the door of the studio. Taunting me.

He gave me a ride to the studio this morning on the back of his bike, dropping me off before leaving to take care of other business.

For a guy so concerned about me being cold, he sure has a funny way of showing it.

The chilly morning air nips at me, but I'm better prepared than I was the other night. I dressed warmer, and Koen lent me a thick pair of motorcycle gloves.

Despite the unexpected company last night, I actually slept okay. I can't remember having any nightmares last night, which is good, considering that would've been fucking embarrassing to have Koen witness.

Mr. Carr has it out for me today. Or all of us, rather. He

spends all morning barking at dancers, terrorizing the tech crew, and his stage manager absolutely went and cried in a closet during lunch break, because when she came back, her cheeks were all red and splotchy.

"Man. Who pissed in his Cheerios?" Mia grumbles to me in between numbers.

I just shake my head, trying to focus while feeling more and more distracted. I'm trying to keep track of all of the quick changes and stage blocking, but my mind keeps circling back to Koen.

He slept in my bed last night. *Koen O'Rourke.* With his arms wrapped around me. Why the hell did he come to my apartment after he got shot anyway? Sure, he made his disdain for hospitals known last night, but surely his brothers or any of his men would have been better equipped to deal with that type of injury rather than me.

As the day wears on, Mr. Carr starts to call me out more and more.

I'm doing better today, but I'm still struggling with one small section of the choreography. Albeit, it's a *critical* part of the choreography, but it's only because I need more practice with it. It's tricky, the footwork incredibly tedious. I'll get it.

"Miss Ralston, either do it correctly or get off my stage!" Mr. Carr shouts, throwing his hands up in exasperation where he sits third row, center stage when I fumble the footwork on that section again.

I stop. "I—" I start, but he waves me off, motioning to cut the music.

"I don't want to hear it. I can't watch this again today, you're done—off." He points offstage and I obey, tears burning in my eyes.

"Can I have everyone in the Giselle excerpt to the stage?" He barks, yelling more when the dancers don't get to their starting positions quick enough.

I move to push through the small crowd of dancers waiting backstage, halting when Mia catches my arm as I pass. "Hey, don't worry about it. You look really good. He's just being an ass today."

If I open my mouth, I know I'm going to start crying, so I press my lips together and give her a stilted nod, hating the pity I see in her eyes.

She lets me go and I walk quickly through the busy backstage, striding down the hall until I find an empty dressing room to dive into before letting out a choked sob.

I feel the panic attack coming on and curl into a ball. My arms wrap tightly around my knees, and I press my head into them, eyes shut tight. My heart is pounding so hard I hear it in my ears.

You don't have time for this.

The lights in the dressing room I've taken refuge in are off, and that helps. My chest feels tight, like there's a pressing weight on it and I can't get enough air.

"You're fine. You're fine. You're fine," I whisper now to myself, slightly rocking back and forth as I count—"One, two, three"—attempting to breathe in deep through my nose, but it comes out shaky, more like a sob.

Three weeks ago, I was drugged, thrown in the back of a van, and almost trafficked. The scars on my back from the whip are still healing, but the mental ones... I haven't even begun to unpack that. I miss my daughter; I miss her laugh, I miss her tantrums over brushing her teeth, and how she turns up her nose at the mere sight of anything green. I miss my best friend, and I miss when dance used to be fun and not my only means of survival. And I hate Koen. I hate him. I hate him so fucking much.

He's so cold, arrogant, manipulative. The way he bosses me around... He's cruel and he's controlling, yet his touch is light and gentle. The way he kissed me the other night... the way he *claimed* me in front of everyone, right before I was drugged... and what did my tattooed nightmare do?

He kept me safe, brought me home to *his bed.*

And last night he slept in *my* bed.

When I woke up this morning, warm, snuggled into his side with his arm wrapped around me... *I didn't hate it.*

"*Fuck!*" I don't realize I've actually screamed it, until I feel my throat burning.

I dig my nails into my thigh, and the world slowly starts to come back into focus. It reminds me of Koen's hand around my throat.

Stop thinking about him.

Stop.

I can't sit here anymore. I have to move. My brain needs something else to do other than obsess over the one man I can't have.

Throwing open the dressing room door, I don't stop until I find an empty studio room and once I'm there...

I don't stop.

I've been at it for hours by the time I clock Koen in the ballet studio's mirrors, watching me intently from the shadows in the hall.

It's late. The sky outside is dark. Everyone else has long since gone home. I wonder how long he waited out there before coming to find me.

I don't react to his presence, though I feel his proximity throughout every inch of my body.

He knows I've seen him. I don't miss the disapproving stare on his face when I finish another run-through and drag myself back up to go again.

"You're going to hurt yourself."

I don't bother turning around. "Mind. Your. Own. Business," I seethe between my teeth.

The following scoff is answer enough.

I go again. I landed wrong on my ankle a few run-throughs ago. The pain keeps increasing the further I get into the routine.

I feel Koen's eyes on my back but I refuse to look in his direction.

"Briar." His voice holds a warning as I get closer to the last leap.

I can't let up.

I won't.

Not when the showcase in two weeks is my only way out.

I can't let Mr. Carr cut me. It's Friday. I have the weekend to get that combination right. I just have to stay focused and lock the fuck in.

I run the routine again, coming down a little too hard on my already screaming ankle on the last leap. I breathe hard through my nose to hide the wince. Rolling my shoulders, I walk with a straight face to grab a drink of water from my bottle in the corner.

Over the plastic rim, I chance a glimpse as inconspicuously as I can at Koen. He's leaning on his good shoulder against the wall, his legs crossed at the ankles, and I'm relieved to find him scrolling on his phone, not paying me any attention. His pants are tactical—black, military cut, fitted through the thighs, with a plethora of pockets, and I can see at least one gun strapped to a holster on his waist. His shirt is tight, black and short-sleeved, revealing the dark ink he has snaking up one arm, and the bandage wrapped around his bicep on the other.

He's changed the dressing. No more unicorn Band-Aids.

My nose twitches and I shake my head, taking one last gulp of water from the bottle before dropping it back to the floor. I roll my ankle beneath me. *It doesn't feel that bad.*

One more run-through.

Mistake.

I know it the moment the music starts and I begin dancing. I can feel Koen's eyes on me now; my own toxic stubbornness takes over and I can't do anything else other than finish the routine. It hurts, but it's fine. I'll ice it when I get home, and *it'll be fine.*

That is, until I get to the same jump that gave me trouble last time.

I land and let out a strangled gasp when my ankle buckles,

my feet slipping out from under me. I'm going down, and I'm going down hard.

Except... *I'm not.*

Koen catches me before I hit the ground. Lowering me down as I let out hollow breaths, struggling to keep in the sudden rush of tears set loose by the sharp pain searing through my ankle every time I move my foot.

"Easy, just sit for a second."

Despite the pain, I try twisting out of his arms, growing irritated when he holds firm.

"You don't understand!" I'm yelling now, my heart pounding, and I'm having trouble catching my breath. "It *has* to be perfect—*I* have to be perfect!"

I shove him, and he takes it. His mouth tightens and his eyes let loose a warning but he doesn't look angry, letting me go as he falls back a step, watching me with those unsettling dark eyes of his.

I point a shaky finger in his face but he doesn't even flinch. His eyes don't leave mine as I unleash all of the anger, the frustration, the *pain* on him.

"*You* don't get to tell me when it's enough. I decide. Because it's *my* life." I pause to glare at him while my breathing further dysregulates. "I decide when it's enough, and it will never be enough!" My shouts crack on a sob, and I whirl away from him before he can see me cry. My chest collapses, my lungs constricting, until my breaths are coming in short, shallow bursts. There's no air. I can't get enough air. It's not enough—I can't breathe—I can't...

The pain in my ankle forces me still; Remi, Giovanni, Mr. Carr, the showcase, *Koen* — all at once it's too much, and I'm spiraling. No matter how quickly I draw my breaths, I can't get enough—there's not enough oxygen. The edges of my vision darken right before the world starts to tilt, which only makes me panic more.

I trip when my knees buckle, throwing my hands out, about to crash down onto my knees, but large, strong hands wrap around me before I hit the floor, holding me up. Slowly, they lower me to the ground when my knees give way, and I crumble.

Koen's deep voice echoes somewhere in the distance, but I can't reach it; it's so far away, and I can't—I can't let him see me like this.

"Look at me."

I don't. Dropping my eyes to the ground as the darkness grows, my vision tunnels even further, my heart rate skyrockets and I start to hyperventilate, fighting for breath. My panic only escalates as I start to freak out that he's about to see me like this.

"Briar!"

My name, shouted from the distance. But it's too late. He's too far away. I can't reach him.

"Breathe, little Rose, *breathe*."

Hands cup my face, bringing my chin up. Deep, rich evergreen is all I can see before lips crush down onto mine, stealing my breath, halting the shadows and freezing my racing heart.

My fingers cling onto him, surrendering entirely to the sheer dominance of his kiss. I don't have it in me to fight it. I don't know that I want to. My heart stops when he pulls me closer.

The world shrinks down until it's just the two of us, he invades every single one of my senses, the feel of his lips against mine. I inhale deep, finding comfort in the familiar dark citrus scent of him. I breathe it in, my hands moving up to the back of his head, my fingers running through his hair. It's softer than I thought it would be. A wave of calm settles over me. The warmth from his body leeches into mine, his tight grip on my hair—on my body—grounding me.

When my breathing evens out, he pulls away, and I release a long steadying breath, peering up at him.

"That's it, breathe. Just like that. Good."

The realization of what just happened hits me and I spin away from him. We're both on the ground, he's on his knees in front of me, but I can't look at him.

I need to cry, I need to let it out. My throat is tight, a sob just wanting to escape, but I don't want to. *Not in front of him.*

My back is to Koen now and I know he can see me struggling. I feel him shift and then he's pulling me back—pulling me into him.

I try to fight his hold on me, try to pull away, but his arms lock around me, caging me in. Frustration at not being able to escape finally tips me over the edge, and I release a small sob. I can't hold it now that it's out, and more follow.

Strong arms tighten around my middle and he leans in, resting his chin down on my shoulder. His hold on me is tight, but I no longer feel trapped—I feel *safe*. He doesn't say anything, doesn't ask any questions. He just sits there, holding me. He keeps holding me until the tears stop, and my breathing slows down to match the steady rise and fall of his chest against my back.

I don't know how long we sit like that. I'm emotionally strung out. I feel numb and I nearly jump at the sound of his voice when he finally speaks, though his tone is soft.

"You ready to go?"

"Yeah," I sniff, raising my hands and wiping my cheeks. "I just gotta get my bag."

"I'll get it." Koen lets me go. Getting to his feet, he crosses the studio, picking up my phone and putting it into my bag, before zipping it shut and swinging it over his shoulder.

I rise awkwardly, trying to avoid putting too much weight on my ankle. I use the ballet barre above me for assistance, wincing slightly at the shooting pain when I accidentally lean too far on it. I go to take one step but my foot never lands. My world tilts sideways as my legs are swept out from under me, and I let out a cry of surprise as I fall back. My hands scramble for purchase, and I cling tightly to Koen's t-shirt. He's scooped me up.

I kick out with my feet, attempting to twist out of his hold. "It's not that serious. I can walk!"

But he's already carrying me toward the entrance, tightening his grip.

"Maybe, but you're not going to."

"You were just shot!" I protest, looking around frantically to make sure I'm not leaning against his injured shoulder, feeling no relief despite discovering I'm not. "You're going to make it worse. "

"Then maybe you should stop wiggling."

I do. I stop struggling. Not wanting to hurt him any more than I probably already am.

"You can just take me home," I hedge, as he sets me down in the passenger seat of the SUV. Hoping maybe he forgot about the whole *not having heat* thing in all of the excitement.

"Not a chance, Ballerina. Buckle up. You're staying with me tonight. I'm not fucking arguing with you about it." He snaps when he sees me opening my mouth, "Your heat will be fixed in the morning."

I blink up at him. "Wait, it will? Uh, how?" I've spent most of this fall, and much of last winter, berating the landlord to fix the damn heat, but he couldn't care less.

Koen slides into the driver's seat, shooting me a dark smile. "Don't worry about it."

52

WE DON'T HAVE A GUEST ROOM

BRIAR

Now

"This really isn't necessary," I complain as Koen eases me out of the SUV. We're in the parking garage under his building.

"I don't remember asking if it was," he grumbles, clearly annoyed that I'm not letting him help me.

He picks me up again and I howl.

"Put me down. I can manage fine on my own."

"No."

I blow out a frustrated breath, wrapping my arms around his neck to better support myself, in an attempt to keep at least part of my weight off of his injured arm.

Koen nods at the man at the desk, guarding the elevator, he stands to watch us pass, eyeing me with curiosity.

The elevator doors close and I think I stop breathing, suddenly hyperaware of Koen's hand under my thigh. He's so warm. My hoodie is still in my dance bag; I didn't get a chance to pull it on before we left, and my bare arms are frozen. Heat radiates off of him like he's my own personal oven, and, as subtly as I can, I shift closer, resisting the urge to snuggle deep into his hold and bury my face in his neck.

The doors slide open after what feels like an impossibly long amount of time, and I'm swiftly carried down the long hallway I know leads to his room.

We stop outside his door, and I struggle uselessly in his arms while he has to let go of me with one hand to open it.

"I can just stay in the guest room..."

With one hand, Koen keeps me pressed against him as he crosses the dark space to deposit me onto his bed. He eases me down slowly, taking care to ensure my ankle is safe and I don't accidentally hit it against the frame.

"We don't have a guest room."

I frown. Looking around the space for my options. Remembering how we passed a relatively comfortable looking sectional back in the living room.

"The couch, then?" I propose, with a weak smile he just returns with a look of utter exasperation that almost makes me laugh.

Koen sits down next to me on the bed, pulling my ankle up so it's resting in his lap. Carefully, he pushes up my leg warmer to further inspect my injury. His hands are steady, clinical in their examination, as he palpates my swollen ankle, but my skin burns everywhere he touches.

"Swollen, but not broken. A mild sprain." He nods, looking up at me, expecting relief as though that's *good* news. But his eyes widen when he catches the look on my face. I glance away immediately, embarrassment blooming in my cheeks, wanting anything other than to cry in front of him *again*.

"Hey." His thumb drags my chin back, forcing my eyes up to his, holding them fixed with his penetrating stare. "You're okay. Nothing's broken. A couple days off of it and it'll be good as new."

Still on the edge emotionally, my lips tremble, and hot tears burn at the corners of my eyes, though I fight them off, refusing to let them fall. "It's not fine. I need to practice, I can't afford—

"Briar," he cuts me off, his voice flat and stern. "It's a sprain, not the end of the world."

"I can't get hurt. I can't—*be* hurt," I correct, glaring down at my ankle like it betrayed me on purpose. "Do you have any idea what even a couple days off means?"

His jaw tightens, and when he speaks, there's a sharper edge to his voice. "It means you have a chance to heal. Rest."

I shake my head, unfamiliar with the concept of rest, having been hustling nearly nonstop for longer than I can remember. "I have to be ready for the showcase. You don't understand. If I'm not ready, they'll take it away, they'll—" My heart jumps with a jolt of anxiety and I pull my knees in, hugging them to my chest, curling in on myself out of instinct. "That showcase is *everything*. I can't lose it." The admission has me biting my lip and I look up at the ceiling, blinking the brewing tears away again before they have a chance to fall.

"The world won't end if you take a break." Koen's tone is harder, but his eyes soften when I look back at him.

"But it might," I whisper, dropping my gaze to stare dejectedly at my ankle.

"You have to schedule in time to rest, for recovery, and you need to eat to fuel your body properly." His eyes flash and I feel my cheeks burn, knowing I skipped lunch again today.

"Speaking of needing to eat..." He rises. "I'm going to get you some ice. You're going to stay here and *rest*." His eyes flash with warning and my lips twitch. "And then I'll figure out dinner."

53

FAMILY DINNER

KOEN

Now

I've just brought the vegetables to a satisfying sizzle when I hear her. I turn from the stove, scowling at the little dark-haired girl lingering under the archway that leads into the kitchen.

"You shouldn't be up."

The nervousness on her face disappears, morphing into annoyance, discontent with the idea of me telling her what to do, so naturally, she steps further into the kitchen, with a limp that has me clenching my jaw.

"I'm fine," she says with a steel resolve in her voice. "I don't want to be in there alone." The words are the only thing that stops me from throwing her over my shoulder and carting her back off to my room.

"Well, sit the fuck down or something." My arm waves in exasperation toward the kitchen island stools and the dining table. I take my eye off of her to stir the sauce that's starting to boil, due to my lack of attention to it.

"You cook?" There's disbelief in her voice. I don't turn around, hearing her shuffle toward the island and pull out a stool, satisfied that she's going to sit.

A little smile pulls at the corner of my mouth. "Is that so surprising?"

She doesn't know what to say, tripping over her words, and I turn to face her, leaning back against the counter and folding my arms across my chest to give her my full attention.

"No, I—" she starts, before she lets out a breath. "Yes," she admits, "I guess it is." She shrugs apologetically at me.

"A man's gotta eat, does he not?"

"Yeah, but you're *you*."

I tilt my head, raising my brows. *What's that supposed to mean?*

She leans in, her voice low before she continues. "The head of the Irish mafia." She whispers like it's a secret. "I figured you'd have, I don't know, people for that."

I shake my head, moving to check on the vegetables roasting in the oven. "I don't like strangers in my space. Don't trust 'em."

We exchange a look during a beat of awkward silence. *That rule doesn't seem to apply to her, now does it?* This will be the third time I've had her in the loft. There's a flash of something in her eyes before she looks away. Guilt, maybe? I can't tell.

"Where did you learn to cook?" she asks, pushing on with the conversation.

"Self-taught. Life's too short to eat shit food."

She chuckles. "I guess that's fair."

The elevator pings and her expression drops, alarm in her

eyes, and she presses both palms to the countertop of the island like she's ready to bolt. Her eyes meet mine—waiting for... reassurance?

"It's just my brothers," I tell her. "They live here too."

Liam's familiar loud tone greets us as he enters the loft, talking to, I'm assuming Aidan, seeing as they would have just wrapped up hockey practice together. His wife, Rory, is somewhere in the loft, though I haven't seen her all day. My other brother Alex has been staying with us since his falling out with the Bratva. It felt good for a minute to have everyone under one roof. That is, until my sister decided to flee her "gilded prison," setting off the chain of events that led to me getting shot and the Bratva Pakhan's death. I sent Alex to New York to try and track her down, but so far he hasn't had much luck, and after the text she sent me yesterday, her phone's gone dark.

"Something smells good!" Liam proclaims loudly as he steps into the kitchen.

Briar's head whips to the archway as my youngest brother makes his appearance.

Liam freezes at the sight of Briar sitting at the kitchen island. They met the night I took her from Gio, and he saw her again at the meeting at The Sovereign, but they haven't been formally introduced.

"Oh, hello?" His eyes dart my way, and I shoot him a look, silently warning him to *behave*.

He returns my glare with a look of amusement—*Not a good sign*—and continues waltzing into the kitchen. "How's it hanging, mystery girl?"

Mystery girl? Briar mouths in my direction, and I roll my eyes, hoping my brother won't make me regret bringing her here.

"I'm Liam." He holds out a gigantic hand that Briar stares at for several seconds before taking it.

"Briar." She nods, shaking his hand assertively, while making a point to look him in the eye, leading to a wide smile forming on Liam's face.

"Where's Aidan?" I ask, noticing how he didn't follow Liam into the kitchen.

"Ah, he's checking on little Kostalova—I mean O'Rourke," he corrects with a wince, quickly checking over his shoulder to make sure Aidan didn't hear him. I don't think our brother would appreciate Liam calling his new *wife* by her maiden name.

"Briar's staying the night," I inform him, which earns me two raised brows.

"Is she now?"

I nod slowly. *Don't start,* I warn him with my eyes.

"Roger that," Liam smirks.

I check the meat thermometer on the chicken. It's almost done. Annoyance rolls through me at how easily Briar and Liam have caught on. The two have been chatting nonstop for the past fifteen minutes.

Briar's sitting at the counter, head propped up on her hands as she asks endless questions about hockey, our family, and our life. It's segued into Liam sharing a few stories about us growing up, and I've had to cut him off twice already from sharing too much.

I watch them intently, but my gaze is more focused on Briar. Liam's been asking her questions, too, but her answers are short and stilted like she's holding herself back from giving away too much. Still, it's the most I think I've ever heard her talk.

Liam is good at making her laugh. She's so different when she's happy; her guard isn't fully down, but she's lowered it, and it's giving me a glimpse into the *real* Briar. The girl I remember from the night we spent together years ago. Sharp edges softened, her laugh is light and genuine, and I almost ruin the sauce, because I'm too busy paying attention to her to notice it boiling again.

Aidan appears in the archway, likely drawn in by the scent of dinner that's nearly done.

"How was practice?" I ask.

He comes around the island, his green eyes eyeing Briar and Liam curiously as he reaches behind me and swipes one of the rolls from the bowl I just put out. They haven't seen him yet.

"Fine." He leans back against the counter next to me, taking a bite from the roll. "That the girl you've been pretending doesn't exist?" he asks quietly in my ear.

I scoff and shove him lightly, and he lets out a laugh.

The sound alerts Briar and Liam to his presence, and her reaction is immediate.

She freezes, shoulders stiffening, anxiety flashing in her eyes.

Interesting.

Although, I guess the last time Briar saw Aidan, he was bashing someone's face in with a baseball bat...

I place the dishes and silverware on the island for Liam to set the table. He takes hold of the dishes, but not before Briar swipes up the silverware, turning back to the table as if she means to help.

"No," I say, and Liam looks up. "Don't let her help. She's injured."

Liam moves quick as lightning, snatching the silverware out of Briar's hands before she even realizes he moved.

"Hey!"

Liam just shrugs. "Sorry, mystery girl. Boss' orders."

She turns to scowl at me, and I give her a look.

Briar slides down off the stool. She's so short that when she's sitting on it, her feet don't touch the ground. Slowly, she makes her way across the kitchen to the table.

I lean over the island, snapping to get Liam's attention. Briar's back is to me. *Help her,* I mouth to him, pointing at Briar currently limping across the kitchen.

He drops the plates and silverware on the table and circles back around it, attempting to assist Briar, but she swats him away. He looks between her and me, his hands hovering around her in case she falls, and I can tell he doesn't want to touch her.

I look up at the ceiling. *Lord help me.*

With Briar safely seated, Liam finishes setting the table, and a few minutes later, Aidan helps me bring the food over. But not before swiping another bread roll from the basket.

"Any more word from Reagan?" he asks, once I've set the final dish out.

"No." I clench my jaw while lowering myself into my chair. "I've sent Alex, Garrett, and Jerrad—and a few of their guys— down to New York to see if they can locate her, but they're still trying to pick up her trail."

"I tried calling her, but it just goes right to voicemail," he tells me, and I know he's as worried as I am.

"How's Rory?" Liam asks, and I lean in, wanting to know, too. She's had a rough couple of days.

"She's still kind of shaken up," Aidan admits. "She slept most of the day, but she said she might come down to dinner."

"If she's not up to it, I can set aside a plate for her," I offer, and Aidan nods at me appreciatively.

Briar's been quiet since we all sat down, and I'm surprised when it's she who speaks up next.

"Who's Reagan?"

The table goes silent. Only a few scrapes of metal can be heard from Liam's fork as he stares down at his plate, pushing his food around with it.

I clear my throat. "Our sister," I inform her.

Briar's eyes dart around the table, taking in the sudden shift of mood, recognizing that she's stepped into something complicated.

I start carefully—we've been trying to keep Reagan's disappearance as much of a secret as possible. We're all nervous about what might happen if word gets out in the underworld that she's on her own. *Unprotected.* I can think of quite a few of our enemies who would have a field day with that information.

"She ran away this week."

"Ran away?" Briar's eyes widen and she looks around the table. I notice how she keeps casting nervous glances Aidan's way.

"She wasn't a fan of lockdown," Liam jokes, though Briar doesn't get it.

I lean forward on my elbows, lacing my fingers together over my plate as I try and explain. "I know you are aware that our father died."

She nods, watching me nervously.

"He was murdered." Her eyes widen but I continue, "Tensions in the city have been running high since his death. We know the Russians killed our dad, but we feel it's part of a bigger play to wrestle control of the city." I watch her face carefully; there's fear there but she's still listening. "It appears a few of us have targets on our backs." She swallows, her fingers tightening around her fork. "Until we get to the bottom of it, we've had to tighten security. Reagan, our sister, was not too happy about that, as you may be able to understand. This life —*our life*—is dangerous. As our sister, Reagan will never be safe. There will always be someone, some *threat*, out there looking to get to us by hurting her." My eyes hold Briar's for a moment. It's a reminder to both of us why I pushed her away in the first place.

"Reagan has been pushing back against the increase in security, and I guess she just finally had enough." My jaw works and I pick my fork back up. "She texted yesterday saying she was safe and she was sorry, but then she turned her phone off."

"So you're going to hunt her down?"

"I'm trying to keep her safe."

She cocks her head. "There's a difference."

The table around us is silent.

"Yeah. There is a difference between tracking someone down and dragging them home. Between watching them and caging them. If she wants out, I won't force her back. But I also won't let anyone take advantage of her or put her at risk either."

She studies my face. "You said she turned her phone off. That kinda sounds like she doesn't *want* to be found."

"Maybe," I say, leaning back in my chair and tilting my head. "Maybe she just needs a little space to breathe. But it doesn't change the fact that there are people out there who want to hurt her. I won't let that happen."

"You don't get to decide for her," she says, and her tone sharpens. I'm not so certain we're talking about *Reagan* anymore.

"You're right."

Surprise flickers in her expression as she stares back at me.

"I don't. But I can do what I can. I can keep watch. Make sure there's a way out if she wants one, and I can keep her safe."

Her eyes narrow. "And what if she doesn't want your help?"

I can feel my brothers' eyes on me, as interested in my answer as she is.

"Then I'll back off." Her brows rise. "But I won't stop watching out for her. The reality is our world isn't safe and, once you're in it, there's no escaping it." I shake my head slowly, and she swallows, shifting in her chair. "I protect what's mine. Family or otherwise."

She drops her gaze back to her plate, pushing around the vegetables, and I would kill to read her thoughts right now.

"For god's sake, Briar, eat something," I growl, after several minutes of watching her rearrange her plate.

Her gaze lifts and she glares at me, spearing a piece of broccoli, and holding my eye while she lifts it to her mouth and pops it in, chewing slowly.

She lifts her hands as if to say: *There, happy?*

The corner of my mouth ticks up, *That's a good girl.*

LET HER GO

KOEN

Now

We eat in silence for an uncomfortable amount of time, until Liam decides to save us all with talk of hockey. Briar plays along, even asking a few questions, but when she smiles, it doesn't reach her eyes.

Briar stiffens at the sound of a phone vibrating from some-where. *Hers.* Slowly, she reaches into her back pocket and pulls out the device, eyes scanning over the screen. Her eyes brighten and her lips curve up.

She looks up at the table, careful to avoid looking me in the eye.

"I'm sorry, if you'll excuse me." She stands, a little too fast, the chair legs scraping across the floor. "I have to take this." She eyes me nervously before she turns, sliding the button on her phone to answer the call, but not saying anything before limping out of the room.

I stare after her. She really shouldn't be walking on that ankle.

The moment she's out of sight, I stand, pushing back my chair. Both my brothers watch me as I trail her quietly out of the kitchen.

She retreats back to my bedroom, closing the door, but not all the way, seemingly indecisive over it as her hand hovers over the knob. *Maybe she's afraid if she shuts it, she'll never escape.* Deciding to leave the door cracked, she moves further inside, and I can hear her voice drifting back to me in soft, hushed tones I can't quite make out.

I linger in the hallway, just out of sight, feeling only a little bit guilty for eavesdropping.

Whoever's on the other end makes her laugh, and my chest goes tight. I inch just a little bit closer to the door, trying to make out what she's saying.

"I miss you so much."

My hands ball into fists before I can stop them. *Who the fuck is she talking to?*

Briar lets out another laugh, and I can't help but take a peek through the crack in the door, seeing a genuine smile on her face, though her eyes look sad.

"I can't wait to watch you play hockey!"

She's talking to someone about fucking hockey? Hockey? Her guy's a fucking hockey player? Really?

My fists tighten at my sides, and I'm really hoping whoever the fucker is plays for the league, so I can tell Aidan and Liam to have a field day. It's a struggle to resist the urge to reach for the handle. *I want his name, I want his team, jersey number, home address....*

"I love you too. Always."

Everything stops.

It hits me harder than it should. Something twists deep within my chest. Part rage, part jealousy, and part a raw ache I'm unable to put a name to.

She loves him?

I don't want to hear anymore. Stepping away from the door, I stalk back down the hall.

She has someone.

I don't go back to the kitchen, needing time to process what I've just heard. My body is wired so tight, it's ready to snap. I'm tense, restless energy crawling under my skin. I slam my thumb hard into the elevator button, and it opens right away. Stepping inside, I pace the small, confined space until it opens up to the garage below.

The image of Briar's smile is burned into my brain. The way her whole face lit up, the softness in her eyes as she spoke to *him*. I hate the way just hearing his voice brought that out in her.

I stalk in the direction of my bike, pulling out my phone and sending off a quick text to Liam to let him know I'm going out and to keep an eye on Briar. Under no circumstances should she be allowed to leave the loft.

I reach the bike and swing my leg over, the deep rumble of the motor already quelling the deep-seated rage I feel in my chest.

What the fuck am I doing? What the fuck is this? Jealousy?

I lean forward, revving the bike under me, and making a hell of a lot of noise doing it. Whatever this is between me and her, it wasn't supposed to matter—*she* wasn't supposed to matter.

We made a deal. It was simple—a means to an end. Once

we clean the fucking shit out of this city, and she's safe from a one-way trip in a shipping container across the ocean, we go our separate ways. She'll walk her way, and I'll walk mine. Clean. Done. Over.

That's what I want.

I love you.

It grates, replaying the warmth in her voice when she said it.

My jaw clenches and I release the throttle, my bike shooting out of the garage and onto the street. *I hate her. I fucking hate her. She's not mine. I don't even want her to be mine.*

The engine roars under me, the vibration running straight through my bones as I push through the gears.

Faster.

The city blurs around me, streetlights streaking gold; icy wind tears at my hoodie, and I lean further into the bike; the sound of the engine and wind is almost enough to drown out the sound of Briar's voice in my head.

I love you.

I throttle the bike again, going faster still until my vision starts to tunnel. The fury, jealousy, longing—it's all tangled together.

A sharp curve in the road ahead comes up fast, and I lean into it hard, my back tire skidding out just enough to spike my pulse.

I welcome it. The risk, the speed, the pain—it all might just be enough to shut my brain the fuck up. The road straightens out and I push the bike even harder, chasing the edge, flirting with the kind of recklessness that could end me in seconds, desperate to chase out the pain. Everything I've had to walk away from, all the sacrifices I've been forced to make for the good of the family. The way I know, eventually, I'll have to walk away from her, *again.*

The road is dark, but I've driven this way enough to know there's another sharp curve ahead, this one worse than the last. I throttle the bike again, edging further into oblivion until, at the last second, I yank the bike back under control, muscles screaming as the tires catch, and hold back just before the turn.

I pull off onto the shoulder and kill the engine. The sudden silence hits hard. A relief—even my head has gone quiet.

Briar has someone. She's moved on. She's not stuck in this endless loop of want and pain that's haunted me from the second I laid eyes on her five years ago. I'd been so concerned with ruining her that I hadn't stopped to think she'd ruin me.

The wind blows, and with it comes the cold bitter reality I can't run from: *My beautiful little Rose was, and still is, too good for me. And I'm going to have to let her go.*

55

HER BOYFRIEND

BRIAR

Now

It took some convincing, but Koen finally allowed me to go to the Conservatory so long as I promised him I would not dance. I thought it would be harder to get him to agree, but it was as if he couldn't wait to be rid of me.

He was quiet this morning, distant and hard to read. Like his mind was elsewhere.

He vanished last night. I came back to the table to find him... gone. Liam said there was something that needed his attention, but I saw the look he gave Aidan when they thought I wasn't looking.

I spent the night in his bed. While I strongly considered camping out on the couch, the room was open to everyone else who lived there, and the privacy of Koen's room felt just a little bit safer.

I don't know where he slept. He reappeared early this

morning, cooking up a couple of omelettes in silence. Besides the little battle over the Conservatory, he'd hardly said two words to me. Leaving me to be Mac's problem for the day, he stalked out of the loft. But not before informing me that my heat would be fixed by the time I got home this afternoon.

Whatever warmth had been there yesterday was long gone. That usual cold control was back, and I could feel the wall rising back up between us.

My ankle does feel a lot better today. I'm able to bear weight, and the swelling has gone down significantly. Though, Koen is right, I should probably take another day or two off from dancing, so as to not prolong the healing process.

But this morning was one of the few classes Melanie wasn't able to find coverage for. It's a winter break intensive for the girls in the intermediate program who are still in high school. They're one of my favorite ages to work with. Just serious enough about their craft that I don't have to redirect their attention every five minutes, and in some of them, you can already see it in their eyes how much they really want this, how far they're willing to go.

They remind me of myself.

Like me, the group is prepping for the winter showcase, and their routine is looking really, really good.

I'm sitting with my foot propped up on a chair, a full bag of ice wrapped around it, while calling out counts loud enough to be heard over the music. "One, two, three, four, five, six, seven, eight. Good, Vanessa!"

By the end of the fifth run-through I find no reason to push them further, ending the class on a good note a few minutes early.

"They're really coming along, Briar!"

I look up to see Mia step into the studio. "I came in to get a few hours of practice in, and I was just heading out, but I caught the last run. They look great." She smiles at me, and I return it. Her frown comes next when her eyes drop to the bag of ice on my ankle.

"What happened?"

I quickly snatch the bag off my ankle and stand. "Ah, just a little sore from yesterday. I may have gone a little overboard trying to get that combination in the second half."

"That combination is tricky, and from where I was standing, it looked perfect. Mr. Carr was just being an ass." She gives me a look. "As per usual."

I give her a shrug because she's just being nice. "It could have been tighter. A few more hours in the studio, and I'll get it right."

"It's crunch time." Mia nods with a knowing look in her eye. "We're all feeling it."

"Tell me about it."

"So I was just about to go grab a coffee over at that place on Newbury Street. Do you want to come with?" She gives me an appraising look. "That is—if you can walk?" She eyes my ankle.

"I can walk," I rush out, a tad defensively, and Mia raises her brows.

"But I... I don't know if I should," I mutter, forcing a smile. I'm not supposed to leave the studio. I'm pretty sure Mac's outside keeping an eye out—or maybe someone else, I'm not sure. I haven't checked because, ignorance is bliss and all that.

But after nearly a week of constant surveillance, it's really tempting to sneak out for an hour on my own. It's just coffee, two blocks over.

And it might be my pent-up frustration at not being able to dance, or how Koen made me stay at his place last night and then disappeared, but I'm tired of being told what to do, where to be, and how to act. He's not supposed to be back for two more hours. He's picking me up to go to another club with him. My anxiety over that is probably what pushes me over the edge.

"You know what?" I grin, "Yes. I need a little afternoon pick-me-up. Let me just grab my stuff."

Mia smiles and starts for the door, and I follow.

"Uhm, let's go out the back door," I say as we near the stairs.

Mia arches a brow of curiosity at me but I don't explain, just turn, trotting down the stairs, then turning away from the front entrance and hoping she'll follow. Lucky for me, she does, and even luckier, she doesn't ask any questions.

It's a quick walk from the Conservatory to Central Perk Coffee, but the cold bites straight through my sweatshirt. I didn't pack a jacket, and I'm regretting that decision now. A cold front has moved in to the city and shows no sign of moving out.

The wind is the worst part. If it wasn't for the wind, it might be a nice day. It whips off the river, burning my cheeks until I'm sure they're a bright pink. I shove my hands into the pocket of my hoodie and pick up the pace, my fingertips already numb.

Still, I've got a big grin on my face. The little thrill I get from defying Koen's "*rules*" wakes me up far more than the cold or the coffee could.

The shop is busy, but we find a spot near the back and take a seat. I listen to Mia tell me all about how her routine is going. She's dancing a pas de deux with Devin. I've seen their routine, and I've never seen two people more in sync with each other. Their chemistry is really something else.

"So speaking of Devin," I smile mischievously when I see her blush. "Is there anything going on between the two of you?" I ask, because the smile on Mia's face every time she mentions Devin's name makes it glaringly obvious.

She does, in fact, flush crimson. "No. Of course not! What on earth would give you that idea?" Her words are too rushed to be true.

"No reason." I smirk, taking a convenient sip of my coffee and watching her grow increasingly flustered, nearly spilling hers. I love how normal this feels. I think I needed this more than I realized.

The low rumble of a motorcycle engine echoes in the distance.

My heart stutters.

That sound. My face whips toward the shop windows, but I don't spot the bike I could have sworn I heard.

He wouldn't, he couldn't—

After a few seconds, when no bike, or biker, appears, I blow out a breath and turn back to Mia, who thankfully hasn't noticed my mini heart attack, too busy trying to convince both me, and herself, that she and Devin aren't meant to be together.

The coffee shop door chimes and my head whips up again.

Everything around me fades away when I catch sight of the hulking menace standing in the doorway.

Koen's eyes are a storm of fury, and he finds me almost instantly. His jaw ticks when those dark eyes make contact with mine.

"*Shit*," I whisper to myself.

He crosses the space in long, deliberate strides, and it's an effort not to shrink back into my seat, or worse—hide under the table, because the thought has occurred to me.

How did he find me here?

When he reaches us, I stare down at my coffee, ignoring the glare he levels down at me, his arms crossed, his face as hard as stone. He's dressed in full leather gear from being on his bike, a cowl bunched around his neck that he probably had pulled up over his face under his helmet. *He's really riding in this weather?*

"Uhm, Briar?" Mia hisses in my direction, looking nervously between an irate Koen and me. "Do you know this guy?" Her finger points timidly upward.

I open my mouth to answer, still avoiding Koen's eye, but he beats me to it.

"I'm her boyfriend."

Mia's eyes narrow. *Boyfriend?* she mouths. I catch it out of the corner of my eye, because, after he spoke, my gaze whipped up and I'm now staring wide-eyed up at Koen.

Boyfriend?

"Time to go."

"I was just—"

"Now." His tone is clipped and stern and leaves no room for argument.

"Briar?" Mia's question is laced with concern.

"It's fine," I lie quickly, forcing a smile before my eyes dart back to Koen. "I forgot we have that—err—thing—" Trying to explain his stern demeanor and clear lack of manners.

One of Koen's eyes twitches, but he says nothing, pulling out my chair for me.

"I'll text you later." Quickly, I gather up my things.

I follow Koen through the shop. He holds the door open for me, and when I walk past him, his hand finds the small of my back—firm, possessive—a silent warning.

I swallow hard, the cool air from the street biting against my skin.

"I thought I told you to stay put. You weren't supposed to leave the studio," he growls into my ear, as he guides me with a light grip on my upper arm to where he parked his bike, just a few steps down from the shop.

I *knew* I'd heard it.

"How the hell did you find me anyway?" I ask, looking around for Mac or the SUV but not finding it, thinking maybe he followed me from the studio, though I kept checking over my shoulder to be sure. I'm almost certain no one saw me leave the studio, yet here stands Koen. A very, very angry Koen.

"You're not as clever as you think you are," he says, handing me an extra helmet.

I grimace. *If I thought walking was cold...*

"You need to follow the rules. It's not safe on the streets for you. Last I checked, Giovanni is still in business, and they're pretty eager to replenish their inventory."

My shoulders tighten at the mention of Giovanni. I'm all too aware of how "in business" he is, seeing as he won't stop blowing up my phone.

"Your girlfriend, huh?" I ask, raising an eyebrow.

"Made sense at the time," he mutters.

"Just like old times," I smile, attempting to lighten the mood, but his eyes just narrow as he loses more patience with me.

"Get on the bike, Briar. I'll drop you back at the studio before having a few words with Mac."

I frown. I didn't want to get Mac into trouble. My brow creases; I'm worried what Koen might do to Mac.

"It's not his fault. I snuck out the back, and he never saw me. I made sure he didn't see me," I rush out in Mac's defense.

Koen turns slowly to face me.

"You're—You're not going to hurt him or anything, are you?" I ask, chewing nervously on my lip, helmet still in my hands.

Koen curses under his breath and looks to the sky. "No little Rose, I'm not going to hurt him."

My shoulders fall forward as I deflate.

"Now, will you get on the damn bike?"

R.I.P to my fingertips. But just as soon as I lift the helmet to my head, my phone rings and we both freeze. I hurriedly pull it out to silence it, aware of Koen's heavy gaze on me. I almost drop the stupid phone in my haste.

"You need to get that?" he asks after a long drawn out pause, his words feeling razor sharp.

"No. It's just my roommate."

"Your *roommate* calls you a lot."

I give him a look. "You're very observant."

His jaw tightens. "I am about things that matter."

"And how often my roommate calls me matters?" I smirk, trying to deflect the tension. I don't need him questioning how often Lily calls me.

He doesn't answer. His gaze pinning me before he says, "Don't test me."

Done with the conversation, he turns around, swinging a leg over the bike and starting it up.

I sigh, slipping the helmet over my head, and getting on the *damn bike* without further argument.

OBSIDIAN

KOEN

Now

After picking my little runaway up from the coffee shop, I gave her a ride two blocks over to the studio, only to shove her right into the back of Mac's SUV, sending her back to her apartment to change. I would have taken her there myself, but it's bloody cold out, and she's not dressed to be on the bike in this weather.

While Briar got ready, I went to the loft to shower and change, putting on a dark suit before shooting back over to Briar's apartment to pick her back up. I'm already on a time crunch, thanks to her little escapade this afternoon, but then she has the nerve to delay us even more, locking herself in the bathroom as soon as I arrive to "finish getting ready."

I've tried pounding on the door several times. The inner battle I've been having with myself on whether or not to kick the goddamn thing down is getting harder to manage each time I hear "five more minutes!"

She's making us late on purpose; I *know* she is. She's probably in there, sitting on the sink filing her nails or something. I bet she's taking absolute delight in listening to the way my voice loses a little more control each time I pound on that door.

"Five more minutes!"

It was, in fact, *not* five minutes.

The club we're going to is owned by the Bratva, and, while I do need her to be presentable, I need her out of the goddamn bathroom. Jace's wife, Cara, has been kind enough to help me pick out clothing for Briar, and thankfully, she was able to help again on such short notice.

But when she finally walks out of that bathroom, I don't know whether to fire his wife, or give her a raise, because Briar steps out and everything just... *stops.*

I'm overwhelmed by the sudden urge to rush her and lift her up, those black boots wrapping around my waist while I take her on the bathroom counter. I want to ruin those perfect waves in her hair with my hands, smear that dark plum lipstick she's wearing all up and down my cock while she kneels at my feet, looking up at me under those thick, dark lashes, all while taking me deep, before swallowing every last bit of my cum.

I step back when she passes me, not trusting myself to touch her. We're already late, and if she so much as grazes up against me, we're never leaving this apartment.

She's dressed to kill in a black latex dress. The glossy material catches the light, and the way the dress creases over her curves makes it near impossible for me to look at her. The dress hugs close to her chest, pushing her breasts up and out, and even worse, the dress is short, barely reaching her upper thighs. And then there's the boots... Thigh-high, black suede, leaving just a sliver of skin between where her dress ends and the boots begin.

On the ride over to Obsidian, I have to keep my eyes glued to my phone screen, because just looking at Briar in those boots is pure torture.

Briar looks like the perfect little pet, which is exactly what I want from her, but it still thoroughly pisses me off, knowing no one will be able to resist looking at her.

I keep her close, my hand on the small of her back as we walk in, but after stepping inside, I take her hand in mine and lace my fingers through hers.

I feel her gaze on me, but my eyes are elsewhere, scanning the club, taking in any potential threats. After what happened last time, I'm not taking any chances with her.

Boston's underworld is still reeling from the events of the other night.

A dead Pakhan will do that.

Word hit the streets this morning that Adrik Kostalov, the Bratva Pakhan—Aidan's new father-in-law—is dead. But what they don't know, is how he was shot clean through the forehead *by his own daughter*.

The disaster worked out in our favor, given that Rory's brother, Niko, is taking over as the new Bratva Pakhan. I thought they hated each other, but I guess I was wrong about that, seeing as how he helped his sister save my brother's life.

Now I owe him one.

My hand tightens on Briar as we weave our way through the club.

Aidan brokered somewhat of a truce between Nikolai

Kostalov and Cole DeLuca, the Italians' Capo, that night, ultimately getting us off the hook for murdering the latter's consigliere in cold blood. The truce is tentative and still untested, but the last thing any of us wants is a war.

It's dark in here. Mahogany wood panels line the walls, and there is a thick cloud of cigar smoke in the air. The furniture is also dark wood and leather, where men sit and discuss business. They're all armed, and we all know it.

I follow one of Niko's men deeper into the club, keeping my eyes forward, trusting Aidan and Mac to have my back.

We draw attention as we move through the club. I'm sure everyone here knows who I am. Everyone knows the Irish were out for blood after finding out Adrik Kostalov killed Declan O'Rourke. And don't get me wrong, I'm still fucking pissed about it, but I got my pound of flesh, so it's time to do the hard work and foster alliances, and all that bullshit.

I should be focused on the meeting ahead, but annoyingly, all I can think about is the girl I have trailing on my heels.

"Keep your head down and don't wander." I draw her closer to me, muttering low enough so only she can hear me.

"I'm not an idiot," she snaps back, and it's the bite of defiance in her voice that eases the tension in my shoulders. It tells me she's okay. I wasn't sure how she'd react, walking back into the lion's den after what happened to her last time. When she stops biting back, I'll worry.

"Who are we meeting again?"

"Nikolai Kostalov."

"Is that—"

"Rory's brother? Yes."

"And do we like him?" Briar looks up at me with an expression that's far too innocent for discussing the new Bratva Pakhan. But the way she says "*we*" has me fighting a smile.

"The alliance is new. He's supposed to be on our side, but no, we don't trust him."

She listens carefully, taking in my words and thinking them over.

I didn't want to do this today, though this bar is the perfect place for Briar to see if she recognizes anyone. I tried putting it off, but Niko insisted.

We're led to a private room.

Nikolai is already seated, and he doesn't move to get up, even as I watch his steely blue eyes follow the girl at my side as we walk inside.

"Have a seat." He gestures to the chairs around the table.

Aidan and I each take a seat, and I place Briar on my lap. This time she's not leaving my sight. Mac stands by the door, along with Niko's two men I recognize as Kaz and Ilya, his usual Bratva goons.

"I didn't know you had a girl, O'Rourke?" There's a smirk on Niko's face when he looks from me to Briar.

"I don't."

Niko studies me, drawing out the silence between us. "The way you look at her says otherwise."

My eyes darken while his sparkle.

"How's the arm?" he asks me, tilting his head just slightly to the side.

Aidan tenses beside me, and I just know he wants to sucker punch the smirk right off of the Russian's face.

"It's fine." I shrug. He can't see the bandages through my jacket, and I have full range of motion back. I can deal with the pain. "You should work on your aim."

Briar flinches atop me; my mouth twitches watching Niko's eyes darken.

"Get to the point, Nikolai."

He throws back the rest of his drink, leaning forward, his face growing surprisingly somber.

"The Volkov have put out a hit on you and your brother." His voice is low, despite the private room.

Briar's body tenses, and I place a reassuring palm on her thigh. "Aidan?" I ask, and he dips his chin.

"You see why this is problematic for me."

I nod, rubbing the rough stubble along my chin. Nikolai Kostalov is a royal pain in my ass, but he's made it very clear that he cares for his sister, and given that she's in love with my brother... My problem becomes Niko's problem.

"The good news is that the Volkov won't outsource. Their problem with you is personal. The bad news is that they've sent their reaper."

"Ronan Volkov," Aidan adds, and we exchange a look.

Niko nods solemnly, waving for a waitress I hadn't seen waiting in the shadows to refill his drink. "Krasnyy volk."

The red wolf.

My mouth tightens. "When he makes his move, we'll handle it."

Niko shakes his head, leaning forward in his chair. "You don't understand, Ronan sent his men after my father. You and Ace interfered, killing them, and as far as the Volkov are concerned, you killed my father, too. Those men were Ronan's, so this is personal for him. When he goes after someone, he doesn't just kill them; it's a game to him. He gets off on the hunt." Niko's mouth curves up into an appreciative smile. "He likes to play with his food before he eats it."

Could Ronan be the one behind the recent sabotage? Possibly. I certainly can't rule it out, though disaster started long before Aidan and I took out those men.

"He wants to meet with you." Niko takes his fresh drink from the waitress and points a finger at me.

"Ronan?" I ask, surprised.

"Da." *Yes.*

I narrow my eyes. "He has a price on my head..."

"One night truce," Niko says with a shrug, which has me questioning whether or not I can actually trust him.

"Fine. Set it up."

Niko raises his glass with a nod, and I see his eyes rove over Briar again; my grip on her tightens.

"Was there anything else, or—"

"How's my sister?" Any remaining trace of amusement on the new Pakhan's face is gone now, and his light blue eyes have slid over to my brother at my side, who has been unusually quiet.

Aidan's jaw flexes. He's been watching Niko like a hawk since we walked in here. "She's fine."

Nikolai scoffs, "Fine? I'm going to need a hell of a lot more than that, *puck* boy."

Niko may have helped Rory escape her father, but Aidan and Niko still have a long way to go as far as trusting one another.

Aidan's fists tighten, and he leans forward in his seat, temper flaring, but I reach up, putting my hand on his shoulder.

"Rory's safe," I assure him. "Maybe we'll invite you over for dinner one of these nights."

He huffs out a genuine laugh, "Da, if we all live through

the month." He stands, and we do the same. Niko reaches across the table to shake my hand, his blue eyes sliding over to Briar one last time. "Ronan's out for blood," he says, holding my eye. "Keep your loved ones close."

57

RULE NUMBER ONE

BRIAR

THEN...

"Do you really have to tell him, though?" Lily is practically running to keep pace with me as I power walk off the subway and charge up the stairs, bypassing the escalator to street level.

"Yes, I have to tell him," I insist, to her and to myself, remembering how I spent most of last night pacing my bedroom while wrestling with this very decision. "It's the right thing to do." But Rí will probably tell me to get lost, the fucking asshole.

He still deserves to know.

"We're closed!" the guy behind the bar calls out as I push through the front door of Last Call; his Irish accent is thick. I pull up short at the sight of the wide empty space. Lily follows in after me, crashing into my back, not prepared for me to have stopped so quickly after stepping inside.

"Sorry," she hisses, but her eyes dart around the club the same way mine did.

"Hey! Are ye deaf?" The guy behind the bar sets down the rag he's using to clean it and straightens, giving us a hard look. "I said we're closed."

Lily and I both exchange a look, and she takes a pointed step back toward the entrance, only to sigh when I head for the bar.

The man's frown deepens when he sees me coming.

"Hi. I'm sorry to bother you, but I'm actually looking for someone who works here."

His head tilts to the side, considering me. "Name?"

I exhale. "Uh... yeah, so you see, that's the problem. I didn't get his name..."

The level of annoyance on this guy's face reaches new levels. I feel Lily's anxious energy at my back, but press on.

"So, this guy..."

"Okay..." He repeats in my same tone of voice, and I narrow my eyes at his obvious imitation of me.

"I met him a couple of weeks ago... he said he works here... I don't know—he's tall. Like, really tall, with short, dirty blonde hair..." The bartender stares at me with a blank expression on his face. "Uhm... he had a spider web tattoo across his hand, and he goes by Rí." I trace my fingers over my knuckles and the bartender visibly stiffens, his eyes widening. "I—err—do you know his name?"

He looks at me like I have ten heads.

"Aye, I do," he answers, but offers nothing else other than to give me a quick once-over.

I shift under the scrutiny. "You wanna share it?"

He looks at me for another moment, then to Lily, as if deciding something, before folding his arms across his chest and looking down his nose at me.

"Koen O'Rourke."

Everything stops.

"O'Rourke, as in—"

"Aye, *O'Rourke,* as in..." He holds up two fingers in the shape of a gun before pretending to fire it.

I've only been in Boston a little over a year, but even I know that last name. *And what it means.*

Lily lets out a breath, and I feel her grip my shoulders. "Shit." She takes a step back, attempting to pull me with her. "We should go."

I shrug her off, keeping my attention on the bartender.

Fuck, Rí is Koen O'Rourke. O'Rourke as in the Irish mafia? I suppose that makes sense but like, how high up is he? Like what level of committed are we talking here?

"I—I need to talk to him."

He shakes his head, going back to wiping down glasses. "No, I certainly don't recommend that now, miss. Best you and your friend get on your way, in fact. If Koen didn't give you his name, that's because he didn't want you to have it."

The guy suddenly looks nervous, checking over each shoulder, but the bar is still quiet.

"Briar," Lily hisses in my ear, still trying to tug me toward the door.

"It's important."

Despite my continued insistence, the bartender just shakes his head. "Still can't help you, lass, even if I wanted to. Koen's not here."

"Like... just stepped out, or—?"

"Gone," the bartender confirms. "Back to Ireland."

"*Back* to Ireland?" I repeat.

He nods. "Yep, he's gone to meet up with his fiancée." He eyes me pointedly. "I don't know if, or when, he'll be back, so like I said lass, it's best ye both be on your way."

Fiancée? Koen has a fiancée? Koen's gone back to Ireland, for his work with the Irish mafia?

Fuck me. My head is spinning and I feel nauseous, and I know for a fact this time it's not morning sickness.

Guess that explains why he threw me out of his room that morning...

Lily is just about to succeed in her efforts to drag me away, when another guy walks up from behind the bar. He looks familiar, his green eyes glitter down at me from his insane height of what has to be six four or six five.

Following our gaze, the bartender turns his head and smiles, even though he looks more nervous than he did before. "Oi lass, it's your lucky day. This here is Koen's brother, he may be able to help you out better than me. Best of luck to you." He gives me a final, warning glance, before acknowledging the hulking mass of muscle behind him, and before slipping away. "Liam."

Liam steps closer, looking between us with a wide grin on his face. He looks a bit too young to be working in a bar. "Hello, ladies, I'm a little disappointed to hear you're here looking for my brother." He rolls his eyes and keeps that easy grin on his face, leaning down across the bar. "But how can I help ye?"

My jaw opens, but I snap it shut, staring into familiar green eyes, the same color green as his brother's, but absent the dark shadows and sharp edges.

"No. Uhm—nope. There's just been a little confusion. We don't need anything, thank you so much," Lily blurts out as she wrestles me away from the bar, steering my shocked ass toward the door.

Liam's brows furrow in confusion, the amusement fading from his face as he watches Lily drag me toward the door. "You're sure?" he asks me a little more seriously.

Lily's managed to push me several feet away before I dig my heels in, halting our retreat.

"Briar!" she hisses under her breath, her panicked eyes darting to Liam and back to me.

I give her a little nod of my head before looking back at Koen's brother, keeping my tone as cool and casual as possible.. "Yep. I'm sure. This was... a mistake. We're just gonna go."

I gesture toward the door behind me, and, much to Lily's relief, resume our retreat.

Once we're safely outside, and around the next block, she finally lets out the breath she's clearly been holding in. "Of all the men in the city to knock you up, you pick Koen-Fucking-O'Rourke?"

"I didn't know!" We pass a trash barrel, and I seriously consider grabbing onto it and heaving out my insides. *I feel awful.*

"Girl!" She pinches the bridge of her nose, keeping us en route to the subway. "Rule number one: Don't hook up with the Irish Devils. And rule number two: *Don't* have their *baby*."

Once we're safely on a subway car taking us back to the dorms, I deflate in my seat, rubbing my fingers on my temples.

"What am I going to do, Lily?" The disappointment I feel is crushing. There really was a part of me that hoped I wasn't going to have to do this on my own.

"Well, I'll tell you what we're not going to do... We're not going to tell the Irish Devil King about this." She waves her hand over my belly. Nausea creeps up, and I'm not sure if it's the conversation or the movement of the train. "He's dangerous, B. Like, sociopathic. Haven't you heard the stories?"

To be honest, I hadn't really paid attention. We didn't have warring mafia families back in upstate New York. But I *have* seen the Irish Devils shake down poor Mr. and Mrs. Ashford, who own Mae's diner, for being late on a protection payment. They broke a couple of windows, some dishes, and terrorized Mae and her husband with a dark promise to return if their payment was late again.

The low-lifes.

"He's the *heir*, Briar."

My gaze raises slowly to meet Lily's eyes.

"The heir?"

She nods slowly. And maybe there is something wrong with me, because after everything I learned about Koen today, the only thing I keep thinking about is how he's *gone*. Gone back to Ireland to be with his *fiancée.*

Tears fill my eyes as everything starts to feel real all at once.

"How am I going to do this Lily? Raise a baby? *Alone?* My parents are going to insist I get rid of it."

Some delusional part of me pictured Rí and I raising this baby together. Yeah, he was a jerk afterwards, but that night with him changed my life. I don't want to believe that it was all just a lie to get in my pants. Whatever transpired between the two of us, it was on a deeper level. I felt it. I know he felt it too. But I guess I was wrong.

Lily squeezes me tight, and for once I don't mind the suffocating hug. "You've got me, okay? Whatever happens, we're in this together."

58

TELL ME TO STOP

KOEN

Now

Briar's at it again. Another late night spent in that run-down dance studio over the diner.

She's dancing again. I should've known she wouldn't be able to stay off that ankle. Just like I should've known I wouldn't be able to leave her alone.

I've got a front-row seat for tonight's performance. I blurred the invisible line between us when I climbed in her window the other night. It's messy now, so tonight—tonight I climb the stairs to watch her from inside.

Briar hasn't seen me yet, too caught up in her routine to notice the man, concealed by the dark shadows of the hallway, watching her. She's too focused, lost in the music and emotions, to see anything right now.

I recognize the routine. It's one I've only ever seen her practice here, alone, never at the Conservatory. I believe it's her senior piece, a solo, the one she's choreographing and performing herself. I don't know the criteria she's supposed to adhere to, but the dance Briar has put together is unlike anything I've ever seen.

It's the opposite of the dance she's performing for the showcase... in every way. Instead of a stiff white tutu, she's wearing a simple black leotard with a short, tattered skirt.

Her hair falls loose down her back, free from the neat bun she typically keeps it in when she dances. The movement of her hair is every bit as choreographed as the rest of her body. It whips around, wild and untamed, even tangling into her face, highlighting all the sudden changes in direction the choreography calls for.

She's barefoot, no ballet slippers in sight, and her movements aren't pretty or perfected; rather, they're chaotic and desperate.

Briar's pretty painted smile is gone, too, pain and sadness taking it's place. The raw, unfiltered emotions are a shock to see on Briar's usual carefully schooled face.

Her music, too, is sad and slow, haunted even, the song slowly building into something grander, angrier, with big sweeping cinematic crescendos. Her movements grow more frantic, and instead of landing her jumps, she falls or tumbles out of them. She breaks and doesn't polish her spins, and she doesn't even bother to point her toes. Once she hits the bridge, it looks like she's being torn apart, her body pulled in too many directions at once. The constant change in direction wears on her, and the choreography becomes more and more disjointed, growing in its chaos until she's near desperate to escape it. But each time she tries, she keeps getting knocked down, over and over again, until it's harder to get up, until, eventually, the music stops and she's lying still, alone, in the middle of the room, her eyes closed.

Silence fills the space when the song ends, and Briar sits up, her knees curled into her chest, staring at her reflection in the mirror.

She looks so lost.

I still don't know what she's been through, but I hate it. I hate that anything, or anyone, made her feel this way, and I want to fix it; I want to make it better. I want to scoop her into my arms right now and promise her that nothing, and no one, will ever hurt her again, because she's mine.

And I can just about feel the cut of the blade in my skin when I'm forced to remind myself...

She's not.

"Do you have a boyfriend?"

"What?" Briar flinches at the sound of my voice, scrambling up off the floor as I step out of the shadows. "How long have you been standing there?"

"Answer the question."

She narrows her eyes, wariness in her expression as she takes in the look on my face. "Not that it's any of your business—"

It is.

"—but, no. I don't have a boyfriend."

She doesn't have a boyfriend? I'm faintly aware of something deep inside of me snapping, every muscle in my body tightening, as my reasons for holding myself back from Briar begin to unravel.

I take another step closer. "Then who do you talk to at night? On the phone?" *Who are you saying "I love you" to?*

"Are you spying on me?" Her eyes narrow with the accusation.

Yes.

"No."

Fury flares in her eyes, but I cut her off before she can say anything else.

"You're hiding something from me," I tell her.

Almost instantly, her entire body tenses, and she averts her eyes. She's hiding something, I've known it for a while now. Something happened, something she doesn't want me to know. She doesn't trust me, and that's fucking fair after what I've put her through. So, as much as it's killing me to know, I won't force it out of her, but I want her to tell me.

"I *thought* I was repaying a favor," she sniffs, lifting her chin back up to glare at me while crossing her arms across her chest. "You're not entitled to know everything about me."

I close the gap between us until only inches separate us. She could back up, but she doesn't, holding her ground.

"No, I'm not," I agree. Her eyes pierce into me. And I speak quieter, softer this time. "But I'm asking you; I want to know this."

She's so close. The smell of jasmine is overwhelming.

"Like I said, I don't have a boyfriend; I don't have *anyone*, okay? Are you happy now?" There's a defiant gleam in her eye as she glares up at me. She's unknowingly dancing on the fragile edge of my self-control. Neither of us moves.

"Why do you even care?" she asks, finally, when I don't

answer her, too busy fighting myself. Her voice is barely audible, even though I'm inches away from her.

It's a question I don't have an answer for. I know, because I've been asking myself the same goddamn thing every single day for weeks now, since the warehouse, since I saw her in Wonderland... since that night in the club five years ago, if I'm being honest.

I don't have an answer.

So instead, I kiss her.

My eyes drop to her mouth a split-second before I move in, cupping her face in both hands. Briar doesn't kiss me back. She's frozen, her body impossibly still, caught between shock and disbelief, but years of regret and restraint crash together in a single moment, and I can't stop myself. Everything I can't say, conveyed in a single, devastating crash of my mouth on hers, the last remnants of my control shattering against her silence.

I kissed her before, *really* kissed her, that night at The Sovereign, but she was drugged. I doubt she remembers it, but *I do*. I do, and I haven't thought of anything else since. And after I did it, I spiraled straight into relapse, all those years of convincing myself I'd romanticized what had been between us, how I imagined the dangerous, euphoric high that came with the taste of her. I realized *I hadn't*. But it's darker now; she's a sweet poison that has only grown more addictive with time, and I'm going through withdrawals.

Briar still hasn't moved, and reluctantly, I lift my lips from hers, hovering just over them before I pull back entirely, regret washing through me at what I've done—a slight tremble ripping through my hands before I let her go.

Briar's staring at me like she's seen a ghost, wide-eyed, her lips swollen and bruised from my momentary lapse in control.

She closes her eyes, shutting them tight, hoping—or fearing—I'll still be here when she opens them again. Slowly, hesitantly, she reopens them. She doesn't say a word, and neither do I, but the second her eyes meet mine again, there's no hesitation—it's Briar who closes the gap between us this time, her hand finding my face and tugging it back down, her lips finding mine again.

Fuck. My self-control splinters further, my hands grasping hold of her hips. I yank her body closer as I take back control of the kiss, backing her up until she's pressed against the mirror.

"What are we doing?" she asks in-between kisses. My hands roam her body, while my mouth explores her neck.

"You kissed me back," I tell her.

"But you kissed me first..."

"And you liked it."

Her hands fall to my chest, pushing me back just enough so she can see my face. Her walls are down, and I can see everything she's feeling written all over her face. There's hope... a tiny, fragile flame of it flickering in her eyes, but it's caged by something darker: uncertainty, doubt, fear.

"But I hate you?" Her words sound more like a question than a statement, and I stare down at her.

"Do you?" I arch a brow questioningly, a knowing smirk tugging at the corner of my lips.

"And you hate me?" She looks up at me, her eyes searching mine as if she's desperate to find the answer in them. The usually bright blue is cloudy with all the thoughts running through her mind—confusion, apprehension, and *need.*

She's right. I hate her, but not for the reasons she might think.

"I do," I breathe, leaning back in to trail light kisses and small nips of my teeth up her neck until I reach her ear. The shiver that rips through her when my breath hits the sensitive skin there has my cock straining in my pants. "But I don't have to like you to fuck you, and you can still hate me after I make you come."

I take her mouth again, staking my brutal claim. I can't stop touching her; I can't stop kissing her. The taste of her is not enough; I need to be inside her. She told me she didn't have a boyfriend, and my control didn't just break... it shattered. And even with my mouth on hers, inhaling the scent of her into my soul, it's not enough. There's nothing stopping me now. I'm out of reasons why I should hold myself back.

Except for one.

"Tell me to stop." I release her mouth again, moving lower, my mouth and tongue trailing down the tender flesh of her throat, my teeth grazing the surface, testing, feeling her body respond and arch against me. "Tell me to stop, little Rose, or I swear to god I'm going to fuck you so hard, you'll still feel me days from now."

I drag my lips from her skin to gauge her reaction. She's breathing hard, and while I've got her pinned, she's not trying to get away. There's conflict in her eyes, but there's something else there too—an emotion I can't put a name to.

She's silent, and we stare at each other for a moment. I'm waiting for her to open her mouth, waiting for her to push me away, but when she doesn't, I close my eyes, cupping her face in my hands while I press my forehead to hers.

"It's one word. Four letters," I tell her, my voice tight as I struggle to hold myself back from her. "Say it, and I'll go."

I feel her eyes on me, but she still doesn't say *stop*. She doesn't say *anything*.

"Tell me to stop," I beg her, near desperate to hear the

words. I need her to tell me; I'm afraid I won't stop on my own, and I don't want to hurt her. "Say it!" I shout at her, my dark voice echoing through the empty studio, my eyes still closed tight.

"I can't," she whispers. My eyes fly open, finding her blue eyes on mine, pleading with me... not to stop, but rather... *not to let go.* "I don't want you to."

The last thread of restraint I had left snaps, and my lips crash down hard on hers, slamming her back into the glass wall, not caring if I crack it. Lifting her, her legs wrap around my waist at the same time as her arms tighten around my neck, and I swear I could come from that alone.

Pain rips through my arm where the bullet cut through, but I don't give a single fuck. Adrenaline and obsession drowning it out.

Keeping my lips on hers, I carry her to the back wall, setting her back down on her feet. Her back is again facing a wall of mirrors, but this wall has a wooden ballet barre screwed into it. I spin her in my grip, so now, instead of watching me, she's watching my reflection. I hold her body to mine, my hand wrapping around her throat and forcing her chin higher.

"You want this little Rose?" I ask, my grip tightening around her throat. She needs to know what she's in for. My need to claim her is all-consuming. I've held out for her long enough, and I am not going to be gentle.

"Yes," she breathes, her eyes on me.

"Hold on to the barre," I whisper in her ear. The softness of my voice doesn't match the darkness in my eyes. I release her, standing stone still while Briar steps forward, shakily reaching for the ballet barre in front of her. Her hands curl around the wooden barre, and her eyes lift back to meet mine in the reflection.

Good girl.

I step toward her, placing my palm between her shoulder blades, gently pushing forward, guiding her down. She offers the tiniest bit of resistance before she gives in, bending over, giving me full access to her pretty little ass.

I run an appreciative palm over each cheek, loving the way she flinches at the surprise touch, her eyes drop to watch my hand. I give her left cheek a sharp slap, and Briar's eyes rocket back to mine.

"Those eyes stay on me, Briar Rose. I want to watch the way those pretty blues of yours roll back inside your head when you come all over me."

Her eyes widen, her mouth falling slightly open in shock.

I lift my hand off of her, and the corner of my mouth ticks up when she stays in the position I've put her in.

Using two fingers, I slide them up the sensitive area between her legs, over the thin, black fabric of her leotard. A whimper escapes her, and she rises on the balls of her feet, chasing my touch after my fingers leave her, her grip on the barre loosening.

"Keep those hands on that barre, little Rose, or I'll tie you to it," I warn her, only once, my voice dark.

She stiffens. What she reads on my face lets her know I'm dead serious, and she reaffirms her grip. Licking her lips in anticipation.

She looks so fucking perfect like this, bent over, waiting for me. I want to draw it out, *god...* I want to take my time, but my restraint is in pieces and I'm tired of fucking fighting it—*this*. All those weeks I spent watching her, *wanting* her, weeks of pretending this wasn't inevitable... that *we* aren't inevitable.

My fingers find her slit again, but this time I pull the fabric aside before touching her, savoring the little gasp that escapes from her lips.

Increasing the pressure, I move in small, controlled circles, checking to be sure she's ready for what I want to do to her. I smile, finding she's already soaked; my fingers are slick with arousal after just a few circles. I turn my attention to Briar's face in the mirror to make sure she has her eyes on me when I bring my fingers to my mouth, tasting her, sucking every bit of her off of me while she watches.

I take those same fingers, this time pushing them inside her, watching how her lips part and her eyelids go heavy, slowly pumping in and out of her until she lets out a moan.

"Just like that." I nod approvingly, working her with my fingers, my eyes never leaving her face. She bites her lip, and knowing how wet she already is for me—her blue eyes staring into mine—I need to be inside her right now.

I free myself from my jeans, withdrawing my fingers only to replace them with my cock, hard, fast, and with little to no warning. The sound that comes out of Briar is one of shock, pleasure, and perhaps a trace of pain. I'm not gentle; I shove into her deep, forcing myself to hold still for a moment to let her adjust to me before pulling out again, only to thrust back inside.

"Fuck." My head falls back and I close my eyes, the heat of her around me, the way she's strangling my cock, *she's so fucking tight*, the moans and whimpers coming out of her—it's taking everything I have not to lose myself to her right now.

I pick up the pace, slamming into her harder, not holding

back, and my thrusts are punishing. I keep my hands on Briar's hips to keep her steady; she's holding onto the ballet barre in front of her for dear life. Her eyes flutter closed, and her mouth falls open in a perfect little "O."

I reach for her hair, wrapping it around my fist and pulling her head back, forcing her to arch her back, which drives me even deeper inside of her. Her moans are borderline screams, her eyes going in and out of focus.

"Eyes on me, love," I remind her.

With one hand in her hair, I reach down with the other, playing with her clit while pounding relentlessly into her. I curse, driving into her deeper, harder. Her release builds fast, her mouth falling open in silent ecstasy as she comes, her entire body going rigid. I can feel the pulsating of her clit inside of her. I let go, following her over the edge, burying myself deep before coming hard, spilling into her.

When it's over, I don't pull out, releasing her hair in favor of her hips, keeping myself inside of her. When my eyes drop to hers, she's watching me, just like I told her to. An unreadable expression on that perfect little face.

"So what's the verdict, Briar Rose? Still hate me?" I smirk into the mirror.

"No," she says, her voice soft and maybe even a little sad, her answer putting me right back on the fucking edge. "I'm starting to think... I might not hate you at all."

59

I PROMISE

BRIAR

Now

Koen dropped me off at my apartment a couple of hours ago. He didn't follow me upstairs, and I didn't invite him up. Neither of us said much on the ride over, both of us still reeling from what happened in the dance studio.

What we did.

It shouldn't have happened, and I could kick myself for being so stupid. Hooking up with Koen complicates *everything*.

It's late, close to two a.m., but I can't sleep. So here I am, pacing my empty apartment, feeling unsettled. My head's a mess, and I can't focus. I attempted to read a couple of books that are now overdue from the library, only to lose interest a few pages in.

I've resorted to curling up on the couch, watching trailers

of shows and movies without committing to any. Not finding anything to match this mood I'm in.

He said he'd be back tomorrow to pick me up for the Delacroix Conservatory's charity gala, like it's no big deal. Like he didn't just rearrange my insides and send me to both heaven and hell before dropping me back on Earth.

Gio texted earlier wanting an update on any new information on Koen. I've been feeding him as much insignificant information as I can. I just can't bring myself to give him anything that might hurt Koen or his family, and I can tell I'm starting to piss Gio off, but I just keep playing dumb, claiming Koen's still keeping me at arm's length.

What am I doing?

What. Am. I. DOING?

Koen gave me an out, he begged for it actually, all I had to do was tell him to stop. Why didn't I say *stop*? Why didn't I *want* him to stop? There's no future with him. There's no universe in which he and I live happily ever after together.

This isn't a fairy tale.

I'm pissed off and angry, and I don't even know who I'm mad at. Koen? Myself? I had made peace with it. I had all but convinced myself that Koen O'Rourke was nothing but bad news. Violent, unhinged, and far too much of a risk for me— *for Remi.*

But that little box I'd shoved him into? It's getting harder to keep him inside. Is Koen violent and unhinged? Yes. Absolutely. But he's also gentle, considerate, and protective.

And don't get me started on how the dark Irish King takes time out of his day to make sure his brothers have home cooked meals.

It might be time to rethink my play here...

But where do I even start? *Hey Koen, so real quick... I've been secretly hiding your daughter from you for four years and oh, yeah, since we reconnected, I've also been leaking information to Giovanni Moretti and his cronies about you and your brothers.*

Yeah, I'm sure that conversation will go over just fine.

A pounding at the door has me looking up, instantly tense. It's the middle of the night, and Koen already told me he wouldn't be back until morning, *not that he would use the door anyway...*

Whoever it is pounds again, and slowly, I switch off the television, carefully placing the remote on the coffee table before walking slowly over to the door. It's probably Gio, or one of his men, checking in. I did let that last text go unanswered.

"Open up. I know you're home," a gruff voice barks out, accompanied by more pounding, harder this time. The voice sounds vaguely familiar.

Standing on my tiptoes, I peek through the peephole, feeling myself pale when I recognize who's on the other side. I make sure the door's chain is secured, then I take a deep breath and crack open the door.

A smile creeps across Daniel's face at the sight of me. "Good evening, sweetheart. You wanna invite me in?" His eyes flick to the chain above my head and then back to me.

I do a quick scan of the hallway. He's alone. "What can I help you with?" I ask, leaving the chain in place, keeping the barrier between us.

He frowns, and a look of annoyance flashes across his face before he replaces it with a fake smile. He's not in uniform, or a suit like I normally see him in at Wonderland; instead, he's wearing workout clothes, dark sweats with a ball cap pulled low over his face.

"I have a couple of questions I want to ask you." His smile, while meant to be reassuring, just sends waves of nausea and a chill down my spine.

I narrow my eyes. "Are you here on official police business?" I ask, since there's no sign of a badge in sight. "Do you have a warrant?"

He frowns, and that's all the answer I need. I try to slam the door, but I'm too slow. Daniel lunges forward, shoving his shoulder hard into the door, pushing both me and the door back, and snapping the pathetic little chain.

I fall on my ass from the force of it, scrambling to my feet just as Daniel steps into my apartment, shutting the door behind him. I notice then that he's wearing gloves when he slides the deadbolt into place.

"What do you want?" My eyes dart around the apartment, careful to keep the distance between us even as he comes closer.

"Gio told me what he did." He shakes his head. "How he gave you to *Koen O'Rourke* as collateral. He said you and him have a *deal* and that he'll let you go on your merry fucking way once you've held up your end of the bargain."

I don't say anything, though it's reassuring to hear that Gio might *actually* plan to keep his word after everything is said and done.

Daniel keeps coming closer, while I keep backing up. He's between me and the exit, and my eyes shift to the island, where my phone is charging. I can't get there either, so I start edging toward the hallway, remembering the gun I keep locked in my nightstand.

"I'm up for a promotion next month, you know?" He puffs out his chest, and my lip curls slightly in disgust. "To Corporal."

"Good for you," I offer, though my words fall flat of any actual meaning.

"It is good," Daniel snaps.

"I don't understand what that has to do with me?" I ask, though my voice shakes because I'm pretty sure *I know*.

Daniel frowns, giving me an apologetic look. "You can blame Gio for this. I handed you to him on a silver platter and what did he fucking do? He botched it all up!" I wince when his voice rises in volume, the rage in it setting off my fight or flight. "You should be on a plane, one bound for Dubai, Saudi Arabia, Russia even! But now I have to worry about you running that mouth."

"I won't say anything. Giovanni's made sure of it," I tell him, but he just scoffs. "Bella, Bella, Bella," he laments, releasing a rueful laugh. "I've been around a long time, and there's one thing I've learned; whores can't help but run their mouths. I've been waiting a long time for this promotion, and I'm not about to let some bitch fuck it all up."

There's no mistaking the dark intent in his eyes, I bolt for my bedroom, hoping to get past him, but he's too fast, catching hold of my arm and hauling me backward. He throws me so hard against the wall, it knocks the breath out of me.

He lunges toward me and I scream, the sound raw and desperate. Daniel struggles to shut me up, but I'm fighting hard. He's got me pinned to the wall, while his hands grapple for my throat. I reach blindly to the left, feeling nothing but air, until the back of my hand knocks into the lamp and I grab hold of it, ripping the cord out of the wall, and pitching us into darkness when I smash the ceramic base over Daniel's head.

The lamp shatters and he yells, cursing at me as he stumbles, falling to the floor. I run for the door. But I didn't knock him out, and his hand wraps around my ankle before I can get clear of him. I fall forward, my momentum taking me down hard. He drags me backwards and my fingers claw at the floor, trying to get away.

"Oh no, no—you're not getting away this time you little bitch. Gio should have taken care of you a long time ago. Did you really think he was just going to let you walk away from this?" He laughs, which freaks me out even more, because he's laughing while trying to kill me. *The sociopath.*

I kick and twist but despite my struggles... *he's winning.*

"Take your fucking hands off of her."

Koen.

We both freeze. My gaze snaps up at the sound of his voice, my eyes connecting with his for all but a second before he turns his attention to Daniel. His gun trained on his head.

"Hey now, you don't want to do this," Daniel sneers, his hand tightening around my ankle. "I'm a cop—"

Bang.

Silence.

My ankle falls to the floor and I push myself away from him, eyes wide, staring—staring at Daniel's dead body. *Dead.* He's dead. *Koen killed him.* Holy shit. Everything happened so fast.

"You shot him."

"Aye."

Keeping his gun on Daniel, Koen comes closer, crouching

down to check his pulse, confirming that Daniel is, in fact, *very dead.*

"You killed him!"

Koen looks up at me.

"You just shot him, just like that. He—He's a cop!" I say frantically, pointing down at the dead body in my kitchen. Fuck, *he's a cop.*

Koen's head tilts slightly, assessing my reaction. "Would you have preferred I left him alive?" He frowns, looking down at Daniel's body. "I don't think he had the best of intentions."

He rises, but it only draws my attention to the gun he's still holding in his hand. *He hasn't put it away.* Panic takes over and I stumble to my feet, feeling his dark eyes burning into me. He's standing there, gun in hand, a dead body at his feet and he's looking at *me.*

He killed a cop. He killed a cop, and I just watched it happen.

"Briar—" Koen starts, his voice cautious, reading the look of utter panic on my face.

"No. No." I back up quickly. "Stay away from me!" I glance around for *anything* else I can use as a weapon, but coming up short.

He takes a step toward me, his brow furrowed. "Briar." He reaches for me, but I flinch away. "No! Don't touch me." His hand falls, but he doesn't stop following me, and I move faster, backing my way down the hallway, too afraid to turn my back on him.

He stalks after me like a predator would its prey.

"Don't. Please don't, Koen." My hands come up protectively in front of me, and he freezes, staring at me with a blank expression on his face.

I seize the opportunity, turning and bolting the rest of the way down the hallway.

"Briar, stop!"

I don't wait. *I run,* nearly sliding past the door, my socks sliding on the slick hardwood. Koen must have come through my window, because it's cracked open.

I rush around my bed, my fingers close around the handle of the window, pulling it wider, the cool air hits my face, and it feels like a wave of relief right before it's slammed shut. A tattooed hand is pressed up against the glass, holding it closed.

I scream, terror pumping through my veins, while his arm circles around my waist. He rips me away from the window, tossing me onto the bed. "No!" I yell, thrashing wildly, hitting him. "Let me go! Let me go! Please—"

"Stop, Briar, just *stop*—" Before I can scramble away, he's on top of me, pressing a palm over my mouth while he works to get the rest of me under control. "Stop bloody screaming!"

His palm muffles my sob and I twist, attempting to throw him off of me, but he's too heavy, tears run down my cheeks, and I really start to lose it.

"Briar! Briar, hey!" He lets go of my mouth, trying to get my attention, but I don't want to look at him.

"You shot him, you shot him, you shot him, you're going to shoot me."

Koen freezes. "I'm not going to shoot you."

I start hyperventilating, and he grabs hold of my face with both hands, forcing me to look at him. "Briar, breathe. Just breathe. Okay?" There's concern in his dark eyes. "Listen to me. I'm not going to hurt you. I am *not* going to hurt you."

I close my eyes, shaking my head.

"Look at me. Briar, *look* at me." He keeps his grip on my

face until my eyes finally lift to his. "You're safe, okay? That was really scary, what just happened, what he tried to do... But he can't hurt you." He shakes his head slowly. "And I promise you, I *promise* you, baby, I will *never* hurt you."

He shifts off of me and pulls me up and into his chest, wrapping his arms around me—not to cage, but to comfort me as I'm crying. "I've got you, okay? You're safe."

"But you killed *a cop,* and I—I witnessed it. Aren't you worried about me telling someone?"

"No." He shakes his head, and there's not a trace of hesitation in his voice.

"You're not?" I sniff, looking up at him.

"No." Koen says, looking down into my eyes. "Because I trust you." He gives me a light squeeze and then a little wink. "You're *my girl,*" he murmurs, like he's letting me in on a secret.

His words cleave me in two, remembering that night at the bar all those years ago when he protected me from Ben—called me his girl—and the tears fall freely now.

"You're shaking," he tells me, and it's true. I'm trembling; he *saved* me. He's *been* saving me. Koen's just been protecting me from the beginning.

I can't find my voice, guilt overwhelms me, threatening to consume me. I should tell him now before it's too late. *But what if it already is?*

Koen wraps his arms around me, and I cry harder. The safety of his arms feels like a double-edged sword. *I don't deserve it.* I have to tell him the truth.

But when I do... *will he keep his promise?*

60

EVERY GOOD FAIRY
TALE NEEDS A BALL

BRIAR

I WAKE up in Koen's bed.

Again.

After everything that happened last night, Koen insisted I come home with him. He assured me he would take care of everything: the broken glass, the lock, the *body*. All of it will be gone by morning, and I would be safer with him.

By the time he carried me out to the car, I was numb, emotionally spent, and completely hollowed out. I fell asleep in his arms somewhere along the drive back to the loft. Only to wake back up after he carefully tucked me into his bed.

But when he turned to leave...

Panic set in. I didn't want to be alone, so my fingers caught his wrist before I could think. He stopped, turned back slowly, gazing down into my eyes. Neither of us said anything. Unable to form the words I need to say, I tugged lightly on his wrist. He stared at me for another minute before he sighed, pulled off his shirt, and slid under the covers with me.

Without a word, he pulled me against his chest, the warmth grounding me, and I drifted back to sleep to the soft steady rhythm of his fingers tracing lazy patterns across my back.

A phone is ringing.

Koen groans, reaching blindly to the nightstand to take the call. Not yet realizing I'm awake, he slips out from under me, dressing quickly while grunting out quick answers over the phone.

"No, we're moving the drop." My eyes peek open just as he slides a fresh pair of boxers over a remarkably fine ass. "Port 17, Monday, nine p.m. sharp." Jeans follow, and I chew my lip, debating whether or not I should try convincing him to take them back off again. "Yeah," he mutters, rubbing a tired hand over his face. "I'm on my way."

Our eyes meet, and I smile hesitantly from under the protection of the comforter.

For a moment, he only stares, his gaze lingering on my face like he's memorizing every detail, as if waiting to see if I'll disappear.

"Morning," he murmurs, the corner of his mouth ebbing into a soft smile. "Sorry, I didn't mean to wake you."

"It's okay." I grip the edges of the blanket just a little bit tighter.

"I have to go take care of a few things, but you should get some more sleep. You have to be at the gala early, right?"

I nod, finding it hard to form actual words with the truth burning holes in my tongue.

"You can get ready here. I had the guys grab some of your stuff, I'll have Mac drive you over."

"You're not coming?" I ask, feeling... disappointed, my gaze dropping to my hands.

He steps closer, and two fingers lift my chin until I'm staring into those shadowed eyes of his. "I'll be there. I promise." He kisses me lightly on the forehead before letting me go.

My eyes soften, and I feel myself relax as I dip my chin.

He turns to leave, and a wave of anxiety creeps down my spine.

"Wait, Koen?"

"Yeah?" He stops by the door, turning back and looking at me expectantly. I swallow, trying to work up the nerve. He tilts his head after a few more seconds when I am silent.

"Sorry," I apologize, feeling like an idiot. "I just—I was hoping..." I try again, my voice growing increasingly shaky. "We need to—" I swallow again, but the words just get stuck in my throat, and I exhale in defeat.

"We need to talk, I know." His phone buzzes again, and he glances down at it quickly. "I can't—not right now—but I promise we'll talk later. Okay?"

I nod, relief flooding through me at the thought of having a little more time.

"Okay."

I sip my champagne, my eyes scanning the room for probably the hundredth time.

He's late.

I hear my name and sigh, schooling my face and straightening my shoulders back before walking over with a smile to greet yet another patron.

It's been the same copy and paste interaction over the last hour. I thank them for coming, and for their generous donation; I answer questions about myself and ballet, and comment on how well showcase rehearsals have been going, but no matter how hard I try, I can't help my gaze from drifting over the room.

He said he'd be here.

The Conservatory really spared no expense for the winter gala. The venue reminds me of something out of a fairy tale; crystal chandeliers hang from the high arched ceilings overhead, ornately carved columns line the room, while a string quartet plays all the classics in the corner.

Everyone is dressed to the nines. The room drips of old money and generational wealth. The Delacroix Winter Gala is not an event to be missed by the Boston elite.

Koen really came in clutch with the dress he bought me. I found it hanging in the bathroom this morning with the rest of my things.

Soft, midnight blue silk—its color appearing to change depending on the lighting—could almost be described as black, as it hugs the curves of my body and pools around my feet. Thin silk straps criss-cross across my back, leaving it mostly exposed, which gives me a little anxiety over the whip marks, though they have healed over into thin white scars. The slit cut high up my left leg is a not-so-subtle reminder of exactly who picked the dress out.

The glittery silver heels I found in the bottom of the bag pair well with it, and so had the silver Celtic knot necklace Koen had given me last week, so I left it on, not that I really have anything to swap it out with. I'd pawned any jewelry worth a cent years ago.

After spending nearly an hour greeting patrons in the hallway, the dancers are dismissed to go enjoy the party with everyone else.

I know Koen told me he had bought a table, but nothing, and I mean *nothing*, could have prepared me for what I see when I reach our assigned table thirteen.

"Mystery girl!"

I take a deep breath and step up to the table. In a shockingly gentlemanly display, Liam stands, pulling out the chair next to him before ushering me into it.

"Err—thank you," I say, remembering my manners once seated, finding myself staring across the table at Koen's other brother, Aidan, and the *girl* he has at his side. *She's smiling at me.*

"Mystery Girl, you remember Aidan." I give him a nod of acknowledgement. "And I don't think you've met little Kostalova."

Aidan sits up in his seat, elbowing Liam hard in the ribs.

"Ow, *fuck* Ace," Liam curses, lowering his voice after drawing attention from the table next to us. "Bloody hell, sorry. It's going to take some getting used to, okay?"

Aidan just glowers at him, and I stare wide-eyed at the two of them.

Recovering, Liam clears his throat and puts a smile back on

his face. "Sorry, that's Rory." He points at the girl again, who's desperately trying not to laugh. "AKA the new Mrs. O'Rourke."

My eyes widen further when I realize that *this* is Rory. I take her in; she's pretty, like *really* pretty. Her honey-blonde hair is in an elegant bun at the nape of her neck, and she's wearing a gorgeous pale silvery blue dress that nearly matches her eyes; her cheeks are round and full of color, and she looks... *happy*.

She doesn't look like she's spent weeks chained up in the Irish Devil's basement. What Filip and Dominick from the Polish mafia had suggested Aidan had been doing to her... I shiver just thinking about it.

"Sorry, I didn't catch your name?" Rory says sweetly while throwing a pointed look at Liam, who throws up his hands in defeat while tossing his napkin on the table.

"Briar," I say, hiding a laugh.

"Nice to meet you, Briar."

"You know you two have a lot in common?" Liam says, gesturing between Rory and me.

"We do?" I ask, looking at the petite blonde curiously.

Liam leans back in seat, "Yeah, Rory's a figure skater, Briar does ballet, you're both sassy, and *both* of you were kidnapped by O'Rourke men."

My jaw drops in shock and Aidan elbows his brother again, but it does nothing to deter the shit-eating grin on Liam's face as he keeps his eyes on me.

"So, Briar," he says, shoving his brother away from him, laughing before leaning onto the table with clasped hands to look at me. "You and Koen... what *exactly* is going on there?"

My cheeks heat and I lock up. "I—I'm not sure—"

"Like, are you two dating?" he presses. "Just talking...
enemies with benefits... *situationship*? Because he's been acting
weird as fuck lately, and—"

Aidan kicks him under the table.

"Ouch!"

"Leave her alone," Aidan hisses.

"It's just a question..." Liam says. "And you know you
want to know, too!"

My eyes connect with Rory's when she clears her throat.
"Well, I was just about to make a quick run to the powder
room, Briar..." She stands, giving me a pointed look. "Do you
want to come with?"

I'm already up and out of my chair before she's finished her
sentence.

"Can I come too?" Liam pipes up, and I think Aidan's eyes
roll into the back of his head.

"No," Rory smirks. "Girls only."

Liam sinks back into his chair, looking genuinely disappointed.

Rory links arms with me, and once we're a safe distance
from the table, she leans in. "Don't mind them. They're
harmless."

"The literal Irish Devil siblings, harmless? Yeah, okay," I
huff out, automatically, before snapping my mouth shut and
turning toward her, hoping to god I didn't just offend her.

Rory just snorts. "Okay, maybe not *entirely* harmless," she
amends, and we both laugh.

We step into the bathroom, and I take care of some needs
before washing my hands at the sink. Rory steps out to join me.
I glance around; it's just the two of us in here.

I look over at Rory, wanting to ask her a question, but my nerves are getting the better of me.

She notices when she grabs a hand towel. "You okay?" she asks, eyeing me with concern as she dries her hands.

I swallow. "Yeah, I... Can I ask you something?"

The corner of her mouth ticks up. "Depends..."

"You don't have to answer if it's too personal, but... is it—is it true Aidan *kidnapped* you?"

Her eyebrows rise, her blue-gray eyes going wide, but she doesn't look offended—rather, she looks *amused*. "So, technically... yes."

"Technically?"

"Okay, he totally kidnapped me, but he *never* hurt me, and he *did* let me go."

"He let you go?"

"He did, but only for me to run right back." She smiles softly.

"Why would you do that?" I ask, genuinely trying to understand.

"I was in danger and didn't have anywhere else to go... I know it sounds crazy, but when I was with Aidan... even though he kidnapped me, when I was with him, I felt *safe*—protected. He and his brothers went to war for me, and I—" she trails off.

"You married him?" I finish, studying her face.

"I married him." There's a warm light in her eyes when she smiles. "Listen, I know how they seem... they're good men, intense, overprotective, and a little *possessive*—but good men at the end of the day." She looks me in the eyes. "All of them."

I nod, thinking over what she's told me.

"Do you need a drink?" she asks, shooting me a conspiratorial smile. "I think we're going to need a drink if we're going to survive that table tonight."

"Yes, please," I laugh, following her out of the bathroom.

It's a short wait at the bar before we're both holding full glasses of champagne. We're just about to go back into the ballroom, when Rory's eyes drift to something over my shoulder, and her smile softens. "I'll, uh, leave you to it." She winks at me, taking her glass of champagne and heading back to the table alone.

I immediately glance back over my shoulder, and my breath catches at the sight I see there.

It's *him. He came.*

Koen is crossing the ballroom, his eyes locked on me. He's moving through the room as if he owns it. Power radiates off of him in waves—it's impossible to ignore. People notice him, recognition flashing on far too many faces, those patrons quickly finding somewhere—anywhere else to be.

He's ditched his usual black hoodie, or rough leather jacket, for a sleek charcoal gray suit. The crisp white shirt is a stark contrast to the dark ink you can still see climbing up his neck. No tie, top buttons undone, a subtle *fuck you* to the formality of the gala.

"I thought you might have changed your mind," I half joke when he reaches me, hoping he can't see the sweeping relief I feel now that he's actually here.

The corner of his mouth twitches up, the ghost of a smile. He leans in, his hand grazing the exposed skin on my lower back as he deposits a kiss on my cheek. "About you?" he murmurs, sending shockwaves of electricity down my spine. "Never."

I shiver.

"Cold?" He smirks knowingly, and I give him a playful shove. But as I do, I see something over his shoulder, and my smile quickly falls.

"Shit," I curse, grabbing hold of the lapels on his suit jacket and pulling him closer. "Come here."

"What's wrong?" Koen asks, instantly on high-alert. He allows me to drag him halfway into the little alcove next to us. I'm doing my best to use his body to shield mine, but I'm afraid it's too late. When I don't answer him, he looks back over his shoulder to scan the crowd for the threat.

"Who are you hiding from?" His hand moves for the gun I know he has hidden in his suit, but I slap it away.

"Jesus, no—we don't need that! We should—" My eyes dart for the nearest exit, but it's too late.

"Briar?" The familiar, sickeningly sweet voice sets my teeth on edge.

"*Fuck*," I whisper, just loud enough for Koen to hear, I feel his stare burning through me. I close my eyes, count to three, and release one slow, controlled breath, before stepping back from Koen, wearing my best stage smile.

"Mother."

61

TALK TO ME

BRIAR

"OH, BRIAR SWEETHEART, IT *IS* YOU!" I pale even further when I see my father is with her. They come closer, my father outright refusing to look at me, while my mother does the opposite. Her cold blue eyes take me in, scanning the length of me, while I fight the urge to fidget under the weight of her perusal.

I am all too aware of Koen at my side, feeling his hand move to my lower back protectively.

"I almost didn't recognize you; you look so... healthy." Her smile is polite, but the disapproval in her eyes is glaring.

I inhale sharply. *Healthy* is just my mother's polite way of saying, *You've gained weight.* It's a trigger for me, bringing me back to the days when she used to obsess over my every calorie, every pound, all in her pursuit to have the picture-perfect daughter.

She's watching me with pursed lips, looking as prim and perfect as ever, in Chanel of course, standing at my father's side. Her dark hair is in an elegant chignon, and while she's definitely been overdoing the Botox, she still is *the perfect wife*.

My shoulders are stiff, every inch of me rigid, and Koen's hand tightens on my waist.

My mother's attention shifts from me to him, her smile growing as she looks him over, and she extends her hand.

"Oh, well, hello there. You must forgive my daughter. We raised her better than this, but she's clearly forgotten her manners." She shoots me an annoyed look. "Allow me to introduce myself, Bridget Rousseau Ralston, Briar's mother." She plasters a wide smile on her face before turning to place a light hand on my father's chest, who's at her side but whose attention is elsewhere.

"And this is Briar's father, Eric." At the sound of his name, my father turns, politely offering Koen his hand for a firm handshake. "Eric Ralston. Pleasure." His response is friendly, though short and clipped, as he quickly appraises my date.

"Eric Ralston, as in Senator Eric Ralston from New York?" Koen asks, shaking my father's hand while his eyes slide back my way.

"The same!"

"Koen O'Rourke."

My stomach twists, and I know Koen can feel the tension running through me when his hand falls back to my waist. I didn't want him to find out who my father is; *I didn't want to give him another reason to use me*.

My father looks up at Koen with a contemplative expression on his face. "O'Rourke, you say? You wouldn't have any relation to the O'Rourkes making waves in the Boston real estate market, would you?"

"Oh, Eric dear," my mother interjects, smiling politely, "I'm sure he's not—"

"Yes, actually," Koen interrupts her, and my mother's smile falters.

I pinch my cheek between my teeth in order to hide my smirk. She *hates* when people interrupt her.

"My father started acquiring property around the city, and you could say my brothers and I have taken over the family business."

I scoff at Koen's so-called *family business* comment, drawing everyone's attention by accident. I take a sip from my glass as cover.

I haven't *seen* my parents in over four years, and I've barely talked to them in as much. When I finally gathered up the nerve to tell them I was pregnant, they told me to get rid of it. And while I support that right for other girls, I just—I just couldn't. Plus, by that point, it was already too late. But my parents were clear: if I had that baby, if I didn't give it up for adoption, they were cutting me off.

I left that night, fleeing to Lily's house, and by the time I arrived, they'd already revoked access to my bank account, shut off my credit cards, and contacted Delacroix about terminating the dorm agreement. Only my scholarship saved my spot at the school. They hoped they could bully me into making a different choice, but I was done dancing at the end of their strings.

They didn't give a shit about me or their future grandchild; all they cared about were *the optics*. How would it look if Senator Ralston's daughter turned up pregnant with a *bastard*? And during an election year! Oh, well now, that just wouldn't do.

Oh shit, *Remi*. A bolt of fear rips through me. What if they bring up Remi? My gaze flickers nervously up to Koen, who's listening intently to my father droll on about mutual funds and property taxes. Not that they've ever asked about her before—but things have a habit of not going my way lately....

"Briar." My mother's icy eyes survey me again. "You look like you're eating well."

I stiffen and feel Koen's attention shift back to me, observing our interaction despite continuing the conversation with my father.

"Yes, mother. You mentioned that," I say sharply, lifting my chin.

"You know the winter showcase is right around the corner?"

I blink at her. Seeing as we're at the gala specifically celebrating the upcoming winter showcase... I think I do, yeah.

But I don't say that. Instead, I bite my tongue and respond with a tight-lipped, "Yes."

She hums audibly, and I look away, anywhere else, finding my glittering shoes a marvelous distraction.

"I have to tell you, your father and I were shocked when we saw your name on the literature sent to sponsors. I would have expected the Conservatory would have wanted to go with a fresh face. You know how those young dancers just have so much drive and ambition; they really are a sight to see."

I keep my gaze on my toes. I painted them black; they look good against the silver shoes.

"But then I heard about the original girl... What a shame. Caterina, right?" She clicks her tongue. "A broken ankle right in the middle of the season!" she laments, though her tone is dripping with venom. "But at least it all worked out for you though, sweetheart, right? You were first understudy? Still an admirable position to hold, and now you get to headline!"

The snide smile she's shooting at me down her nose tells me she already knows, so I lift my chin when I say, "No, actually I didn't get understudy. Julia Zhang did." My mother gives me a satisfied smirk. "But one thing led to another, and they asked me to take the role." I shrug, trying my best to look bored with the conversation, but Koen's sharp eyes aren't missing any of it.

"Oh, well, even more exciting!"

Releasing a sigh, I take another sip from my glass and watch a look of horror spread across her face.

"Is that *champagne* you're drinking?"

I nod. Holding up the glass, as if I'm toasting her, before taking another sip. "Yep."

"There's a lot of sugar in that, don't you think?" If she were wearing pearls, she'd be clutching them right now. The thought comes out almost involuntarily, but then she catches herself, adjusting her shoulders. "Well, I suppose it *is* a party, good for you on indulging."

I stop drinking, lowering my glass in front of me.

But my mother doesn't stop there. She's enjoying herself far too much. "Briar dear, did I tell you I ran into the Ashfords?"

I shake my head because *no, of course she didn't, we haven't talked in four years but sure... do go on.* "Their daughter Emilia —you remember Emilia, of course? You two were in dance lessons together back in grade school? She's now touring with the Premiere Ballet in Paris! A prima ballerina! I told your father we must fly out and see her next show. I think they're doing Giselle next!"

430

"That's great for Em. I'm happy for her," I say, and I mean it. Emmy is a talented dancer. We haven't talked in a while, but I'm sure she deserves it.

"She was always such a responsible girl. Goes to show what you can accomplish if you stay focused and don't throw your life away." My mother's tone sharpens on her closing words, staring at me pointedly.

I avoid her gaze, turning my attention back to Koen and my father. "Of course, a man with your portfolio could do well partnering with us," my father continues, oblivious to the conversation playing out to his right. "You'll have direct access to, well, I really can't say, but I am telling you, opportunities like this don't present themselves every day! You know, I could really go for a cigar right now; why don't we leave the ladies to it, and we can continue this discussion in the gentlemen's room over some smokes? I'd love to hear your thoughts on the new zoning policies on the table for next year." He glances about the room. "And I know I saw Senator Jeffries around here somewhere. I'd love to make an introduction..."

I shift uncomfortably and subtly step out of Koen's hold on my lower back, freeing him up to join my father and his friends for more shop talk, but just as I slip out from under his fingers, he reaches down, without even looking, catching my hand and stopping me from getting any further away from him.

"My apologies, Senator, but I actually need to steal Briar away for a few minutes."

"Briar?" Confusion fills my father's face as he looks my way for possibly the first time all night, possibly even forgetting I was here at all.

"Yes, *Briar*," Koen confirms, his tone cold before finding

my widened eyes. "Who also, by the way, is quite a sight to see. If you'll excuse us." Both my mother and father stare at him in disbelief. But Koen doesn't seem to care, tightening his hand around mine and pulling me away from them.

"Koen."

He moves us quickly down the hall, going the opposite direction of the ballroom, and I'm struggling to keep up with him in my heels, holding my dress up with my free hand to keep from tripping over it. He doesn't answer me, continuing to pull me down a maze of hallways until we reach an elevator, where he shoves his thumb into the button as if the button itself personally offended him.

"Koen," I say again.

He still doesn't look at me, but his mouth tightens, just as the elevator doors open, and he drags me in. Another couple appears behind us, attempting to board as well, but he holds up a hand, glaring at them.

"No."

They freeze as he hits the button for the doors to close.

"Where are we going?" I whisper, but he doesn't say anything, doesn't *look* at me, doesn't let go of my hand. My brain is racing through what could have happened. I'd been trying to monitor his conversation with my father and heard nothing damning. However, Koen clenches his jaw, and his eyes burn. He's *angry*, but I don't know why.

The elevator dings, and he takes off, stalking quickly down the hall, my hand locked in his. We reach a door, and he pulls a card out of the inside pocket of his jacket. I stare at it; the door lock blinks green to allow him access.

My throat goes dry. "Please talk to me," I say quietly.

He pushes open the door, letting go of my hand, and holds

it open for me to walk inside on my own. I stare at the door and then at him, trying to read him, but, as always, he's a closed book. I can still sense the simmering anger burning under his skin, but he promised he'd never hurt me, so against my better judgement, I step into the room.

Koen follows me in, the door clicks shut behind him, and slowly, I turn back around, looking at him with a mixture of nerves and anticipation, when he finally speaks.

"Truth or dare, Briar Rose?"

62

STRIP

KOEN

"You can't be serious." She stares at me incredulously.

I shrug, leaning against the wall of the hotel room with my hands in my pockets. "It's your turn."

She chews her bottom lip, her eyes darting between me and the door.

My eyes narrow, and I step closer, watching as her breath catches but she holds her ground. "Truth or dare, Briar Rose?" I repeat, letting my eyes soften when she searches my face for reassurance.

She swallows hard. I see the memories playing out in the shadows of her eyes. *The last time we played this game.*

"Dare," she whispers finally.

A slow smile tilts up the corners of my mouth. "Strip," I tell her. There's no mistaking the command in my voice.

Her mouth falls open, and I have to force my eyes to stay on hers.

"W-what?" she says, taking a step back from me, folding her arms across her chest, immediately uncomfortable.

I take another controlled step forward, taking off my suit jacket and hanging it over the back of a nearby chair, slipping my hands into my pockets.

"You heard me. Strip. Take off that dress. Right now." I take another step until I'm fully invading her space. She won't look at me, her eyes on the floor. I place two fingers under her chin and slowly lift.

Her eyes close in defeat.

"Briar, look at me."

She does, but there's ire in her eyes that wasn't there before. After everything her mother just said to her, she thinks I'm being cruel.

"I hate you," I tell her, watching the hurt flash in her eyes, revealing all the broken pieces she's been killing herself trying to keep together.

"You hate me?" she repeats softly, her bottom lip quivering slightly.

"I do," I tell her unapologetically. "You've haunted me, little Rose." I release her chin, letting my fingers lightly trace the skin on the side of her neck, traveling south. I run my thumb over the Celtic knot at her throat. "Since the night we met, you've haunted every dream, every nightmare—you've lingered in the deepest shadows of my mind, a divine sin I can neither escape nor forget. *My sweet damnation.*" I stare down into her eyes, feeling the rapid beat of her pulse against my thumb, before my mouth finds her ear. "Take off your dress."

I step back, watching her spiral with brutal intensity. Her arms wrap tighter around herself, searching for comfort while shaking her head no.

"I hate how fucking beautiful you are," I continue, starting to circle her. She trembles when my fingers brush against one of the faint white scars across her back. "I hate the way you draw attention everywhere you go because of it. I hate the addictive taste of you, the rarest of drugs, nearly impossible to get my hands on." I smirk.

Briar's staring up at me, her eyes wide. "I hate the way you look at me." I reach out and grab one of the curls framing her face, running the silky strand through my fingers. "How it makes me forget all the reasons I shouldn't touch you." I move behind her. The backs of my fingers stroking her still silk-covered side, before reaching up and smoothly tugging down the zipper of her dress.

"The dress, Briar," I remind her. "Take it off."

I come back to stand in front of her, sliding my hands into my pockets while I wait.

Her eyes stay on mine, uncertainty shining through them, but there's something else there now too... She *wants* to trust me. For a few long seconds, she battles with her inner thoughts, until she takes a deep breath and lifts her shaking hands to her shoulders. Slowly, while averting her eyes, she hooks her thumbs through the straps of her dress and drags them down.

The silk glides over her porcelain skin as it drops, pooling at her feet, leaving her in just her panties and glittering heels. No bra. Briar's arms quickly wrap around herself to hold her chest, hiding it from me.

I look her over slowly, purposefully, appreciating the literal goddess standing before me, as she's meant to be appreciated. She won't look at me, keeping her gaze trained on the floor, trembling.

I freeze when my eyes come across the dark ink, just above her right hip bone.

My mark.

She still has it.

I reach out to trace the tattoo with my fingertips, the little black club, the letter "K" just above it, and then, of course, the crown.

"It's my turn," I say, feeling Briar's eyes lift. "And I pick truth."

Her eyes are on me.

"You were too good for me back then." My fingers brush against the tattoo one last time. "You still are." I move my hand to her arms, gently pushing them down, away from her chest. She resists slightly before giving in, her arms falling to her sides. There's nothing but raw vulnerability in her eyes when she looks up at me.

I glance down, taking my time, my fingers skimming the underside of her breasts. They're fuller than I remember; her body is different from five years ago, softer, curvier, but her ribs still poke through far more than I'd like. All the times she "forgot" to eat—or skipped meals—hit me like a punch to the gut, and I clench my jaw, thinking of how she has her mother's horrible voice in her head.

"You are perfect. Every. Single. Inch." My eyes darken as they linger on hers, making certain that she's listening. My fingers travel further south, down the lean muscles of her stomach, until they find the hem of her panties

"Briar Rose." She shivers as I play along the fabric's edge. "I pushed you away because I didn't want my shadows to darken your light. You were too untouchable for hands like mine— cold, rough, and forever drenched in blood. I couldn't let myself ruin you, *so I let you ruin me instead.*" I hold her gaze, letting her see past the walls in my eyes.

A tear breaks loose, running slowly down her cheek.

"But darkness came for my little rose anyway, and in it, you didn't wither and die; you grew thorns in the shadows; you got stronger, sharper, and unforgiving. Now, you aren't just beautiful, you're *dangerous*, but I would bleed a thousand times over just to touch you."

Tears run down her cheeks as my hands grip her hips, walking her backwards until she's up against the wall. I stare into her eyes for another second before I drop to my knees, sliding her panties down with me, carefully lifting each leg to slip them all the way off, leaving the sparkling heels on her feet. *And fuck, if that's not the most attractive thing I've ever seen.*

Unlike the last time I touched her, I take my time. My fingers run up her inner thigh, and she shivers. "Beautiful. Now, hold still so I can show you *exactly* how you should be appreciated."

I kiss her inner thigh, my mouth trailing north until my lips find her pretty, pink center. I get a taste of her with a single swipe of my tongue, and the sound of her little gasp is music to my ears. Of course, one taste is not enough, and soon I'm exploring every inch of her, finding her clit and circling it slowly with my tongue.

Briar's head falls back, and the sounds escaping her only encourage me more, the way her body responds to me... going rigid and taut, to squirming and shaking when she gets close.

I grip her hips, holding her to me, grabbing her leg and throwing it over my uninjured shoulder to give me greater access.

She hooks her knee over my shoulder, and when my fingers join my tongue at her clit, her back arches off the wall and she cries out, her body trembling, but it's when I start to suck that she really starts to writhe and scream.

I'm lost in her, utterly consumed by this beautiful, dark-haired girl that I'm on my knees for; my only goal to please her.

Briar comes hard, and I don't relent until she's a whimpering mess in my arms.

I pick her up. The tension I usually feel in her is gone. Her body is limp and trusting as I lay her down on the bed. She's breathing hard, working to catch her breath while watching me slowly unbutton my shirt. Her cheeks, flushed a light pink.

"Truth or dare, Briar Rose?"

"I don't think it's my—"

I give her a hard look, and she sighs in defeat. "Truth"

"How many men have you been with since me?"

Her eyes widen, her cheeks flaming a brighter shade of pink before she presses her lips together, not wanting to say.

I reach the last button and let the shirt drop to the floor, moving on to unbuckle my belt.

Her breath catches, and I watch her blatantly check me out. Her gaze lingering on the single drop of color, the little red rose tattooed just over my heart.

"There's no wrong answer. I just need to know," I tell her, sliding the belt off and making quick work of removing my pants.

She chews her lips nervously and, okay, right now, she's making *me* nervous, too. *Just how many guys am I going to have to hunt down and kill for touching what's mine?*

"Do you want to switch to dare?" I ask, but after seeing the dark glint in my eye, she wisely shakes her head no.

"Then out with it."

She stares at me for another second before releasing a sigh.

"None."

I freeze, and my gaze turns molten.

"Lying is against the rules, little Rose."

She swallows once, blinking up at me, the picture of innocence, her voice soft and quiet when she says, "I'm not lying."

"Oh, Briar Rose." I click my tongue, a dark smile curving up my face as I toss my boxers to the floor. "You should have lied."

63

WE DO NOT SLEEP WITH OUR BABY DADDIES!

BRIAR

PACING my apartment for what is probably the thousandth time today, I glance up anxiously again at the kitchen clock. Lily and Remi are coming home today. Or, well, they were supposed to be home—an hour ago.

Lily texted a little bit ago, warning that they'd hit traffic coming into the city, which is really not a shocker, but I'm stuck in pause mode. Unable to do anything else until they walk through that door.

After everything that happened last night, I need to hold my daughter in my arms, but most of all, *I need my best friend.*

Koen and I spent the night together, *and* most of the morning. We didn't sleep. What we did, instead, felt like crossing a line that can't be uncrossed. And when he finally dropped me off at my apartment, I hated how much I didn't want to get out of his car.

Koen has an important meeting today that's supposed to keep him away all day. I have rehearsal tomorrow, but he's supposed to pick me up after. We're supposed to go out to dinner. Our very first date. And I—I am going to tell him *everything*.

I can't keep going like this. It's not fair to *him*; it's not fair to *me*; and most of all, it's not fair to *Remi*.

Koen isn't the cold-hearted mafia king I thought he was. He deserves to know he has a gorgeous, sassy daughter who looks just like him.

I wring my fingers together as I pace the apartment some more. After tomorrow night, the truth will be out and, hope-fully... *hopefully*... Koen can forgive me.

A few more painfully long minutes later, the doorknob jiggles violently, which may have been scary if it weren't the exact way Remi attacks the door before you can get your key through the lock.

I rush for it, throwing it open wide.

"Mommy!" Remi squeals, dropping the many stuffed animals she's carrying to leap into my arms.

I pull her tight, inhaling her sweet scent, before planting kisses everywhere I can reach.

"No kisses!" Remi screeches, trying to twist out of my arms.

"Nope!" I squeeze her tighter, increasing my kiss rate across her cheeks. "You've been gone too long. I demand my right to kisses."

My daughter lets out a sound of dissent but stops fighting, accepting my bout of kisses until I'm ready to release her. "Mom..." she grumbles, wiping at her cheeks like she can wipe them away.

"I missed you. I'm sorry," I shrug before pointing at the floor. "Do you want help with those?"

At my prodding, Remi suddenly remembers the armload of stuffed animals she walked in with. "No, I've got it!" She snatches up the lot. "I'm going to put them in my room."

"No running!" I call after her as she sprints down the hall, far too chaotically for my taste, seeing as how she can barely see over her haul.

"I think running is her default speed."

Smiling, I look back toward the door, finding my best friend shoving their two suitcases over the threshold.

"I would have helped you with those!" I chide, reaching out to grab both bags from her.

"It's fine," she huffs out, collapsing onto one of the island's stools, out of breath and *clearly not fine*. "I needed the workout."

"It's five floors."

Lily recovers quickly, and I notice how her eyes dart around the tiny space. "Is he here?" Lily whispers, looking curiously around the apartment.

"No," I whisper back, checking for Remi before continuing. "But one of his guys is probably parked outside."

Lily bolts for the window, peeking excitedly out.

I scramble for her arm, trying to drag her back. "Don't look!"

"Why?" she asks, pressing her nose up against the glass to better see the street. "Where is he? Is he hot?" She scans the street quickly, spotting the blacked-out SUV on the corner.

"Lily, for god's sake." I toss my hands up, giving up. "I don't know whose rotation it is... Mac, maybe?"

Koen does have an exceptionally good-looking group of guys in his crew. "I wouldn't say any of them are your type though..." My voice is teasing, and it gets her attention, drawing her away from the window.

"What's that supposed to mean?"

"Koen's guys are seriously scary, and you like 'em pretty and helpless." I wonder for a minute if my comment is a little too harsh, but she lets out a laugh.

"I know. But seeing how *well* that's been working out for me, maybe it's time for a change." She grins, leaning back slightly to peek out at the street again.

Shaking my head, I set about unpacking the bags littering the tiny foyer space, hearing the telltale sound of Remi's racing feet coming back down the hall.

"Remi?" I call out, craning to see her past the island blocking my view.

"Just getting a snack!"

"Hold on, I'll help you."

I'm in heaven for the rest of the afternoon, playing games with Remi, and listening to Lily catch me up on all the hometown drama with her brothers.

"Okay, so don't hate me..." Lily side-eyes me as she drinks her mug of hot chocolate from the batch we all made together.

I narrow my eyes because that's never good.

"We took Remi to Dash's hockey game, and she's been begging to play ever since. Dash and Sam took her out on the lake, and I've never seen her so happy."

I know this. Remi and I have talked a few times about hockey over the phone.

"She still wants to play?" I ask, sighing. Part of me hoped she would have lost interest. I don't know anything about hockey. Lily bites her lip and nods. "I tried to talk her out of it, but you know how she is."

Remi gets free dance lessons at the studio since I work there, but hockey... "Hockey's *expensive*, isn't it?"

Lily's wince tells me everything I need to know. "I checked around, and the Edge Arena has a learn-to-skate program starting up soon. A hundred bucks for the lessons, and it includes the gear and skates."

I sigh. It's doable... but I worry about how her asthma would handle the cold arena air. She's done okay in ballet, but cold air makes her wheezy.

Doing the bedtime routine with Remi is a kind of therapy I didn't know I needed. *I missed her so much.* I make the most of it, drawing out the time in the bath, and adding a few extra stories. She falls asleep almost instantly at my side, but I stay next to her for a while. Just staring at her, gently running my fingers through her long blonde hair.

I have to tell him.

Walking back out into the living room, I find Lily perched on the sofa, television on, watching another video on her phone, a carton of ice cream in her lap.

I wander into the kitchen. Pulling open the fridge, only to stare into it for a minute, before shutting it again without taking anything out. I exhale deeply, pacing the kitchen before I even realize I'm doing it again—running circles in my mind and in life. I keep turning over the same impossible question— what the hell can I possibly say to Koen that would keep him from *hating* me?

"Briar?"

Lily's voice pulls me from my head. I glance over, seeing her watching me, head slightly tilted. "What are you doing?"

My thoughts are still a jumbled mess, so I run a hand through my hair, not really having a good answer. "I, uh, was just looking for a snack?"

Her eyes narrow, and I realize I framed it as a question.

"You're acting weird."

"Am I?" I reply almost absently, my mind drifting back to the need to tell Koen the truth.

"And you've *been* acting weird."

"Well, I mean, it could be the daily threats to our lives and that sort of thing..." I reply ruefully.

But she shakes her head, her face uncharacteristically serious. "No, that's not it..." I feel her scrutiny and shift uncomfortably, avoiding eye contact. "Oh, my god, you *slept* with him!" Lily's eyes widen and her face lights up with both shock and excitement. "Briar Elizabeth! We do not sleep with our baby daddies!" she chastises.

She's so loud.

I shush her, rushing closer, glancing around quickly to make sure Remi didn't get out of bed, but her bedroom door is still shut tight.

"Shhh, she could hear you!"

Lily rolls her eyes, waving me off. "Please, that kid could sleep through the end of the world once she's out."

It's true.

"I didn't—sleep with him," I wince.

"Briar," she frowns, "you are the worst liar the world has ever seen. Now, go get a spoon from the kitchen, and then get your fine ass back over here so we can discuss how you *totally* slept with Koen!"

My head drops back, looking to the sky for help before spinning around, giving up, and following her instructions. Plopping down on the couch next to Lily, I dig my spoon into the ice cream carton and scoop out a mouthful, while ignoring her wickedly annoying grin of glee.

"Okay, I want all the tea." She settles in deeper into the cushions, ready for a full debrief. "Spill!"

"I don't even know where to start..." I grumble between bites.

"How about when you fucked him?"

"Lily!"

"What?" She just blinks innocently at me, and I shake my head.

"Which time?" I slip my spoon back into my mouth, smiling slyly.

"Briar! You little slut!" She leans forward, slapping my arm teasingly. "Was he good? As good as you remember?"

I cover my face with my hands. "I am *so* not giving you a play-by-play."

She rolls her eyes again, with irritation this time. "Ugh, you're such a prude!"

"Am I a slut, or am I a prude?" I tease. "I'm pretty sure I can't be both."

447

"Shut up. You have to give me something!"

"Fine," I relent, quickly giving her the PG-13 version of what went down at the ballet studio the other night, and then again and *again* at the gala. I leave out the part about Koen shooting a guy in our apartment.

"Holy shit," she whispers when I'm finished. Dropping the ice cream carton down on the coffee table, completely forgotten. "You're falling for him," she says softly.

The words land heavier than I expect. My chest tightens, and suddenly it isn't fun anymore. "I don't know what I feel."

She softens, the amusement on her face fading. "Hey. That's okay. But, babe, sleeping with your baby daddy isn't exactly *casual hookup territory.* It means something. Even if you're not ready to admit it."

I sit back against the couch cushions, blowing out a breath while hugging a throw pillow to my chest. "It's complicated."

Lily stays quiet, letting me work through my thoughts.

"What if it was a mistake?" It shouldn't have happened. I shouldn't have let it... I release a shaky breath and hug the pillow tighter against me like it alone might hold me together. "It wasn't supposed to happen. One second he's being his usual grumpy, irritatingly bossy self and then... I don't know. It was him, it was me, it was—*everything*. And it felt..." My voice catches, breaking the word in half. "It felt like more than it should have." I chew my bottom lip. "It's a bad idea; *he's* a bad idea—"

"Stop trying to convince yourself of all the reasons you two shouldn't be together. Putting everything else aside, how does Koen make you *feel*?"

"He makes me feel..." I think about it for a second. "He makes me feel safe, protected, and when he looks at me..." My heart warms in my chest and I bury my face in my hands again, sinking deeper into the couch cushions. "I know what this sounds like..." I trail off, cutting off my stream of crazy.

"It sounds like love," Lily says, and I look up, meeting her eyes.

I shake my head, looking back down at my feet. My stomach twists. I don't want to say it. But the truth is there, raw and impossible to deny. "I think I'm falling for him. And it terrifies me."

"Because of his connections?" Lily asks, her voice careful as she brings up Koen's line of work.

"Because it's not just about me," I whisper. "He doesn't know about Remi. And every day I don't tell him, it gets heavier. He deserves to know. But if I tell him and he hates me, or if he doesn't care at all... If he walks away again..." My chest caves in. "I don't know if I could survive that," I admit quietly.

"I thought I was protecting her, protecting me..." The image of Koen I'd curated in my head all these years, the constant reminders I gave myself that who he was that night had just been an act, and that the news reports and the word on the streets detailing the cold, ruthless leader of the Irish mob was the *real* Koen O'Rourke. But now, having spent the past couple of weeks with him...

"I think I got it wrong." Tears sting the corners of my eyes, and my lower lip quivers slightly before I bite down hard on it to get it to stop.

Lily, not one to miss a thing, lunges forward. "Oh, honey," she breathes out, wrapping her arms around me in a tight hug. She squeezes me again. "Then maybe it's time to stop running. Secrets like this... they don't stay hidden. And if he really loves you back, he won't walk away. He'll fight for you. *Both* of you."

"We're supposed to go out tomorrow night after rehearsal. I'm—I'm going to tell him." I look up at Lily. "I'm scared."

"It'll be okay," she sighs. "And if it's not... we'll figure it out."

"I hope so."

64

THE RED WOLF

KOEN

I walk back into Obsidian, and the mood is tense. It's just Mac and I. Aidan and Liam have a Breakers game this afternoon, and Alex, Garrett, and Jerrad are still combing the streets of New York, trying to track down my sister, who's still in the wind after running away last week.

New York was Reagan's last pinged location before she disabled the tracker I use to keep tabs on her.

Honestly, New York makes sense. She wants to vanish, and in a big city like that, it's the equivalent of searching for a needle in a haystack.

She texted her apologies, citing her need for space, and dipped. But the longer she's out there on her own, the more danger she's in. And even though searching for her is spreading the Irish thin, family is more important.

Jace is on Briar duty. She had rehearsal all day for the show-case, and either way, after what Niko said, I don't want her anywhere near the Volkov. We already know they're funding

Giovanni's little sex trafficking organization, but to what end, I'm not yet sure.

I don't owe the Volkov shit; they are Nikolai's problem. They don't have a stake in Boston yet, but their influence in the recent trafficking ring could signal a newfound interest. The Volkov primarily run Russia, though their reach and influence stretches far across the ocean to the States.

The Bratva is more structured than the Irish Mob as a whole. Though, still not anywhere near as organized as the Italians. Where each Irish mob organization is its own entity, the Bratva has higher-ups they answer to.

Each Bratva organization answers to its own Pakhan, like Nikolai Kostalov in the Boston Bratva, or Andrei Vasilyev in New York. All of those different organizations bow to the Volkov back in Russia. A vast organization run by Pakhan Oleg Volkov.

Ronan Volkov is the third son of Oleg. His older brother Maksim will inherit that throne, but Ronan... Ronan is their reaper. Judge, jury, and executioner.

Krasnyy volk. *The red wolf.*

I'm anxious to get this meeting over with. While I trust Jace, I haven't seen Briar since yesterday afternoon. The Devils have a big shipment arriving tonight that cannot go wrong. I spent all day yesterday prepping and readying everything, and I personally vetted all the men working the shipment to ensure no leaks.

Liam and Mac will be on site tonight to make sure all goes smoothly. I would join them, but I have other plans. I trust they can keep it locked down.

Tonight, I'm taking Briar out to dinner. Just the two of us. Tonight, I make her mine. She's already mine. She's *always* been mine. But after tonight, everyone else will know it too.

I stalk through the club, meeting Niko outside of the private room we met him in a few days back. He gives me a stiff nod of acknowledgement, which I return.

"Weapons."

Silently, I hand over the two guns I have on my person, along with the knife at my belt—and the one tucked into my ankle, after Niko gives me a hard look when I try to get away with keeping it.

"He's already here," the Bratva Pakhan informs me, and I nod again, indicating for Mac to wait here before I head inside.

Ronan is standing near the middle of the room, a lit cigarette in his hand. I've never met him in person, but his reputation precedes him. He's around my age and looks every bit as deadly as the rumors suggest he is. His features are sharp, unforgiving, like he'd been carved from stone. The pale blue eyes glinting in the low light are a sharp contrast to his inky black hair, slicked back neatly atop his head.

He's sharply dressed—in a suit, all black. All clean lines and expensive taste, and not a drop of ink in sight.

I take a few steps into the room, letting the door close behind me before greeting him.

"Volkov."

I don't sit.

And neither does he. Ronan doesn't answer me either, just stands there, all predatory, sizing me up. The way he moves is quiet, deliberate, controlled, and immediately I can tell the most dangerous part about him is his *mind*. He keeps his eyes on me as he brings his cigarette up to his mouth and takes a drag.

"O'Rourke."

I've been around a lot of bad men in my life, the worst of the worst, but something about Ronan just doesn't sit right with me. There's a wrongness that makes the hair on the back of my neck stand on end. His eyes are cold and there's a deadness to them. They're light, yet full of darkness—empty, like there's no soul behind them. I fold my arms across my chest and wait. *He* called this meeting, after all.

"You killed my men."

"Aye," I say, with a dip of my chin. I did, a few weeks ago, when his men were terrorizing the Kostalov estate, threatening Aidan's soon-to-be wife, so I did what needed to be done.

Ronan has no reaction, though I think I see his jaw clench. "They were good men."

I can't help but scoff, "Not what I hear." Ronan's dead expression flames suddenly into a glare. But considering that Aidan killed one of Ronan's men after he tried to assault Rory, I respectfully disagree with that statement.

Ronan stares at me for a long moment, the silence thick between us, his expression unchanging. "Where is your pretty little pet tonight?"

I try not to react, pulling my phone out of my pocket to check the time, acting bored with the conversation. "I don't see how that's any of your business."

Ronan's mouth twitches. "Somewhere else to be?"

"Yes, actually. I'm a busy man," I say, staring him down. "Get to the point, Volkov. What is it that you want?"

"You should have stayed in your own lane, *Ri*." My eyes narrow when he uses my nickname. "You stuck your nose where it doesn't belong, and now Moscow wants you dead for what you've done." He inhales the last of his cigarette, flicking away the embers before dropping the butt into the ashtray sitting atop the table between us.

I keep the same cool, indifferent expression on my face. "Okay," I reply calmly, because someone wanting me dead isn't out of the ordinary day-to-day, but the threat from the Volkov is certainly one we need to take seriously. "And what do *you* want?" I tilt my head to study him, because Niko had warned me; this is *personal* for Ronan, but what I can't figure out is why? Men die in this dark world we've built every day. It was a risk all of us knew going in.

"I want your death." He glares at me, the flames in his pale eyes turning to ice. "But I want your death to be a mercy, after I take everything else from you first."

"The last thing this city needs is a war, Ronan," I warn. If the Volkov come for Boston, we'll have to throw everything we have at them to stand a chance. That tentative alliance between the Irish, the Boston Bratva, and the Italians will be put to the test.

"Make no mistake, Rí, this isn't a war." He uses the name again, and I clench my jaw. His hands slide into his pockets, and he looks down at me. He's taller, nearly the same height as Liam, who's around six five. "This is a consequence." He pauses, his eyes gleaming with veiled amusement. "Tell me, how is your family?"

I stiffen, despite myself, and my hand twitches for the gun I don't have at my belt. "Don't go there, Ronan," I warn him, my eyes impossibly dark. "Whatever this is, it's between you and me. Family is off limits, you know that." It's an unspoken rule in this world, but the one most frequently broken.

Ronan's eyes gleam. "Such loyalty," he purrs, and my fists

tighten. "You should be careful who you let close, and beware the snake in the grass."

"What's that supposed to mean?"

He doesn't answer me, just walks past, headed for the door, but pauses before he reaches it, looking back over his shoulder.

"Enjoy what you can, Irish King, because I'm going to burn your kingdom to the ground, and the only thing you're going to be able to do is watch."

65

YOU'RE ALREADY DEAD

BRIAR

It's another long day of dress rehearsals at the theater. Mr. Carr is still on another tear, and each number is taking painfully long to get through. I spend most of my time backstage on the floor, my eyes on the clock, either stretching or thinking about what I'm going to say to Koen later.

He's supposed to pick me up at nine, so he's not due to be here for another hour, but at the rate we're going... rehearsal is undoubtedly going to run late, and I'm going to be the reason we miss our reservation.

The dress I borrowed from Lily to wear tonight is tucked into my dance bag, back in Studio A where I did warm-ups, with the rest of my things. It's cute, green velvet, and falls to my knees. But right now, I'm in full costume for the run-through; a beautiful white tutu with brushes of pink sequins that sparkle each time the lights hit it.

I still have one more number to perform, but they're still on the one three-ahead of me. I sigh, growing impatient. I've already stretched as much as I can possibly stretch, and the nervous energy in my body requires movement.

I lean in toward Mia beside me, "I'm going to go grab my new pointe shoes out of my bag. Might as well break them in now since we aren't going anywhere, anytime soon."

"Take me with you," she sighs, bored out of her mind, but her number is next up.

I laugh, "I'll be right back. Do you want some water?"

"Yes, please," she hums, and gives me an appreciative smile.

Getting up, I dodge bodies of other dancers, stagehands, and lighting assistants to slip out the back end of the theater, which leads to the hallway most of the studios are on.

After weeks of dancing every day on my current shoes, I finally had to admit to myself that I needed a new pair, so I broke down and bought some from the shop downstairs this morning. Most dancers, if dancing every day, swap them out every one to two weeks, but at over one hundred dollars a pair, I do what I can to make mine last.

Money is tight right now, especially since I haven't gotten any tips or lesson money flowing in, and the slippers cost me just about my last hundred bucks.

I don't know how everything is going to work out with Koen tonight, but in one week, our deal will be over, and I'll have the money for Remi's meds, I'll be free of Gio, and I'll be able to get a job at another club or bar, and with the showcase next week...

The studio lights are off when I enter, but there's something off about the room. After weeks of being stalked by Koen, I trust my instincts, and I am certain I'm not alone.

I get halfway to the bag and freeze. My eyes scan the dark edges of the studio until I see Giovanni step out into the light.

I narrow my eyes, unsure why he's here. I've been keeping up with his texts, even though I've been feeding him all but useless information.

"Bella, Bella, Bella." He looks me over. "Long time, no see."

I'm not in the mood for his games. "But *not* long time, no talk. What do you want, Gio?"

He clicks his tongue at my attitude. "Have you seen Daniel?"

"No." I stiffen, but try and play it off.

"Interesting..." His eyes scan my face. "Because the last time I talked to him, he was on his way to see *you*."

I just shrug, doing my best to keep a blank expression on my face.

"It's a rough neighborhood..."

"Mmm." Gio considers, staring at me hard.

I stare back, my face carefully schooled.

He looks away first. "There's a shipment coming in tonight," he says, changing the subject, but my entire body tenses further. "Nobody seems to know where."

"That's too bad," I say, trying to pretend this has nothing to do with me.

He smiles. "It is. Because, Bella, I need to know where that shipment is arriving. And I think you know *exactly* where that is."

I shake my head *no*.

"You've been spending an awful lot of time with the O'Rourkes; I know you've heard more than you've let on."

"No," I tell him, still shaking my head.

He sighs, disappointed. "Did you forget my threat, Bella? We had a deal, but if you're not going to deliver, I'll have to consider our deal off." He frowns. "But you do work best with a little incentive..." Gio pulls out his phone, holding it up, the screen facing me, and my blood goes cold.

It's a picture of Remi and Lily curled up on the couch, watching a movie. Only in this photo, they're in the middle of a rifle sight, the angle of the camera shows it was taken by someone perched on the fire escape across the alleyway.

The photo is from tonight. Remi's wearing her favorite unicorn pajamas, and in the background I can see the suitcases that are still in the living room from yesterday.

"I don't know anything," I say, quieter.

Gio pulls the phone away, giving me a bored expression. "I really hope you do, Bella, because I'm not walking away without what I came for. And if you really don't know... well then that's a pity. Because then there's only one use for you—and your pretty little daughter."

My chest burns with rage and I blink away angry tears, curling my hands into fists at my side.

"You're not going to lay a finger on her," I growl, even though my voice shakes along with the rest of me.

Giovanni makes a show of checking his watch. "Well, that depends on you, Bella. Where is the Irish shipment dropping tonight?"

I'm going to kill him.

He laughs when he sees the glare on my face. *I amuse him.* He knows I know.

"So, what's it going to be, Bella? Do we *remember* any new details?" He waves his phone at me, the picture of Lily and Remi still on it. "Or do I need to make up my money elsewhere?"

"Yes," I bite out. Everything in me rebelling against giving Gio the information.

"That's the answer I was looking for! You're learning, Bella."

I don't respond. Too busy glowering at him.

"Where and when, beautiful? That's all I need."

"The docks," I bite out, watching as he lifts his phone, typing something into it.

"I hope you have more than that." He raises an eyebrow at me expectantly.

"Port 17. Nine p.m. Tonight," I clip out between clenched teeth. My shoulders sag with the weight of what I've just done. I eye the clock; it's almost eight-thirty. Maybe Gio won't have time to intercept the shipment, or divert it, or whatever the hell he's planning to do on such a short timeline.

The smile that curves up his face tells me otherwise, and he presses his phone to his ear.

"Did you get my text?" He listens to whoever is speaking on the other end. "You were right about the docks. Get the sniper in place." He checks his watch. "There's not a lot of time."

I freeze.

"Liam O'Rourke is the target."

My heart skips a beat. *Liam?*

"Call me when you have eyes," he says, before ending the call and smiling at me like we're friends.

I inch toward the door. *Liam can't die. I have to warn them.* But I left my phone backstage when I came to get my shoes; it's not in here. Gio's still in front of me, and he moves to block my path out of the studio.

"Not so fast, Bella. I have to make sure you're telling me the truth. Once my guy confirms the intel, I'll be on my way."

We wait, just like that, in uncomfortable silence, for what feels like an eternity but is really only ten minutes, until his phone rings.

"Hello?" The dark smile on Gio's face sets me on edge. "Excellent. Excellent."

He hangs up the phone, straightening his jacket before eyeing the look on my face with a look of confusion. "Chill, Bella, I thought you'd be pleased! If all goes to plan tonight, you'll have one less O'Rourke to worry about."

My knees feel shaky. "What do you mean?"

"My guys have confirmed the drop location. Liam O'Rourke is on site."

"You're—you're going to *kill* Liam?" I blurt out, the gravity of what I've done hitting me all at once. My heart is racing, and my head spins, but I have to keep it together.

"Me? No." He shakes his head, his lips curling in distaste. "I'm just the middleman, a broker of information, but I do have a Russian client who is very highly motivated." He smiles with a nod.

"I thought *you* were vetting them as potential clients," I say, still trying to come up with a plan to fix this in my head.

Gio just shrugs, finally making his way toward the door. "I'm a businessman, Bella, and my client came to me with a lucrative deal for information. Very lucrative." His smile is dripping with grease.

"Lovely chatting with you, Bella. Until next time!" Gio calls, exiting the studio, and leaving me alone in my mental turmoil.

The docks... a sniper... Liam.

They're going after Liam! *And it's all my fault.*

I chance a look at the clock; it's almost quarter till nine. There's still time.

I dart for the door, looking out into the hallway quickly first to make sure Gio is gone. The hallway is clear and I race toward the theater, flinging open the rear door, and jumping over dancers sprawled across the floor as I dart for my phone, scooping it up from where it's lying next to Mia, fumbling it in my hands as I try to unlock it.

"Briar, are you okay?" Mia asks, looking up at me with concern.

They're going to kill Liam. I like Liam. *I set him up.* I told Gio where he'd be; I might as well have loaded the fucking gun myself.

I have to stop it.

My fingers freeze over the screen. *He'll know.* There's no way I can warn him without confessing what I've done. *What I've been doing.*

Tears stream down my face as I finally unlock the screen, finding Koen's contact, my finger hovering just over his name before pressing down to connect the call.

"Pick up, pick up, pick up," I plead with the sound of the ringing phone in my ear, but it just rings and rings. Just as I fear I'm about to be sent to voicemail, the line clicks open.

"Yeah?"

I almost drop the phone.

"Koen?" I rush out, my brain moving too fast for my mouth to keep up.

"Briar Rose, where are you? I'm waiting for you."

I freeze. *He's here.*

Half in a daze, I dart between the thick curtains out onto

463

the left wing of the stage. Mr. Carr is in the middle of reaming out the orchestra, so he doesn't notice me, my eyes scan the rows of chairs in the audience.

"I see you."

I see you too.

Through tears, I locate Koen across rows and rows of empty seats; he's all the way at the top of the theater, by the rear double doors; I see my dark shadow waiting for me.

I choke back a sob, trying to clear my throat.

"Koen, listen to me. There's no time. I don't know..." *Fuck, just spit it out, Briar.* "They're going to kill Liam," I rush out, sucking in a breath. "They—they know where the drop is tonight. Port 17 at nine p.m. It's an ambush."

There is only silence on the other end of the phone, and I try to hold back the sobs that threaten to rip out of me.

"Koen?" He's staring at me. I can *see* him staring at me, but I can't hear anything.

I check the phone, thinking maybe we got disconnected, but we didn't.

"Who?"

I flinch at the dangerous edge in his voice.

I swallow. "Giovanni... and some Russians, he said. I swear, Koen, I didn't know. I didn't know what they were going to do." The image of Remi and Lily in that rifle sight flickers back through my mind, and tears soak my cheeks. *He has to go. He has to save Liam. But he's not moving... He's just staring at me.*

"How does Giovanni know about the drop tonight, Briar?"

I suck in a breath, my lip trembling, my heart shattering into a million pieces.

"Because I told him."

Silence.

Deafening, cataclysmic, screaming—silence. I meet his eyes, and with each second he looks at me, I feel the knife of his gaze cut through me. He looks torn between going to save his brother and coming down here to strangle me.

"I'm sorr—"

"Don't." My words seem to snap something inside of him.

"Koen..."

"Oh, little Rose," he purrs; his voice sounds *strange*, darker, borderline unhinged. "You don't know, do you? You're already dead."

Tears stream down my cheeks, and he backs away, moving toward the doors behind him, but still his eyes never leave mine.

"Don't cry. *Run*. Run, little Rose, *I dare you*, because when I find you... I will show no mercy. I will take my time, and I will make sure you know exactly who the fuck you betrayed."

He disappears, and the line goes dead, and I fall to my knees.

66

DO IT. I DARE YOU.

BRIAR

I GO HOME.

I go home because I have a child, and I can't just head for the fucking hills after the Irish Devil King threatens my life.

"We have to go!" I shout, nearly incoherent, into the phone as I lose time navigating the fucking subway system. I'd get a rideshare, but I don't have any money.

I don't have any money.

"What happened?" Lily asks on the other end of the phone, her tone instantly serious.

"*He knows,*" I half sob. "Koen knows about Gio."

"*Fuck,*" Lily breathes.

"Pack what you can; I'll be home in ten."

Bolting through the door fifteen minutes later, I quickly secure the locks and race for my room.

I rip the backpack out from under my bed, and start tearing through drawers, stuffing the bag with what I think are the essentials. *Underwear, right? I'll need clean underwear for my life on the run from a fucking mob boss.*

I'm sure Giovanni and his men will find out I tipped off the Irish, if Koen can actually warn Liam in time. So, we can add *them* to the list of people hunting me down... you know, for *funsies.*

I sense Lily before I see her standing in my doorway.

I sniff, struggling to keep in the absolute devastation that's ripping through me. "Koen knows I betrayed him."

She pales.

"We have to get out of the city. *Tonight.* It's not safe."

She nods solemnly. "I'm going with you."

I freeze, looking her way. "I can't ask you to do that."

"You're not asking, I'm telling."

"Lily—" I start.

"Briar Elizabeth Ralston, if you think for one second I'm going to leave you and that precious little angel baby to face the Irish Devil on your own, you've got another thing coming!"

I almost smile, despite myself. "Fine."

God, if anything happens to Lily because of me, I will never forgive myself. She can't stay here either; someone will probably hurt her to get to me.

"Grab what you can. I can get us a car," she shouts, darting between the bathroom and my room, grabbing stuff.

My head shoots up in her direction. "A car? From who?"

Lily just shakes her head. "A friend. Just be ready to go when I get back." She's halfway out the door before she adds,

"My backpack's on my bed but... pack me some clean underwear, will ya? I forgot. And it's a road trip, baby! Don't forget the snacks!" She hollers as she runs down the hall, and I hear the door slam shut behind her.

I roll my eyes, laughing through my tears, tearing open my bottom drawer to grab an extra pair of leggings. Only Lily could find the fun in *running for your life.*

Ten minutes later, I've got one backpack for me, one for Lily, and another one filled to the brim for Remi. I've also left the suitcases full of clean laundry (thanks to Lily's mom) that we still haven't fully unpacked, to take as well.

Remi is still sleeping the night away, blissfully unaware that her entire life is about to be upended.

The plan is that when Lily gets back with the car, we'll load it up first, and then I'll grab Remi. She's a heavy sleeper, so once we get her into the car and start driving, Lily and I can figure out what the fuck the rest of the plan is.

I take a minute to use the bathroom, not knowing how long we'll have to drive before it's safe to stop. After that's done, I decide to do one more pass over my room to make sure I've packed everything important.

My handgun is already tucked safely into my backpack, loaded and ready to go. Extra bullets in the side pocket.

I make it two feet into my room before I freeze. *Literally.* My eyes go right to the broken window in the now cold, but *empty,* room.

One of the first things I did when I got home was seal up that stupid window latch with duct tape. It should have prevented him from running his knife through and flipping it open, but I didn't consider he could just break it...

A chill, that has nothing to do with the cold air, runs the length of my spine.

The gun.

It's in my backpack, sitting just beside the kitchen island by the door.

Slowly, I turn back around, walking on leaden feet towards the kitchen.

I step into the room, stopping the second I see him.

Looking every bit the dangerous mafia king that he is, Koen waits in the darkest corner of the living room. I know it's him, despite the mask obscuring his face. His dark eyes are on me, and he's leaning far too casually against the back wall. My eyes drop to the blade he's playing with in his hands. The red glow of the neon sign outside glints off of the hard steel, and I inch closer to my backpack. *It's only a few feet away...*

"Is Liam okay?"

It's a dangerous question to ask, but I ask it anyway. Koen is nearly impossible to read at the best of times, and I need to know what I'm walking into.

Koen's eyes glint in the dark, which is no comfort. "He's downstairs."

I let out a breath of relief and feel a bit of tension release from my shoulders.

Liam's okay. He's okay.

"And he's just as eager as I am to find out why the fuck you set him up," he says, his eyes reflecting red like the knife in his hand.

I open my mouth to refute his statement, but no sound comes out, because after he speaks, he steps forward, into the kitchen light.

Blood.

He's covered in it. Both hands are stained crimson, with smears of it all over his clothes, neck, and on the mask itself. There's a wild look in his eyes that has me moving closer toward the kitchen. The way his head tilts is predatory; the way he's watching me has me fighting an overwhelming urge to scream in terror.

"What's the matter, Briar? Surprised to see me?" His voice is so cold, so dark, he barely even sounds like himself.

I freeze. Holding up both of my hands, I attempt to reason with him.

"Koen... wait, you don't understand," I say, shaking my head. I can't move; his icy stare alone has me frozen in place.

"Oh, I think I understand perfectly, little Rose. I was just a payday to you. A job," he snarls at me, and I wince. The knife is still in his hand, and he just continuously runs his finger up and down the blade while glaring at me. "But I thought you understood the rules—*no one* touches family."

I swallow, and the tiny movement is enough to snap the cord between us. He lunges for me just as I make a dive for my bag. It's still open, and my fingers close around the rough grip, just as Koen's hand closes around me.

He quickly redirects me, slamming my back up against the kitchen wall, and holding me there by my throat.

The knife pressed against my jugular doesn't even waver when I cock the gun in my hand. I press it just under his chin, and click off the safety with shaking fingers.

Koen *laughs,* tipping back his head.

"There are those thorns." His gaze drops back to me, ice cold, no trace of amusement left in his eyes when he leans in, burying the barrel of my gun deeper into his chin.

"Do it."

I stare up at him with wide eyes, hating how my hand shakes, hating how the scent of him is both a comfort and a terror; the metallic scent of the blood he's drenched in has my stomach in knots.

"You want to kill me, Briar Rose? Fucking do it!" he half shouts. "Or do you need me to turn around first so you can get a clear shot at my back?"

I wince, and he leans in even closer until his mouth is just over my ear, and his voice drops to a whisper, "Do it. *I dare you.*"

My grip on the gun tightens, and I let out a whimper of frustration. I can't. *I can't do it.* He's going to *kill* me, but yet I can't pull the fucking trigger.

I'm shaking, crying now, tears once again stain my cheeks. "I can't." Exhaling in both surprise and resignation, I lower the gun.

"Should've taken the dare." Koen tilts his head; his eyes look almost—*disappointed?*

A sharp prick in the soft skin of my neck is a surprise. I'd been so preoccupied with the gun, and with him, I didn't notice he'd swapped out his knife for a... *needle.* Fear unlike anything I've known before fills me, as my body immediately goes weak; the edges of my vision are already darkening.

There's pity in Koen's eyes as I tremble under him; his grip on my throat is all that keeps me upright. He plucks the gun out of my hands easily, taking his eyes off of me for a second to study it.

"No," I breathe out, my eyes locked on him. My panic alone is all that's keeping me from going under.

"Koen, don't—"

His dark eyes slide back to meet mine, and he cocks his head. His fractured eyes reveal a fractured soul. "Don't what, little Rose? Don't *hurt* you? Don't *kill* you?" he mocks. "I hate to break it to you, darling, but—"

My eyes dart to the hallway and back. *I can't fight it any longer.* I can feel the powerful pull of whatever he injected me with dragging me under.

"*Don't leave her alone!*" I shout. The words spilling out of me just before it all goes dark.

A CAT?

KOEN

WHO THE FUCK is she talking about?

I stare down at Briar in my arms. I caught her before she fell, passed out cold. Her mouth is still tight and pressed down into a frown as though, even now, she still fights the sedative I gave her.

I swing her up into my arms, carrying her out of the apartment, down several flights of stairs and toward the back exit.

Aidan is waiting at the back door of the apartment building and holds it open for me as I pass, making my way to the SUV concealed in the dark alley next door.

The trunk opens, and I lay Briar down inside, not bothering to tie her up. The drugs I gave her will keep her unconscious for a few hours yet. Long enough to get where we're going.

I brush the hair out of her face with a frown. *Don't leave her alone.*

Don't leave *who* alone?

Lily already left—Mac and Alex are out tracking her down.

After my meeting with Ronan, I was forced to call back my crew from New York. They made good time, too, arriving just in time to help clean up the mess down at the docks.

But a nagging feeling settles over me, and I glance back up at Briar's window, quickly running over what I remember about her apartment. *She doesn't have a dog, but maybe a cat?* Though I'm pretty sure I would've seen it sitting in the window or on the sofa at some point...

I shut the trunk, halfway to the passenger seat before I shake my head, cursing under my breath before turning around, and heading back into the decrepit brick building. Something about what she said—and *the desperate look on her face* when she said it. I just—

"Rí."

I stop. My head snaps up in Liam's direction. He's behind the wheel, twisted around in his seat, watching me through the open window with narrowed eyes. "What are you doing? Let's go." He scans the street as he talks, seeing as how we're in the middle of a kidnapping.

I turn back to look up at the apartment again, making my decision. "I'll be right back."

"What the fuck? Where is he going?" I hear Aidan ask Liam as I stalk back into Briar's building, before taking the stairs two at a time until I reach her door again. Cursing for the hundredth time their lack of an elevator.

The apartment is as I left it—empty. And eerily quiet without Briar.

I spot her phone on the counter and pick it up, tucking it into my back pocket. I move through the space, keeping my eye out for a laptop or other electronic device I can have Liam scan. Who knows what other information she's passed on to the Italians, or whatever else she may have sold us out on?

Moving slowly down the hall, there's no sign of movement, and *no sign of a fucking cat,* in either the kitchen or the living room.

My eyes scan Briar's room from the hall. There's not much inside. Her pathetic excuse for a mattress is on the floor, no closet, and it looks like she's already torn through her bureau. The drawers sit half askew, clothes everywhere, with one drawer pulled out entirely, sitting overturned on the floor.

I take a quick inventory of Lily's room next door.

Also empty.

Lily's room is a direct contrast to Briar's. The color pink dominates the space. Soft and feminine. Nothing jumps out at me, and seeing as I have no beef with Lily, I leave her room alone, prowling back out into the hall.

That leaves only the bathroom, and the closet across the hall from Briar's room.

Something doesn't feel right about this situation and I take out my gun, clearing the bathroom before moving in on the closet. Silently, I twist the nob, nudging the door open with my foot, before peering inside. I enter slowly, surprised to find it's not a closet at all... but actually *a third bedroom.*

The floor is a landmine of toys, so I stay in the doorway, my eyes scanning the small space.

Colorful drawings and paintings are taped rather haphazardly to the walls. A pink tutu and a hockey stick lie abandoned on the floor in front of a small wooden bed.

A small wooden bed containing a tiny sleeping *child.*

The kid is buried so deep under the covers, I might have missed her if I hadn't been so taken aback by the room.

Don't leave her alone. Briar's terror-filled plea.

I quickly holster my gun at my waist.

"Fuck."

Not taking my eyes off of the sleeping child, I pick up my phone, dialing Liam before pressing the device to my ear.

"I need your help," I mutter as soon as the call connects, keeping my voice as low as possible.

"Fucking hell." I hear him slam his palm down on the wheel in frustration. "I'm coming."

I eye the child warily while I wait for my brother. Dodging toys, I risk a closer look.

It's a girl.

She looks to be around three, maybe four? With a mess of blonde curls strewn across her face, clutching a pink, stuffed unicorn in her hands. Sleeping peacefully.

Relief courses through me when, upon closer inspection, she looks *nothing* like Briar. But with that blonde hair... she *does* look an awful lot like *Lily.*

Not sure what else to do, I retreat back into the hallway, lightly pacing the space outside, standing guard over the room while watching the little rise and fall of the blankets, until I hear the front door open.

Liam moves swiftly through the apartment, mask on, gun in hand, seeing as I gave him no context as to the *help* I required.

He gives me a look of mild irritation when he finds me, just standing in the hallway waiting for him, and puts his weapon away.

"Aidan is with Briar?"

"Yeah, but what—"

He's loud. *Too loud.* I press a finger to my lips, pointing silently into the bedroom.

Liam arches a brow, but humors me, coming closer and taking a peek around the corner.

"Oh, fuck," he breathes out, glancing back at me, his eyes wide.

"Yeah," I clip out, still working out what to do about this situation in my head.

"Is she—?"

"Lily's," I answer. "I think." Or maybe we can add nannying to the seemingly never-ending list of Briar's part-time jobs.

"We have to go." The urgent look in Liam's eyes reminds me we've long since overstayed our time here.

"I know."

"We can't leave the kid here." His eyes dart from the child to me.

He isn't wrong. We're not the only ones after Briar. It's only luck we beat Gio and his crew here, and I have no idea where Lily is.

I sigh. "We have to take her with us." I pull out my phone and send out a few quick messages. "Mac and Alex are already out looking for Lily. I'll have someone monitor the apartment in case she turns up here. You get the kid." I shoulder past him, headed toward Briar's room. "I need to find Briar's laptop."

Liam nods, rolling back his shoulders and cracking his neck before stepping into the child's room. I should go look for the computer, but I wait in the doorway for my brother to reemerge. The child looks even smaller in his arms; he scooped her up, covers and all.

He gives me a silent nod before heading down the hall. As he does, she stirs, letting out a soft sigh, eyelids fluttering for a second. We both freeze and lock eyes, holding our breath. I can only imagine the sight if the kid wakes up right now... two strange men in masks, both of us still drenched in blood from our earlier altercation. But thankfully, her eyes remain shut, a deep sigh escaping as she burrows deeper into Liam's arms. The pink stuffed unicorn slips out of her grasp and falls to the floor.

Not noticing the stuffed toy, Liam moves as swiftly and smoothly for the door as possible, disappearing with the child down the hall.

Once they're gone, I stare at the little pink unicorn on the floor for a few seconds before heading back into Briar's room, finding nothing, and then following Liam back outside.

"So we're kidnappers now?" Aidan asks when I slide wordlessly into the passenger seat. He's now in the driver's seat; Liam is in the back, the girl still asleep in his arms.

"You're one to talk," I shoot back, so not in the mood for anyone's shit right now. I rip off my mask.

"Is it Briar's?" Liam asks, and I feel his eyes on the back of my head, but I'm too busy scanning the street outside.

"*It?*" Aidan scolds, turning around in his seat to give our brother a disappointed look.

"The kid's got to be Lily's," I say, with only half a mind on the conversation, too preoccupied thinking about the little dark-haired liar I have in the trunk.

"Are you sure?" Liam presses, looking down at the girl asleep in his lap.

"Briar doesn't have a kid."

"But what if..."

"*Briar doesn't have a kid,*" I snap, and Liam wisely shuts his mouth.

A minute goes by and nobody speaks, and the car doesn't move either.

"Drive," I growl out, and Aidan makes a show of putting the SUV into gear.

"Where?" he asks me.

"The warehouses." I turn back to Briar's building, throwing one last glance up at her window. The same one I've watched her through too many times now to count. It's dark inside. "It's time to get some fucking answers."

68

LITTLE TRAITOR

KOEN

It's quiet now in the interrogation lockers at the warehouse.

There had been a flurry of activity when we first arrived, our guys unloading the last of the shipment Giovanni and the Volkov had hoped to intercept earlier today—or well, yesterday now, seeing as it's a little after four in the morning.

Liam and Aidan have the kid we took from Briar's apartment back in Aidan's office. The child stayed asleep on the drive out and is now curled up on the couch next to Rory, who Aidan insisted we pick up on our way out of Boston. After what the Volkov tried with Liam, he wasn't leaving the city without her.

I took over driving from Aidan. Still sleepy-eyed, Rory climbed into the back of the SUV without a word, even when she saw the kid asleep on Liam's lap. She just gave Aidan a questioning look before falling back asleep on his shoulder before we even hit the highway.

Lily managed to evade Mac and Alex, turning back up at the apartment with a car shortly after we left. She led them on a brief chase through the city before they backed off, not wanting her to get hurt on our account. Mac's working on trying to track the car, or her phone, as we speak.

I lean my back against the cold cement wall in one of the lockers and wait. My jaw is clenched so tightly it aches. I haven't left this spot since I brought Briar down here, limp and unconscious in my arms. She hangs from the ceiling by her wrists, just high enough so her toes barely scrape the concrete below.

I want to see her break. I want to see the fear in her eyes when she finally realizes the consequences of her betrayal.

She lied to me.

She's been working for Giovanni this entire time, and has likely betrayed me in ways I don't even know about yet. And tonight, *she nearly cost me my brother.*

My chin lifts as the chains overhead clink softly as Briar stirs.

Her eyes are still closed, and she's gagged—a thick cloth in her mouth to keep her quiet—but it doesn't stop the small whimper that escapes as she begins to wake. Briar's body trembles slightly, a shiver running through her, reacting to the cold before fully coming to.

She's wearing what she had on when I took her, but it's not doing her any favors. An old, ripped, cut-off t-shirt that exposes her stomach, with a black sports bra visible underneath, along with a pair of black leggings and leg warmers that have fallen down over a pair of worn sneakers. She must have changed back into her warm-up clothes before fleeing the theater.

I'm still angry with myself, because I *should* have stripped her. That's protocol after all; every person we bring back here for questioning ends up naked, exposed, and humiliated. It serves a purpose: access, control, *fear.*

But I couldn't.

My jaw clenches even harder as I try to force myself into that cold, lethal void of detachment I know all too well—the place in my mind I retreat to when things need *taking care of.*

I wanted this. I wanted her helpless. I wanted her chained. I wanted her to feel a mere fraction of the betrayal she'd carved into me. But now, seeing her like this, she looks so thin, so vulnerable, with tear-stained cheeks... my anger sits differently. It's heavier. I thought I'd feel satisfaction seeing her at my mercy, *but I just feel pain.*

She did this, I tell myself, and steel myself for what comes next.

Briar shifts again, fighting her way to consciousness. Her eyes flutter open, connecting with mine, and I smile.

"Hi, *little traitor.*"

She jerks back violently, screaming through the gag in her mouth. Losing her footing, her sneakers claw for purchase on the slippery cement floor below.

Fully conscious now, her eyes dart around the space. It's dark; the room itself is lit by only a single bulb overhead. She's in what used to be an old freezer that we've converted and soundproofed for the Devils' interrogation needs.

She tugs on her hands that are bound over her head, but it's no use; she's properly restrained.

Briar steadies herself on the balls of her feet, chest heaving, when her eyes come back to meet mine. I hear my name—a muffled version of it anyway—through the gag as she looks up at me, searching my face—my eyes—for any shred of humanity I might have left in me.

I click my tongue at the look in her eyes. "Ah, ah, ah, none of that, darling. You think those puppy-dog eyes will save you?" My eyes narrow into a glare. "Tell me, little Rose, do you know what the Devils do to traitors?"

The way her entire body shudders tells me she at least has an idea.

"It's okay if you don't," I say, bringing the knife up. "I'll show you." The blade is the same one I held to her throat earlier, and while I don't touch her with it, she flinches away violently when I bring it closer. The movement knocks her off the precarious position she's in atop her toes, and she has to scramble to get her feet back under her again.

I circle her, and she trembles, another terrified whimper escaping her.

Maybe I should have gone with duct tape... The sound slices through me, fracturing something deep within my chest.

I shove the feeling away, reaching for that void again.

"I want to play a game. Do you want to play a game with me, baby?"

She murmurs something incoherent, her eyes pleading with me.

"Truth or dare, little Rose?"

Briar stares into my eyes for another second before she looks away, turning her gaze to the ground, refusing to even humor me.

I click my tongue in disappointment. "Fine. I'll choose."

She doesn't react, staring hard at the floor below.

Annoyed, I slip the tip of my blade under her chin and lift. Her head tilts up, but she keeps her eyes down, refusing to look at me.

Something inside me snaps.

"Look. At. Me," I growl, my tone lethal.

She won't.

I step closer, and she closes her eyes. Her body tenses, as if she's bracing to take a blow.

My hand snaps out, and I grab her jaw, jerking her face closer to me.

"Briar," I snarl. "Look at me."

Her eyes slowly lift, and I regret my words.

Her blue eyes are stained red, and wet with tears she's trying to hold back. She looks up at me, broken, fragile, and—fuck, she might as well have stabbed the knife through my chest. I see *everything*—fear, guilt, shame—but worst of all is the tiny flicker of *hope* I find deep within her eyes. Misplaced trust that, despite my anger, and her actions, *I won't hurt her.*

"You were playing me this whole time?"

Tears finally fall as she loses her battle to hold them in.

My grip on her jaw tightens until her eyes open again, but I hold her there, refusing to let her look away from me again.

"Why, Briar?"

She searches my eyes. Something breaks in her from whatever she finds there, and the tears flow harder and she releases a muffled sob.

"And don't you fucking lie to me now. *One truth.* You owe me that much. I want you to tell me *why.*"

I slide the knife through the cloth that's keeping her quiet, letting it fall to the floor between us.

She swallows. "You don't understand..." Her voice cracks, coming out rough and scratchy, and I loosen the grip I have on her jaw. "It's complicated."

"Either an explanation comes out of that mouth, or a bullet is going in your skull," I warn her. Rage is boiling inside of me, and I'm on the verge of tipping over the edge. But I think I'm more pissed about how much control she still has over me, how after *everything* she's done, I still feel an overwhelming urge to protect her, to keep her safe, even when *I'm* the one threatening her.

"I never meant for any of this to happen. I—"

"Never meant for this to happen?" I cut her off. "Briar, you *planned* this. You were working with Giovanni from the beginning. And the Volkov, the *whole fucking time.* You knew *exactly* what you were doing when you betrayed me, and crying now won't save you." Disgusted, I release her, leaving her trembling.

"I wasn't—I didn't have a choice."

"There's always a choice," I snarl, coming at her again fast. She shies away from me, recoiling as far as the chains allow her to. My chest tightens, feeling as though it might burst, as if my ribs can't contain the catastrophic damage being done inside. I point the tip of my blade at her. "You *chose* wrong."

Her eyes drop to the knife, the cold steel glinting in the dim lighting as I pace the space in front of her.

"You won't hurt me. You won't," she says, shaking her head.

"You sound pretty confident about that." I step forward, placing the sharp end of the blade against her skin, a few inches above the little Celtic knot at her neck. The silver charm glints in the low light, *taunting me,* and I'm tempted to rip it from her throat.

"You won't hurt me," she repeats. Her voice shakes with the words, and there's uncertainty in them, and in her eyes when she looks up at me. Especially when I press down harder, aware that she can feel the bite of the blade against her skin.

The small prick of blood that appears unleashes a wave of nausea through me. "You *promised*," she whispers, almost as if the words are a prayer.

I lower the knife, pacing the room once again, my chest tight, trying to walk off the anger burning through me before I do something I regret. Coming for her again, I pull her toward me by the back of her head until our foreheads meet, and I press mine to hers. Her sweet scent fills my lungs, giving me air to breathe.

"Tell me why, Briar Rose, *please*."

"I had to. I didn't have a choice!" she says again.

"Stop saying that!" I shout, stepping away from her. "*You* had a choice, you *chose*, and you didn't choose *me!*"

Briar's eyes flash, giving me a small glimpse of those thorns I love. "No, because I chose *her!*" she screams back at me, looking like she wants to throttle me, and fall apart, all at the same time.

There's a pounding on the door that I ignore, staring at Briar as I try to work out what she just said.

"Koen."

The pounding at my back intensifies. "Go the fuck away, Liam!" I shout through the metal.

Two seconds later, the door slides open anyway.

"What the fuck?" I whirl on him. "I'm a little fucking busy right now."

"I know, I'm sorry, but..." his eyes trail over my shoulder to look at Briar. "It's an emergency."

"It can wait," I growl, turning away from him.

"No."

The unusually somber tone in my brother's voice has me turning slowly back around.

"It can't."

I want to ask him what's so goddamn important, but Liam's not looking at me. Instead, he's watching Briar, and there's a silent conversation passing between the two that sets off a spiral of rage inside me.

Tears fill her eyes as she stares at my brother, and she gives him the tiniest imperceptible shake of her head.

"There's something you need to see," Liam tells me, his voice tight.

"Just tell me what it is," I say, losing my patience.

"No." Liam rolls his shoulders back, looking me in the eye this time. "You have to see for yourself." *Bloody fucking hell, he's not letting this go.*

"Aidan's office," Liam adds quietly, sneaking another weighted glance at Briar.

"Fine." I storm out of the locker, leaving Briar and taking my brother with me. I slam the door behind us, because there's no fucking way I am leaving the two of them alone together after whatever the fuck just went down between them.

Stalking into the office, I find Aidan and Rory standing by his desk in quiet conversation, both of whom tense and go silent when I enter.

"Someone care to tell me what the fuck is so goddamn important that it couldn't wait—"

My mouth snaps shut when I follow their gaze to the old sofa in the corner, where I find the child we technically kidnapped from Briar's apartment sitting up.

She's awake.

The office is silent.

Big, round eyes stare up at me, with a mixture of curiosity and apprehension in them. I have to give the little one credit;

she hasn't screamed or cried yet, but under my hard gaze, tears well up in those big green eyes and—

No.

Her eyes aren't green... not all the way...they're fractured in half, right down the middle, one side a dark evergreen, and the other... a dark brown.

I can feel everyone looking at me, but I can't look away from the little girl's eyes—*my eyes.*

Mine.

She's mine.

69

REMI

BRIAR

No, no, no, no, no, no, no....

Not like this.

Please, god, not like this.

Of all the ways he could have found out about her, this is, without question, the worst possible one.

Koen reappears in the doorway, his eyes on the floor. His expression is unreadable, but not empty. He stops a few feet from me, and his gaze slowly lifts, and he just... shatters everything inside of me with a single look.

He knows.

"It's not true." He steps forward, shaking his head. "Tell me it's not true, Briar. Whose kid is that?"

Tears stream down my face, and I know he can see the truth written in my eyes. *The guilt.*

Koen shakes his head. "Tell me she's not mine. Tell me you haven't been hiding my *daughter* from me this whole time."

The way his voice breaks...

There's so much to say—so much to explain—but it's too hard to put it into words, *and I can't stop fucking crying.*

"She's mine?"

It's a simple question, but I can't breathe; the words stay caught in my throat.

"Briar, I swear to god if you lie to me right now..." Koen's tone sharpens and I look away, unable to look him in the eye.

"She's *mine*," I say quietly. "My secret. My beautiful little secret." I look up at him. "And she's *yours,* too."

His jaw flexes. Once. A small, controlled movement, and then he nods, a single, tight dip of his chin.

"*I'm sorry.*" I regret the words as soon as I say them—because they're not enough... not nearly enough. But I am... *I am so sorry.*

"Don't." His words are quiet, and I can sense the storm brewing behind his eyes.

I press my lips back together as I try to pretend everything inside of me isn't falling apart.

"What's her name?"

I take a sharp intake of breath.

His eyes slide back to mine. "What's. Her. Name?" His question is raw and desperate, like he's never needed to know anything more. "My *daughter*?"

"Remi," I say quietly.

He exhales—just once, staring at the ground again. Silence fills the air between us long enough that I gather up the nerve to ask the one question I *need* an answer to.

"Where is she?"

"She's here."

His answer doesn't put my mind at ease.

"Is she... *okay?*"

Koen's chin lifts, and his gaze finds mine, and I almost feel guilty for having to ask.

"She's safe."

I nod my head, falling silent. The ropes holding my wrists bite into my skin, and I shift. The chain clinks above, and I feel the weight of his eyes on me.

"That's why you ran." I look up to find myself caught in the wild intensity of his gaze. Watching as he works it out— *works it all out.*

"That's why you ran from me at the warehouse—and again when I found you at Wonderland. You've been pushing me away this entire time. You really hate me that much?"

"I don't hate you." I stare at him, eyes wide with surprise.

He scoffs.

"I don't. I don't hate you... I was going to tell you—"

"Don't." Koen's eyes narrow into slits and he glares at me. "You were going to tell me?" His laugh is cold and cruel. "You had *weeks* to tell me... *Years!*" He throws up his hands. "But you didn't." The anger and rage inside of him rises back up to the surface. "But you know what you did do?" He steps closer, his eyes darkening. "You got me to *trust* you, all while you were *lying* to me. And then you betrayed me."

"I—I can explain—"

"Stop." He holds up a hand, cutting me off.

"I didn't know if I could trust you!" I rush out.

"You're working for Giovanni."

"No, I'm not! I—"

"You set Liam up."

I'm shaking my head, my lip quivering under his sharp glare, and I feel the mental wall slide back up between us like a sheet of solid steel.

"It's complicated."

"Uncomplicate it," he orders, biting out every syllable, reaching the limits of his restraint.

"I didn't—I didn't want to! I had to keep her safe! I told you I didn't have a choice!"

He sniffs. "Safe from me." He steps forward, his hand shooting out, and I feel his grip tighten around my throat. "There's always a choice. You *chose* to sell out Liam. You *chose* to betray me. You *chose* to keep my child a secret."

He stares down at me. Rage and raw fury blazing in his eyes.

"*Your* choices Briar. And every choice bears a consequence. And this is yours." He releases me, and my breath quickens, on the verge of hyperventilating when he turns, stalking back toward the hallway. *Leaving me here.*

No.

"*Koen.*" I barely get his name out, a choked whisper on my lips. He's so far away but he freezes just before he hits the threshold.

"*I'm sorry.*"

He doesn't turn, doesn't look at me, before he says, "You're not sorry, Briar Rose, but you will be."

70

BOOM!

KOEN

I'm on my way back to Aidan's office, but I stop just before I reach the door. My daughter is inside.

I have a daughter.

Just as I reach for the handle, gunfire sounds out, and bullets tear through the thin metal sheeting of the outer warehouse walls. Shouts and screams fill the air, and I reach for my gun just before an explosion rocks the building, the metal groaning overhead. It came from outside. *Liam's SUV, if I had to wager a guess...*

Automatic rounds continue to pelt the building for another minute before the guards in the warehouse can return fire.

I rip open the office door, finding myself face-to-face with the barrel of Aidan's gun before he lowers it.

"What's happening?" Rory shouts, tucked behind her husband. I look to my right to find Liam holding Remi tight to him.

Remi.

"We're under attack," I growl, listening to the persistent sounds of the firefight down in the bay. The bullets can't reach the office; it's set too far inside. "Fucking Volkov," I mutter venomously. *Ronan's going to regret this.*

I push open the door at my back and look at both of my brothers.

"Get them out," I urge, stepping aside as they move into the hallway, Aidan pulling Rory by the hand behind him, and Liam carrying a sobbing Remi. "Out the back. They already blew the front."

Liam gives me a quick nod, something unspoken passing between us, before they disappear toward the back of the warehouse.

I grab two more guns from Aidan's closet, strapping them across my chest before taking off, headed for the bay. The lights flicker and go out, and I move forward silently in the darkness, edging around the corner and taking out two Russians as they attempt to come through the front door.

Two of my men are already down. The two left alive hit the ground alongside me, just as another round of automatic gunfire sweeps the room.

I move in closer, firing blind through the warehouse walls; the glow from the burning SUV outside flickers through the thousands of tiny holes.

I've just about reached one of my men, Byrne, I think, when the other one shouts.

"Grenade!"

We dive. I roll behind a forklift just in time. The grenade explodes, ripping through the loading bay. Metal shrieks, and everything plunges into smoke and chaos. The blast leaves my ears screaming—a high-pitched, painful whine.

Shaking off the buzzing in my head, I peer out from behind the heavy machine.

Walsh is dead.

Byrne is at my side in an instant, his gun cocked and ready. I nod at him, and together we move in on the entrance. Firing at anything that moves.

Byrne's hit and he goes down, but I keep shooting, switching guns when my clip runs empty, until every single fucking Russian is dead.

Letting out a heavy breath, I keep my gun in my hands, on high alert before turning to assess the damage.

Bullet holes pierce just about every inch of the outer face of the building. Liam's SUV sits not far off, engulfed in flames. An orange glow also lights up the warehouse from the inside.

Fuck.

I race back in, pulling up short at the sight of an entire pallet of wooden crates on fire. The flames are spreading too fast; the fire is too far gone to stop now.

The shipment we just brought in... at least half of it was explosives.

I run.

Throwing open the locker door with a clang, Briar flinches, a look of absolute terror on her face until she recognizes me. My face is likely covered in a mix of blood, dirt, and ash.

I don't waste any time, reaching up and releasing the chain that's holding her up. "I've got you," I breathe, catching her when her legs can't handle the weight. My ears are still buzzing from the explosion, so it takes a minute for me to realize she's screaming something at me.

"What?" I shake my head, trying to listen more closely.

A *name*... she's screaming a name.

"Liam's got her. Liam's got Remi," I assure her, our eyes meeting, exchanging a weighted look.

"Can you walk?" I set her down on shaky knees, but she stays on her feet. Nodding at me.

Her hands are still bound with rope, but there's no fucking time.

"Come on." I grab her arm and drag her out of the room. She tries desperately to keep up with me as I run us down the hall, and at some point, I scoop her up to carry her since she's slowing us down.

We crash out of the back door, and dash across the lot. The garage door of the warehouse next door is already open, thanks to Aidan and Liam. We own this entire industrial park.

I set Briar down and grab a key off of the hook. Liam and Aidan will have taken the extra SUV, leaving only a couple of bikes parked further in the garage.

Briar stands by the entrance, shaking, trembling. I take out my knife, cutting the ropes from her hands before she even sees the blade, pulling off my sweatshirt and shoving it over her head before going for the bike.

There's no time. I glance up at the black smoke billowing out of the warehouse beside us as the bike starts up. Swinging my leg over, I rocket forward. Briar jumps when I stop short at her side.

"Get on!" I shout.

She does, wrapping her arms around me tight before I gun it out of the open bay, speeding down the narrow road between buildings, leaning hard into the turn. We only just clear the access road when the night erupts.

We both glance back, Briar's hair flying in the wind since we didn't have time for gear.

It's like a war zone at our backs; plumes of dark smoke black out the stars overhead. The warehouse is gone, twisted metal is all that remains.

Briar clings tighter to me as I throttle the bike, accelerating us faster into darkness.

71

IS THIS WHAT YOU WANTED?

BRIAR

THE WIND STINGS my cheeks as we ride through darkness, but it's nothing compared to the sting of silence between us. Koen keeps us speeding along winding back roads at a terrifyingly high speed. We haven't spoken since he carried me out of the warehouse, saving my life.

Again.

He's only pulled over once, to make a quick call to his brother before speeding off again. It's still dark, but the sky has begun to lighten; dawn is approaching.

Without warning, Koen turns off the main road, slowing as he takes us down a narrow dirt road I never would have noticed, leading us deeper into the dark expanse of woods.

I haven't seen a single light for nearly sixty minutes. We are completely and totally *alone*. The dirt road we're on is lit up only by the bike's headlights.

Once we're well out of sight from the main road, he brings the bike to a stop, killing the engine. And then there's only silence. Nothing but trees on either side of us.

"Get off," he says, his voice flat.

Trembling from fear, and shivering from the cold, I slowly let go of him, climbing stiffly off the bike; my limbs are border-line frozen from the ride.

I walk a few feet. The frozen leaves crunching underneath my sneakers make a sound far too loud in the oppressive silence of the woods around us. I look back to see Koen still on his bike, reading something on his phone before slipping it back in his pocket, and for a moment, he just stares down at his hands, and even though it's dark, I can't help but see the look of absolute devastation written across his face.

My heart constricts, but before I can say anything, he's up, and instinctively, I back up a few steps. When he looks at me, his eyes, now burning with rage, show his fury, which has replaced any trace of devastation that was there before.

"Come here."

I swallow, but take a few cautious steps forward.

His hand comes out from behind him—*he's holding a gun.*

I freeze, inhaling sharply.

"Get on your knees."

"Koen..." I shake my head in denial, wrapping my arms tightly around myself.

"On your knees, little Rose," he says again, quieter this time, controlled, his eyes dark.

I look away from him, first to the ground, and then out into the shadowed forest surrounding us. I think about running, but there's nowhere to run to. My eyes slide back to his, and I don't look away while lowering myself to my knees.

"You saved me..." I say, when I hit the dirt. *He pulled me out of the warehouse... he could have left me there to burn.*

Koen steps forward, and my eyes flicker between his face and the gun in his hands.

"Because your death belongs to me."

I'm shaking, trembling at his feet from the cold... from the look in his eye... But there's *conflict* there. I can see it, past the steel wall he's built to hide it. He wants to kill me, *and he doesn't....*

I swallow hard. "Everything I did, I did to keep her safe," I say slowly. He still has that lethal edge in his eyes.

"From whom?" His eyes flash, daring me to say the words.

I sigh. "From everything... from Gio..." I look up to face Koen's dark eyes. "From you."

His jaw flexes right before he raises the gun, leveling it at my forehead, holding it just inches from my face. As if to prove my point.

I don't flinch, but I lift my chin, as if daring him to do it.

He calls my bluff, stepping closer until I feel the cold metal ring press up against my forehead. Rage and fury gone, but the cold detachment that takes its place is far worse.

I don't run, and I don't cry, not even when I hear him click off the safety. I just *look* at him.

I search the dark void of his eyes for any sliver of the man I know is somewhere buried inside, choosing to believe that the Koen I've gotten to know over the last couple of weeks is the *real* Koen O'Rourke. That it wasn't just a game, or an act to gain my trust to use me as a pawn to his own end. I want so desperately to believe that deep down, under that cold and brutal exterior, and through all of his anger, *he loves me, too.*

But all I see is *darkness.*

"You lied to me. You hid my child from me. And you

betrayed me, almost getting Liam killed." His voice is cold and devoid of emotion, as he lists my transgressions.

"All true," I admit softly.

"You played me."

My mouth opens to refute that last statement, but he keeps going before I can get a word out.

"What do you have to say for yourself?"

I make sure I'm looking him straight in his eyes when I say, "*I'm sorry.*" And I mean it, it's not a lie. But Koen's gaze is still ice cold, and his gun stays pressed against my forehead. I exhale slowly, a calm resignation settling over me. "If—if you're going to do it, then just...*just listen first.*"

He tilts his head to the side, silently, but I take that as an invitation.

"*Her favorite color is pink.*"

His brow furrows.

My voice is shaking. "She has asthma; her inhaler is in her backpack in my apartment." Koen's eyes narrow, and he tightens his grip on the gun. "She needs to see Doctor Haven at Boston Children's Hospital once a month." I nod, tears filling my eyes. "Her favorite food is pancakes, she has your temper, and she's afraid of the dark, so you need to leave the light on at night. Okay?" He doesn't answer me, but I nod like he did anyway, a single tear sliding down my cheek before I drop my gaze from his. "*Okay...*"

The long stretch of silence that rings out after that feels infinite, until I feel the cool metal of the gun drop away. Shocked, I chance a look up at him. Koen is dragging a rough hand down his face.

"*Fuck.*"

He turns, shaking his head and storming back over to his bike, trading his gun for his phone.

I stay, frozen in the dirt, feeling like the slightest of movements could still cost me my life.

After exchanging a couple of messages, Koen swings his leg over the bike and starts it up, the rumble of the engine cutting through the silent night.

By the time I notice he's put the bike in gear, it's too late. *He's already gone.*

I scramble to my feet, screaming, "No! Stop! *Please!*"

But Koen doesn't stop; he doesn't even look my way before shooting down the road, back the way we came.

Leaving me alone.

72

SOMEWHERE SAFE
BRIAR

I RUN after Koen's bike like I stand a chance of catching him, before stumbling over a rock and hitting the ground hard. I press my ripped-up palms against the unforgiving dirt, and scream.

He left me.

He left me, and he took *her*.

Remi.

He could have killed me, but instead he left me out here. The temperature has been steadily dropping, and the smell of snow is heavy in the air. This could still be a death sentence, just not one at his hand.

I have no idea where I am, and I'm not dressed for the weather. I'm thankful, at least, that Koen didn't take his sweatshirt back before he bailed. I barely survived the ride on the back of Koen's bike; at least then I had the heat emanating from him to get me by. I could freeze before I find my way out of these woods. Taking my chances on the main road is a risk.

Giovanni—or the Russians Koen keeps talking about—may be after us and out scouring the roads for survivors.

Even if I make it out alive, I know, without a shadow of a doubt, *I'll never find her.* Not if he doesn't want me to.

I don't get up.

Instead, I punch the earth. Experiencing instant regret when searing pain shoots through my knuckles, unleashing the waterworks I've been holding at bay.

Not like this.

All I can think about is how scared Remi must be. And how she won't understand when I just disappear from her life.

Light floods the road up ahead, and holding up a hand, I have to squint my eyes to deal with the sudden brightness.

Headlights.

I freeze, uncertainty washing over me. *Headlights on this abandoned road in the middle of nowhere?*

A black SUV comes into focus, traveling slowly down the narrow road, coming to a stop just in front of me. I sit back on my heels, knowing there's no way a random car just stumbled across me. No, this has got to be the Irish back for more, or Giovanni's men have tracked me down, and I'm not overly eager to find out which.

The driver's side window rolls down, and a familiar face pops out of it.

"Get in the car, B!" Liam calls, and I can hear the SUV's doors unlocking.

He doesn't have to tell me twice. I scramble to my feet, running for the back door just as it swings open.

I can't help the sobs of relief that escape me when I find Remi's anxious face staring back at me.

"Mommy?"

"Baby!"

I dive forward, scooping my daughter off of who I think is Aidan's lap and hugging her close. She clings to me, her arms and legs wrapped around me tight. *She's okay.* She looks tired, but no worse for wear, considering. My sense of self slowly returns, as the initial flood of relief ebbs away. Peeking over Remi's hair, I find four faces staring back at me.

Liam is driving, and Alex sits up front—the O'Rourke's unofficial brother. I've met him a couple of times with Koen. Liam's grinning as he watches me, and I eye him nervously— seeing as how I almost got *him* killed, he has even more reason to hate me than his brother does.

Looking into the back, I confirm I did, in fact, rip my daughter off the lap of Aidan O'Rourke, and I recognize his wife, Rory, sitting on the other side of him, giving me a reassuring smile.

"Everybody remembers Briar, right?"

My eyes narrow at Liam's introduction, internally debating whether or not hightailing it through the woods while clutching my daughter is a sensible plan, given the circumstances.

"And Briar, you remember everybody?"

I grip Remi tighter, and she lets out a little groan of protest.

"Make room for Briar, guys," Liam prods, and I watch as Aidan and Rory vacate the second row in favor of the third, but I stay frozen outside in the cold, paralyzed with indecision.

He left me...

He left me but sent *them*?

Apprehension must show on my face, and surprisingly, it's Aidan who speaks up, leaning forward to look in my eyes, "Listen, you have no reason to trust us, I get it—I do. But you have my word; no one in this car is going to hurt you or your daughter. *My niece.*" His green eyes drop to Remi in my arms, and I shift uncomfortably under the weight of his statement—and his *claim* to her.

"Mommy, I'm cold," Remi whines. She's only wearing her pajamas. No jacket. But I spy her comforter and Rainbow Cupcake, her pink unicorn, on the floor of the SUV.

I sigh, ignoring the smirk on Liam's face when I reluctantly climb in the back, shutting the door behind me. Immediately thankful to Alex when he subtly turns up the heat, having not realized my teeth are chattering.

But instead of reversing back out onto the main road, Liam continues forward, taking us deeper into the woods.

A few more minutes of rough terrain, and the woods thin out, and I see a house, backlit by the orange glow of the sunrise just starting to peek over the mountains. A large frozen lake stretches out for what must be miles just behind it.

"Where are we?" I ask, reaching for Remi's blanket.

"Somewhere safe."

73

IMPOSE

KOEN

IT's late at night by the time I pull my bike up to the lake house, every muscle in my body aching and raw from the freezing ride.

I'd been doing recon with Mac and Jace all day, trusting Aidan, Liam, and Alex to keep shit locked down here. My father purchased this cabin years ago as an escape from the violent chaos back home. It's a secret—one of our safe house locations.

The house itself sits perched on the edge of a lake, nestled deep in the woods of northwestern Massachusetts, far away from everyone and everything. As kids, we spent summers cannonballing off the dock, and winters playing hockey out on the ice until our toes went numb.

We have other safe houses, but this one will always be my favorite.

Word hit the streets that the Irish Devils, *the O'Rourke brothers,* are dead. That the warehouse blast took us all out.

I let it ride for now. It buys us time; *nobody goes hunting for ghosts.* My uncle Seamus is doing a good job holding things down, stepping up in our absence to keep everything running.

Someone had to have given up our warehouse location. We chose an industrial park outside of Boston for a reason. No one outside of the Irish should know about it. But yet, someone has been feeding the Russians intel for weeks—months even. Whatever information Briar gave Giovanni, he'd turned around and sold it to the Volkov, but even she didn't know about the warehouses.

And the Volkov aren't wasting any time.

The house is quiet.

It's been a while since the last time I was here, but the familiar scent of cedar and wood smoke is an instant comfort, and I feel a little bit of tension ease out of my shoulders. I spot the massive stone fireplace as soon as I walk in. Someone's lit a fire, casting the entire floor in a warm glow.

Alex looks up from the book he's reading on the couch, giving me a silent nod before his attention falls back to the pages. His relaxed stance tells me he clocked my arrival minutes ago when I first pulled up the driveway. He must've drawn the short straw for first watch.

I make a beeline for my room on the lower level, exhausted, in desperate need of a shower, and ready to pass the fuck out for a few hours. I tread lightly down the stairs to my room. It's tucked into the back corner, where the sliding glass doors open right out onto the stony back patio overlooking the lake.

I shove the door open, ripping off my shirt, only to stop dead when my eye catches on the dark hair spilled out across my pillow. *Briar,* passed out, asleep in my bed—she and the kid, curled under my blankets like *they belong there.*

Briar looks like she fell asleep attempting to keep up her

own version of a watch, half propped up on the pillow, her face to the door, her body curled protectively around her little girl.

I stare at the two of them for another beat. The unexpected sight hits me deep in my chest, sharp and unexpected, before anger flares.

My bed.

I know without a doubt this is Liam's doing. *My brother knows better.* I clench my teeth, quietly turning and stalking back out of the room while cursing under my breath.

"I'm going to fucking kill him."

Storming back through the living room, I narrow my eyes at the smirk I catch on Alex's mouth as I hunt down my target.

My boots thunder on the stairs heading to the upstairs bedrooms, not bothering to be quiet now.

Liam wakes with a start when I kick open his door, his hand relaxing off the gun he grabbed on a reflex off his nightstand, when he recognizes me glowering at him from the hall.

"Jesus fuck, Koen. Can't a guy get a wink of sleep around here?" He groans, burying his head under his pillow and rolling away from me.

I cover the room in just a few steps, glaring down at him just before leaning over to grip the underside of his mattress. The corner of my mouth ticks up when I lift it, dumping my brother's ass onto the floor.

"Argh."

Liam faceplants onto the hardwood with a groan, and I'm not the least bit sorry, crossing my arms and watching him flail about, tangled in the sheets.

"You're an asshole," he grumbles irritably.

"Why the fuck is *Briar* in my bed?"

My brother sighs deeply, pressing his forehead back into

the floor. "That's what this is about?" Grumbling out a few more obscenities, he pushes himself up, crawling back onto the mattress, the look on his face meant to warn me off of dumping his ass again.

My fingers twitch at my sides.

"The little one didn't want to sleep alone, and Briar wasn't about to leave her side. *Your* bed is the biggest."

"Why didn't you put them in the guest room?"

"The guest room is across the hall from Aidan and Rory..."

"So?"

He levels me a look. "You've clearly never had to share a wall with them."

I roll my eyes. "You still could've put them there."

"Aye, I could have. But I didn't," he replies flatly.

I glare at him, my gaze dropping to the gun he's left sitting out on his nightstand.

"Put the fucking gun away; there's a kid in the house."

Liam grumbles something about being a moody asshole as I stalk back toward the door.

"And why don't you relieve Alex on watch while you're at it?"

The corner of my lip twitches at the colorful string of curses he shoots at my back, dodging the incoming pillow he hurls at me before slamming his door shut.

Liam had no right putting them there, *in my room—in my bed.* But yet, I can't bring myself to wake them in order to drag them out of it.

Irritation courses through me as I shove open the guest room door—the bedroom, across the hall and over one from Liam.

I drop onto the mattress, staring up at the dark ceiling. I'm so fucking exhausted, but my chest feels tight, and my blood hot, my jaw aching from clenching it so damn hard.

I'm angry. I'm mad at Liam, furious at Briar, but most of all... I'm angry with myself.

I let her get too close... *I know better.* I told myself to keep her at arm's length, and then I let her break all of my rules, strike a match, and light them on fucking fire.

I pride myself on being prepared for every scenario before it happens, but *nothing—and I mean nothing—*could have prepared me for finding out I have a *daughter.* And what the fuck am I supposed to do about it?

I'm not handling this well, and I know it. My head is a mess of emotions I haven't even begun to untangle. And instead of dealing with it—dealing with *her.* I did what I always do...

I walked away.

74

MY WORST FEAR

BRIAR

MORNING COMES TOO BRIGHTLY ONCE AGAIN. The ice outside reflects the early morning sunlight, and I let out a groan, pulling the thick comforter up and over my head, trying to give myself a few seconds reprieve from facing the day.

It's been two days.

Two days have come and gone since Koen left me in the woods. There are so many unanswered questions, and in typical Koen fashion, he didn't stick around to give any answers.

I'm anxious, my stomach is in knots, and I've been walking around this house like the floor is made of glass.

The first morning here, we arrived early. Liam brought Remi and me to a bedroom where she slept for a couple of hours in my arms while I kept watch. *It's Koen's room.* I'm sure of it. Everything is neat and clean; there's no clutter; dark woods and walls are offset by the sunlight streaming in through the wall of windows facing the lake. And the faint scent of him lingers on the sheets and in the air.

I don't know what to expect. I'd been a prisoner the night before. *Was I their prisoner still?*

Guest, captive, unwanted intruder—exiled to this house in the woods to live out the rest of my sorry existence caged and alone? All of it bleeds together into a deep pool of anxiety that's made its home deep within my chest. I'm on edge, tense, ready for my world to come crashing down at any given moment... even though the days have been—*peaceful.*

I sat in the bedroom for hours that first afternoon, doing my best to appease an energetic Remi, with nothing to entertain her, watching the door and wondering if it was locked. I didn't have it in me to try, and I certainly wasn't brave enough to venture out of it with Remi's safety at stake. The sliding doors are locked, from the inside, but she doesn't have a jacket or shoes, and it snowed while she slept, a couple of inches quieting the world around us.

Sometime in the early afternoon, a knock sounded at the door. I stiffened, instinctively reaching for my daughter and pulling her close, though she failed to notice the imminent threat of danger.

The door cracked open, and Liam leaned casually against the frame. Easy in a way that made me even more wary. "The door is not locked, you know; you two can come out."

I opened my mouth, but words didn't come, because *what do I even say?*

But Remi didn't have to be told twice. She slipped from my grip, running for the door and darting out under Liam's arm.

He tracks her, smiling softly.

I rise slowly, my motherly instincts screaming at me to run after Remi, but all too aware of the danger standing in my way.

Liam's gaze trails back to me, green eyes softening when he

sees the fear in mine, reaching up to rub the back of his neck uncomfortably.

"Listen," he says, remaining in the doorway. "You're safe. Nobody here is going to hurt you. Not last night, not this morning. You don't have to worry about that, okay?"

I want to believe him, and I genuinely want to believe that none of them would hurt Remi now that the secret is out, but I'm not certain the same can be said for me. *I saw that look in his eyes.*

"Where's Koen?" I ask, the words coming out lower and scratchier than intended, my throat dry from the stress.

"He's not here."

I catch the unspoken addendum. Nobody *here* is going to hurt me. *The jury is still out on Koen.*

Liam reads my face and shrugs. "Koen's... complicated, but he'll come around. Give him time." He pushes the door open wider. "Hungry?"

That was two days ago, and I still haven't seen a trace of Koen. He's left me to linger in this frozen purgatory, trapped inside this beautiful house with the rest of his family. I'm cautious, too well aware of every rule I don't know, every expectation I'm bound to break.

I'm trying my best to keep Remi quiet and out of their hair, but no matter how hard I try to shield her, she's wormed her way into all of their rooms and hearts.

She beats Liam in endless games of checkers; he swears

she's cheating, and she cackles every time he pretends to throw the board in frustration. Alex is able to find Remi's favorite cartoon on the television, and sometimes I catch Liam or Alex watching it after Remi's lost interest and left the room.

Rory found some markers and paper in one of the drawers, so while Remi is occupied, happily scribbling nonsense, I leave her with Rory. Hurrying to the bathroom and nearly having a heart attack when I come back to find my daughter coloring in Aidan's *tattoos*.

Aidan O'Rourke, Irish Devil Enforcer.

"Remi!!!" I chastise, racing over to pick her up, but Aidan raises a hand, stopping me.

"It's fine," he says, before pointing to an area she's missed. "I think we need some more green over here, Rem."

I shoot Rory a look, who's got her hand clasped over her mouth looking like she's trying not to die from keeping the laughter in.

She's great. I spend a lot of time with Rory. We have a lot in common; she's a figure skater and has certainly spent a fair bit of time in a dance studio. We bond over relentless practice schedules, and overly-critical instructors—and complicated O'Rourke men.

But nothing can make me forget that I'm in Koen's world now, under *his* roof and at *his* mercy. Even if everyone else is kind, Koen's shadow is never far off. Like a guillotine blade hanging over my head, the torture of it is far worse than anything he could've concocted back in that grimy little room.

By the end of the second day, the lake house had... against my will... grown more comfortable, familiar, and dare I say, even *safe*.

That is... until *he* walks into it.

Aidan, Liam, and Rory have just disappeared upstairs. They're leaving early in the morning for a Breakers game tomorrow afternoon. It's a long drive, but Rory promises me they'll be back tomorrow night.

I'm sitting in the large plush armchair by the fire, hands curled around a mug of hot chocolate. Remi is at my feet, wholly consumed by the last game of checkers she has going with Alex on the rug. She's dragging it out with the threat of bedtime hanging over her.

The front door opens, and suddenly *he's there*. Koen's cold eyes scan the room as he moves through it, bringing the frost in with him from outside. His dark eyes fall on me, and I hold my breath, while they linger for the briefest of seconds before he looks away. There's no anger, no rage; there's just—*nothing*.

Koen continues walking through the main floor and up the stairs, as if *I don't even exist*.

I stare after him.

Alex is quiet, and I feel his eyes on me.

I've been sitting here, waiting for Koen's anger, preparing for it, but this—his... indifference? The way he looked right *through* me as if I didn't even matter... barely a blip on his radar, ignoring me, ignoring *Remi*?

It was my worst fear come to life.

75

BEG FOR ME

BRIAR

KOEN'S GONE by the time we wake up.

Remi and I stop by the kitchen for breakfast. I'm tense, rounding the corner like I'm walking to my execution, expecting to find him standing there.

But the kitchen is empty, except for Alex. He's leaning over the counter, eating a bowl of cereal, eyes on his phone.

I ask him, because I have to know...

"He left early this morning."

Oh.

My face falls, and Alex's jaw ticks at the sight. I recover quickly, forcing a smile on my face when I offer Remi options for breakfast: frozen waffles or cereal?

The disappointment is crushing, because as scary as Koen is, and the threat of what he could do to me if he so decides... I'd take it. I'd take his anger—his malice, his fury—over his *silence.*

The day ticks slowly by, and I feel myself slipping away. The flicker of hope that Koen might care about the fact that he has a daughter is slowly suffocating, and my worry over what's to come of us is taking over.

It's late. Remi's long since fallen asleep beside me. I stare out the glass doors across the frozen lake outside. The moon is full tonight, and the silvery glow reflecting off the shiny surface lights up the darkness.

The showcase was tonight.

I missed it.

But strangely, I can't bring myself to even care.

I startle at the low whine of the bedroom door as it opens, locking eyes with Koen just as he freezes in the doorway.

He doesn't say anything, but his impassive eyes darken at the sight of me before he looks away. Stalking purposefully over to the dresser on the far wall, he wrenches open the drawers, pulling out what looks to be some clean clothes, before turning, to leave again.

"Wait," I call out, keeping my voice low so I don't wake Remi, but loud enough to know he heard me.

He doesn't, disappearing back through the door. He's barely got it closed before I'm shoving off the covers, and chasing after him out into the hallway.

"We need to talk!"

"No, we don't," he bites out, not bothering to look back as he's closing in on the stairs.

A surge of frustration spurs me forward, and I run after him, grabbing hold of his arm to stop him from leaving.

"Stay, *please.*" The words sound pathetic—*but I am pathetic*—and desperate. I *need* him to put me out of my misery, one way or another.

Koen growls at my touch, and I release him almost as soon as I have him, but it's too late; he whirls on me, fury flaming through indifference. I back up, hitting the wall, and his arms come up, caging me in.

Words flood out of me, but he looks away, his hand curling around my arm, moving me roughly out of the hall and into another room—another bedroom. He shuts the door behind us.

"Don't." His eyes flash as he reels on me, his fist clenched tight at his side. "Don't stand there and pretend this was ever anything more than what it was. *You used me.*"

"That's not true," I argue, but he's shaking his head, refusing to hear me out.

"You want to know what the worst part of all of this is?" My lips press together, and my heart is thundering; the edge in his voice is sharper than a knife. "It's not the way you betrayed me, or lied... No, the worst part isn't what you *did*—but how I actually believed you *wanted* me."

There's a raw bit of vulnerability in his voice, and the sound of it cleaves my heart in two.

"It was just a lie." He shakes his head, backing away, moving toward the door.

"It wasn't a lie... Not *all* of it," I say quietly.

"Stop lying!"

"I'm not!" My voice breaks. "I wanted to tell you! I wanted to tell you *all of it* because I *do* care about you. I wanted—" I shake my head because it doesn't matter anymore. *None of it matters anymore.* He'll never forgive me after what I did, but I can still apologize. "I'm sorry, Koen." His name on my lips stops his retreat from the bedroom. "I'm so, *so sorry.*"

He turns back, striding toward me, closing the gap between us in less than two strides, grabbing hold of my jaw to stop the words from coming out of my mouth.

"I don't want to *hear* how sorry you are." His voice is hard and full of malice, and he holds me there, looking down at me, the dark edges of his eyes glinting in the light. "I want you to *show* me."

He releases my jaw, his fingers finding the zipper of his jeans, dragging it down slowly.

I swallow hard.

"You said you *wanted* me? That it wasn't just another lie? That you're *sorry*?" I try not to flinch at the venom dripping from his words.

"Then prove it. Get on your knees, open that pretty little mouth, and show me just how much you *want* me." His tone is cold, his words a *challenge*. He doesn't think I'll do it—doesn't think I'll take the bait.

Surprise flashes in the dark shadows of his eyes when I sink down to my knees, holding his gaze as I do. His eyes go fully black at the sight.

"You want *this*?" The doubt in his tone is clear. He's holding himself back. Despite his anger, maybe even his desire, he doesn't want to take more than I'm willing to offer.

"I want *you*," I say clearly. "I always have."

"You don't know what it is you're asking for, Love."

He frees himself, and he's already hard. "Beg for it. I *dare* you," he commands, his eyes alive with the challenge. "Convince me you're *mine*."

He still doesn't think I'll go through with this.

"I *am* yours," I breathe out, holding his hard stare. "I'll do anything—"

"Anything?" His head tilts to the side. The little smile that tugs up the corner of his lip is unnerving, and I feel the first pang of fear, but shove it away. *He promised me*, and I'm certain that no matter how much Koen hates me, he won't hurt me. *Not physically, anyway.*

"Open," he says, stepping towards me. His hand fists in my hair, holding my head steady as he guides the tip of his cock between my lips. "Suck."

My cheeks hollow, letting him slide into my mouth, looking up at him as he does.

"Change of heart?" he asks, and I shake my head no.

"Wider."

I stretch my mouth, opening it as wide as it can go, and then I lick and suck him until his head rolls back and he lets out a groan. I take this as encouragement, and pick up the pace, turning myself on as I work him. My fingers slide down, dipping beneath the waistline of my borrowed boxer shorts. I whimper when I find my clit, and my throat tightens.

Koen tugs my head back, pulling out, and I look up at him, confused.

He clicks his tongue while shaking his head. "Hands behind your back, little Rose."

The glare I shoot up at him is sharp enough to cut glass, but I obey, lacing my fingers behind my back.

"There's a good girl."

His fist tightens in my hair as he drives back into my mouth. But this time, *he's* in control, and he doesn't let up for anything. He pushes deep, thrusting down into my throat. He doesn't relent, even as I choke and gag around him. My throat burns, and tears leak down both cheeks, but I tilt my head back, giving him more. My eyes find his, and his body tenses right before he spills down my throat.

I swallow every drop.

When he's done, he lets go of my hair, pulling out and tucking himself back into his jeans while looking down at me.

"This—*this* is all you're good for. Remember, little Rose, *you belong to me.* I will never be *yours*, but you will always be *mine.*"

My heart shatters, and I cannot hide the hurt from my face when he takes one last disgusted look at me before stalking out of the room.

Leaving me again.

76

TURN TO STONE

KOEN

I LEAVE Briar on her knees, stalking out of the bedroom before my emotions can get the better of me. I head for the stairs, fully intending to get the fuck out of here, when something big steps into my path and I come up short, finding myself face to face with *Liam*.

"Where the fuck do you think you're going?"

"Out. Do you mind?" I motion with my hand for him to kindly *get the fuck out of my way*.

"I do, actually." He lifts his chin, drawing attention to the fact that he's got three inches on me. "We need to talk. Family meeting. Now."

He turns and stalks down the hall and up the stairs, not bothering to look back, knowing full well that he's got me. Family meetings aren't optional, and there's only one rule: when someone calls a meeting, you show up.

Always.

I follow Liam upstairs, finding Aidan already waiting in the living room for us. Liam moves to lean up against the kitchen island that separates the rooms. His temper is already running hot, judging by the redness on his face and the clenched fists by his sides. Neither of them sits, so neither do I, stopping by the door I'm itching to get out of and staring them down.

"Where's your *wife*?" I ask Aidan, not seeing Rory anywhere.

"Upstairs. She agreed it was better if we talked alone."

"I've got Alex on the line." Liam holds up his cell, coming closer to drop the phone on the coffee table, center to all of us, before retreating back to his spot by the island. With things settling down, I sent Alex back out to look for our sister.

"Any luck tracking down Rea, Alex?" Liam asks.

"No. Not a trace," Alex replies, with resignation in his tone, sounding more tired than I've ever heard him.

"I sent her a text," Aidan speaks up, "about this meeting, but her phone is still off."

I work a muscle in my jaw. As much as I don't want to deal with this fucking meeting right now, not having Rea here feels wrong.

So much for rule number one.

A long silence rings out and no one says anything, but the weight of their stares on me is heavy.

"Someone want to tell me what we're meant to be discussing? I've got shit to do."

Liam frowns. "You can't avoid her forever, you know."

I roll my eyes, fists tightening at my side. *Of course,* this is about *Briar.*

"I'm not avoiding her. I was just with her," I bite back, although my words lack any conviction, and both my brothers pick up on it.

"You have to deal with this, Koen. It's been over three days." Aidan says calmly.

"Weren't you like... stalking her?" Liam asks, and I fix my glare on him.

"Yes," I say, my tone clipped and short.

"But you didn't know she had a kid?"

"No," I bite out, clenching my jaw.

He laughs, *the fucker.* "Don't take this the wrong way, but... you're a *terrible* stalker."

"Shut the fuck up, Liam," I growl. "She betrayed me. Betrayed us. *Briar* is the reason you were almost *killed* the other night, in case you've forgotten that little fact."

My bite doesn't dim his swagger, and he leans back further. "Aye, she is. I haven't forgotten, because *Briar* is also the reason I wasn't. She *called you,* she *confessed;* that's got to count for something..."

I scoff, refusing to look at either one of them.

"She lied to me for *years.* Would she ever have even told me if I hadn't—" I stop myself. *Kidnapped her?* Christ, that's hardly a defense. "Who's to say she's not still lying? Is that kid really even mine?" My words come out bitter, and I regret them almost instantly, but I'm too stubborn to take them back.

"Don't even start with that shit," Liam snarls. "She's got your eyes, your attitude; that little girl is your spitting image, and you know it. And her *name* is *Remi.*"

I look away because I *know* he's right. There was never any doubt in my mind, from the second I looked into that child's eyes—*Remi*—I knew she was mine; I *felt* it deep in my bones.

"Christ, you've gone ice cold." Liam pushes off the island, crossing his arms and shaking his head, looking down on me.

"On Briar, on the kid... You don't get to freeze her out, Rí. Not when there's a kid in the middle. You've spent your whole life fighting for this family, *bleeding* for it, and now, when it's your own flesh and blood, you're going to stand here and pretend she doesn't matter?"

My throat tightens. Anger and guilt eating me alive. But the betrayal still burns hotter. *Briar hid my kid, lied to me, spied on me, sold my brother out to the fucking Italians and Russians, and I'm just supposed to move past it? Get over it?*

No.

"What do you want to do?" he continues, when I stay silent. "Kill your kid's mom?" Liam asks me point blank. The gloves are off; he's not holding back.

My shoulder twitches, and I roll it back, cracking my neck to release the growing tension. *Yes.* There is a part of me that wants to wrap my hands around Briar's throat, a part of me that wants to put a bullet between her pretty blue eyes for what she's done. For the *years* stolen, how she'd been playing me for *weeks*... who knows what information she's been feeding to Gio —and for how long. *It was all a lie.* Everything about this girl was a fucking lie. Every instinct within me screams for blood, demands I make her pay.

But when I picture it—her body still, bright eyes dark— something inside me reels back. I couldn't, even in the moments I find myself blind with rage, I know I could never bring myself to hurt her. And it goes against everything I was taught, how I was raised. *Betrayal means death.* There are *no* exceptions. It's weakness. *She's* my weakness. And for the first time in my life, I don't have a plan. I don't know what to do or how to move forward.

Briar *ruined* me. Even now, with her locked away down the

hall, *I can't fucking shake her*. I can't kill her, but I'll never be able to forgive her.

"We all know you're not going to touch her," Aidan says, finally breaking the simmering tension between Liam and me. My hot-headed little brother coming in as the voice of reason in this situation—who would have thought? "But now what? You've got the two of them locked up here. Your issues with Briar aside, Remi is innocent; punishing Briar only hurts Remi in the end."

"I missed everything," I mutter, my throat raw, finally meeting Aidan's eyes.

His hard stare softens before he speaks again. "Then don't miss another second. You can't get those years back, but you can damn well decide what kind of father you're going to be now."

Silence hangs heavy in the room, the truth staring me right in the face.

They're right.

"I'll deal with the kid—*Remi*," I say finally. My voice is hard, final. "But *her*? Briar made her choice when she kept the truth from me. She betrayed my trust when she sold us out to Giovanni. She doesn't get another chance."

Aidan's jaw tightens, but he doesn't argue. I hear Liam mutter something under his breath, but I let it go, stalking for the stairs leading to the guest room on the upper level, since apparently, I'm staying the fucking night.

77

PANCAKES

KOEN

IT'S EARLY, but seeing as I can't sleep, I decide to get an early jump on breakfast.

A quick glance at the clock shows it's about five thirty a.m. I leave the lights off in the kitchen, the dim glow from the rising sun illuminates the kitchen just enough to see.

I started cooking breakfast for the family just after our mother left; our father didn't handle it well. He spent most of his time out of the house, seeing to mob business, and leaving me in charge of the family.

It was my responsibility to keep them in line.

Keep them *safe*.

He'd offered to hire cooks or maids, but I didn't trust them. I didn't want strangers inside our home or anywhere near my siblings, and besides, I enjoy cooking. The slow monotony and normalcy of the routine grounds me.

Even now, the turmoil inside my head quiets as I pull out the eggs, ham, and cheese—deciding to keep it simple today with omelettes. There is still so much work to do after everything that went down the other night. Giovanni's gone under-ground. I have my men out scouring the streets for both him, and Volkov, too.

Needing more cheese for the omelettes, I head for the fridge, grabbing the cheese and closing the door, but as I go to turn back to the stovetop, I freeze.

The tiniest flicker of motion catches my eye. So small, it's possible I imagined it, a trick of the light even, in the stairwell leading from the lower level to the kitchen.

I move slowly, carefully placing the cheese on the counter and reaching for a knife from the block on the island. Pulling open the drawer just below me, I casually rifle through the silverware in there to cover me while I keep my eyes on the doorway.

I left my gun in the guest room.

The house is well-protected—well-guarded—and I'd doubled the guards since the Volkov's attack, but while the odds of an intruder are low, they're never impossible.

A shadow shifts in the hall, and my spine goes rigid, my hand tightening on the knife. But just as I go to step around the island to face this intruder head-on, a pair of round green-brown eyes peek quickly around the corner.

They catch me looking, and disappear just as quickly as they appeared.

I freeze.

Remi.

My heart pounds in my chest, and I slide the knife back into the block as I debate what to do. I reach back, bringing my bowl of eggs over to the island so I can monitor the stairs while I work. As I go back to whisking the eggs, I see her—from the corner of my eye—peeking in again.

Curious eyes scan the kitchen, keeping one eye on me the whole time. When I dip out of view to pull out the salt, she darts inside, hiding behind one of the chairs at the kitchen table. *Watching me.*

She inches closer when I pull out the pancake mix.

"Hey Remi," I say casually, "do you like pancakes?"

Her eyes widen when she realizes *I can see her.* She rises slowly, her eyes flickering between me and the door, contemplating making a run for the stairs.

I try again, pulling a bag of chocolate chips out of the baking cabinet and holding them up. "What about *chocolate chip* pancakes?"

Green-brown eyes flash with excitement, making her decision even harder. She inches forward another half a step, coming into full view as she sizes me up. Her face is serious as she watches me measure out the pancake mix. Her eyes drop to my tattoos, and I see the way her eyes linger on the spiderweb on my hand.

The weight of her gaze is heavy, and my heart beats harder.

Close up, I can see she looks like her mother. At first glance, Remi is the spitting image of me, same dark blonde hair, green-brown eyes, *but Briar is there too...* I can see her in the way Remi's sizing me up as a threat.

"Who are you?"

Ouch.

"My name is Koen."

She sniffs, and I can't tell if the sound is approval or dismissal. I'm getting the sense that Remi is hard to impress.

"Are you friends with Liam?" She tilts her head to the side as she awaits my answer, in a perfect imitation of myself. *It's unnerving.*

"He's my brother." I fight the mild irrational jealousy that rears up when *my own daughter* is vetting me up against my brother. How he's already managed to weasel his way into her good graces.

Remi visibly relaxes, wandering to my side of the kitchen island to closer inspect my work on the pancakes. "You guys talk funny."

I can't help the chuckle that escapes me. "That's because I'm Irish." Of all of us, my accent is the strongest. My siblings were young when we moved to Boston from Ireland; their accents have a tendency to come and go, but mine always had a tendency to linger. "You don't like it?"

She thinks for a moment, holding my full attention. "No, I do," she decides. "I wish I were Irish too."

I look down at her, studying her face, memorizing her blonde curls, the fractured eyes that mirror my own. "I think you might be," I say softly.

Remi beams in response. "You think so?" she asks excitedly.

I let out a small laugh as I nod, "I do." An unexpected rush of warmth floods through me at Remi's approval.

"I think I might need help." Changing the subject, I frown down at the pancake mix in front of me. "It's still pretty lumpy." I look over at Remi. "How are your stirring skills?"

"They're good." She nods, her face deadly serious.

"You're sure?" Narrowing my eyes, I feign uncertainty. "I don't let just anyone into my kitchen. I've got a reputation to uphold."

She furrows her brow, meeting my eyes, hers coming alive with the challenge. "I can do it," she practically growls, and I let out another laugh.

531

"Okay, you're hired."

I drag one of the island stools over to our side and pause when she holds up her arms, waiting for me to lift her onto it.

Oh.

I swallow hard, bending down and carefully lifting her, wondering if she can feel my hands shaking. She's so tiny—so breakable. And once she's on the stool, I drive myself mad—continually hovering around her, checking to ensure she's not about to slide off or crash to the floor.

Remi stirs the batter, and I finish up the omelettes before prepping the griddle for pancakes.

"Alright, let's see how you did." I peek over her shoulder. There's batter *everywhere*. On the counter, on Remi, and somehow even on me, but admittedly, she did a good job. "I think they're ready to cook." I peek at her over my shoulder and nearly melt when I find her looking up at me. Clearing my throat, I ask her, "I'll flip, you chip?" Then I hand her the bag of chocolate chips.

She takes the bag and grins, dropping a chip on her tongue with a smug look that makes me think that somehow she planned this.

"Okay!"

78

LUCKY GUESS

BRIAR

I WAKE TO AN EMPTY BED.

"Rem?"

"Remi?" I say with increasing panic, as I tear through the covers on the bed, like maybe she's just tucked under them.

She's not.

I practically fall out of the bed, checking the room for any sign of her. Fear paralyzes me when I see the hall door is *open*.

I bolt through it, anxiety rising when there's no sign of my daughter in the hallway.

"Remi?" I whisper-shout. It's still early, and with any luck, everyone is still asleep. We've been out and about in the house, but I've always been with her. I don't even want to think what kind of trouble she could get into on her own.

The sound of her laugh sends me running down the hall, relief ebbing through me when I find her sitting atop one of the stools, her feet swinging under her as she stuffs her mouth full of—*are those pancakes?*

The relief is short-lived when my eyes slide to the guy sitting beside her.

"Mommy!" Remi waves wildly, and I look between the two of them. "We made pancakes! They're chocolate chip!" She stuffs another huge bite into her mouth.

Koen.

Koen's eyes find me over the rim of his coffee cup as he takes a sip. He leans back in his seat as I search the kitchen, looking for Liam, Aidan, Rory... desperate for the presence of *literally anyone else.*

"You made her pancakes?" I ask, stunned.

"*We* made pancakes, Mom." Remi rolls her eyes, not to be ignored. "He flipped, and I chipped," she announces proudly.

I look to Koen for confirmation, but he just shrugs. "You should try some." I follow his fork to a breakfast spread that could put a five-star restaurant to shame. Plates of pancakes stacked high, along with omelettes and a bowl of fresh-cut fruit.

"I—um." I'm frozen where I stand. Unsure what to do—how to act—especially after what he *said* to me last night.

"Coffee?" I manage to get out.

"Behind you." Koen lifts his chin, and I back slowly over to the coffeemaker, not wanting to take my eyes off of the two of them.

She was out here. Alone. With him...

I find a mug, and pour myself a cup of coffee with shaking hands.

I'm saved from the awkward moment with Koen by the arrival of his brothers.

"Princess Remi!" Liam exclaims, throwing out his arms as if in complete surprise to see her here.

Remi giggles, "I'm not a princess!"

"Debatable." Liam breezes by, winking at me on his way to the pancakes.

"Briar." Aidan dips his chin as he trails in after his brother.

"Hi," I clip out, sliding over a few steps so he can get to the coffeepot, immediately overwhelmed by the two brothers towering over me, both north of six feet.

"Make sure you eat something," Koen calls after Aidan, who's already retreating out of the kitchen with two cups of coffee.

"I'm on my way to right now," Aidan smirks over the rim of his cup, disappearing up the stairs to the bedrooms, and I blush on his behalf.

"Gross," Liam mutters, as he finishes piling layer upon layer of pancakes onto his plate.

"All done with your pancakes, Remi Rose?"

My eyes snap up at the sound of Koen's voice.

Remi tilts her head, confusion on her face. "How do you know my middle name?"

Everything stops.

The kitchen is so silent; I swear you could hear a pin drop when Koen's eyes slide to meet mine, holding my gaze for a moment, before answering her. "Lucky guess."

My mouth opens at the exact time Koen pushes his chair away from the table. "I've got work to do." He walks past me on his way to clear his plate, and I hold my breath when he passes by me, debating on whether to—

"Koen!" I call, trying to catch him before he disappears out of the kitchen. "Can we—can we talk?"

He turns to scowl at me, and nervously I chew my bottom lip, waiting for his answer.

"No."

"Koen, stop."

He doesn't.

"Please?"

That does it. I swallow the lump in my throat that forms at the glare he gives me when he turns back to face me.

"What?" he bites out.

Bravery fails me and I straighten my spine, crossing my arms, which turns more into hugging myself than anything else. "Um," I swallow again, reminding myself that the worst thing that can happen is he can say no. *Except that isn't the worst thing Koen could do*—not by a long shot. I lift my chin, paling under his full attention. "Remi needs stuff."

His brow furrows, and for a moment that icy glare ebbs— slightly. "Stuff?"

I rub my elbow, uncomfortable, hating that I have to ask him for things. "Yeah, like clothes, pajamas... she didn't have any shoes when she got here and she's been wanting to go outside..."

"Right," he says, running a hand through his hair. "I'll take care of it." He turns to leave.

"Thank you," I say sincerely, and he pauses, his head turning slightly back in my direction, before he nods once, and disappears out the door.

79

IF YOU CAN'T PLAY NICE, PLAY HOCKEY.

BRIAR

SOMETIME IN THE EARLY AFTERNOON, Remi-sized snow boots appear on the mat beside the back door of the cabin. *Pink snow boots.* I notice them as I'm coming up the stairs after Remi's nap.

The house is quiet.

Liam and Aidan are out playing hockey on the lake, and I'm not sure where Rory is.

I pick the boots up, looking them over.

"Are those for me?"

I jump, realizing Remi is right under me. I thought she was still across the room.

"Umm, I think so?" I can't think of another reason tiny pink snow boots would suddenly just appear.

"Can we go outside and play?" Remi's jumping up and down at the thought. It's been a few days, and as much fun as she's having at the house, she's been near desperate to go outside and play in the snow.

I hesitate, my eyes lifting to find a matching pink winter jacket on the hook.

"Please, please, please, pleaseeeeeee," Remi persists, until I finally sigh out a *yes*.

Grabbing the coat and boots, I bring her back downstairs and get her dressed. While she's admiring the adorable new winter footwear on her feet, I find my sneakers. Rory was nice enough to lend me some clothes to wear, so I have on her leggings and sweater, but I don't have a jacket. I pick up the hoodie Koen gave me back at the warehouse and pull it on.

"Okay," I tell Remi, before unlocking the sliding door out to the stone patio behind the house. "But just for a few minutes, okay?" She nods in agreement. The jacket and boots are a good start, but she still doesn't have gloves or a hat, and it's *cold*. An icy blast of winter air catches me right in the face as I pull the door open and I tuck my fingers further into the sleeves of Koen's sweatshirt.

I shiver watching Remi run straight for the snow, laughing while she jumps up and down in the soft, white, fluff. After a few minutes of playing happily, she notices the guys down on the lake.

"Mom, look! Hockey!" I glance down the hill. Aidan and Liam have shoveled out a clearing and dragged a hockey goal out onto the lake, and are skating around, shooting pucks.

By the time I see her running, she's already too far ahead of me.

"Remi, no!"

I take off after her, but for having such little legs, Remi is goddamn fast, charging full speed ahead for the lake, and my sneakers keep slipping in the snow.

Aidan and Liam hear the commotion and look our way,

seeing the little pink blur flying at them down the hill. Liam pushes forward on his skates, intercepting her at the edge of the lake just before she careens out onto the ice.

"Princess Remi! What do you think you're doing?"

"I wanna play! Can I play? Liam pleaseeeeee! I love hockey!"

"You do?" Liam asks, eyebrows lifting in surprise. He looks up at me when I finally catch up to them, fighting to catch my breath.

"It's new," I explain. "She just got back from New York. My friend's brothers play, and I guess she fell in love."

Koen's youngest brother's eyes light up. "There's a youth league at the Edge Arena that Aidan and I help with sometimes. You should sign her up!"

"Umm, yeah, maybe," I say, shifting uncomfortably, still uncertain what the near-distant future looks like for me.

"But can I play now? With you and Aidan?" Remi pleads with him.

The other O'Rourke brother leans on his stick a few feet behind Liam, watching us.

"It's okay with me, but we gotta ask your ma..." Two sets of green eyes flick up to me, and I'm surprised that Liam would even care to ask my opinion.

I squat down until I'm at Remi's level. "You don't have any skates, Rem..." I wince, certain we're heading straight for a tantrum.

But before Remi can cue the tears, Liam pipes up. "No, we do! Back up at the house."

Confused, my eyes shift to him, but before I can question it, he's unlacing his own skates and leading us back up the hill.

Liam guides us through the house and up two flights of

stairs to a small room on the second floor that has shopping bags covering just about every surface. He rummages through the mess, snatching up a bag with Power Hockey printed on the side, and pulls out a brand new pair of hockey skates. *Teeny-tiny hockey skates.*

"Here we are." He hands the skates to my daughter, who takes them from him with a look on her face like he just gave her the world.

"Where did those—?"

"There's probably a helmet around here somewhere too," Liam says absently, scratching his head, poking through some more bags. "Maybe even pads, if I know Koen..."

"Koen?" I can't hold in my gasp. "All of this is from *Koen?*" I'd just asked him for stuff for her this morning... And I certainly didn't ask for all of *this.*

"Mom, look!" Remi's eyes light up as she drags a pink helmet out of a bag by the edge of the bed, holding it up for me to see.

Liam looks up, catching the expression on my face for the first time, and he just smirks. "Yep," he says with a nod of approval while he appraises the pile with me. "He *may* have gone a little overboard..."

"A little?" I say, looking it all over.

Liam laughs and then changes the subject. "So this is the guest room. Apologies for not setting you guys up in here right off the bat. I *thought* Koen would have wanted you in *his* room, but, alas..." His green eyes sparkle with mischief, and mine narrow. "So if you guys want to move up here..."

"Yes," I say, almost too eagerly, anxious to get out of Koen's space.

"I can take Remi off your hands for an hour or two if you want to get... unpacked?"

I look around, suddenly anxious at the thought of being separated from Remi, although Liam has looked after her before.

Sensing my hesitation, he points to the large window overlooking the lake. "You can see us from here. But you're more than welcome to come hang out—or skate, if you want?"

"I don't know how."

"You don't know how?" Liam blinks at me like I just told him pigs fly or something.

I ignore him, eyeing the great expanse of ice warily. "Is it safe?"

"The lake?"

I nod.

"Oh yeah, four inches solid—gotta be careful about some of the hot springs out in the middle though..." He laughs to himself. "Rory learned that the hard way."

My eyes widen, and he immediately backpedals.

"Er—you have nothing to worry about. She'll be perfectly safe. Promise."

"I don't know—" I look between him, Remi, and the lake, but the way Remi's looking at me...

"Okay," I sigh, and they both shout, "Yes!"

Liam digs out a pair of hockey gloves and pads, to go along with the skates and helmet, before they head outside. I stand, watching them like a hawk from the guest room window for another solid thirty minutes.

While Liam gets Remi geared up, Aidan goes and retrieves a contraption—two milk crates that look to be zip-tied together—from the garage, that Remi's now pushing around the ice on her own.

The crate gives her stability but still allows her to tear around the ice like a maniac.

She's crashed a lot.

The first time nearly gave me a heart attack, but before I could race down there, she was back on her feet, laughing, careening around with the milk crates until crashing again twenty seconds later.

Having the time of her life.

Finally, content that Remi is safe outside, I turn my attention to the bags.

So many bags.

There are clothes for Remi, toys, games, and *clothes for me... he thought of everything.*

Glancing out the window, I laugh when I spy Remi practicing her checking skills on Liam and Aidan. Both dramatically fall to the ground when she hits them, and I can almost hear her laugh.

After I put everything away, I take a deep breath and head back downstairs to grab the few things we have in Koen's room, but I freeze when I cross the threshold.

Koen is sitting on the bed, elbows on his knees, watching Remi on the lake outside with his brothers.

He doesn't turn, but I know he's aware I'm behind him, and for a while, neither of us says anything. We just watch our daughter play, smiling and laughing, on the ice below.

"You kept her from me," he says after a while. His voice is... *sad.*

I swallow hard, mentally preparing myself to have the conversation I know we need to.

"I did what I had to do."

He turns toward me. "What you *had* to do? You had my child and didn't think I deserved to know?" He rises off the bed. "I would have protected you both, but instead you *hid* her, you hid her from *me*." His dark eyes burn into mine. "What gave you the right to decide for me? You had no right, *no fucking right*, three birthdays, her first steps, her first words —all *gone*."

I search his face—his eyes—but for the first time, I don't see anger; I see *grief*. Tears threaten the corners of my eyes.

"I tried to tell you, but you left."

He scoffs, glaring at me, but I continue, "*You* pushed *me* away, remember?"

"I was protecting you; I didn't know she existed!" he shouts.

"And that's not my fault!" I shout right back, and we both stare at each other, chests heaving.

"Koen, you made it very clear you didn't want *me*... why would I ever think you'd want *her*?"

He just shakes his head, looking anywhere but at me, turning away and pacing the room, as he fights to maintain control over his emotions.

"What was I supposed to do? You were *gone*; I was nineteen, I was *alone*, and I was terrified. *This isn't a fairy tale*, remember?" I say quietly, and he stops, his eyes darkening. "When I found out your name, found out *who* you were, *what* you were capable of... I made a choice and I'm sorry—I'm sorry that I got it wrong, but I thought I was protecting her. And I did try. I *tried* to tell you—*once*. I didn't know your name, or have your number, so I went back to Last Call after I found out

I was pregnant... looking for you, only to be told you were with your *fiancée* in Ireland."

His gaze sharpens. "You're *lying*. I was never engaged."

"Why would I lie about that?" I give him a hard look. "You know what? Ask Liam; he was there that day in the club."

"Because you lie about everything—you were selling us out to Giovanni the whole goddamn time!"

"No, I wasn't!" I almost scream. "It started with money. I had to borrow it from him because I got behind on bills, but the interest rate was impossible, and before I knew it, I was working at the club to try to catch up, and then that night at Wonderland happened and I saw something I shouldn't and... he made me spy on you, but I *swear*, I did what I could to protect you—your family, but when I found out they were going after Liam..." Tears start to fall and my voice breaks. "I *tried* to fix it... I tried to make it right..."

"You *can't* fix this, Briar! You still betrayed me. I will never be able to *trust* you again, and there's no coming back from that. What can't you understand?"

"I didn't have a choice!"

"Stop fucking saying that!"

"They were going to hurt Remi!" I scream.

Koen goes very, *very* still, and he steps toward me, slow, deliberate, his eyes are darker than I've ever seen them when he says, "Who?"

80

FEAR

KOEN

BRIAR'S MOUTH opens to give me an answer but snaps shut, her eyes darting to something over my shoulder.

I look back to find Liam hauling open the sliding glass, panic written all over his face, Remi in his arms. Briar runs for them.

"What the fuck happened?" I wince after cursing, suddenly aware of little ears.

Remi's breaths are coming in ragged little gasps that follow each other in quick succession. Her usually pink lips have an unnatural blue tinge to them. I'm by Liam's side in an instant, looking at Briar, who's also gone alarmingly pale.

She seems torn between snatching Remi out of Liam's arms and something else... she starts and stops in various directions, not getting anywhere.

"Oh my god, Koen, did you bring any of her things?" The panicked expression on Briar's face has me on edge. "Her backpack! Do you have her backpack?" Her blue eyes plead.

"What is it? What's wrong with her?" The questions

flood out of me even as I set into motion, because *yes*, I grabbed the bag. Running for my closet, I open the door and look between the bags I grabbed from Briar's apartment earlier today, but Briar's hot on my heels. She reaches for the smallest one, and once she has it, she immediately drops to the floor, tearing through it in her haste to get whatever it is she needs out of it.

Meanwhile, Remi's choking gasps pull my attention up. *Is she getting worse?* Liam and I exchange a helpless look as Remi wheezes sharply, her breaths coming fast and shallow. *Okay, yes, she's definitely getting worse...*

Below me, Briar curses, resorting to dumping out the contents of the bag on the floor, unable to find what she's looking for.

I feel useless.

Another wheeze, and I can't stand it anymore. I stride toward Liam, closing the gap between us in seconds. "Can I have her?" I ask, holding out my arms.

Liam doesn't hesitate, gently transferring Remi over to me. "Aidan was calling an ambulance, I'm going to go check on that."

"Okay, thank you." My brother gives my shoulder a reassuring squeeze before running back outside.

I look back down to find Remi staring up at me with wide eyes full of fear. Her little body is trembling with the effort it's taking her just to *breathe*. I feel so fucking helpless. If she needed me to, I'd burn the whole fucking city down for her, but that's not what she needs right now.

"Hey, hey," I say as gently as I can, running my fingers through her hair, like I did for her mother that day in the dance studio. This isn't a panic attack—something is really, *really* wrong—but that look of fear in Remi's eyes softens, even as that horrifying wheeze intensifies, rattling now into her chest.

"Briar?" I call, unable to hide the fear in my voice, while doing my best to keep it from my face, holding Remi's gaze.

"I got it. It's here. I have it." The relief in her voice is palpable, even though I still don't know what *it* is. Briar rushes toward us, and I take a seat on the bed so she can better reach Remi, seeing the little L-shaped plastic device in her hands.

An inhaler.

Right, Briar said Remi has asthma, but I never imagined...

"Okay, Remi-roo, you know what to do." Briar looks down at Remi, and she nods, a serious look on her face. "Deep breaths in," Briar instructs, releasing the spray, and Remi inhales just as Briar instructed. "And slow breath out."

The rattle in Remi's breathing lessens, but doesn't go away like I was hoping it would.

"One more time." Briar nods, and I watch them go through the process again. "Asthma," Briar explains, and I realize she's finally answering my question from earlier. "She has asthma."

Another minute passes with both of us monitoring our daughter's breathing, but she's still wheezing, though the color has come back slightly in her lips, and that terrifying rattle is gone. "Shouldn't that have worked better?" I nod to the inhaler Briar's holding tightly in her hand.

Briar sighs, "She has *complicated* asthma." I take my eyes off Remi long enough to see the pain on Briar's face, the heavy weariness in her eyes.

Voices float in from the hall, and we both sit up straighter. I'm still holding Remi in my arms when the EMTs step into my bedroom. They made pretty good time, considering the remote location of the cabin. Briar answers questions while two EMTs converge on Remi and me, listening to her breathing and taking her oxygen levels.

"Alright, Dad, I'm going to put this mask on her just like this." The female EMT slips a small plastic mask around Remi's face, adjusting it until it fits snug. "Oxygen," she informs me. "That should help until we get to the hospital."

Out of the corner of my eye— I feel more than see—Briar's gaze snap to me at the word *hospital*. She's well-acquainted with my thoughts on the place. I hate the way she looks uneasily between me and the EMT.

"No." My grip tightens around the little girl in my arms when the male EMT pushes the gurney in our direction, and everyone stiffens when I stand. "I'll carry her out."

The ride to the hospital goes by in a blur. After carrying her out to the ambulance, I handed her back over to Briar but climbed in immediately after them, refusing to let either one of them out of my sight for a second.

The albuterol from the inhaler and the oxygen from the EMTs have stabilized Remi, but she's far too pale and still wheezing. She's stable, but not out of the woods yet. The local hospital isn't equipped for the kind of treatment Remi needs, and the decision is made to transport her straight to Boston Children's.

I listen closely as Briar updates the EMTs with our daughter's medical history. My body only growing more tense when I learn about the *frequent* hospitalizations and the *monthly* injections.

Upon arrival at the hospital, Briar and Remi sit atop a gurney together, disappearing behind a set of double doors. I go to follow but pull up short when I suddenly find a stout, but stern, nurse in my path. I go to circle around her, but she moves with me, holding up her arms.

"Sir, Sir." The nurse addresses me more sternly the second time when I ignore her, bravely pressing a palm to my chest to hold me back. "It's family only past this point."

"That's my daughter," I growl, spending extra effort to slide the nurse as *gently* as possible to the side, instead of shoving her like I want to, and proceeding through the damn doors.

The doctor is already in the room by the time I catch up with them, and I slip in as quietly as I can. Remi is still on Briar's lap, but they're on a hospital bed now. She sees me looking and gives me a little wave.

I wave back.

"So, have you given any more thought to what we discussed last time?"

I cock my head in confusion when, instead of answering the doctor's question, *Briar looks at me.* There's uncertainty on her face. "I—um," she stumbles, "I don't—"

"What did you discuss last time?" I ask, anxious to know what has Briar tongue-tied all of a sudden.

The doctor's gaze slides to mine. "I'm sorry, I don't believe we've had the pleasure..." She sizes me up. "I'm Doctor Haven, Remi's pulmonologist," she says curtly, "and you are?"

"Koen O'Rourke. What did you discuss last time?" I reiterate. The anxious look on Briar's face is *stressing me the fuck out.*

Surprise shines on Doctor Haven's face; she *recognizes* the name. "I'm sorry, I didn't realize—-" She doesn't finish her sentence, instead looking to Briar for confirmation before continuing.

Briar nods, reluctantly.

"There's a new drug on the market. An injectable, but it's given yearly instead of monthly, with a much higher success rate at minimizing and preventing these types of attacks altogether."

"Do it." I push off the wall I've been leaning on, rising to my full height and crossing my arms while eyeing Briar with confusion. The two nurses in the room each take a step back, and Doctor Haven rolls back her shoulders, gripping tightly to her laptop. "If she's such an excellent candidate, what are you waiting for? Give her the drug." There's a tension emanating from everyone in the room. *I'm missing something*, and it's starting to piss me off.

"Well, it's very expensive, and we do require the payment up front in order to proceed." She lifts her chin, but catching a glimpse of the ire in my eye, she loses a bit of bravado.

"You have a medication that will make my daughter's life infinitely better, and you're *withholding* it until you get the cash?" Doctor Haven's eyes widen, and she gulps, shifting uncomfortably. "Am I understanding that correctly?" I ask, well aware of the intensity of my gaze on her.

She mumbles something about policy, but I wave her off.

"How much?"

"I—uh—" Doctor Haven fumbles with the laptop in her hand, sensing my growing irritation with every second passing. "The estimate for the injection alone is $10,700, and then—" I don't hear anything else she says after that. A quiet realization spreads through me when I hear that number.

That very *specific* number.

My eyes slide to Briar, but she's staring at the floor. Remi's watching me with a little smile on her face, not a fan of *Doctor Haven,* it would seem.

"It doesn't matter," I cut off the doctor's whole spiel. "I'll take care of it, just give it to her now."

The room is a flurry of activity as the hospital staff set Remi up for her injection, and people are in and out, continuing to monitor her breathing and oxygen levels.

I learn Remi is not a big fan of needles.

They have to hold her down, and it takes everything in me not to fight every one of those nurses when I hear her screams.

Remi has to stay at the hospital for a couple of hours to monitor her progress, but she should be able to go home tonight. She falls asleep in Briar's arms not long after she gets her injection, exhausted from all the excitement.

Briar and I sit in silence. There's a lot that needs to be said, but now is not the time.

My phone rings and I pull it out to answer quickly, not wanting to wake Remi up.

"Giovanni's surfaced," is all I hear on the other end of the call.

"I'm on my way," making eye contact with Briar as I speak the words before I hang up the phone.

"I've gotta go." I see a flash of hurt in her blue eyes, and it's almost enough to make me sit back down. *Almost.* I was ready to burn the world to the ground a couple of hours ago, but right now, I'm willing to settle for a very *small* piece of Italy.

"Have someone call me if anything changes," I tell her.

Briar's face is carefully blank again, mask back in place when she nods absently toward me, pretending not to care if I stay or go.

"I'll be back," I promise both of them, hovering by the door for another second, before stepping out into the hall where I find Liam, Aidan, Mac, and Jace, all guarding the door to the hospital room. Their towering forms—and pissed-off expressions—seem to be keeping everyone who doesn't need to be in this *particular* hallway out of it, seeing as it's dead quiet. I spy Rory, too, nearly hidden behind Aidan where she's curled up in a chair reading a book.

"Rory, could you stay with Briar while I'm gone? I don't want her to be alone." She nods and stands, reaching out to squeeze my hand before disappearing into the room.

My eyes connect with Liam, and with a slight nod of my head, he follows me a few feet down the hall. I lower my voice. "Briar says she showed up at Last Call when she first found out she was pregnant... that she was going to tell me—about Remi," I swallow hard, "and that *you* were there..."

Liam's eyebrows knit together in confusion, and I can see him thinking, though he looks doubtful.

"When was this?"

"It would have been a couple of weeks after the bar first opened."

He thinks about it for a minute.

"During the day?"

I just shrug, because I didn't get any details.

"I don't think—wait!" His eyes widen. "*Yes*, two girls came in once, during the day, one blonde and one with dark hair. But they didn't stay long... actually they left right after I came up, but they were—" I lift my brows, waiting for him to finish. "They were talking to Uncle Seamus."

My jaw clenches, and I rub my temples. Suddenly, Briar's story that I had a *fiancée* when we met holds a lot more merit.

Seamus and my father had been doing just about anything possible to push me and the Quinn girl together around that time. They wanted to secure a much-needed alliance with Ireland, but I couldn't be talked into it.

"Thanks, Liam." I clasp him on the back, and he nods before I turn to address the rest of the guys in the hall. "Mac and Jace, you're with me. Aidan and Liam—"

They both nod. Aidan leans back against the wall, and Liam drops back onto a doctor's stool he stole from somewhere, parked right next to Remi's door.

"Do everything I wouldn't," Liam bites out venomously, which isn't saying much, seeing as there is very little Liam *wouldn't* do.

"And more," I promise.

81

WHAT DID YOU JUST SAY?

KOEN

"WEAPONS," the broad Italian at the door growls at Mac, Jace, and me, blocking our path when we try to enter the restaurant.

I glare at the man.

"No exceptions. You understand?"

I do. But that doesn't mean I have to like it. Begrudgingly, I draw out my gun and place it on the table, watching Mac and Jace do the same. I also deposit my knife, and my backup pistol from the strap on my ankle.

Then, I barely tolerate the required pat down before finally being allowed admittance into the quaint little Italian restaurant.

Another man in a suit shows us to a back room, where I find just the man I'm looking for.

"Koen." Giovanni's midway into his dinner. "This is a surprise! Won't you join me?" He gestures to the seat across from him, and I slide into it. Mac and Jace hang back by the door, keeping their eyes on the two men standing along the wall—the ones watching Gio's back.

"I heard you were dead."

"Sorry to disappoint."

"What can I—"

"Let's cut the bullshit," I say, leaning forward over the table. "I know you sold me out to the Russians—The Volkov —Almost cost me my brother."

Gio's expression sours, and he leans back. "That fucking bitch," he mutters. "Couldn't keep her goddamn mouth shut."

Giovanni's head snaps back past his shoulder from the impact of my fist.

His men push off the wall to come after me, but Gio raises a hand, waving them off, and they back away, the promise of violence dancing in their eyes.

"I suppose I deserved that." He spits blood out onto the floor, adjusting his jaw.

"You sent her to spy on me."

"Is there a question in that statement?"

My fist tightens at my side, but I resist the urge to hit him again.

"Why did you send the girl to spy on me?"

"You're a hard man to get eyes on, and I'm a simple businessman. When you showed an interest in the whore, I saw an opportunity."

"You almost got my brother killed."

"Hey now," he says, holding up his hands. "I did nothing. I'm simply the messenger—the point of contact, if you will. You know how it is. Your issue is with the Volkov. Not with me."

I sigh, leaning back in my seat. "Last question: What does Briar get out of this deal?"

I've saved it for last, having gone back and forth over whether I even want to know.

His smile is stained red when he shrugs, looking bored with the question. "She had a debt—a couple thousand. She helps me, and I make it go away."

My heart sinks and I stare at the table. *Briar sold me out for a few thousand dollars...*

"I should've known she'd fuck me over with that bleeding heart of hers," he sighs irritably, reaching for his drink. "I should've held the kid as collateral instead of just threatening her."

I freeze. My gaze slowly lifts back up to find Gio, still muttering in his seat, oblivious to the storm brewing in my eyes.

"What did you just say?" My words are quiet—*dangerous* —but he doesn't notice.

He shoves a mouthful of steak into his mouth before pointing his fork at me. "You want to get back at her? Go after the kid. It's the only thing she fucking cares about," he adds, rolling his eyes. "She's pretty too, like her mum, she'll fetch a nice price on the market I'll tell you," he laughs.

The motherfucker *laughs*.

I move like lightning, snatching the fork out of his hands before ramming it through his eye.

Giovanni screeches as blood pours down his face and his hands come up, trying to pull the piece of silverware out.

His men rush forward. Mac's already intercepted one, but the other is nearly on me. He draws his gun while I pick up a steak knife, sending it flying. It finds its target in the man's forehead, and he drops, his gun sliding across the floor, stopping right in front of me.

I scoop it up and fire two rounds into the man grappling with Mac at my back, and another one into the man I just impaled with my knife. *Making sure.*

Rolling back my shoulders, I turn my attention back to Giovanni; he's on his knees, blood coats his face while he screams frantically at me. Mac and Jace move to stand behind him.

"What the fuck are you on about? I only sold some information! I didn't do anything to you!"

I keep a straight face as I crouch down by Gio's head.

"You threatened my *daughter*," I say softly, tapping the fork sticking out of his eye with the barrel of my gun.

The man screams in agony and then visibly pales, finally connecting the dots.

"I didn't—I didn't..." His pathetic pleas erupt into screams of bloody murder when I yank the fork from his eyeball. He's breathing hard in between sobs, both hands pressed to the eye gushing out blood. I hold the fork up, inspecting it casually, while Gio writhes at my feet. It's looking none the worse for wear, all four tines still straight. My gaze drops back down to Gio.

"That was for Briar," I say, my jaw flexing.

He stills, his good eye finding me, filled with confusion.

My mouth tightens, and I wave the fork above him. "For the way you looked at her that night at Wonderland." My head tilts slightly to the side, which is Giovanni's only warning before I jam the fork through his throat. "And that's for calling her a whore."

Gio's scream cuts off, turning to gurgles as he drowns in his own blood.

I stand, looking down at him in disgust before I finally take the stolen gun and aim it at his head. I pull the trigger and the gurgling stops, but it's not enough. Shot after shot after shot, I empty the clip into the motherfucker's head, his body jolting with each new bullet.

"Okay, Rí, I think you got him," Mac says when the shots turn to clicks.

Slowly, I lower my arm.

"And that's for Remi."

82

YOURS

KOEN

I HEAD HOME. They discharged Remi from the hospital while I was out, somewhere around 2 a.m.

My brothers brought both Remi and Briar back to the loft in Boston, and after a quick shower, I find Remi sleeping peacefully in the guest bedroom.

Briar is keeping a quiet vigil. She's dragged the armchair over to the side of the bed, and there she sits, resting her head on the edge of the mattress, silently watching the rise and fall of Remi's chest.

Standing in the doorway, I watch them both for a minute or two before I speak.

"How's she doing?"

Briar startles at the sound of my voice, and her eyes are cool when they take in my shadowed form half lurking in the hall.

"You left." There's a trace of accusation in her tone, and hurt shines in her eyes.

"I had business to attend to."

"Right." She looks away from me.

"Can we talk?"

She shifts uncomfortably.

"Privately?" I add, looking over a sleeping Remi, not wanting to wake her up.

"I don't know," she hesitates, "I don't want to leave her..."

"I'll have Liam sit with her. Give you a break? You need sleep, too, Briar."

For a second, I think she might fight me on it, but to my surprise, she relents, trailing me out of the room. She must be more exhausted than I thought.

"Meet me in my room," I murmur, as I stop at Liam's door.

She nods absently, walking past me, her eyes heavy.

A few minutes later, I walk into my bedroom.

Briar's standing in the middle of it, looking out at the city, her arms wrapped around herself. She's still wearing my hoodie, the one she had on earlier today.

I move closer, reaching out to touch her cheek, but she flinches away from me. A deep, unfiltered and raw pain tears through me at what I've done. *I became the monster she always thought I was.*

"I'm sorry."

Her gaze snaps up, and she just stares back at me as if in disbelief of the words she's hearing come out of my mouth.

I risk taking a step closer, moving slowly, not wanting to scare her.

"Truth or dare?"

She just stares at me.

"Truth or dare, Briar Rose?" I say, softer this time.

"Truth," she whispers, wrapping her arms tighter around herself, curling her fingers into the frayed edges of her hoodie. *My hoodie.*

"Why?"

She swallows hard, her eyes darting around, marking the exits.

"Why did you give us up to Giovanni?"

She inhales a deep breath, steeling herself against me.

"Why, Briar?" My voice raises in volume, and she jumps. My heart constricts, and I say, softer this time, "I *need* to know, Briar Rose, please."

She nods stoically, letting out a shaky breath. "I had to make a choice... he was going to hurt her; it was you or Remi, and in this, there was no choice. I had to do it, Koen, I'm sorr—"

I step forward, pressing my palm over her mouth, feeling her tremble under my fingertips, her eyes shining bright in the moonlight.

"I *never* want to hear you say that again."

Tears fill her eyes, but I don't stop.

"You have *nothing* to be sorry for, do you hear me? You protected your daughter—our child... it's all you've ever done. You did everything you could to keep her safe—*even from me.*"

Tears leak down her cheeks, wetting my hand, and I pull it away to kiss the top of her forehead, holding her face in my hands.

"I'm sorry. I'm so fucking sorry."

"But I kept her a secret—"

I shake my head. "You kept her *safe*." I stare into her eyes, brushing her hair out of her face. "And I can't hate you for that."

Her breath shudders, and she looks up at me.

"I was wrong—about all of it. I didn't listen, I didn't even try to understand, and I punished you, god, I—" I rub my hand down my face, remembering how I held that gun to her head in the woods.

I lower myself and my knees hit the ground. I look up and watch as silent tears leak down her cheeks.

"I'm *sorry*," I repeat, hanging my head, my forehead falls against her stomach, holding her to me one last time before I let her go. "I can't take it back—what I did—how I treated you when I should have been protecting you..."

I pull back from her, letting my hands fall away.

"If you want to go... if you want to take her..." I choke on the words, but force them out anyway, "I'll let you go." I swallow hard. "Anything you need, wherever you want to go, I'll take care of it. No threats, no guards, no dark shadow watching you—*haunting* you in the night. I won't force this on you if you don't want it. If you want me to stay away... I will."

Briar's red-rimmed eyes burn into mine.

"But that's not what I want," I whisper to her, shaking my head and trying to keep my composure. "I want you. *I've always wanted you.* I want you by my side and tangled in my sheets. I want it to be me you run to when you're scared or overwhelmed. I want to be there for *you*, and I want to be there for *Remi*. In every way I should have been from the start." My throat locks and I drop my gaze. "I missed *so much*, and I can't get that back, but I want to try. I want to hear her adorable little laugh every morning when I wake up. I want to be the one who gets her to smile when she's sad. I want to tie her skates and teach her a proper slap shot, and god, I might be shit at it but... I just—I want to be her *dad*." My eyes flick up to meet Briar's. "If you'll let me?"

She's got a hand pressed to her mouth, trying to stifle the sound of the choked sob as it rips through her, but I can't stand it, and in another second I'm on my feet, with my arms around her.

Briar buries her face in my chest, tears falling freely now, but she's holding on to me tight; something inside of me breaks, and I feel a tear slip away.

"I'm here," I whisper, my voice breaking, wishing with all I have that she doesn't push me away. "I'm here, baby, and I'm not going anywhere unless you tell me to."

"No," she says, and at the sound of the word, my spine goes rigid; my hands shake slightly when I draw back from her but without letting go, searching her face.

"I don't want you to go." Her fingers curl into the fabric of my shirt. "I want you to stay."

"Are you sure? After everything... you don't have to decide right now."

She just looks at me, fingers locked in my shirt when she says, "I'm sure. I want you." Her eyes search mine. "*You*. I just want *you*."

I lean down and kiss her gently, holding my lips to hers as long as I dare before picking her up, carrying her over to my bed, and laying down with Briar on top of me. She's exhausted, she needs sleep, but I don't want to let her go. So I hold her, running my fingers through her hair until her breaths come even and her grip on my shirt loosens.

"I'm yours, baby, *I'm all yours*."

83

1, 2, 3, 4, 5

KOEN

LEANING AGAINST THE DOOR FRAME, I watch Briar sleep. She needed it; it's been a long twenty-four hours. I've only been watching for about ten minutes before she stirs, as if sensing my presence.

Her eyes blink slowly open. I enjoy the little snapshot of peace on her face before it's gone. Briar shoots up, her hand going to the other side of the bed—*the empty side.* Panicked, she looks around, freezing when she meets my gaze.

"Where's Remi?"

"She's fine. She woke up a couple of hours ago and went wandering into the kitchen, hungry for breakfast. Liam took her to the rink for a tour of the Breakers' locker room before the game tonight."

She exhales, having held her breath while I talked, her shoulders relaxing.

"What time is it?" Briar rubs her face, trying to push off the heaviness of sleep that still clings to her.

"It's past ten."

"What?" Her hands drop and she gapes at me. "Why did you let me sleep so late?"

"You needed it," I tell her honestly, and for a moment we just stare at each other before she lets out a short laugh.

"Yeah, you're probably right." And then my words from earlier hit her. "Wait, did you say there's a Breakers game tonight?"

"Aye. And we're going."

"We?" She blinks at me.

"We," I confirm, unable to suppress the half smile on my face. "You, me, and Remi; Aidan and Liam hooked us up with tickets for tonight's game, and Rory'll be cheering."

"Oh, wow!" Briar exclaims. "Remi—Remi's going to love that," she says softly.

"I hope so," I say. "I have a lot of making up to do. With Remi and with you."

Another long moment passes between us, the silence in the loft becoming very apparent.

"Where is everyone?" she asks.

"Out," is my only response, and my eyes track her hard swallow.

Hoping to break the tension, Briar moves to get out of the bed.

"Oh no, darling, you stay right where you are." She stills, the hand holding the blanket hovering mid-air. "You need to eat."

"I can do that in the kitchen," she replies, but I shake my head.

"Don't you move," I warn, before disappearing out into the hallway to retrieve the breakfast tray I prepared for her. It only takes a minute, and I'm pleased to find her still in the bed when I return, though, with a slightly miffed expression on her face like she's mad at herself for listening.

I come closer and notice her body tense—not in fear, no, this is a different kind of tension altogether. Setting the tray down on her lap, I return to my full height. "Eat."

Briar makes a little face at me, and my fist tightens as I resist the urge to grab hold of her chin. *Not yet.* I have to readjust myself before taking a seat in the armchair across from the bed. Looking up, I find Briar watching me. My eyes narrow, and I point to the tray in her lap. "I said *eat.*"

Another roll of her eyes, and she's finally exploring the tray, eating a few bites of eggs and bacon and all of the toast. I wait patiently. She must have been hungry, because by the time she's done, the plate is just about clean. It's the most I've seen her eat. *Ever.*

Setting the tray aside, she takes another sip of coffee, her eyes on me. "Thanks for breakfast."

I just nod. Now that she's properly fed, I can proceed with my plans for the day. I rise from my chair, stalking toward her with purpose. Without warning, I scoop her up, out of the bed and into my arms.

"Hey!" She twists, half fighting being taken down the long hallway. "What are you doing?"

We cross the living room and down another hall and we're in my bedroom. "Putting you back where you fucking belong." I drop her onto my bed, a little less gently than I probably should have.

She lands on the soft mattress with a grunt, immediately scrambling for the mattress's edge.

"Ah." I hold up a finger and she stops, eyes flickering between my finger and me. "Don't move."

She sits back, folding her arms across her chest, and rolls her eyes. "Did anyone ever tell you how bossy you are?"

I step back, admiring the sight of her in my bed. It looks right—*she* looks right. She's wearing a plain t-shirt and shorts, no bra, dark hair down and messy from sleep, no makeup. *And god, she's never looked more beautiful.*

"So how long am I supposed to sit here exactly? I've got things to do, you know." She tosses her long dark locks over her shoulder, and oh, how I want to wrap the length of it around my fist.

I take a step toward her, my eyes darkening. "You're not leaving this bed until you understand just how sorry I am."

Surprise shows on her face, and her eyes widen. Noticing my increasing proximity, her eyes soften just before I reach her. She goes to reply, but when she opens her mouth, I take that as my invitation. My lips are on hers, my tongue sweeping mercilessly through her mouth, devouring her. She had her breakfast, and now I'm going to have mine too.

I release her lips, and she lets out a gasp, her eyes watching as I circle around to the end of the bed.

"Remember how I was the first to make you come?"

She swallows, her cheeks burn pink but she nods.

I grab hold of her ankles, twisting her flat on her back and dragging her down to the end of the mattress. "And remember when you told me you haven't been with anyone since?"

Her eyes are huge, pupils blown wide, but she nods again, though this time it's more stilted.

"And you should know, I'm also going to be your last." Her mouth parts at my words, but I keep going. "You're *mine*, Briar Rose; *you've always been mine*, but I've been negligent in my duties as *yours*," I admit to her, my face serious.

Grazing my fingers against her skin, my hand travels up her outer thigh until I reach her shorts, slowly tugging them down the length of her legs. *She's not wearing any panties.* Briar doesn't stop me. Her shorts hit the floor, and my hands make their way back up her legs. My gaze is locked on hers as I slowly force her thighs apart. "Do you wish to see me on my knees, darling? 'Cause for you, I'll fucking bend."

I sink down, and she sits up, trying to stop me. "No, you don't have anything to make up for—" One of my hands pushes her back down onto the mattress, while the other finds her slit, smiling when she releases a little whimper at the contact. *Already so sensitive.* Leaning in, I give her a taste, and the way she shivers when my breath hits her skin..."Oh, baby. I have so much to make up for. And I'm starting right now. So lie down. Shut up. And fucking come for me, darling."

I take the subsequent whimper that escapes her as agreement and go in on her. I'm not gentle, there's no teasing; I devour her like a man starved. She gasps and wiggles when I hit the right spot. I grip her hips, keeping her in place. Her legs wrap around my head, her back arches off the mattress—the sudden rush of sensation too much for her to handle.

Dragging my tongue higher, I suck on her clit, and her body goes rigid. *She's close.* Alternating between licking and sucking, I focus my full attention on her clit until she trembles. Moving my fingers up and fully exposing her to me before sucking hard, I continue to torment her as she comes apart on my tongue. An orgasm rips through her, and it's intense. I left her wanting last time, and she's shaking fully as I force her to ride it out, the sensations overwhelming her. I feel her clit pulsating on the tip of my tongue.

Before she's had a chance to catch her breath, my hand

presses between her thighs, avoiding the still too sensitive clit; as I slide a finger inside of her, my cock tightens, aching for her, but I ignore it. This isn't about me—this is about *her*. I rise, pushing her higher up the bed with me as I crawl onto it, keeping one finger inside of her before dragging her against me. I pin her feet under mine and grip her throat until she's stretched out against the length of me; her back to my chest gives me full access to that sweet, sinful body of hers.

Her ear is beside my mouth, and her body tenses when I whisper, "That was one."

I use my free hand to push her shirt up until she's naked beside me, stretched out and at my mercy. I run my hand up the length of her, exploring every inch until I find her breasts. I keep my fingers light, tracing them just where the skin swells, taking my time before finding one of her nipples. My touch is delicate, and a direct contrast to the firm grip I have on her throat. I roll the taut bud between my fingers, my teeth finding her neck, biting down before flicking my tongue.

She gasps and squirms, grinding her backside into me, needing my attention lower. I breathe out a soft laugh, "Oh, little Rose, that was quick. *Do you want to come again?*" I circle her nipple with my fingers before giving it a sharp pinch.

She inhales sharply, biting her lip and nodding quickly.

My hand moves to her other breast, the one I've ignored up until now. The hardened nub straining for my attention. I flick it with my thumb, and Briar arches her back, her backside grinding into me again, harder this time, until she freezes. My mouth curves into a smile. *She felt it*—I'm hard as a rock and impossible to ignore. I pull her closer, my cock jerking with the contact, desperate to be inside of her. "You feel that? What you do to me?"

Briar clamps her thighs together, but I shove them back apart, using my feet to pin hers while keeping her pressed up against me. She jumps when my fingers find her sensitive slit, using four fingers to rub deep circles just over her now desperate clit.

She squirms in my arms, her ankles trapped under my feet, keeping her in place, so she resorts to thrusting her hips, trying to inch my fingers lower so they make contact, but I keep teasing her until she lets out a desperate whimper. My mouth finds her ear again at the same time my fingers slide down an inch, forcing out a squeal at the sudden burst of sensations as I finally give in to her. "Ready for number two?"

There's no hesitation this time; my hand is still around her throat, but she nods her head quickly. "Please—*fuck*—please, I need it."

Working my fingers around, I slide my thumb inside her and enjoy the sharp cries when it finds the other side of her clit. She comes again, screaming louder this time. I release my grip on her throat to hold her chin. Sliding two fingers into her mouth, her choked-out screams cut off when her lips close around them and she sucks. And dear god, I nearly come in my jeans, my jaw clenching so hard it aches, continuing to stroke her until her body sags against mine and she goes limp.

I release her, leaving her lying on the mattress, naked and spent. She's on her stomach with her eyes closed; she doesn't see me go for my top drawer, doesn't see me pull the ribbons out.

The bed shifts under me when I climb on top of her; it's too late by the time I grab hold of each of her wrists, pinning them at her back. She thrashes in surprise, and I sink deeper, easing more of my weight onto her to keep her trapped underneath me. Carefully, I wind the ballet ribbons I stole from her bag around each wrist, binding her tight. The smooth satin kisses her skin, but the high-quality fabric refuses to give as she twists—testing the knot—struggling against it.

I roll her onto her back so I can see her face. It's a tense mixture of surprise, anger, and fear as she still fights against the ties. When she inches for the edge of the bed, I grab hold of one ankle, tugging hard so that she falls back, dragging her toward me.

"What—what the hell?" Her voice trembles slightly with shock and apprehension. "You tied me up?"

"Aye, can't have you trying to run off now, not when we're about to go for number three?"

Her mouth drops, and she shakes her head, body tensing. "I can't—not again."

"I told you. You're not leaving this bed until you know *exactly* how sorry I am. Not until I've decided you've had enough."

She gulps, watching me as I move back toward my top drawer, careful not to put my back to her, certain she's about to bolt. Her eyes widen, face paling at the same time her cheeks flush a bright pink when she catches sight of what I've pulled out.

"That's not—"

"Yours?" I smile, holding up the wand I stole from her bedside table back at her apartment. Her throat tightens, fear flashes in her eyes, but so does *anticipation*.

"You've been making yourself come with this thing by yourself for too long. It's *my* turn now."

Briar's eyes go black, and a little shiver travels through her. "You're insane."

I tilt my head as I take a step toward her. "Maybe," I admit, smirking at the way she squirms when her eyes drop back to the toy in my hands. "But you like it."

Reaching her, I drop one of my hands to graze my fingers against the skin of her inner thigh, and she quivers. My fingers travel higher, and her breath hitches.

"Look at me."

She doesn't.

"Briar."

The sound of her name brings up her eyes. "If you want me to stop, tell me to stop. And I will," I promise her. "But I have a feeling—" I lean in, switching on the wand and pressing it to her already soaking cunt, "—you won't."

Briar's eyes widen, her back arching involuntarily at the feel of the wand against her, the low hum vibrating through her, her mouth forming a small O as she pants out, "Oh, fuck."

I tease the wand just over her entrance, keeping it far away from the little bundle of nerves at the top. Without warning, I pull the wand back so it no longer touches her skin.

"Wider." I tap the wand between her thighs, watching intently to see what she'll do. If she'll continue to resist and ask me to stop, or if she'll submit. *If she'll beg me for it.*

Her hips chase the missing wand, and she lets out a groan of disappointment at the sudden loss of pleasure. Blue eyes stare up into mine as she makes her decision, lifting her chin when she spreads her legs wider, helpless with her hands bound behind her back. Her breasts push forward, rising and falling with her breaths as she waits to see what I'll do next.

Bringing the wand back down, I drag it in slow, deliberate circles, rewarding her obedience, enjoying the way her back arches off the mattress; her body squirms as she chases the wand, trying to get me to stay where she wants me. Each time the wand passes over her sensitive little clit, engorged and tender, her body tenses, going rigid, and her eyes roll back with the pleasure it brings—the wand working too well to bring her close again until I pull it away.

By the third time I've teased her, working her up just to drag it away again, she whimpers, fighting against the ribbons binding her wrists together, needing that release. She's distracted when I flip her onto her stomach, my fingers wrapping around the ribbon holding hers, and drag her back until she's on her knees, facing away from me. I drive the wand in between her thighs and she screams, falling forward into the mattress, that perfect pussy propped up for me to play with.

This time I bring her right to the edge until her body is shaking with her need for release before I slip the wand down, and she nearly screams, "No!"

"Beg for it." My voice is quiet, dark, but I know, by the way she tenses, she heard it.

She tests her restraints again, her hands shifting where they're trapped at her back, keeping her wrapped up like a pretty present, and she flexes on her knees. Pushing the sensitive apex of her thighs higher, trying to find the tip of my wand.

Slowly, deliberately, I drag the wand farther away from where she needs it before I repeat my words, even darker this time. *"Beg for it."*

She doesn't—at war with herself, on her knees, face first in my bed.

I drive the wand over her again, giving her just enough that she trembles, and just as I go to pull it away again, I hear her voice, "Please! Please—I *need* it—I, I can't take it!"

I move the wand in a circle, giving and taking, until she's panting, "Koen." My hand stops at the sound of my name; I'm fixated on the way it sounds strangled under her breath. *"Koen —please—"* she begs, and I relent. Fisting her hair, I drive her head deeper into the mattress as I give her what she wants, muffling her screams with my sheets. Her legs spread wider as she climaxes, her clit throbbing desperately under the wand.

Briar's screams grow louder, and her chest heaves as she pants, moans mixing with sobs as the force of her climax rips through her, the pent-up frustration from my continued edging lets go all at once, overwhelming her. "Please—please —" she screams, twisting to get away from the wand, fighting under my hold, this time begging for a whole new reason. "It's too much!" Another scream rips through her as another wave of climax leaves her body trembling. But my grip on her hair only tightens, pushing her face deeper into the mattress, clicking the button on the wand and bringing it up another level.

"Beg me all you want, baby; you know I don't show mercy."

Strangled cries escape her, tangled with moans, as I work her through her orgasm, forcing her to stay right there, to ride it out; she's both desperate for it and desperate to escape it. I give her everything I denied her—made her wait for.

"No, no, no, please! I can't—it's too much! I—"

I flip her over so she's on her back. "You can," I assure her, looking into her blue eyes before kissing her neck, then moving lower and taking one of her breasts in my mouth, my tongue flicking over the sensitive little bud, loving the way she arches under me, pushing more of her into my mouth.

I press the wand harder, relentlessly, mercilessly, watching as she comes apart. She's a frantic, panting, whimpering mess, begging me with her eyes, but even as she begs me—pleads with me—she doesn't tell me to stop.

So I don't.

Briar squirms and thrashes; screams and sobs erupt out of her as she tries to shake me off of her sensitive clit. Her climax follows in quick succession after the third—hard, violent—her body shaking uncontrollably while her eyes roll back. And when I finally release her, switching off the toy, her body sags in quick relief, no resistance left.

I leave her lying there, hands still trapped behind her back, her breaths coming hard, but she's looking at me, staring me down as I slowly remove my belt, freeing myself as I slide my jeans down, kicking them to the side.

My cock twitches under her scrutiny, yearning to claim her, *to be inside of her.*

"One more." I kiss her lips, leaving her chasing after me when I pull away again to speak. "This time, you come with *me.*"

I reach behind her, carefully untethering the knot that holds her hands, freeing them, freeing her.

"I've taken too much from you already," I whisper. My need for her—I can feel it, the tension in my chest, the ache in my cock, the inexplicable urge to claim her as mine. "This— this has to be yours. Not because I need it. Not because I can't hold myself back for another second. But I want you to *choose* me, even after everything I've done. I want to make you mine, but I won't steal that from you. If you want me inside you, if you want *me*, I need you to tell me. If not..." My forehead falls against hers and my eyes close, inhaling her sweet scent, savoring this moment, the feeling of her breath against my skin.

"Say it?" I whisper, so low my voice is like a ghost against her skin—this time, it's not a demand, but a question.

For a moment, she just looks at me, really looks, and I let her. I let her see *everything*.

"I want you," she whispers. Her hand comes up to cup my face as she reaches in to kiss me. "Even if it breaks me. I want you."

The second the words leave her lips, something inside me shatters. For the longest time, I've been closed off, cut off from my emotions, behind a wall I'd built so high I thought I'd never see the other side. That is, until I met Briar. With her, I feel everything, every emotion, every ounce of pain—hurt, happiness... *love*.

I kiss her with the kind of urgent tenderness that tests the edges of my restraint. Her arms come up and wrap around me, her body arching up into mine.

"Christ, you'll be my undoing," I breathe out before I kiss her again, the world narrowing to the feel of her soft lips on mine, her hands in my hair, around my neck, the warmth of her body when she grinds up against me. I ease into her carefully, reverently, like she is glass in my arms. When I finally enter her, it's not the brutal claiming she expected, but something deeper—slower—every movement, every thrust, threaded with apology.

I kiss her jaw, her throat, each of her wrists I'd bound in satin, murmuring words between ragged breaths, "I'm sorry... you're mine... I'll make it right..."

Briar clings to me, her soft cries not torn from her this time, but given, willing offerings that light my chest on fire. I work her up slowly, patiently, her body meeting mine as if she's finally giving in, letting herself fall, surrendering herself to me.

And when she comes, it's not violent, not frantic like it was before; it's more of a slow burn, a sweet, torturous release that has her moaning my name like it's a prayer. And when it's over, I don't let go. I stay inside her, running the tips of my fingers down her arm, not wanting to let her go, afraid if I do—even for a second—she'll disappear.

"I'll keep paying—atoning," I whisper, kissing her forehead, my voice raw. "Every time you need me, I'll be here. I promise."

It doesn't make it right—the dark things I've done. How I abandoned her, stalked her, tortured her when I thought she had betrayed me—but it's a start.

Finally, I pull out of her, careful not to crush her when I move to the side. And when she curls up against me, exhausted, her body relaxed in a way I've never felt, my arms tighten around her, pulling her closer—not in a possessive way, but protective—holding her until she falls asleep.

84

DROP THE GLOVES

BRIAR

AFTER WHAT MIGHT'VE BEEN the best nap of my entire life, I'm awakened by the quick and familiar sound of Remi's feet racing down the hall. There's a second of hesitation, giving me just enough time to fully ensure maximum blanket coverage, before she crashes through Koen's door.

Koen rockets out of the bed, and I'm instantly grateful that, at some point, he slid on a pair of shorts.

However, Remi is staring at me with eyes wide open in surprise. "Mommy, are you sick?"

I run my hands down my face, once again checking the blanket and tucking it tighter under my arms. "No, baby, Mommy's not sick."

She tilts her head to the side, her clever little eyes studying me. "Then why are you in bed?"

"Mommy...Mommy was just so tired and cranky she needed to take a little nap." I smile, careful not to make eye contact with Koen.

Remi's eyes slide to him. "And *Koen* was helping you sleep?"

"Mhmm." My tone goes up in inflection, and I'm hoping my face is not as red as it feels. "Listen, baby, why don't you go pick out something to wear to the game tonight, and I'll come help you in two quick minutes, okay?"

Remi's eyes narrow for another long moment of silence before she shrugs, spinning on her heel so fast it almost knocks her over. "Okay!" she yells, disappearing back out into the hall.

"Ohmygod," I breathe, looking over to find Koen hiding a laugh behind his hand, the one *not* hiding a gun behind his back. Annoyed, I throw a pillow at him. He lets it hit him straight in the chest, arching one brow as if shocked at my audacity. "You don't lock the door?" I grumble, shoving out of the bed while attempting to keep the sheet over me, half tripping over it in the process.

"Why would I lock the door in my own house?"

"Umm, for reasons similar to what just fucking happened."

He smirks, sliding the gun back into the drawer in his nightstand, before frowning and taking it back out again. "I guess I have some childproofing to do..."

I stare at the drawer in open horror. "Yeah, I say you do." I quickly retrieve my clothes from the floor and pull them on. Shaking my head, I move to follow Remi back out the door, stopping at the sound of Koen's throat clearing behind me.

"Er—that chest of drawers there is yours."

I freeze, following the direction of his finger, to a dresser tucked up against the door to the bathroom.

Koen runs a hand back through his hair, and I can tell he's

uncomfortable. "It — uh—it's got some clothes in there." He stares at me. "For you," he clarifies.

"Oh." I stare at the drawers before cracking a smile. "Awfully presumptuous of you, wouldn't you say?" I turn back with a grin, only to be hit square in the face with the same pillow I'd thrown at him earlier.

"Get dressed, Briar Rose. We've got a hockey game to get to."

Remi spends nearly the entire car ride to the game telling me all about the Breakers' arena, what the locker rooms look like, the bench, how to work the scoreboard, how good the burgers are at the Chill Zone... *everything*.

"Wow, it sounds like you really got the full tour!" I say, finally getting a word in after she's forced to take a sip of water after almost thirty minutes of non-stop banter.

"Mommy, I have a question?"

I open my bottle of water and take a drink. "Yes, baby?"

"Is Koen driving us to the game because he's my dad?"

I choke, falling forward in my seat to recover. Koen might as well have crashed the car for how my heart stops in my chest.

"What?" I croak out. "Where did you—why do you think that, Rem?"

I shoot a look at Koen, who shockingly looks just as rattled as me. *What do I do?* I mouth at him from behind my water bottle so Remi can't see.

Koen just shrugs, tightening his grip on the steering wheel until his knuckles are white.

Remi tilts her head briefly in thought. "Well, he has the same eyes as me." I raise my brows, genuinely impressed she put that together on her own, until she continues, "And Liam called him my dad... but then he freaked out! And he told me to keep it a secret. But when I told him I'm not allowed to keep secrets, he freaked out even more!"

Koen exhales slowly, "*Liam* talks too much."

I cover my mouth to hide the laughter bubbling out of me as I watch Koen's eyes narrow.

"If Koen is my dad, does that make Liam my uncle?" Remi continues, completely oblivious to the gravity of the topic we are discussing.

"I—uh." My eyes dart over to Koen, who's staring straight ahead, his jaw locked tight.

"Like Uncle Dash and Uncle Sam?"

That breaks Koen out of his thoughts. He glances in his rearview mirror at Remi before giving me a sharp look. "*Uncle Dash and Uncle Sam?* I thought you were an only child?"

I'm torn between answering my daughter and answering Koen.

"Yes." I wince, turning around to face Remi. "That makes Liam your uncle, and Aidan and Alex too. I look back at Koen. "Dash and Sam are Lily's brothers," I explain.

There's an unreadable look, *not unlike jealousy*, on his face before he turns his attention back to the road. We pull into an underground parking garage meant for just the players and their families.

Remi claps, sitting back in her seat. "Yay! We're going to watch my *uncles* play!"

"Yes, we are..." I blow out a breath, sitting back in my seat and trying to get my heartbeat to regulate, while Koen finds us a spot to park.

One thing about a hockey game... It's loud.

So loud.

Once inside the massive arena, I half expect Koen to lead us up to a box, or somewhere private, but we head down. Down and down until we're at the glass level, right in between Boston's bench and goal.

We're early enough to catch warm-ups. Music blasts from the overhead speakers, and when the players race out onto the ice, Remi shrieks with excitement. More players spill out of the doors until both teams are moving in massive circles around each end of the rink before breaking apart. Some come over to stretch near us while others practice their shots on the goalie.

Remi's got a huge smile on her face, jumping up and down before she, too, starts banging on the glass at the players skating around like she sees others doing around us.

She's bundled up in layers: long sleeves, with her new jacket underneath her brand new #26 Boston Breakers jersey, courtesy of #26 himself, Liam O'Rourke. And honestly, she looks adorable in it. I even found some green ribbon to tie in her hair. Koen bends down, picking her up and holding her so her toes rest on the top of the boards. Both of her hands press up against the glass, and she squeals ecstatically. I think my heart might burst at the sight of the two of them together.

Liam skates by, and Remi bangs harder, trying to get his attention.

Koen gives me a look, mumbling, *"I'm gonna kill him,"* under his breath at the same time Liam spots us. Grinning ear to ear, he peels out of the warm-up circle, coming straight for the glass, green eyes fixed on Remi. He holds up his glove and gives her a high five through the glass.

In true Liam fashion, he doesn't notice Koen glowering at him as he bends down to pick up a puck off the ice. He taps it against the glass twice in warning before he reaches up and drops it over, right into Koen's open palm.

Koen's hand closes around the puck, and he hands it to Remi, who takes it from him like she's just been given the holy grail.

You're dead, I spy Koen mouth to Liam while Remi is distracted. Liam cocks his head, pointing his green glove to his ear while mouthing back a helpless *I can't hear you,* but the shit-eating grin on his face suggests otherwise.

Koen's jaw clenches, and I can't help but laugh, earning myself a wink from Liam, and a scowl from Koen at my side.

Liam gives Remi one more fist bump through the glass before he turns his attention back to the ice, warm-ups nearly over. Not half a minute later, Rory takes his place, waving at Remi with her green pompoms. Remi holds up the puck Liam just gave her, showing it off, and Rory's mouth drops open in exaggerated shock and awe.

Rory makes eye contact with me before she, too, tosses something over the glass. I catch her shimmery, green and silver pair of pompoms, which elicits another squeal of excitement out of Remi, who snatches them right up, holding them high and shaking them like the rest of the Belles are doing out on the ice.

"Thank you!" I shout to Rory, hoping she can hear me through the glass.

"Anytime!" she yells back. I can hear her perfectly fine. "Have fun at your first game, guys!"

I've seen hockey on TV before, but to experience it in person, and right at ice level, it's a completely different experience entirely.

They are so *fast*! And when they hit each other, they hit *hard*, pushing the glass outward with force each time. We're not five minutes into the first period before we spot Aidan, right before he slams one of the Chicago Bolts players into the glass right in front of us.

I scream, jumping back, and Koen laughs. I spy Aidan shooting Remi a little wink before skating off.

"Do you think there will be a fight?" Remi asks Koen. The look in her eyes tells me she's hoping he says yes.

Koen smiles, tilting his head while looking over the players on the ice. "Well, Aidan's on the ice tonight so statistically... probably, yeah."

Remi claps excitedly, jumping up a few times before resuming her spot against the glass, shouting for Aidan to "drop the gloves."

"She craves violence," Koen chuckles, sitting back in his seat, which puts him right next to me.

"She gets that from you." The words are out before I can think them through, and my eyes widen when I realize what I've said, but Koen just grins back at me.

"That she did. That she did."

My heart warms in my chest, and I smile before changing the subject, not wanting tonight to get too heavy.

"So why do they keep blowing the whistle every time they're about to score?" I ask with genuine curiosity. It's happened at least three times, where one of the Breakers is dominating the ice, moving in on the Bolts' goal, and just as he's about to let it rip, the ref blows the whistle, halting the play.

"Oh, 'cause they're offside," Koen tells me before noticing Liam skating by. "'Cause it's amateur hour out there!" he shouts, cupping his hands around his mouth.

Liam rolls his eyes before lining up for the puck drop right in front of us.

"Make him go boom, Uncle Liam!" Remi shrieks through the glass. I don't think he hears her until the play starts, and Liam tears at the forward on the other team who gets the puck, going in for a massive open ice hit.

I wince at the brutality of it, while Koen and Remi clap and bang on the glass.

I do my best to follow the game, but it's pointless, so instead I watch Koen and Remi bond.

After the game, Remi's climbing into the backseat of the SUV. Koen's standing by her door, holding the hockey stick Aidan slipped her after the game. Once she's settled in her seat, she looks up at him, locking him into one of her intense Remi stares.

"Dad?" She tries it out, and I hold my breath, my eyes flying to Koen, who's giving her his full, undivided attention, but I see him swallow nervously before he answers.

"Yeah?"

"Can you teach me to play hockey like that? Uncle Liam said you taught him and Uncle Aidan, and I want to be just like them someday!"

"Yeah, Remi." He swallows again, and his eyes look shiny in the light. "I would love that," he says softly, his eyes finding mine. "I would really love that."

85

HE'S A RED FLAG...
BUT A HOT RED FLAG

BRIAR

I'M SITTING on the couch, catching up on missed texts and e-mails on my phone Koen gave back to me, while Remi watches cartoons at my feet, when the elevator door dings, and shouts immediately grab my attention.

"Stop. Squirming!" someone shouts.

"I'm not squirming; you're manhandling!" a furious but familiar voice shouts back.

Koen appears from down the hall at the sound of the commotion, but his relaxed stance is reassuring.

The elevator doors are fully open now, and I blink rapidly, not sure if what I'm seeing is real life.

"Put me down, you oversized tree!" the girl yells, kicking her legs wildly from where Mac has her tucked under his arm, carrying her into the loft like she's a rolled-up carpet.

"No," he says flatly, looking to Koen, who's watching the exchange with amusement on his face.

"Lily???" I shout in disbelief, rising off the couch. "Oh my god—is that you?"

Lily stops struggling in Mac's arms long enough to lift her head.

"B?"

Lily resumes her struggling. "PUT ME DOWN, YOU CANCEROUS OAF! THAT'S MY BEST FRIEND!"

"Stop wiggling, or I'm going to drop you!"

"That's the whole point!" Lily huffs, attempting to kick him but failing miserably.

Mac releases a long-suffering sigh and, after Koen gives the okay, he lowers her to the ground while doing his best to avoid her fists.

Lily hits the ground and seconds later, I'm wrapped in a soul-crushing hug. "Oh my god, I thought you were dead!"

"I'm so glad you're safe!" I squeeze her tighter.

"Auntie Lily!" Remi squeals, running over and tackling Lily out of my arms.

"Remicoaster!!!" Lily picks Remi up, spinning her around before settling her on her hip and booping her nose. Remi laughs.

"I think I need a tetanus shot..." Mac mutters, looking over his hand.

"Cry me a river, you wanna-be-action-figure," Lily shoots back at him.

"You bit me!" Mac growls.

"Because you grabbed me!" Lily snaps.

"You were running!"

"I was just trying to go home!"

"Your apartment isn't safe."

"You're telling me! I got kidnapped the second I walked into it!" Lily turns her attention back to me, shifting Remi higher on her hip before she drops her voice to a whisper.

"Okay, what's the plan? Who are we fighting? I'd say I'll take the big man, but he's way faster than he looks..."

The expression on her face is dead serious, and I can't catch my breath. It's not funny, but I can't stop laughing, and trying to stop it from coming out is just making it worse.

While I struggle, Lily gives me a quick once-over, and Remi too, noting the cartoons on the television. "Are you okay? You look okay..." Her eyes narrow, darting around at the luxurious loft around us.

"Yes, we're fine, look, it's a long story but—"

Koen steps closer, and I watch as Lily sizes him up.

"Hey, you! Yeah, you!" she says when he raises his brows at her, stealing a glance at me. "Are you the one in charge around here?"

"Jesus Christ..." I mutter under my breath.

"Don't start that again," Mac mutters from behind us, looking like he's lived a thousand lives since I've seen him last.

I grab Lily's arm, hoping to call off my attack dog. "Lily—Lily, that's Koen."

Lily's head turns slowly in my direction. *Koen???* she mouths, and I nod slowly, my eyes flashing with hidden meaning. She drops her voice, talking into my ear while keeping her eyes on Koen ahead of her. *"Oh my god, he's hot. I hate that he's hot. Do we still hate him?"*

But Mac's still close enough to hear her. "You think everyone's hot."

"Not you," she snips back, giving me an irritated look.

"Sorry, I think we've gotten off on the wrong foot," Koen says, giving me an amused look as he steps forward to offer Lily his hand. "I'm Koen."

"Careful, Rí, this one bites," Mac warns, watching Lily carefully.

Lily sighs audibly and tosses her hair before taking Koen's hand. "Lily, a pleasure," she says haughtily, glaring at Mac before giving Koen a smile. "So you're the one who kidnapped my bestie." She shifts Remi on her hip. "And my mini-bestie."

"Ahh—" Koen's dark eyes dart between Lily and me, not quite sure how to respond. "Kidnapped is a strong word..."

"Is it?" My attention narrows on Koen, remembering everything he put me through.

Don't start, he says with his eyes, and I keep my mouth shut. *For now.*

"You. Took. My. Best. Friend." Lily's hazel eyes flash, and I'm suddenly nervous she might hand Remi off to me so she can go fight my boyfriend.

"Yeah, but—"

"You chased me through half the state of Massachusetts!" Lily continues, cutting him off.

"Okay, that wasn't *technically* me..." Koen's eyes flicker to Mac.

"Your *goon* manhandled me!"

"Don't make me regret saving you." Mac pinches the bridge of his nose, closing his eyes.

"*Saving me?* You kidnapped me!" Lily argues.

"Yeah, those two words are synonymous in this world, apparently..." I mutter, and Koen's eyes sparkle.

"Okay, listen here, Captain Kidnap." Lily straightens, lifting her chin and glowering at Koen. "Yeah, I'm talking to you." She nods when Koen arches a brow. Mac coughs a laugh at our back. "A repeat offender, it would seem..." She sniffs, and I have to hold a palm over my mouth, tears of laughter tearing at the corners of my eyes. "If you ever so much as *think* about scaring Briar like that again, I will beat you to death with your own *skull!*"

"I don't think that's..."

I cut Mac off with a little hiss and a shake of my head.

"You're right, Lily," Koen says, his voice deadly serious, and we all freeze. "Briar didn't deserve what I put her through. I fucked up, but I'm ready to spend the rest of my life making up for it. I wasn't there for her when she needed me, but I'm here now for whatever she needs, and Remi, for as long as they'll have me." His eyes connect with mine, and I feel myself melt.

Lily blinks, surprise catching her tongue. "Well, great. Fantastic growth arc. You're temporarily forgiven." Lily sniffs. "On probation."

"Is the probation term negotiable?" Koen asks.

"No."

GIRLS NIGHT

BRIAR

"ONE MORE MOVIE! Please! Please! One more!" Remi begs, before the credits are even rolling on the movie that just finished. "We can make ice cream sundaes!"

"I don't know... it's getting kind of late." I check the time on my phone.

"C'mon, Mom!" she whines.

"Yeah! C'mon, Mom!" Lily echoes, throwing popcorn at my face.

I narrow my eyes at her. "You're not helping," I mutter, before chucking a piece of popcorn back at her.

"I mean, what's another ninety minutes?"

"Rory!" I whip my head around, clutching my chest at the unexpected betrayal.

The newest member of our little girl squad just shrugs her shoulders. "What? Ice cream sundaes sound amazing right now..." She winks at Remi, who beams back at her.

"It looks like you're outvoted!" Lily teases, reaching over and swiping the clicker out of my hand.

"Ugh, fine!" I relent, sinking deeper into the couch cushions. "But only if there are cherries for the ice cream sundaes..."

Remi's eyes go wide and connect with Rory's.

"Race you to the fridge!" Rory shouts, launching herself off the sectional, with Remi tearing after her, giggling up a storm.

I laugh, watching Remi try to dart under Rory before they reach the door, and Rory almost falls trying not to trip over her.

"Be careful!"

We're having a girls' night. Liam and Aidan have an away game in Chicago tonight, so Rory has the night off, and while Koen was supposed to be here, something urgent came up and he had to step out.

We've done it up proper with pizza, and a fresh batch of cookies we baked using store-bought dough—because none of us can bake worth a damn—and a fresh coat of glittery black nail polish adorns my fingernails. And of course, a movie marathon, popcorn, and now apparently ice cream sundaes.

A crashing sound from the kitchen has me up and on my feet.

"You guys need help in there?" I ask, already moving.

Both Remi and Rory respond in unison, "Yes..."

"Don't get up," I snap playfully at Lily, who's scrolling through movies with her feet propped up on the coffee table.

"Don't worry, I won't," she replies without looking up.

Shaking my head, I enter the kitchen, finding a mess of bowls scattered all over the floor from where they must have fallen out of the cabinet.

It's quick work to pick them up, and I help Rory gather the

rest of the ingredients for the sundaes, setting Remi up at the kitchen island to make them.

A faint bang echoes from somewhere below us, maybe on the street outside, and Rory turns around to look at me.

"Was that you?" she asks over Remi's head, who is fully absorbed in dropping as many chocolate chips as she can onto her tiny scoop of ice cream.

I shake my head slowly. "No. I thought—"

The elevator dings, and both of us lock eyes. Koen made it seem like he wouldn't be back until late. There's another noise. A heavy thud and then boots on the hardwood in the living room. I hear voices, *Irish* accents, but I don't recognize any of them.

Rory slides a kitchen knife out of the block as I creep toward the archway separating the kitchen and living room. Remi, still blissfully unaware, is still filling her mouth now with more chocolate chips since I'm not policing her.

Heart racing, I chance a quick peek around the corner and see four men I don't recognize. One of them has got Lily by the hair, his hand pressed over her mouth. One of the men is saying my name over and over to her while she shakes her head frantically.

I rocket back into the kitchen, moving as quickly as I can while being silent about it, and grab Rory's arm. "I need you to hide her."

Rory blinks at me. "But what about you?"

I shake my head slowly, my gaze heavy. "They're looking for *me*."

Rory grips the knife tighter, looking conflicted, but I turn my attention to Remi. "Hey Rem," I whisper, holding my finger to my lips to show that she should, too. "We're gonna play a little game, okay? Hide and seek?" Her eyes light up, but I tap my finger again to my lips when her mouth opens. "You have to be super duper quiet, and you can be on Rory's team, okay?" I'm desperately trying to keep the tears out of my eyes but failing.

Remi looks up at me, her brows creasing with concern before she nods.

"Okay, good. Go with Rory, okay, and remember..." I press my finger to my lips one more time, and she nods.

Quietly, she climbs down off the stool, but as her feet touch the ground, I wrap my arms around her tight. "I love you, okay? I love you so much." I kiss the top of her head before letting her go.

She stares up at me. I can tell she wants to say it back, but I told her to be quiet. There's fear in her eyes now because I'm doing a terrible job at hiding my own.

"It's okay, it's okay, go with Rory." I nudge her in Rory's direction, who takes Remi's hand in hers, and the two of them retreat deeper into the kitchen.

I inch closer to the living room.

"She's here. Search the house," I hear and close my eyes.

Opening them, I spot Rory quietly opening the door out onto the courtyard that sits in the middle of the loft. Good thinking. Even if Remi makes a sound, it'll be harder to hear since they'll be outside. Rory pulls Remi into some bushes. Crouched down with the knife still in her hand, she'll be able to see the kitchen, but it's unlikely anyone will see them if they didn't know they were there.

Releasing a shaky breath, I roll back my shoulders, making eye contact with my daughter one last time before I step into the living room.

I have their attention immediately, and I freeze, recognizing the man who appears to be calling the shots.

"Ah, well if it isn't my lucky day," he says, his Irish accent thick.

One of his men pulls out a gun and presses it to Lily's head. I raise my hands, stopping in my tracks.

"Who are you?"

The man motions for one of his men to grab me. I don't resist, but he's still rougher than he needs to be.

The man frowns at me, pretending to look disappointed. "Ah, now Bella, I'm hurt." He holds his hand to his chest like I shot him. "I *know* you recognize me." He smiles, and it's all too familiar.

I swallow because I do. *I do recognize him.* He was there *that* night. At Wonderland. He was in the back in that meeting with all the important clients... *and he winked at me. Salt and pepper hair, broad shoulders.* But nothing else easily identifiable. I didn't hear him speak that night, but his Irish accent has my stomach sinking.

The guy holding Lily cocks his gun, and my attention whips to them.

"No, no, no—we'll keep the Kostalov girl. I'll take care of two problems for the price of one." He smiles again, and I shiver. *He thinks Lily is Rory.* They do sort of look alike; they're around the same height and blonde, but that's about where the similarities end, and Rory's eyes are blue and Lily's hazel...

Lily and I lock eyes, but she keeps her mouth snapped shut. *My ride or die.* She knows what's at stake and she's not going to correct them.

"Ladies, allow me to formally introduce myself. I'm Seamus O'Rourke, Koen and Aidan's uncle."

87

GONE

KOEN

MAC and I have just pulled into the parking garage of the loft when Aidan calls.

"Yeah?"

Aidan's frantic on the other end, and I sit straight up, causing Mac to look over. I only hear a few words before I'm out of the car and sprinting for the elevator. The sight of the body lying a few feet from the doors hits me like a fucking truck.

"*No.*"

For a second, my brain blanks out, and I freeze, not believing what I'm seeing. In the next second, I'm at his side. *Jace.* My hands shake as I move aside the collar of his jacket to press two fingers to his neck, confirming what I already know by the bullet lodged in the side of his head, and *his unseeing eyes.*

He's gone.

"What the fuck?!" Mac curses, falling down beside me and shaking Jace as if trying to wake him up. His voice breaks, sharp and jagged. "Wake up. C'mon, man, wake the fuck up!" When he realizes what I did only seconds before, he releases Jace, standing up and pacing behind me, letting out a sound that's somewhere between a roar and a sob.

My throat is tight and my eyes are burning, but I reach up, fingers shaking, and lightly press Jace's eyes closed. Leaning forward, I press my forehead to his, closing my own eyes, just for a moment before I lift my head. Rising, I wipe the tears from my cheeks before drawing my gun and moving for the stairs, but not before calling back to Mac.

"Stay with him."

"But, Ri…" Mac's face is red and a mess of tears himself, but he pulls out his gun, moving to follow me.

"No." I cut him off sharply, freezing with the door to the stairwell half open. "Stay with Jace. Don't leave him alone."

He halts, nodding, his gaze falling back to my cousin—*our friend*.

"Call *everyone*," I say, my voice low and lethal. "Whoever did this, dies tonight."

The loft is silent.

The sound of my heartbeat is loud in my ears after sprinting up the stairs, faster than the elevator. I step into the hallway. The television is still playing some movie, and aside from the spilled popcorn all over the floor, there's no sign of a struggle.

My gun is drawn, and I clear the area, moving into the kitchen—*also empty.*

"Rory?"

There's no answer.

Aidan said she was here...

I check over the courtyard before turning down into the first hallway.

"Rory?" I call again, louder this time, still on high alert.

I catch the faint sound of sobs before a door opens. I lift my gun but let it fall when Rory emerges out of her and Aidan's bedroom, holding Remi tight to her.

"Daddy?" Remi calls, wiggling out of Rory's arms and running to me when her feet hit the ground. I drop down, scooping her up and holding her tight against my chest while she cries.

"I've got you; you're safe now," I whisper to her, but my voice breaks.

"I want Mommy," she sobs, and something inside of me cracks, my grip on her tightening.

"I'm going to get her too, baby," I promise her. Running my fingers through her hair before looking up at Rory. She's pale, shaking, but looking me in the eye.

"Who?" I try to keep my voice calm and steady, but all the grief and pain is funneling into rage and it's only getting worse.

"I don't know..." Rory says quietly, coming closer. "I didn't see them—we were—Briar told us to hide." She swallows. "They were—they were here for *her.*"

My jaw flexes. Just once.

"He took Mommy."

My attention falls back on Remi in my arms.

"Who?" I ask her, but she's quiet. "Baby, who took Mommy?"

"A bad man," she whispers, burying her face in my chest again.

"Koen..."

My head lifts at the tone in Rory's voice.

"I didn't see them, but before we hid out in the courtyard, I—I could hear them, and they—" Her stormy eyes burn into mine. "They were Irish."

88

A FAVOR

KOEN

I MAKE a single call before I put Rory and Remi in the back of my car.

"I need a favor."

They're both quiet in the back of the SUV on the ride, exhausted and emotionally drained. It allows me the time to go over what we know.

Jace was shot at point-blank range. *He didn't even draw his gun.*

Rory said they had Irish accents...

All signs point to betrayal. Jace knew who shot him—he trusted them. And knowing someone he trusted pulled the trigger shatters me, and my heartbreak twists into something sharp and deadly.

Liam texted that he and Aidan caught a flight out of Chicago; they should be home in two hours. Alex and Garrett are on their way back from New York, and Jerrad is helping Mac take care of Jace.

I'm not sure I can wait much longer. Remi is the only

reason I'm not tracking Briar down as we speak. I can't leave her until I know she's going to be safe.

We pull up outside the iron gates, a few beats pass, and they open, allowing us access into the gated compound.

Nikolai Kostalov stands at the bottom of the front steps, a hard look on his face, hands in his pockets, blonde hair pulled back into a knot at the back of his head.

I get out of the car, making eye contact but not exchanging a word, as I circle around the vehicle, opening up the back door.

Rory climbs out, Remi in her arms, and I see Niko's expression shift. His sharp blue eyes take in every detail: the look on his sister's face, the look on mine, and the curious look Remi is giving him as she peeks out from behind Rory's protective grip.

I don't trust Niko. *Not entirely.* But there is one thing I know for certain: he would go to the ends of the Earth to protect his sister. Rory will be safe here. *And I trust Rory with Remi.*

Niko lifts his chin toward the house behind him, and Rory starts for the steps, but Remi twists in her arms, reaching back for me.

"No! I want to stay with Daddy!"

Niko's eyes and mine connect for a split second before I move toward Remi, taking her from Rory. Her little arms lock tight around my neck, like her grip alone can keep me with her.

"You gotta stay with Rory, Rem," I tell her, my tone gentle, my fingers tracing lightly down the side of her tear-stained cheeks.

"But I want to stay with you…" she whispers, her grip on my neck tightening.

Fuck, I don't want to leave her.

I shake my head anyway. "I've gotta go—I've gotta go get Mommy."

She looks up at me, her dark eyes staring into mine.

"I gotta go make the bad men pay," I promise her, my eyes intense.

She stares at me for another half a second before she nods. "Okay," she agrees.

I give her one more hug and a kiss before handing her back to Rory.

"I love you, Remi Rose."

"I love you too, Daddy," she whispers back, before Rory starts up the steps and into the Kostalov mansion.

I watch them disappear before my eyes slide back to Niko. He's been standing silently by, watching, his arms folded across his chest.

"I owe you one," I say, my words both a threat and a promise.

The corner of his mouth ticks up just a hair before he lets out a deep sigh, his Russian accent heavy when he says, "This one is on me, O'Rourke."

I nod once before getting back into the car and peeling out through the gates. Itching to finally unleash the dark rage that's threatening to consume me.

You took the devil's rose. Don't be surprised when he sets the whole garden on fire.

89

HOUSE OF HORRORS

BRIAR

LILY AND I are shoved forward through the back entrance of a ghastly estate. A dark mansion, long since abandoned, judging by the vegetation overgrowth and the musty smell that hits us when we enter the ground level.

"I don't like this. It's like a scene straight out of a horror movie.."

"Shhh," I hiss at Lily at my side. "Keep your head down and your ears open."

The man who took us from the loft leads the way. *Seamus O'Rourke.* Koen's *uncle.*

"What do you think, ladies? Pretty grand, eh?" he says as he marches us through the foyer. A chandelier lights the space overhead, but it's covered in cobwebs and hanging slightly askew.

There are voices up ahead... and music... We get closer, coming up to what must be the ballroom, and I catch a glimpse of... *yes, it's a fucking party.*

"What the fuck?" Lily whispers, and I just stare.

"My idea," Seamus boasts as we walk by the entrance. The room is filled with mostly men, but some women, dressed to impress, drinks in hand, while servers circle with trays of hors d'oeuvres. "A little fun before the games begin." He raises his brows in excitement and I feel bile rise up in my throat.

The auction.

I swallow hard and exchange a look with Lily.

"Ah, not to worry, ladies, it truly is your lucky day. You get to escape all of that pomp and circumstance." A sharp tug on my elbow and I'm redirected, both of us dragged downstairs into what looks to be the basement. Something tells me that *lucky* is not quite how I would've phrased it...

"I should really kill you," Seamus prattles on. "You two have been nothing but a problem from the start, especially you." He turns to glare at me. "But unfortunately, for now, you're worth more alive than dead," he laments.

Koen promised me the Irish had nothing to do with any of this. *He swore it.* And I believe him. *I still believe him.* I don't know what Seamus is up to, but I'm certain that, whatever it is, Koen doesn't know.

We walk down a long hallway, and he pushes open another door. The smell wafting out is horrid, and I wince. I can't quite place the scent, but I'm able to isolate the over-whelming stench of urine. But even that horrible smell alone could not prepare me for what's on the other side of that door.

Cages.

Actual cages.

Row after row after row of them. And inside of each... *girls.*

I crowd in closer to Lily, and feel her grip on my arm as we dig our heels in at the sight, but it seems our party is coming to a stop. A couple of men step forward to greet us.

Seamus gives them a nod. "Strip them to their underwear. They've already been sold, and their buyer doesn't want *any* marks." He gives the men a hard look. "He paid a pretty penny for this set, and he is not to be displeased. Is that understood?"

"Yes, sir."

"When you're done, room three," Seamus instructs, and he receives a nod in return.

What happens next is downright dehumanizing. Seamus leaves and the men grab us, dragging us down the long aisle between cages and into another room where we're both stripped of our clothes.

Lily panics, thrashing in their hold, and they resort to ripping hers off. Cold, practiced and fast. They continue until we're left with nothing but our underwear.

A man steps forward with a tray of numbered plastic tags. Tiny. *Like cattle tags.* I struggle in the hold of the two men who have a grip on me, when he picks one up, loading it into some sort of gun.

"No." A man with a clipboard steps forward. "The buyer requested they not be tagged."

A breath of relief escapes me as the man with the tray disappears out of the room, and I am thankful to whoever the fuck *the buyer* is for that, and *that alone.*

Clipboard Man gives both Lily and me a once-over before nodding in approval.

"Take them to room three."

It's probably our only opportunity to escape, but like the well-oiled machine that this place is, *they know that.* We're both handcuffed and escorted by more than enough guards, up two flights of stairs and into a bedroom. Except there is no bed. It's been replaced by a four-by-six-foot steel-barred cage that Lily and I are pushed into, the door locked behind us.

Then they leave us there.

"*Are you okay?*" I ask Lily after several minutes when she's still quiet. She's tucked into a ball in the corner, staring at her knees.

"Mhmm," she murmurs, without looking up.

I sit down next to her, throwing an arm around her and pulling her into me. They took the handcuffs off when they shoved us in here. "It's going to be okay," I tell her.

"I don't know, Briar..." The seriousness of her tone is unsettling.

I finger the silver chain around my neck between my fingers. The men overlooked it when they stripped me. "Koen's on his way," I tell her.

She looks up at me. "B..."

"He's coming," I say, staring at the door. *I've never been more certain of anything in my life.*

The door to the room opens, and we both jump.

It's been a few hours. I have goosebumps all over my body; the two of us have been huddling together for warmth. There's no heat in this decrepit mansion.

My heart sinks when the man that steps inside of the room is *not* Koen.

The room seems to grow colder with his presence. Lily

curls into a tighter ball, but I rise to my feet, stepping up close to the bars.

"Briar Elizabeth Ralston." The man comes closer, giving me an appraising look. He's tall, about the same age as Koen or Aidan, and terrifyingly beautiful, a walking nightmare: pale blue eyes that remind me of ice; dark hair; nice suit—violence wrapped in elegance. He's playing with a small silver lighter in his hand but makes no attempt to touch me. There's no warmth in his eyes, just cold, detached assessment.

"Who the fuck are you?" I bite back at him, figuring there's no need for manners since I'm locked in a cage. His use of my middle name sets me more on edge, and my eyes narrow. I don't recognize the man—I've never seen him before.

"Ronan Volkov," he tells me, his voice cold.

My heart catches in my throat, and a faint smile appears on that hard, stony face.

"You've heard of me?"

I force a swallow and nod my chin, staring up at the monster who's become utterly fixated on Koen and his family.

"Good." He smiles. *It's worse than his frown.* "Because I've heard a lot about you." He takes a turn about the room, dropping the lighter into his pocket before wiping a single finger down a nearby table, looking disgusted at the dust he pulls up.

"What do you want?" I'm shaking, half from the cold and half from the trauma of it all, but I still glare at him defiantly.

"I'm a collector," he turns toward me, "of a very *particular* type of woman." He steps closer, but I refuse to back up, the bars still separating us. "One the Irish just go *mad* for," he purrs out in his Russian accent, forcing my stomach to do a flip. *He wants to hold us over Koen and Aidan's heads.*

He tilts his head to look behind me, where Lily is curled in the corner, and the cold deadness of his eyes flares to life with a quick flash of rage.

"That's not Aurora Adrikova Kostalova," he growls, and I can't help but smile a little.

"No, it's not," I say quietly, taking what pleasure I can in *ruining his fucking day.*

Pissed, he stalks to the door, pounding on it hard before it opens. "Tell Seamus I want a word before I leave." He checks his watch. "I have a flight to catch." He points at the cage—at *Lily.* "I'm no longer in need of *that one.*"

My lips curl as I glare daggers at him.

"The other one, you will deliver?"

"Yes, sir." The guard nods, and Ronan looks satisfied, giving me one last look.

"I'll see you soon, *little rose,*" he mocks, and my eyes flame. "Try not to lose too much hope; it's far more fun to shatter it in person." With a cruel smile, he steps out into the hallway, replaced almost instantly with several of the mansion's guards.

"No! No! No!" I shout when they go to unlock the door to the cage.

Two of them grab me, and I fight them, clawing, kicking, biting, but it's over in seconds. They have me pressed hard up against the bars as more guards drag a sobbing Lily out of the cage.

I scream blood-curdling screams, thrashing in their hold, but I can't get them to budge. I can't stop them from taking her, and our eyes meet just before she's dragged out into the hall.

And no matter how many times I scream her name, *she doesn't come back.*

GOOD GIRL

BRIAR

I PACE THE CAGE. Trying and failing to formulate a plan to save us. The cage feels smaller without Lily in it.

It starts to feel like I can't breathe.

I scream—begging, *pleading*—for them to let me out. I fall down to the ground, wrapping my arms around my knees where I hyperventilate, panic taking over.

The door opens, and I hear Seamus' voice from outside the cage, but I don't look up; just continue to cry, keeping my head buried in my knees.

"Pathetic. She'll be lucky if she lasts a day with Volkov." He pauses and then speaks again, "Get her bagged for transport. The auction is about to start, and her *whining* is going to disturb the other clients."

The door closes, opening again a short while later, and I steal a peek, seeing a single guard enter, prepping a needle. He unlocks the cage and steps closer, taking his time given my current state, and just when he leans down to jab the needle into my neck, *I move*. Snatching the needle right out of his hand.

We stare at each other, shock on both of our faces, before I drive the needle full force into his neck.

"Fuck!" he curses, shoving me off of him, succeeding in flinging me against the bars. The back of my head slams hard against the metal, but he stumbles, and in another breath, he goes down entirely.

Keeping one eye on the door, I quickly search him. He's got a gun, a knife, and a set of keys. I'm still only dressed in my underwear, so I grab the gun and the ring of keys and stand up.

"Yeah, how do you like it?" I say to the guard passed out on the floor before I kick him. My feet are bare, so it hardly suffices. I kick him one more time— this time in the balls. *He'll feel that when he wakes up.*

Taking a few steadying breaths, I open the door to the hallway and peek out. There's no one standing immediately outside, which is reassuring, so I peer out further.

The sound of male voices down the hall draws my attention, and I duck my head back in, listening carefully before ever so slowly peeking out again.

Seamus stands at the end of the hall, addressing a couple of guards. Shaking his head in irritation, he heads back down the hallway toward *me*.

Panicking, I draw back, my heart pounding in my chest. Looking around the room, there's nowhere to hide, and while there *is* a window, we're on the second floor and it's a straight shot down to the stone patio below. I don't even know if he's coming in here, but at the last second, I dart behind the door, just before it opens.

Seamus steps inside. The door closes fully behind him before he notices the guard's body in the cage.

I point the gun at the back of his head. He must see the movement out of the corner of his eye because he turns to look at me, giving me a quick once-over, a slimy smile creeping up his face.

"Get in the cage," I warn him, trying to hold the gun steady.

"Briar, darling..." he starts, but I pull back the hammer.

"I said... Get. In. The. Cage." I jerk my chin toward the metal cage next to him, lifting the gun higher, training it on his forehead. He's not far from me, so even if I'm a bad shot, it would be *really* hard to miss.

His jaw flexes, reminding me of Koen, before he starts to do what I've told him to, backing up toward the cage, while lifting his hands in front of him. "Listen, your friend—"

"Where is she?" I demand, my voice shaky, but it's making me appear more unhinged. Seamus' gaze turns wary as he finally backs fully into the cage. I follow him, quickly slamming the door shut once he's inside.

"She's downstairs. Now listen here, I can help you—"

"Give me your gun," I demand, and he narrows his eyes. "Throw it out," I say, my voice a little steadier this time. I catch a glimpse of the glint in Seamus' eye as he pulls the gun from his waistband. I lift the barrel of the gun, firing a warning round into the ceiling. I flinch from how *fucking loud* it is but bring it back to Seamus, holding it steady while staring him in the eye. "Don't. Even. Think. About. It."

He considers me seriously for, perhaps, the first time all night, holding one hand high while the other takes his gun and tosses it through the cage bars.

"Now get on your knees."

Seamus glowers at me, holding his hands up a little higher before slowly sinking down to the floor. "You're out of your damn mind," he hisses at me.

"Maybe," I admit—I don't have much of a plan put together. I'll never make it to the basement on my own. I know that. But one thing's for certain... *Seamus needs to die.*

Before I can say anything else, the door slams open violently at my back. I sidestep quickly to the right, keeping the gun on Seamus, while shifting so I can see the door as well.

Koen.

I blink, just in case I've truly gone mad and I am, in fact, imagining him, but when I open my eyes again, *he's still here.* Standing in the threshold, gun raised, chest heaving, with nothing but dark violence dancing in his eyes.

"Koen! Koen! Thank god, you needed to see this!" Seamus cries from the floor. "I'm so sorry you have to find out this way, son, but she's working for them! It appears she's more clever than she looks." He frowns at me, and I glare down at him. "She's been playing you the whole time, got you wrapped around her little finger, that one." He glares up at me. "She never stopped feeding information to the Volkov."

"He's lying," I say, keeping my gun on Seamus.

Koen's face is a stone mask, and he remains in the doorway, cold eyes flickering between his uncle and me.

"What are you doing here, Seamus?" Koen's eyes narrow on him. "Did Garrett text you?"

"Well, like the rest of you, I came to help, of course," Seamus says, throwing up his hands like it should be obvious. "And yes, yes, Garrett texted me," he adds nodding his head, looking up at Koen, while eyeing me as if I'm a wild animal. "Get me out of here Koen, *before she kills me too.*"

Koen stares at Seamus for a long second before he drops the gun he has on him; my heart dropping right alongside it. And then he turns his dark gaze on me.

"Koen..." I start, my voice cracking.

"Briar, give me the gun," Koen says, holding out his hand and taking a step toward me.

Tears fill my eyes, but I shake my head, tightening my grip on the gun I keep steadily pointed at Seamus' forehead. "No." I whip my head back to Seamus in front of me. He's looking awfully smug all of a sudden on his knees. "*No,*" I say again, shaking my head. "No, he's behind all of it. He created this—this *nightmare.*"

Images flash in my head: *all the girls in cages, Lily's clothes being torn off of her, her screams when they dragged her away.*

I push the gun closer to Seamus, faintly aware of Koen entering the room, circling around behind me, *closing in.*

"He betrayed you." My finger feathers the trigger, staring down at the man on his knees before me.

"She's *lying,* Koen. She's never been anything other than a lying *whore.*" Seamus spews more vitriol from the ground, and my eyes fill with tears. "She killed Jace."

Kill him. Kill him now. He deserves to die. He betrayed Koen, Liam, Aidan... *He killed Jace...* A single tear leaks down my cheek. *Do it. You can do it. Just pull the trigger.*

"I can do this," I say aloud, willing myself to pull the goddamn trigger. The hand holding the gun to Seamus' head trembles. Even with Koen closing in behind me, my eyes stay fixed on his uncle, who's sneer grows wider with every inch Koen closes between us.

I know the second he reaches me, feeling his warmth at my back. Koen reaches up, his fingers slowly trailing down my arm until they reach the gun, and he gently pries it from my shaking fingers, *taking it from me.* His other arm snakes around my waist, pulling me into him, and his warm lips find my neck, where he deposits a light kiss before he whispers, "I know you can baby, but you don't have to."

"Look at me," his low voice whispers in my ear again, and I turn in his arms until I'm looking up into his eyes. "Cover your ears, baby."

I do.

"Good girl."

I jump at the loud bang at my back as Koen fires the gun, falling forward and burrowing deep into his chest, where the tears finally fall, unbidden and soaking into his sweatshirt. Warmth floods into me when he wraps both of his arms tight around me.

"Are you okay?" he asks, running a hand down my hair. "Did he—did any of them touch you?"

The fear in his voice guts me like a knife. I shake my head. "No. No, I'm okay."

Relief lets loose some of the tension in his body.

"How did you find me?"

Koen reaches down, picking up the silver chain around my neck, holding up the little Celtic knot on the end. "You never took this off."

My brows furrow in confusion; he just watches me expectantly until I work it out.

"You—" I gasp in shock. "You put a *tracker* in it?"

The corner of his mouth ticks up.

"I said you would always be safe, so long as you kept this on."

God, I want to hug and punch him all at the same time.

"I told you, Briar Rose, there's no escaping me. *Not this time.*"

STAY

KOEN

I'VE GOT HER... She's okay... *She's okay.*

Part of me still can't believe it as I hold Briar's hand, her fingers swallowed by the sleeves of my sweatshirt, pulling her behind me, gun out, as we move through the hallway and down the stairs.. Gunfire and screams fill the air around us. I turn right for the door but stop short, meeting resistance.

Glancing back, I find Briar, feet planted and shaking her head. "Where are we going?" she asks.

"I'm getting you the fuck out of here," I tell her, stepping again toward the front door, but she doesn't budge.

"Briar..."

She shakes her head, taking a step backwards. "No. No, I'm not leaving Lily."

My eyes scan the foyer, constantly looking for threats. "The others will get her out."

She looks at me, and when my eyes meet hers, my jaw tenses at the steely defiance I find in her hard blue eyes. *Fuck.* I stand there thinking for a moment, contemplating just how mad she'll be if I throw her over my shoulder and force her out.

"Please, Koen," she begs, and I sigh, knowing I've already lost.

"Fuck. Fine!" I relent, turning left. "But stay behind me."

We pass several bodies on the way to the basement, and I pull out my radio. "Anyone have eyes on Lily?"

Both teams report back a "negative," and I internally curse before starting downstairs.

The cavernous basement of the mansion has erupted into a war zone. The cages have all been opened, and most of the girls have fled or are hiding, but some still crouch inside, too afraid to leave, hands covering their ears as gunshots continue to ring out from further in.

"Stay close!" I shout at Briar behind me. Every muscle in my body is coiled tight, doing my best to keep her body shielded with mine.

Two guards appear around the corner up ahead and they raise their guns, but it's already too late—I drop them both.

There's more gunfire up ahead near the processing rooms and I move toward it, until it stops. Freezing, I keep my gun trained on the doorway, letting out a breath when a familiar face steps through it.

Alex has his gun trained on my head, but he drops it as soon as he realizes it's me, and steps toward us. Mac follows closely behind with Lily in his arms.

"*Lily,*" Briar breathes out in quiet relief at my back, and immediately I switch us into reverse.

"Where's Aidan and Liam?" I call to Alex at my back.

"They're right behind us." And sure enough, Aidan and

Liam appear a second later, in the doorway Alex and Mac just emerged from.

"Time to go."

Aidan and Liam push past us to walk in front; Briar, and Mac with Lily, are at my back, with Alex watching our six.

We move quickly down the hallway and up the stairs into the foyer.

A door slams open to our right and three more men pour out, guns firing. I lift my gun and fire, alongside Liam and Aidan. I realize my mistake too late, not noticing the hallway door that opens to my left... and the man standing there, the barrel of his gun fixed on me.

But Briar does.

She screams my name and I twist back, right before she shoves me with two hands pressed to my chest, pushing me out of the way as the man fires, the bullet whizzing past, just narrowly missing us—

No.

Not missing *us*—missing *me.*

Briar lets out a gasp as she falls into my chest, her eyes wide, pupils blown out in shock as she slowly realizes what's happened.

Her knees buckle, but I catch her before she goes down.

Shouts sound around us, and bullets fly as my brothers take out the bastard, but I can't look, my attention is wholly fixed on the girl whose breaths are coming too sharply in my arms.

"*No. No. No. No. No. Why would you do that? Why would you do that?*" I grab her face, blood quickly coating my left hand. Panicking, I search the side of her head, looking for the source... *holy shit, there's so much fucking blood.*

I find it, just above her left ear, and I press my palm down hard, doing my best to stop the stream of blood pouring out.

Briar's watching me, her blue eyes bright against her paling skin.

"Hey—hey—hey—Briar—look at me," I beg. "You're going to be okay—alright? We're going to get you out of here."

Not willing to wait another second more, I scoop her into my arms and take off running, not stopping until I reach the car, throwing open the door and sliding into the backseat. Alex appears at the wheel a second later.

Briar's heartbeat is faint; her breaths are shallow, *but she's still breathing.* She's still conscious, looking up into my eyes, with fear in her own.

"*Breathe,* baby, breathe for me, okay? That's it! You're going to be okay, alright? Do you hear me?" I brush the hair out of her face, the blood on my hand smudges her cheek.

"Drive!" I scream, and Alex puts the car in gear, flooring it.

Briar's eyes begin to flutter open and shut, and my free hand grips her chin, the other continuing to apply pressure to the wound. *There's so much blood.*

"Don't you dare," I growl, tightening my grip on her chin. "Don't you fucking dare leave me, Briar Rose."

Her eyes open again but they're out of focus. "I just need to sleep it off—" she mumbles, before her eyes fall shut, but this time they don't reopen.

"Fuck!" I scream. "*No—no—no—no—no,* Briar! Don't go to sleep. Stay awake, baby. Stay with me." My voice breaks. "Stay, baby, please." She's covered in blood; it's soaking into my shirt, the leather seats... No-no, *fuck,* I can't lose her, not like this, *not when I just got her back.*

She's pale.

So pale.

"Stay with me, baby." I'm sobbing now, my tears mixing with blood as I press my forehead to hers.

"*Please.*"

R.I.P.

KOEN

THREE DAYS LATER

It's raining.

The grey sky and heavy mist captures the very essence of the grief weighing heavily on us all.

The rain falls in a steady but relentless drizzle. It soaks my hair, darkens my suit, and I see it pool into beaded droplets atop the mahogany woodgrain of the casket before they grow too large and roll off.

In my hand, I roll the stem of the rose I stole from one of the bouquets back at the church. A rogue thorn pricks my thumb, the pain welcome within the deep sea of numbness I'm currently drowning in.

Father Lucent steps up to the head of the casket and, with a single nod from me, he begins.

Everyone's silent as he starts with the prayers. I'm aware of Alex and Aidan at my side, Rory next to him. Liam's watching with a somber expression on the other side of the casket—holding Remi, next to Mac and Lily. Garrett and Jerrad, Conor and Jimmy, the circle of people thick around us, everyone showing up to pay their respects.

Sniffles and tears start to fall at the delivery of the Lord's Prayer, but I remain silent, jaw locked, eyes trained on the dark casket, stoic, controlled. I don't need to speak; I need to *feel*. I need to say *goodbye*.

The priest's words float through the heavy drizzle "... beloved husband, son, brother, cousin and friend..."

I inhale softly when the coffin is gently lowered down, bringing with it a heavy sense of finality.

Jace.

Jace is gone.

A few minutes after the ceremony concludes, I step forward, letting the rose fall as I say *goodbye*.

I step back, paying my respects to Conor and Jimmy and finally... *Cara*, Jace's wife. Her eyes are red-rimmed and swollen from crying, and I pull her in for a hug, letting her know she'll be taken care of; we'll look out for her. *It's what Jace would have wanted.*

Before turning to leave, I find Liam and Remi, and give my daughter a quick kiss before I turn and walk out of the cemetery.

There will be a gathering after, but I won't attend.

I've already been away for too long.

And there's somewhere else I need to be.

I stride with purpose through the busy hospital, all the way to the third floor, where I find Nikolai Kostalov, the Bratva Pakhan himself, leaning against the wall in a quiet hallway, right where I left him.

"Any change?" I ask, and he shakes his head slowly.

My jaw tightens, and I nod once before clasping him on the shoulder.

"Thanks, Niko."

He gives me a silent nod before I leave him behind and step into the room to his left.

Before today, I hadn't left it.

Not for three days.

Hadn't left *her*.

But with the funeral today, Niko offered to watch out for Briar so all of us could attend. Jace was close to each and every one of us, and asking anyone to stay behind wouldn't have been fair. We are still in the midst of untangling the web of deception Seamus had woven within the Devils, so there are few in my circle I truly trust right now.

On the night everything went down, Niko kept his word. He kept Rory and Remi safe, and when he offered again, just for a few hours so I could say goodbye to my cousin—my *friend*—I reluctantly agreed.

I stand at the end of the bed, watching her sleep.

She got lucky.

That's what the doctors said anyway. The bullet had just grazed her skull. While the damage wasn't devastating, she'd lost a lot of blood. And she had a concussion, either from the bullet itself, or the wound at the back of her head where she must have hit it. There'd been some swelling in her brain, and they induced a medical coma hoping to minimize the damage done.

They lifted the coma yesterday morning, but Briar *still hasn't woken up.*

The rain picks up outside, the pitter-pattering of the drops hits up against the window, the sky darkening as if in tune with my mood.

A clean white bandage is wrapped around Briar's head, with cute little unicorn stickers stuck all over it, courtesy of Remi from her visit this morning before we left for the church.

"I can't bury you too," I murmur softly, letting out a deep sigh before reclaiming my spot in the chair beside her head, leaning in to trace my fingers down the side of her cheek.

"On the night we first met, you asked me to play a game. Do you remember?" She doesn't say anything—doesn't move. "I picked truth." My voice is soft as I recall the memory. "You called me a coward and then you asked me what my biggest regret was." I move closer, tracing my fingers over hers. "I told you I didn't have one, and that was true... *then*. But if you asked me today, I'd confess that my biggest regret... was ever letting you go."

"Truth or dare, Briar Rose?" I say, my voice rough.

She doesn't answer me, blue eyes closed, her chest rising and falling alongside the routine beeping of the machines.

"It's okay, I'll choose." I move to stroke my fingers gently through her hair.

"Dare," I whisper softly into her ear.

"I dare you to *stay*."

93

IF I LAY HERE...

BRIAR

I'M MET with darkness when I finally manage to pry my eyes open.

My lids are heavy, and it's a struggle to hold them up, and for a moment, everything is blurry.

I focus on the sounds—the persistent beeping of a machine, the sound of rain hitting glass—*and the feel of a large, warm hand wrapped around mine.*

The blurriness clears, and I blink a few times, ignoring the pounding in my head to slide my eyes over, looking for *him.*

Koen's hunched over in his chair, leaning his chin atop one hand while the other holds onto mine.

He's a mess.

Dark circles ring his eyes, the collar of his shirt is undone, his tie loose, and his hair is mussed like he's been repeatedly running his hands through it.

He's awake, just staring at our linked hands with familiar quiet intensity.

I squeeze his hand, and he *flinches.* Dark eyes rocket up,

and there's an indescribable look of relief in his when they meet mine.

"*Briar?*" He whispers my name, reverent, cautious, as if uncertain what he's seeing is real.

"Hi."

Koen releases a breath, and it's as if an immense weight falls off his shoulders. Part of me wonders how long he's been holding it. And it might be my vision blurring again... but his eyes look... *shiny*—and red.

"I thought I lost you again."

I squeeze his hand, looking him in the eye. "I'm not going anywhere."

"Remi?" I ask. My voice is scratchy, and he quickly grabs a cup of water from the table beside me and puts the straw between my lips.

"Safe."

"Lily?" I ask before drinking anything.

"She's okay. They're all okay..." he assures me, and I relax, taking a small sip of water to relieve the burning feeling in my throat.

We're interrupted by the arrival of the floor nurse, and then the doctor, who checks me over before explaining everything that happened and their plan of treatment. By the time they all clear out, my eyes feel heavy again.

"You should sleep," Koen says, noticing my yawn as he exits the bathroom. He's changed into a pair of sweats—clearly he's not going anywhere.

"Lie with me," I say, and I watch him freeze.

He shakes his head. "I don't want to hurt you."

"You won't," I assure him, scooting over to make room on my right.

He looks conflicted.

"Please?" I blink up at him. "I just want to fall asleep in your arms."

He lets out a sigh but comes over to the right side of the bed anyway, carefully sliding into it, holding his breath when I lay my head down on his chest.

He's so warm—solid. We lay like that in silence for a few minutes while I listen to the sound of his heart racing inside his chest. It's so loud.

After a few more minutes, I feel his body relax and his heartbeat slow, his arm coming around to hold me closer to him.

"Don't go, okay?" I say, afraid he might try and sneak back to the chair once I'm asleep. "Stay with me?"

Koen works his jaw, tightening his arm around me while pressing a light kiss to my forehead.

"I'll stay, baby. I promise."

Satisfied, I snuggle deeper into his chest, and while exhaustion ebbs at me, I force myself to stay awake until I hear his breathing even out and his heartbeat slow to a gentle rhythm.

He's asleep.

And after listening to a few more beats, I join him.

94

HOME

BRIAR

TWO WEEKS LATER

"This is a bad idea."

"Shut up."

"It's a bad idea."

"Well, it's a good thing I didn't ask for your opinion," I sass, the corner of my mouth ticking up.

Koen grumbles something unintelligible behind me, all while keeping a firm grip on my waist as I fight for my life on top of frozen water.

"Stop moving your feet so much!"

"Stop telling me what to do!" I growl at him while trying to slow down, my feet skittering like crazy under me.

"I'm going to tell you what to do as long as you don't know

what you're doing!" he cries out, exasperated as he prevents yet another catastrophic fall.

We're at the annual Boston Breakers Family Skate at the Edge Arena, surrounded by Breakers players and their families.

Remi's living her best life, tearing up the ice with her stack of milk crates at high speed. Just ahead of us, she careens wildly into the boards, knocking herself off her feet, only to cackle maniacally before getting back up to do it again.

"She's got a future in hockey," Koen says, watching her.

I smile.

"You guys doing okay?"

The sound of Rory's voice has my head turning, causing me to trip over my own blades again. Koen curses at my back as he catches me just before I hit the ice.

"Yes," I say at the same time Koen growls, "No."

"Do we intervene?" Rory looks up, asking Aidan at her side.

Aidan's brows furrow. "You sure you're cleared for this? Didn't the doctor say—"

"He said, 'return to normal activity after two weeks while exercising caution,'" I repeat flatly.

"I wouldn't consider *ice skating* to be a *normal* activity..." Koen challenges, but I wave him off.

"But I *am* exercising caution," I say, patting the arm he has locked around my waist.

Aidan and Rory exchange a look. "Good enough for me." Aidan shrugs, deftly avoiding Koen's glare.

Ice skating, it turns out, is much harder than it looks, and honestly, I could actually use a break.

"Maybe we could get some water?" I throw out there, and

the next thing I know, Koen's swept me up into his arms and is skating for the bench.

"Hey!" I cry. "I could've made it on my own!"

He rolls his eyes. "We don't have all *week*, Briar Rose."

I huff, allowing him to carry me off the ice and deposit me onto the bench. There's a bottle of water in my hands a minute later, and I take a few quick sips, searching for Remi on the ice.

I find her with Liam. They've ditched the crate, and instead he holds her up, pushing her in front of him while she squeals, a huge smile on both of their faces.

"So, I have something to tell you," Koen says, sitting down next to me.

"Well, that sounds ominous..." I reply, shifting until I'm facing him.

"I talked to the director of the Boston Ballet."

I nearly spit out my water. "You WHAT?!"

He just continues talking. "I explained how you missed the showcase because you were kidnapped—"

"Did you tell them *you* were the one who kidnapped me?" I say, cutting him off.

Koen waves the thought away. "*Details...*"

I smirk.

"Anyway, they're still *very* interested in having you audition, so, as soon as you're fully healed, they'll arrange it." His eyes search my face, hovering over my frown. "I thought you'd be happy?"

"I don't want anything I didn't earn..." I say. My voice is low.

He holds up both his hands innocently. "All I did was explain why you weren't at the showcase. The audition... that's between you and them," he says, his eyes sincere. "It's really not a surprise considering the only reason they were coming to the showcase was to see *you*."

My eyes narrow. "What do you mean?"

"Briar, you haven't headlined a performance in *years*. They thought you stopped performing, stepped back from ballet. They only committed to attend after word broke that *you* would be taking over the role."

"Oh," I breathe, too shocked to say anything else.

Koen takes my hand in his. "You're an *incredible* dancer. You have talent, *genuine* talent, and whatever you choose to do with it, I'll be here for you." He reaches up to brush a lock of hair from my face. "Promise me you'll at least think about it?"

That warm feeling creeps into my chest again, and I squeeze his hand. *That explains the dance studio...*

After I was released from the hospital, Koen set to work on renovating a couple of the empty loft apartments directly beneath his. His plans include: an apartment just for me, him, and Remi; an apartment for Lily next door; and then across the hall... a dance studio. For Lily, Rory, and me to use whenever we want.

"Okay, I'll think about it," I relent, while secretly plotting how soon I can convince him to let me resume training.

There's been a little pressure from the heads of the other clans for Koen to *make it official* and get married, but he's pushed back. Given what happened recently with Seamus, they've backed off—for now. Especially since Koen is adamant; he won't get married without his sister... *who's still missing.*

And honestly, I need time. *We* need time to just *be* together, without any of that added pressure.

"Daddy?" A little voice calls, and we both look up, seeing only ten tiny fingers clinging to the top of the boards.

"Remi?" Koen gets up, lifting our little blonde menace onto the bench. She's wearing her #26 jersey; it looks super cute paired with her pink helmet and gloves.

"Will you skate with me?"

Koen's face lights up and he nods. "Absolutely I will, but *only* if your mommy *promises* to stay right here and that she will not, under any circumstances, step back out on the ice alone."

I roll my eyes. "You're being dramatic."

He arches a brow, and I can't help but laugh.

"Fine." I stand up, only to sit back down again but while making a show of it. "I'm staying put. Now go have fun!"

"Okay, Remi Rose." Koen smiles. "Let me show you how it's done." He takes her hand, helping her through the gate and onto the ice.

"And you," he looks over at me, "I'll be back for you."

"I'll be here," I tease, and watch them skate off. My heart swells when he puts his arm around our daughter, keeping her steady while still letting her lead.

It's not long before I spy Koen sending one of his brothers back to check on me. I laugh, shaking my head.

This family, this chaotic, messy, terrifying family, had staked their claim on us, *both of us*. And for the first time in what feels like forever, I let myself relax—being here, with them, with *all* of them... it feels like *home*.

READY FOR MORE?

This story may have ended, but the war is far from over.

Turn the page for an exclusive sneak peek at the first chapter of
The Devils & Darlings - Book 3

Expected Winter 2026/2027

CHAPTER 1 : REAGAN

FIVE WEEKS EARLIER

I wake to movement.

The irregular swaying motion elicits a violent wave of nausea.

Holy hell... how much did I drink last night?

It's hard to breathe. I'm on my stomach and I try to roll over, but I can't quite seem to manage it.

Air.

I need air.

As in, there isn't any fucking air.

I suck in hard through my nose, but it isn't enough. I try to open my mouth to get some more oxygen but—I can't open it. Oh my god, my mouth is stuck closed! My lips stick to the adhesive; I try desperately to get my mouth open, but it holds firm.

636

Tape... there's tape over my mouth!

I can't see anything either. My eyes are open, but I'm still in darkness. There's something over my eyes, too! I panic. Thrashing around, the panic worsens when I realize my hands and feet are bound behind my back. *Hog-tied.* They're hog-tied behind my back!

Holy fucking shit, am I being kidnapped?

Please god, whatever this is, just please don't let my brother be right...

My heart is racing, but I don't have the oxygen for that; I struggle to get what I can in through my nose. *Okay, don't panic Rea, it's very important that you don't panic.*

I scream, but it's severely muffled by the tape across my mouth, and then I thrash violently against my bonds, part tantrum—part attempt to loosen them.

It doesn't work.

Okay, that *might* fall into the realm of panicking...

Regaining my composure, I focus on breathing because *I'm going to fucking suffocate.*

Awkwardly, I'm able to push myself onto my side, and breathing comes easier; my chest is no longer compressed.

Okay, okay... now what?

I rub my head against the carpet underneath me, over and over until I start to slide the silk tie covering my eyes up, centimeter by centimeter until I'm able to see. Which doesn't help much, seeing as how wherever I am is pitch black, but it still makes me feel better.

I'm in a car.

I'm in the *trunk* of a car, I gauge by the movement and the sound of the wheels on the asphalt below.

I let my eyes adjust to the dark, looking around for anything I can use, but besides me, the trunk is empty. There's no glow-in-the-dark release tag either... whoever owns this car likely ripped it out, which tells me they've probably kidnapped people before.

Great.

I try piecing together the last memory I have before waking up here but it's really fuzzy. You'd think I'd remember being hog-tied and shoved into a trunk, but alas... I'm coming up blank. I don't even remember leaving the club...

I'd snuck out... We'd been on lockdown for *weeks,* and my brother Koen was being an ass. I've done it before... climbed down the fire escape, met up with some friends, partied, and then I was back in enough time so that no one was the wiser.

What made this time any different?

I rack my brain but come up with nothing. The last memory I have is of dancing in the club with Effie and Margot, and then it all goes dark...

I wiggle some more, sadly coming to the conclusion that I can't even kick out the taillight like they do in the movies, with my feet bound like they are. I sigh deeply, laying my head back down on the floor, but still refusing to just give up.

The trunk isn't very tall, and I try propping myself up on my elbow and knee to examine the roof above me, still searching for the likely nonexistent emergency release. I've just about managed it when the car hits a bump, sending my head straight into the unforgiving roof of the trunk. Pain splits my head, and I let out a groan.

Okay... ow!

The car slows to a stop, and I freeze.

The car doors open—two people getting out, if I'm

hearing correctly. One of them shuts the door so hard it shakes the car.

A meathead, probably.

In another couple of minutes, the trunk opens, revealing two men dressed in black, staring down at me.

Unable to say anything, I just stare back.

"She's awake," the smaller of the two says. And that description is relative... *They're both fucking giants.*

"I can see that," the taller one says.

They're both Russian, too, judging by their accents.

The smaller one fiddles with his bag. "She sure burned through that sedative quickly."

"It's the red hair," the taller one says, tilting his head a little as he looks into my eyes with a cold intensity.

I give him my best withering stare, but I don't think he appreciates it the way he should.

"You should have stayed in your tower, princess." His pale blue eyes lock on mine. "Now look at you—bound, gagged, and wrapped up like a pretty present."

My eyes burn with anger, while his seem to grow even colder. He reaches into the trunk, turning me slightly to inspect my wrists and ankles, releasing me when he's satisfied I'm still thoroughly caught in his net.

My eyes dart to the man next to him, who draws out a needle, but the taller of the two puts his hand over it, shaking his head. He's clearly the one in charge.

"She's not going anywhere; let her stay awake. It's more fun that way."

My fists tighten in the ropes when his eyes meet mine again.

"My name is Ronan Volkov," he says, and my pulse picks up, my eyes going wide.

His icy blues are the last thing I see before he reaches out, dragging the silk blindfold back down over my eyes.

"Welcome to Hell, Little Devil."

ACKNOWLEDGMENTS

First and foremost, to my editor Nicole—without whom this book would still be a mess of half-finished chapters, unhinged notes and vibes. I genuinely do not think I would have finished this book on time, or maybe at all, without her. She is my rock, my reality check, my #1 cheerleader, and a total badass. I am endlessly grateful for her talent, patience, and belief in this story. And for all the Heated Rivalry DMs. I want 'em all!

To my family; my parents, step-parents, siblings, grandparents, etc. thank you for your endless support and encouragement. I am so lucky to have all of you. I can't believe how much love you have for this story/series and for encouraging me to chase this dream. My #1 hype team, honestly.

To Michaela and Susanne, thank you for being there to bounce ideas off of at any hour. Your creativity helped shape this story more than you know—and to Michaela for coining the nickname Rí (King) to keep my playing-card theme alive.

To Cody, Kayla, Kristina and all the girls in the "Booktok Besties" group chat for your love and support and of course to Amanda for forever haunting me in the comments of just about every video looking for this book. And to Taylin, my wonderful PA, for her endless love for No Promises No Lies and for all her help running Dare Me to Stay's ARC team.

And of course, to the readers, for taking a chance on an unknown indie author's book, I am forever grateful. Dare Me to Stay quite literally would NOT exist without you. I was going to go in a completely different direction until you guys jumped in with an overwhelming love for the O'Rourke family and requests for their stories. You not only took the time to read it, review it, post about it, you told your friends about it and got THEM to read it, and that is just so incredibly insane to me. I love you guys so much.

And a huge thank you to my street team and ARC team—legends. I truly do not have words to express how grateful I am to you. You hyped, reviewed, shared, shouted and showed up over and over again—before this book was even out in the world. Thank you for reading early, loving it loudly, catching things I missed, and helping this story reach readers I never could have reached on my own. I am endlessly grateful for your time, your energy and your enthusiasm for this story.

To my audiobook narrators Alyssa Avery and John Hartley, thank you for bringing these characters to life in ways I never could on the page. Hearing No Promises No Lies out loud was surreal in the best possible way, and I am so grateful for the care, talent, and heart you poured into every scene—yes, even the spicier ones. I cannot wait to hear what you do with Dare Me to Stay! And to my audiobook publisher Podium, thank you for believing in this series and helping bring it to an entirely new audience. Your trust, support, and willingness to invest in this series means more than I can say.

To my husband and my kids, I have to thank you for your patience, your love and your understanding of how much time writing and marketing takes away from you. The late nights, pizza for dinner, baskets of unfolded laundry, the giant white-board on wheels in the middle of the dining room. Thank you for understanding when my brain was elsewhere and for supporting me as I chase this dream.

And finally, to all my new author and reader friends—I started this year with a published book and ended it with an entire community. I've made so many new friends and made so many unexpected, and possibly lifelong connections, I will be forever grateful for.

Thank you.

ABOUT THE AUTHOR

Aj writes dark romance because therapy is expensive, it's cheaper than revenge, and slightly less illegal...

She lives in New England, where the winters are cold, the hockey is endless, and the coffee is non-negotiable.

When she's not busy writing, you can find her reading way past her bedtime, at the hockey rink, or pretending her third cup of coffee doesn't count.

Her books are full of morally gray men, tough-as-nails women, and just enough spice to ruin your sleep schedule and your moral compass.

She believes in messy emotions, happily ever afters, and that nothing says "I love you" like a well-placed threat.

Chaos is her love language.

Buckle up.

JOIN THE WILDING STREET TEAM!

Did you love Dare Me to Stay?
Consider joining "Aj Wilding's Street Team and ARC
Readers": A private group on Facebook

https://www.facebook.com/share/g/182Cjtrjvx/

This is our cozy little corner to connect, share, and gush about
all things books (and maybe a little behind-the-scenes magic).

As a member of this group, you're not just helping me get
the word out about my stories—you're part of the journey. I'll
be sharing:

📚 **Exclusive sneak peeks** and bonus chapters.

✏️ Behind-the-scenes look into my writing process.

🎁 Fun challenges, giveaways, and rewards for your
support.

📖 Advanced Reader Copies (ARCs) of my upcoming
releases!